PRAISE FOR THE MAGNIFICENT NOVELS OF JULIE GARWOOD

PRINCE CHARMING

"A wonderfully exotic book with both grand characters and grand deception."

—*The News-Commercial* (Collins, MS)

"Fans of Julie Garwood's highly amusing light-hearted romps will find a real emotional uplift in her latest offering, *PRINCE CHARMING*. . . ."

—Harriet Klausner, *Affaire de Coeur*

SAVING GRACE

"[A] rollicking adventure. . . . Garwood endows *Saving Grace* with a first-rate setting, a splendid supporting cast and witty dialogue. . . ."

—*Publishers Weekly*

"Julie Garwood is a gifted writer whose rich descriptions and unforgettable heroines have made her a perennial favorite. . . . *Saving Grace* is another winner."

—B. Dalton's *Heart to Heart*

CASTLES

"A charming, sweet, funny romance, brimming with sparkling dialogue, delightful characters, and a story that flies."

—*Romantic Times*

"The story is splendid, the characters are wonderful, and the dialogue excellent. . . . A keeper."

—*Rendezvous*

THE SECRET

"This story abounds with love, passion, joy, and faith—it certainly gave my life a lift. . . . Judith is a wonderful heroine."

— *Rendezvous*

"It is no secret that Julie Garwood is one of America's favorite romance authors. . . . One of her strongest assets is her ability to tell a story honestly but with great beauty. *The Secret* is a delight."

— *Greater Springfield Business Journal*

"Woven into Judith's story is an intriguing, almost heretical message for a romance novel: a woman needs more than the right man to have a full, happy life. That Garwood can argue this point and still deliver a delightful tale is an accomplishment."

— *Publishers Weekly*

THE PRIZE

"A delight. . . . Mystery, betrayal, divided loyalties, gentle love, *The Prize* has it all, along with a heroine who will steal your heart."

— *Affaire de Coeur*

"Ms. Garwood brings to sparkling life an age when men had the opportunity to prove their mettle and women their wiles. . . . Engrossing, romantic, funny, adventurous. . . . Excellent."

— *Rendezvous*

BOOKS BY JULIE GARWOOD

Gentle Warrior
Rebellious Desire
Honor's Splendour
The Lion's Lady
The Bride
Guardian Angel
The Gift
The Prize
The Secret
Castles
Saving Grace
Prince Charming
For the Roses
The Wedding
Come the Spring
Ransom
Heartbreaker
Mercy

The Clayborne Brides
One Pink Rose
One White Rose
One Red Rose

PUBLISHED BY POCKET BOOKS

JULIE GARWOOD

PRINCE CHARMING

POCKET BOOKS

New York London Toronto Sydney Singapore

This book is a work of fiction. Names, characters, places and incidents are products of the author's imagination or are used fictitiously. Any resemblance to actual events or locales or persons, living or dead, is entirely coincidental.

 POCKEY BOOKS, a division of Simon & Schuster, Inc. 1230 Avenue of the Americas, New York, NY 10020

ISBN: 0-671-87096-3

First Pocket Books paperback printing February 1995

19 18 17 16 15 14 13

POCKET and colophon are registered trademarks of Simon & Schuster, Inc.

For information regarding special discounts for bulk purchases, please contact Simon & Schuster Special Sales at 1-800-456-6798 or business@simonandschuster.com

Cover art by Lisa Falkenstern

Printed in the U.S.A.

To Marilyn Regina Murphy.
My sister, my champion, my friend.

Know what it is to be a child . . .
To see a world in a grain of sand
And a heaven in a wild flower,
Hold Infinity in the palm of your hand
And Eternity in an hour.

—William Blake, *Auguries of Innocence*

1

Virtue is bold, and goodness never fearful.
—William Shakespeare,
Measure for Measure

London, England, 1868

The vultures were gathering in the vestibule. The salon was already filled to capacity, as was the dining room and the library above. More of the black-clad predators lined the curved staircase. Every now and then two or three would bob their heads in unison as they gulped from their glasses of champagne. They were watchful, expectant, hopeful. They were also vile and disgusting.

They were the relatives.

Quite a few friends of the earl of Havensmound were in attendance as well. They were there to show their support and their compassion over the unfortunate tragedy about to take place.

The celebration would come later.

For a brief spell, everyone tried to behave in a dignified manner befitting the solemn occasion. Liquor soon loosened both their thoughts and their smiles, however, and it wasn't long before outright laughter could be heard above the clinking of their crystal glasses.

The matriarch was finally dying. There had been two false alarms in the past year, but many believed this third attack would turn out to be the charm. She was simply too damned ancient to keep on disappointing everyone. Why, she was already past sixty.

Lady Esther Stapleton had spent her life accumulating her fortune, and it was high time the old girl died so her relatives could start spending it. She was, after all, reported to be one of the richest women in England. Her only surviving son was also reported to be one of the poorest. It wasn't right, or so his sympathetic creditors announced whenever the lecherous earl was within earshot. Malcolm was the earl of Havensmound, for God's sake, and should have been allowed to spend as much as he wanted, whenever he wanted. Granted, the man was a blatant squanderer, and a rake as well, whose sexual appetite ran to the very young, but those flaws weren't frowned upon by the moneylenders. Quite the opposite in fact. While the more respectable bankers had long ago refused to loan the licentious earl any more money, the street corner lenders were more than happy to accommodate the man. They were jubilant. They thoroughly enjoyed their client's debauchery. Each had charged an exorbitant amount of interest to shovel the earl out of his latest gambling fiasco to say nothing of the staggering amount they'd had to fork over to silence the parents of the young ladies their client had seduced and then discarded. The debts had piled up all right, but the patient creditors were soon going to be richly rewarded.

Or so they all believed.

Thomas, the ailing butler's young assistant, pushed yet another creditor out the entrance, then took great delight in slamming the door shut. He was appalled by their behavior. He was certain they knew better. They just didn't care.

Thomas had lived in the household since he was twelve, and in all that while, he didn't believe he'd ever seen anything as shameful as this. His dear mistress was above the stairs, struggling to hold on until all her affairs had been properly settled and her favored granddaughter, Taylor, arrived to say her farewell, while down below, the dying woman's son was holding court as pretty as you please, laughing and carrying on like the cad that he was. His daughter, Jane, clung to his side, a smug expression on her face. Thomas guessed the gloating look was due to the fact that she knew her father would share his wealth with her.

Two rotten peas in the same pod, Thomas thought to himself. Oh, yes, father and daughter were very alike in both character and appetite. The butler didn't feel he was being disloyal to his mistress because he harbored such dark opinions about her relatives. She felt the same way. Why, on several occasions, he'd heard Lady Esther refer to Jane as a viper. She was that, all right. Thomas secretly called her much worse. She was a vicious young woman, full of clever plots, and it seemed to him that the only time he ever saw her smile was after she had deliberately crushed someone's feelings. It was said by those in the know that Jane ruled the upper crust with a malicious hand and that most of the younger men and women just stepping into their places in society were actually afraid of her, although they knew better than to admit it. Thomas didn't know if the gossip was true or not, but one thing was certain in his mind. Jane was a destroyer of dreams.

She'd gone too far this time, however, for she'd dared to attack that which Lady Esther most valued. She'd tried to destroy Lady Taylor.

Thomas let out a loud grunt of satisfaction. Very soon now, Jane and her disreputable father would be made to realize the ramifications of their treacherous deeds.

Dear Lady Esther had been too occupied with ill health and family losses to notice what was going on. Since the day Taylor's older sister, Marian, had taken her twin babies to live in Boston, Lady Esther had begun her decline. She'd been failing ever since. Thomas believed the only reason she hadn't completely given up was because she was determined to see the child she'd raised as her own daughter married and settled first.

Taylor's wedding had been canceled, thanks to Jane's interference. A bit of good came out of the godawful humiliation, however. Lady Esther finally had her eyes opened. She used to be a forgiving woman until this latest outrage. Now she was just plain vindictive.

Where in heaven's name was Taylor? Thomas prayed she would arrive in time to sign the papers and say her farewell to her grandmother.

The servant paced and fretted for several more minutes. He then turned his attention to ushering the guests lounging so insolently on the steps into the already crowded solarium at the back of the house. He used food and additional liquor as an incentive to gain their cooperation. After he crammed the last of the vile creatures inside, he pulled the door closed, then hurried back to the foyer.

A commotion coming from outside drew his attention. He rushed over to look out the side window. He recognized the crest on the black carriage still rocking to a stop in the center of the circle drive, let out a sigh of relief, and then said a quick prayer in thanksgiving. Taylor had finally arrived.

Thomas looked into the salon to make certain both the earl and his daughter were still occupied with their friends. Since their backs were turned to the entrance, he hurried over to shut the salon doors. If luck stayed on his side, he would be able to get Taylor across the foyer and up the stairs before her uncle or cousin noticed.

Taylor was threading her way through the crowd of opportunists camped out on the drive when Thomas opened the door. He was pleased to notice she completely ignored the scoundrels trying to gain her attention. Several actually shoved their cards into her hands with loud boasts that they were the best investment counselors in all of England and could get her a triple return on the money she would soon inherit. All she needed to do was hand the inheritance over to them. Thomas was disgusted by their theatrics. If he had had a broom handy, he would have gone after the rabble.

"Here! Here! Get away from her." Thomas shouted the order and rushed forward. He latched onto Taylor's elbow in a protective gesture and glared over his shoulder at the offenders while he escorted her through the doorway.

"Criminals, if you ask me, every one of them," he muttered.

Taylor was in full agreement with his pronouncement. "You were ready to pounce on them, weren't you, Thomas?"

The servant smiled. "Cecil would box my ears if I

were to lower myself to their station," Thomas remarked. "If I am to follow in his footsteps, I must refrain from boorish behavior. A butler must always maintain his dignity, milady."

"Yes, of course," Taylor agreed. "How is our Cecil doing? I sent him a note just last week, but I haven't heard a reply yet. Should I be worrying?"

"No, you shouldn't be worrying about Cecil. As old as he is, he's still as tough as leather. He rallied from his sickbed to say his farewell to Lady Esther. Your grandmother already pensioned him. Did you know that? She set him up as grand as can be, Lady Taylor. Cecil won't be wanting for anything the rest of his days."

"He was Madam's loyal butler for almost thirty years," Taylor reminded the servant. "He should have received a handsome pension. What about you, Tom? What will you do? I doubt Uncle Malcolm will let you stay on here."

"I've already been given an assignment by your grandmother. She wants me to look after her brother, Andrew. It means moving to the Highlands, but that doesn't matter. I would go around the world to please Lady Esther. She set aside a parcel of land and a monthly allowance for me, but I'd wager you already knew about that. It was your idea, wasn't it? You have always looked out for Tom, you have. Even though I'm your elder."

Taylor smiled. It had been her idea, but she was certain Madam would have come up with the notion if she hadn't been so busy with other matters.

"My elder, Tom?" she teased. "You're barely two years older than I am."

"I'm still older," he countered. "Here, let me take your wrap. I'm pleased to see you're wearing white

6

just as your grandmother requested. It's a lovely dress, and if I may be so bold as to add, you're looking ever so much better today."

Thomas was immediately sorry he'd added the compliment, for he didn't want to remind her of their last encounter. Not that Taylor would ever forget, of course. Still, it wasn't gentlemanly to bring up *the humiliation*.

She did look better though. No one had seen her since that afternoon six weeks ago when her grandmother had taken her into the salon to give her the news about her fiancé. Thomas had stood sentry inside the room with his back pressed against the doorknob so no one would dare intrude. He saw how devastated Taylor was by the announcement. To her credit, she neither wept nor carried on. Such behavior wouldn't have been appropriate for a lady. She'd kept her expression contained, but the proof of the injury done to her was evident all the same. Her hand shook as though with tremor as she nervously brushed her hair back over her shoulder, and her complexion turned as white as fresh snow. Her blue eyes, such fair, enchanting blue eyes, completely lost their sparkle, as did her voice when her grandmother at last finished reading the foul letter she had received and Taylor responded, "Thank you for telling me, Madam. I know it was difficult for you."

"I believe you should leave London for a spell, Taylor, until this little scandal blows over. Uncle Andrew will be happy for your company."

"As you wish, Madam."

Taylor excused herself a moment later. She went up to her bedroom, helped pack her own bags, and left for her grandmother's estate in Scotland less than an hour later.

Lady Esther hadn't been idle during her grand-daughter's absence. She'd spent her time with her solicitors.

"Your grandmother is going to be happy to see you, Lady Taylor," Thomas announced. "Since she received the mysterious letter the other day, she's been in such a fretful state of mind. I believe she's counting on you to know what's to be done."

The worry in his voice was quite pronounced. He noticed the name cards she was clutching in her hand, deposited them in the waste receptacle, and then followed her across the foyer to the staircase leading upstairs.

"How is she, Thomas? Has there been any improvement?"

The servant took hold of her hand and patted it with affection. He could hear the fear in her voice. He wanted to lie to her but didn't dare. She deserved the truth.

"She's failing, milady. There won't be a reprieve this time. You must say your good-bye to her now. She's most anxious to get everything settled. We can't continue to let her fret, now can we?"

Taylor shook her head. "No, of course not."

Tears filled her eyes. She tried to will them away. It would upset her grandmother if she saw her weep, and crying wouldn't change what was happening anyway.

"You aren't having second thoughts about your grandmother's grand plans for you, are you, Lady Taylor? If she believed she had truly coerced you into . . ." Thomas didn't finish voicing his concern.

Taylor forced a smile and said, "I'm not having second thoughts. You should know by now that I would go to any length to please my grandmother. She wants all the loose ends tied up before she dies, and since I happen to be the last of her loose ends, it has become my responsibility to help her. There will be no getting around that duty, Thomas."

A burst of laughter came from the salon. The sound jarred Taylor. She turned toward the noise, then spotted two strangers garbed in black attire lounging in the back of the hallway adjacent to the stairs. Both men, she noticed, held champagne flutes in their hands. She suddenly realized the house was packed with guests.

"What are all these people doing here?"

"They're getting ready to celebrate with your uncle Malcolm and your cousin, Jane," Thomas told her. He added a nod when Taylor looked so infuriated, then hastily added, "Your uncle invited a few friends . . ."

Taylor wouldn't let him finish his explanation. "The vile man doesn't have a single redeeming quality, does he?"

The anger in her voice inflamed his own. "It appears not, milady. Your father, God rest his soul, seems to have inherited all the good qualities, while your uncle Malcolm and his offspring . . ." Thomas paused to let out a weary sigh. He noticed that Taylor was about to pull open the salon doors and hastily shook his head. "Both Malcolm and Jane are inside, milady. If they spot you, there's bound to be a scene. I know you want to chase everyone out, but you really don't have the time. Your grandmother is waiting."

Taylor knew he was right. Her grandmother came first. She hurried back across the foyer, took hold of Thomas's arm, and started up the steps.

When they reached the landing, Taylor turned to the servant again. "What does the physician say about Madam's condition? Isn't it possible she could surprise all of us once again? She could get better, couldn't she?"

Thomas shook his head. "Sir Elliott believes it's only a matter of time now," he told her. "Lady Esther's heart has simply worn out. Elliott's the one who notified your uncle Malcolm, and that is why everyone has gathered here today. Your grandmother was fit to be tied when she found out, and I do believe Elliott's ears are still ringing from the tongue-lashing she gave him. It's a wonder his own heart didn't quit beating then and there."

The picture of her grandmother berating such a giant of a man like Elliott made Taylor smile. "Madam is an amazing woman, isn't she?"

"My, yes," Thomas replied. "She has the ability to make grown men shiver with fear. I had to remind myself I wasn't afraid of her."

"You were never afraid of her," Taylor scoffed at the notion.

Thomas grinned. "You wouldn't let me be afraid. Do you remember? You told me all about Madam's bluster while you were dragging me home with you."

Taylor nodded. "I remember. Madam didn't raise her voice when she berated Elliott, did she?"

"Good heavens, no," Thomas replied. "She's a lady, first and always," he boasted. "Elliott flinched as though she were shouting. You should have seen his expression when she threatened not to leave him any money for his new laboratory."

Taylor started down the long corridor with Thomas at her side. "Is Sir Elliott with Madam now?"

"No. He stayed the night through and only just left to get a change of clothing. He should be back in an hour or so. That gives us sufficient time. Your grandmother's guests are in the parlor adjacent to her chambers. She suggested I usher them up the back stairs so no one would see them. Your uncle Malcolm won't have an inkling what's going on until it's too late."

"Then Madam is still insistent we carry through with that plan too?"

"Yes, of course," Thomas answered. "My dear, a word of caution if I may. It will upset your grandmother if she sees tears in your eyes."

"She won't see me cry," Taylor promised.

Lady Esther's suite of rooms was located at the end of the hallway. Taylor didn't hesitate at the threshold to her bedroom. As soon as Thomas opened the door for her, she hurried through the entrance.

It was as dark as midnight inside. Taylor squinted against the darkness while she tried to get her bearings.

The bedroom was gigantic. Taylor used to believe it was at least half the size of Hyde Park. The square platform with the four-poster bed was on one side of the long chamber. On the opposite side were three wing-backed chairs and two small end tables, placed at an angle in front of the heavily draped windows. Taylor had always loved this room. When she was a little girl, she would jump on the bed, do endless somersaults across the thick Oriental carpets, and make enough noise to wake the dead, or so her grandmother often remarked.

There weren't any restrictions inside the chamber. When her grandmother was in an accommodating mood, Taylor was allowed to play dress-up in Lady Esther's wonderful silk gowns and satin covered shoes. She would put on a wide brimmed hat with clumps of flowers and feathers perched on top, drape mounds and mounds of precious jewels around her neck, and don white gloves that came all the way up to her shoulders. Once she was all dressed up in her finery, she would serve tea to her grandmother and make up outrageous stories about the pretend parties she had attended. Grandmother never laughed at her. She went right along with the game. She would diligently wave her painted fan in front of her face, whisper, "I declare" at the appropriate moments, and even gasp with mock dismay over the scandals Taylor would conjure up. Most involved a Gypsy or two and Ladies in Waiting. Occasionally Madam would even make up a few outrageous stories of her own.

Taylor cherished this room and all the wonderful memories, almost as much as she cherished the old woman who lived here.

"You took entirely too long to get here, young lady. You will now give me your apology because you made me wait for you."

Her grandmother's raspy voice echoed throughout the chamber. Taylor turned and started forward. She almost tripped over a footstool. She caught herself before she was pitched to her knees, then cautiously edged her way around the obstacle.

"I apologize, Madam," she called out.

"Quit dawdling, Taylor. Sit down. We have much to discuss."

"I cannot seem to find the chairs, Madam."

"Strike light to a single candle, Janet. That is all I will allow," Lady Esther instructed her maid. "Then leave the chamber. I wish to be alone with my granddaughter."

Taylor finally located the chairs. She sat down in the center seat, straightened the folds in her dress, and then folded her hands together in her lap. She couldn't see her grandmother. The distance and the darkness made it impossible to see much of anything. She still kept her posture ramrod straight. Her spine was as stiff as a starched petticoat. Grandmother hated to see anyone slump, and since she happened to have the vision of a cat, or so Taylor believed, she didn't dare relax.

The light from the candle on her grandmother's bedside table became a beacon in the darkness. Taylor felt rather than saw the lady's maid cross in front of her. She waited until she heard the click of the door as it was closed, then called out, "Why is it so dark in here, Madam? Don't you wish to see the sun today?"

"I do not wish to," her grandmother replied. "I'm dying, Taylor. I know it, God knows it, and so does the devil. I won't make a fuss. It wouldn't be ladylike. I won't be accommodating, however. Death is going to have to stalk me in the dark. If fortune stays on my side, he won't find me until all of my business here has been concluded to my satisfaction. Light might give him an advantage. I fear you're ill prepared for the tasks ahead of you."

The switch in topics took Taylor by surprise, but she was quick to recover. "I beg to differ with you, Madam. You have trained me well. I am prepared for any eventuality."

Lady Esther snorted. "I left a good deal out of your training, didn't I? You know nothing about marriage or what it takes to be a good wife. I blame my inability to discuss such intimate topics on the times, Taylor. We live in such a restrictive society. We must all be so very prim and proper. I don't know how you came by it, but you have great compassion and love inside you, and I will tell you now, I'm thankful I wasn't able to take those qualities away from you. You never caught on that you were supposed to be rigid, did you? Never mind," Lady Esther continued. "It's too late to change. You're a hopeless dreamer, Taylor. Your infatuation with those dime novels and your love for the ruffian men is proof enough."

Taylor smiled. "They're called mountain men, Madam," she corrected. "And I thought you enjoyed listening to me read the stories."

"I'm not saying I didn't enjoy the tales," Lady Esther muttered. "But that isn't the issue now. The stories of Daniel Crockett and Davy Boone would entice anyone, even rigid old women."

She'd mixed up the names. Taylor thought it was done on purpose so that she wouldn't think Madam had become as fascinated by the mountain men as she had. She didn't correct her again. "Yes, Madam," she said, guessing she wanted to hear her agreement.

"I wonder if I'll meet up with those mountain men in the afterlife."

"I believe you will," Taylor replied.

"You're going to have to get your head out of the clouds," her grandmother warned.

"I will, Madam."

"I should have taken the time to teach you how to train a man to be a good, caring husband."

"Uncle Andrew explained everything I need to know."

Lady Esther snorted again. "And just how would my brother be knowing anything about that topic? He's lived the life of a hermit all these years in the Highlands. You have to be married to know what it's all about, Taylor. Don't pay any attention to anything he told you. It's bound to be wrong."

Taylor shook her head. "He gave me sound advice, Madam. Why didn't Andrew ever marry?"

"Probably no one would have him," Madam speculated. "The only thing my brother was ever interested in was his giant horses."

"And his guns," Taylor reminded her. "He's still working on his patents."

"Yes, his guns," Madam agreed. "I'm curious, Taylor. What did he tell you about marriage?"

"If I wish to turn a rascal into a fine husband, then I must treat him very like a horse I'm trying to train. I should use a firm hand, never show him any fear, and dole out affection only sparingly. Uncle Andrew predicted I would have him eating out of my hand within six months. He will have learned to value me and treat me like a princess."

"And if he doesn't value you?"

Taylor smiled. "Then I should borrow one of Uncle's fine guns and shoot him."

Madam's smile was filled with tenderness. "There was a time or two I wanted to shoot your grandfather, but mind you, child, only a time or two."

Her mood turned from jovial to melancholy within the space of a heartbeat. Her voice shook with emotion when she said, "The babies are going to need you. Dear God, you're little more than a baby yourself. How will you ever get along?"

Taylor hurried to soothe her. "I'll do just fine," she insisted. "You think of me as a child, but I'm a fully grown woman now. You've trained me well, Madam. You mustn't worry."

Lady Esther let out a loud sigh. "All right then, I won't worry," she promised. "You have given me your love and your devotion all these years while I . . . do you realize I have never once told you I love you?"

"I do realize it, Madam."

A moment of silence followed Taylor's acknowledgment. Then Lady Esther changed the topic again. "I wouldn't let you tell me why your sister was so desperate to leave England. I'll admit to you now it was because I feared what I would hear. My son was the reason Marian left, wasn't he? What did Malcolm do to her? I'm prepared to listen, Taylor. You may tell me now if you're so inclined."

Taylor's stomach immediately tightened into a knot. She took a deep breath before answering. "I'm not so inclined, Madam. It all happened such a long time ago."

"You're still afraid, aren't you? Even the mention makes your voice tremble."

"No, I'm not afraid any longer."

"I gave you my complete trust and helped Marian and that worthless husband of hers leave, didn't I?"

"Yes, Madam."

"It was difficult for me, knowing I would never see them again. I certainly didn't trust Marian's judgment. Look at the man she married. George was only slightly better than a street beggar. He certainly didn't love her. He latched onto her for her money. She wouldn't listen to reason though, would she? I disowned the both of them. It was a spiteful thing to do. I realize that now."

"George wasn't worthless, Madam. He just didn't have a head for business. He might have only married my sister for her money, but he stayed with her after you took her inheritance back. I think he learned to love her, if only just a little. He was always good and kind to her. And from all the letters he sent us, I also believe he was a wonderful father."

Lady Esther nodded. "Yes, I, too, believe he was a good father," she admitted grudgingly. "It was you who convinced me to give them some money so they could leave England. I did the right thing, didn't I?"

16

"Yes, you did the right thing."

"Did Marian want to tell me what happened? Dear God, she's been dead eighteen months and I'm only just now able to ask you that question."

"Marian wouldn't have told you," Taylor insisted, her voice urgent now.

"But she confided in you, didn't she?"

"Yes, but only because she wanted to protect me."

Taylor paused to take another breath in an attempt to hold onto her composure. The topic was so distressing, her hands started shaking. She didn't want her grandmother to know how upset she was. She tried to keep the tremor out of her voice when she spoke again. "You showed your love for her by protecting her without demanding reasons. You helped her leave. She and George were happy in Boston, and I'm certain Marian died at peace."

"If I ordered you to bring her daughters home to England now, would they be safe?"

"No." Her answer was quick, forceful. She softened her tone when she added, "The little girls should be raised in their father's country. It is what George and Marian both wanted." *And not under Malcolm's guardianship,* Taylor silently added.

"Do you believe the cholera has taken the babies as well? We would have heard by now, wouldn't we?"

"Yes, we would have heard. They're healthy and well," she said. She made her voice as emphatic as possible and said a quick prayer that she was right. The babies' nanny, Mrs. Bartlesmith, had written with the tragic news. She hadn't been at all certain cholera had killed George, and since the physician refused to expose himself to the possibility of catching the disease by coming to the house after George had died, no one could be sure. The nanny kept the babies

17

away from their father while he was so ill. She protected them as best she could. God had already taken Marian, and now George, and He wouldn't be so unmerciful as to take the two-year-olds as well. It was too upsetting to even consider.

"I trust you, Taylor." Madam's voice was weary now.

"Thank you, Madam."

"Did I protect you growing up?"

"Oh, yes," Taylor cried out. "All these many years you've protected me."

Several minutes passed in silence. Then Lady Esther said, "Are you prepared to leave England?"

"I am."

"Boston is a world away from us. Tell the babies kind stories about me, even if you have to make them up. I wish to be remembered fondly."

"Yes, Madam."

Taylor tried desperately not to cry. She stared at her hands and took several deep breaths.

Lady Esther didn't seem to notice her granddaughter's distress. She went into detail once again about the money she had had transferred to the bank in Boston. Her voice was weak with fatigue by the time she finished her instructions.

"As soon as Sir Elliott returns, he'll announce I've had yet another miraculous recovery. He may be an imbecile but he knows who is buttering his bread. You'll attend the ball tonight and act as though everything is as right as ever. You will laugh. You will smile. You will celebrate my good health. You will stay until the chimes strike the midnight hour. No one must know you're leaving at first light. No one."

"But, Madam, now that you're so ill, I had thought to stay here with you."

"You'll do no such thing," her grandmother snapped. "You must be away from England before I die. My brother, Andrew, will keep me company. I won't be alone. Malcolm and the others will be told that you've gone after you've set sail. Agree with me, Taylor. It's your duty to make this old woman die content."

"Yes, Madam." Her voice caught on a sob.

"Are you weeping?"

"No, Madam."

"I cannot abide tears."

"Yes, Madam."

Her grandmother sighed with satisfaction. "I went to a great deal of trouble to find the right one. You do know that, don't you, Taylor?" she asked. "Of course you do. Now then, there is just one more document to sign and witness. One last ceremony for me to see through. Then I'll be at peace."

"I do not wish for you to die, Madam."

"One doesn't always get what one wishes, young lady. Remember that."

"Yes, Madam."

"Tell Thomas to fetch the guests he's hidden away in the parlor. Then come and stand next to me. I want to watch you sign the paper before I witness it."

Taylor stood up. "You will not change your mind about this?"

"I will not," her grandmother answered. "Will you change yours?"

The challenge was there in her clipped, no-nonsense tone of voice. Taylor managed a smile. "No, I will not change my mind," she answered just as forcefully.

"Then hurry up, Taylor. Time's wasting away, and time, you see, is my enemy."

Taylor started for the door connecting the bedroom

to the adjacent parlor. She was halfway across the chamber when she suddenly stopped. "Madam?"

"What is it?"

"Before Thomas brings the others inside . . . we won't be alone again and I . . . may I . . ."

She didn't say more. She didn't need to. Her grandmother understood what she was asking.

A loud sigh filled the chamber. "If you must," her grandmother grumbled.

"Thank you."

"Get it said, Taylor."

"Very well," she agreed. "I love you, Madam, with all my heart."

He couldn't believe he'd done it. Damn it all, he almost hadn't been able to pull it off. He shook his head in disgust. *What kind of man would demand one brother buy another brother's freedom? A real bastard, that's who,* he thought to himself . . . a real son of a . . .

Lucas Michael Ross forced the raging thoughts aside. What was done was done. The boy was free now and ready to start a new life. That was all that mattered. The son-of-a-bitch heir to the family fortune would eventually get his reward. As far as Lucas was concerned, his older half brother could rot or thrive in England for all he cared.

His anger wouldn't go away. Lucas leaned against the pillar near the alcove in the majestic ballroom and watched the couples twirling around the marble floor in front of him. He was flanked on both sides by his brothers' friends, Morris and Hampton. They both held titles, but Lucas couldn't remember what they were. The two men were in the middle of a heated debate on the merits versus the perils of capitalism in

America and why it would never work. Lucas pretended interest, nodded whenever he thought it was probably appropriate, but otherwise pretty much ignored the men and their discussion.

It was his last night in England. He didn't want to savor the evening; he wanted to finish it. He didn't have any particular fondness for this bleak country and was in fact confused by those who chose to make their home here. After living in the wilderness deep in America, Lucas couldn't imagine why anyone would deliberately choose England. He found most of the inhabitants to be as pompous and pretentious as their leaders and their monuments and every bit as stifling as the air they breathed. He detested the closeness, the endless smoke stacks, the gray-black film that hung over the city, the gaudiness of the women, the prissiness of the men. When he was in London, Lucas felt penned in, caged. The sudden image of a dancing bear he'd once seen when he was a boy attending a country fair on the outskirts of Cincinnati came into his mind. The animal had been dressed in men's britches and was prancing in a circle on his hind legs around and around the owner who controlled the beast by holding onto a long, heavy chain he'd secured around the bear's neck.

The men and women circling the dance floor reminded Lucas of the trained bear. Their movements were jerky, controlled, certainly rehearsed. The women's gowns were all different in color but otherwise identical in both cut and style. The men were just as silly looking to him. They all wore their black formal uniform. Hell, even their shoes were identical to one another. The rules and regulations of the restrictive society in which they lived were their chains, Lucas supposed, and he found himself feeling a little sorry for them. They would never know real adventure or freedom or wide-open spaces. They would live, then die, and never realize what they had missed.

"What has you frowning, Lucas?"

Morris, the older of the two Englishmen, asked the question. He looked up at Lucas while he waited for his answer.

Lucas nodded toward the dance floor. "I was thinking there isn't a maverick among them," he replied in that soft Kentucky drawl that seemed to amuse the men so.

Morris obviously didn't understand what he'd meant by the remark. He shook his head in confusion. Hampton was more astute. He nodded agreement. "He's referring to the couples dancing," he explained.

"And?" Morris prodded, still not comprehending.

"Don't you notice how alike the women are? Every one of them has her hair all bound up tight at the back of her head, and most of them have those ridiculous feathers sticking out at all angles. The gowns are quite identical as well," he added. "With those wire contraptions hidden underneath the skirts to make their backsides look so bizarre. The men aren't any better. They're all dressed alike, too."

Hampton turned to Lucas. "Breeding and education have taken all our individuality away."

"Lucas is dressed in formal attire, just like we are," Morris blurted out. He acted as though the thought had only just occurred to him. He was a short, squat man with thick glasses, a receding hairline, and firm opinions about every possible topic. He felt it was his sole duty to play the devil's advocate and argue against any view his best friend held. "The clothing you've suddenly taken exception to is appropriate attire at a ball, Hampton. What would you have us wear? Boots and buckskin?"

"It would be a refreshing change," Hampton snapped.

Before Morris could come back with a rebuttal, Hampton turned to Lucas and changed the topic. "Are you anxious to get back to your valley?"

"I am," Lucas agreed, finding his first smile.

"Then all of your business has been completed?"

"Almost all," Lucas replied.

"Aren't you leaving tomorrow?"

"Yes."

"How can you finish up your business with so little time left?" Hampton asked.

Lucas shrugged. "There is only one small task to take care of," he explained.

"Are you taking Kelsey back with you?" Hampton asked.

"He's the reason I came back to London," Lucas answered. "The boy's already on his way to Boston with his brothers. They left the day before yesterday."

Kelsey was the youngest of Lucas's three half brothers. The older two, Jordan and Douglas, were already seasoned frontiersmen working their land in the valley. Kelsey hadn't been old enough on Lucas's last trip back, and so he'd left the boy with his tutors for two more years. Kelsey was almost twelve years old now. Intellectually he'd been nurtured, Lucas had seen to that, but emotionally he'd been neglected to the point of starvation. The son-of-a-bitch heir to the family fortune had seen to that.

It no longer mattered that Kelsey was too young for the harsh life in the wilderness. The boy would die if he stayed in England any longer.

"It's a pity Jordan and Douglas didn't stay on in

London a little longer," Morris remarked. "They would have enjoyed this affair tonight. Quite a few of their friends are here."

"They wanted to get a head start with Kelsey," Lucas replied.

They were also determined to get their brother out of England with all possible haste. As soon as the son-of-a-bitch heir had signed the guardianship papers, they booked passage. They were concerned he might change his mind or increase the amount of money he wanted in exchange for his own brother.

He was getting angry again. Damn but he wanted to get out of England. During the war with the South he'd been locked up in a prison the size of a broom closet. He'd turned claustrophobic then and thought he would go out of his mind before he escaped. The torments weren't over yet, however, and he'd been forced to endure another atrocity he still couldn't think about without breaking out in a cold sweat. The war had changed him all right. He couldn't stand close quarters now. His throat would start to tighten up on him, and he'd have difficulty taking a deep breath. The feeling was welling up inside him again. London was rapidly turning into a prison in his mind and all he could think about was breaking free.

Lucas pulled out his timepiece, flipped open the latch, and noted the time. Twenty minutes until midnight. He could last, he told himself. He had promised to stay until midnight, and twenty more minutes wouldn't kill him.

"How I wish I could go with you to your valley," Hampton suddenly blurted out.

Morris looked appalled. He squinted up at his friend through thick glasses. "You can't be serious. You have responsibilities here. Do your title and your lands mean so little to you? I don't believe you really mean it, man. No one in his right mind would give up England and all she has to offer."

Morris was gravely offended by what he considered to be extreme disloyalty to his homeland. He hurled himself into a lecture meant to shame his friend Hampton. Lucas wasn't listening. He'd just spotted the son-of-a-bitch heir across the hall. William Merritt III was the legitimate firstborn son. Lucas was three years younger. He was the bastard. Their father had visited America when he was a young man, and while he was there, he swept an innocent country girl off her feet and into his bed. He gave her his pledge of love, bedded her every night of the month he spent in Kentucky, and then thought to mention he had a wife and a son waiting for him back in England. The son had grown up to be just like his father. He was a self-indulgent demon who thought only of his own pleasures. Loyalty and family values held little meaning for him. Because he was the privileged firstborn, he inherited the land, the title, and whatever funds were left. His father hadn't bothered to make provisions for his other legitimate sons, and his firstborn wasn't about to share the wealth. Jordan, Douglas, and Kelsey weren't just left out in the cold. They'd been thrown there.

Jordan was the first to track Lucas down and ask him for help. He wanted to come to America and start a new life. Lucas hadn't wanted to get involved. Jordan and his brothers were strangers to him. He felt disconnected from the world of privilege they lived in. He was an outsider, and though they shared the same father, he didn't feel any kinship to his half brothers. Family was a concept altogether foreign to him.

Loyalty, however, was another matter.

He couldn't turn his back on Jordan, and he refused to take the time to figure out why. Then Douglas came along, and by then it was too late for Lucas to change his mind. When he traveled to England and saw how Kelsey was being treated, he knew he wouldn't be finished with his duty until he'd found a way to free the youngest from bondage.

The price Lucas had had to pay was well worth his own freedom.

The waltz ended with a crescendo of sound just as Morris finished his spontaneous lecture. The men in the orchestra stood up, then formally bowed to the sound of thunderous applause.

The clapping was suddenly, inexplicably cut off. Couples still lingering on the dance floor turned to the entrance. A hush fell over the guests. Lucas was intrigued by the behavior of the crowd. He turned to see what attraction held everyone so spellbound just as Morris nudged him.

"Not everything in England is tainted," Morris announced. "Have a look, Lucas. The proof of England's superiority stands at the entrance."

From the enthusiasm in his voice, Lucas didn't think he would be surprised to find the queen of England standing there.

"Hampton, get out of his way so he can see," Morris ordered.

"Lucas is a good head taller than every other man here," Hampton muttered. "He can see well enough. Besides, I can't take my gaze off the vision long enough to even consider moving anywhere. God love her, she showed up," he added in a whisper, the adoration in his voice unmistakable. "She's got courage, I'd say. Oh, yes, courage, indeed."

"There's your maverick, Lucas," Morris announced in a voice thick with pride.

The young lady under discussion stood on the top of the steps leading down into the ballroom. The

Englishmen hadn't exaggerated. She really was an incredibly beautiful woman. She wore a royal blue evening gown with a scooped neck that was neither overly revealing nor overly concealing. The dress wasn't molded to her figure, yet it was impossible not to notice her softly rounded curves and her creamy white skin.

She was all alone, and from the faint smile on her face, she didn't seem to be the least bothered by the stir she was causing. She didn't seem to care that her clothing wasn't considered fashionable either. Her skirt wasn't all poofed out at odd angles, and it was apparent she wasn't wearing one of those wire contraptions underneath. Her hair wasn't bound up tight in a braid. The long, golden-colored curls fell in soft waves around her slender shoulders.

No, she wasn't dressed in the uniform of the other women at the ball, and perhaps that was one reason she held every man's rapt attention. She was a refreshing diversion in perfection.

Lucas was certainly affected by the sight of such loveliness. He instinctively blinked. She didn't disappear. He couldn't see the color of her eyes, but he already knew they were blue . . . candlelight blue. They had to be.

He was suddenly having difficulty drawing a breath. A tightness settled inside his chest, and his heart started slamming a wild beat. Hell, he was acting like a schoolboy. It was humiliating.

"She really is a maverick," Hampton agreed. "Will you look at the marquess? He's standing directly across the ballroom. I declare I can see the lust in his eyes even from this considerable distance. I imagine his new wife sees it, too. Look how she's glaring at him. Lord, this really is quite delightful. I do believe justice is finally being served to the blackheart. He's getting his due now. God, I'm sorry, Lucas. I shouldn't be talking about your half brother with such disrespect."

"I don't consider him family," Lucas replied in a hard, unbending voice. "He disowned the rest of us years ago. And you're right, Hampton," he added. "Justice has been served in more ways than even you realize."

Hampton gave him a quizzical look. "You've made me mighty curious, Lucas. What is it you know that we don't?"

"He probably heard all about *the humiliation,*" Morris speculated. He didn't wait for Lucas to confirm or deny his statement but hurried on to give the full report just in case he hadn't heard every single little detail.

"The beautiful vision in blue smiling so sweetly was engaged to your half brother, but I'm certain you already knew that much of the story," he began. "William could have had it all. He was quite smooth while he courted her, and she, so young and innocent, surely found him attractive. Then, just two weeks before the wedding was scheduled to take place, William eloped with his fiancée's cousin, Jane. Over five hundred people had been invited to the celebration, and of course, all had to be notified of the cancellation. It was going to be the bash of the season all right. Can you imagine the disgrace of having to call the thing off at such a late hour?"

Hampton nodded. "Do you see how Jane is clinging to William now? Oh, this is priceless. It really is. William isn't even trying to hide his lustful thoughts. I wouldn't be surprised if he started drooling. Jane's a pale shadow next to what he gave up, isn't she?"

Lucas wasn't amused. "He's a fool," he muttered.

Hampton agreed with a nod. "I despise William

Merritt. He's a crook and a manipulator. He duped my father, then publicly boasted of his cleverness. My father was humiliated."

"Look what William did to his own brothers," Morris said.

"He almost destroyed Jordan and Douglas, didn't he?" Hampton asked.

"He did," Morris answered. "William's getting his just reward, all right. He's going to be miserable the rest of his life. Jane's every bit as vile as he is. They make a frightening couple, don't they? Rumor has it she's carrying his child. I pity the babe if that gossip is true."

"She could be carrying," Hampton agreed. "The two were blatantly carrying on while he was engaged. Jane's going to be sorry, too. She thinks William has quite an inheritance left."

"Doesn't he?" Lucas asked the question.

Hampton shook his head. "It will soon come out with the wash. He's as destitute as a beggar. The fool speculated and lost every pound he had. The bankers own his land now. He's probably counting on Jane getting a fat inheritance when old Lady Stapleton dies. She was ailing, but I understand she made another miraculous recovery."

The music started up again. The crowd was forced to quit gawking. Taylor lifted the hem of her gown and walked down the steps. Lucas couldn't take his gaze off her. He took a step toward her, then stopped to look at his timepiece again.

Ten more minutes left. He could last that long. Just ten more minutes and then he would be free. He let out a loud sigh of satisfaction and smiled in anticipation.

Lady Taylor was also smiling. She was following her grandmother's orders to the letter. She had forced a smile on her face the second she'd walked through the doorway, and by God, no one was going to do or say anything to make her frown.

She would smile. She would celebrate. It was agony. She was so sick inside over the mockery of it all, her stomach felt as though it were on fire.

Taylor forced herself not to give in to despair. She must look forward to the future, she thought, echoing her grandmother's words to her. The babies needed her.

Young, unattached men came rushing forward. Taylor ignored them. She looked around the ballroom, trying to find her escort. She spotted her cousin, Jane, then William, but refused to allow herself to stare at either one of them. Her heart started pounding. Dear God, what would she do if they came over to her? What would she say to them? Congratulations? Oh, God, she'd die first or throw up. She hadn't considered the possibility they would attend the affair. Her mind had been consumed with her worry about her grandmother. There hadn't been room for lesser concerns. Ironically, Madam had made quite an improvement that afternoon, and when Taylor had taken her leave, she was hopeful her grandmother had truly been given another reprieve.

An eager young man she knew she'd met before but couldn't remember where or when begged her for the honor of escorting her onto the dance floor. Taylor graciously declined. He had just turned away from her when she heard Jane's distinctive high-pitched laughter. She turned to look, spotted Jane's malicious smile, and then noticed a young lady turn and hurry toward the exit. Taylor recognized the girl. She was Lady Catherine, the youngest of Sir Connan's offspring and barely fifteen years old.

Getting married hadn't improved Jane's disposition. Catherine had just become her latest victim, Taylor decided, when she saw the look of devastation on the poor girl's face.

Taylor was suddenly overwhelmed with melancholy. Cruelty was a sport some of her relatives thoroughly enjoyed. She was sickened by their meanness, and in her present state of mind, she simply didn't know how to combat it any longer. She felt useless, inept. She had always known she didn't fit in with the upper crust of England's society, and perhaps that was why she always had her head in the clouds and her nose in the dime novels. Yes, she was a dreamer, just as her grandmother had accused, but Taylor didn't think that was so terrible. Reality was often quite ugly, and it would have been completely unbearable if she hadn't been able to daydream every now and then. It was escapism, pure and simple.

She loved romantic stories most of all. Unfortunately, the only heroes she'd ever known were those dashing figures she'd read about. Daniel Boone and Davy Crockett were her favorites. They were long dead now, but the romantic legends surrounding their lives still enchanted writers and readers alike.

Madam wanted her to become a realist, and all because she believed there weren't any heroes left.

Lady Catherine was in such a state of despair, she very nearly knocked Taylor down on her way to the steps. She was thinking only of running away from the cruelty.

Taylor grabbed hold of the distraught girl. "Do slow down, Catherine."

"Please let me pass," Catherine begged.

Tears were already streaming down her face. Taylor refused to let go of her arm. "Quit crying," she

31

ordered. "You aren't going anywhere. If you leave, it will be all the more difficult for you to show your face in public again. You can't allow Jane to have such power over you."

"You don't know what happened," Catherine wailed. "She said . . . she's telling everyone I . . ."

Taylor gave her a little squeeze to get her to calm down. "It doesn't matter what vile things she's saying. If you pretend to ignore her and her slander, no one will believe her."

Catherine pulled a handkerchief out of the sleeve of her gown and mopped her face. "I was so mortified," she whispered. "I don't know what I did to cause her to turn on me the way she did."

"You're young and very pretty," Taylor answered. "And that is why she turned on you. Your mistake was getting too close to her. You'll survive, Catherine, just as I have. I'm certain Jane's already looking for someone else to try to make miserable. Being cruel amuses her. She's quite disgusting, isn't she?"

Catherine managed a weak smile. "Oh, yes, Lady Taylor. She really is disgusting. You should have heard what she just said about you. The sapphires you're wearing should belong to her."

"Is that so?"

Catherine nodded. "She says Lady Esther's gone dotty and . . ."

Taylor cut her off. "I'm not interested in anything Jane has to say about my dear grandmother."

Catherine peeked over Taylor's shoulder. "She's watching us," she whispered.

Taylor refused to look. Lord, just a little longer, she thought, and then she could leave this godawful place.

"Catherine, would you do an enormous favor for me?"

"Anything," Catherine fervently promised.

"Wear my sapphires."

"I beg your pardon?"

Taylor reached up to unclasp the necklace from the back of her neck. She removed her earrings next.

Catherine was gaping at her. The look on her face was quite comical. Taylor smiled in reaction.

"You cannot be serious, Lady Taylor. They must have cost a fortune. Jane will scream if she sees me wearing them."

"She will become upset, won't she?" She drawled out her question and smiled again.

Catherine burst into laughter. The sound echoed throughout the hall. It was cleansing, honest, joyful. Taylor was suddenly feeling much better.

Taylor assisted Catherine in putting the jewelry on before speaking again.

"Never be ruled by possessions, and never, ever make wealth more important to you than your self-respect and your dignity. Otherwise you're bound to end up like Jane," she warned. "You wouldn't want that, would you?"

"Dear heavens, no," Catherine blurted out, appalled by the very idea. "I promise I won't be ruled by possessions. At least I'll try not to be ruled by them. I feel like a princess wearing this necklace. Is it proper to feel that way?"

Taylor laughed. "Yes, of course. I'm glad they bring you such joy."

"I shall make certain Papa hides these in a safe place. Tomorrow I shall personally deliver them to you."

Taylor shook her head. "I won't need them tomorrow," she explained. "They're yours to keep. I'm not ever going to need such jewels again."

Catherine almost fell over. "But . . ." she began. She was clearly too astonished to continue. "But . . ."

"They're my gift to you."

Catherine burst into tears. She was obviously over-whelmed by Taylor's generosity.

"I didn't mean to make you cry," Taylor said. "You look beautiful, Catherine, with or without sapphires. Wipe your tears away while I find a suitable dance partner for you."

Milton Thompson caught her eye. Taylor motioned to the young man. He came running. A scant minute later, Catherine was being escorted onto the dance floor.

She looked radiant. She was giggling and flirting and once again acting like a fifteen-year-old.

Taylor was content. The feeling didn't last long. Where was her escort? She decided she would circle the ballroom, being sure to make a wide arch around her cousin, of course, and if she came up empty-handed, she would simply leave. She had arrived fashionably late and would leave fashionably early. She had smiled enough for one evening, and Grand-mother would never know she only stayed fifteen or twenty minutes. Yes, Madam would approve of her performance.

Taylor was waylaid from going anywhere by three well-meaning friends. Alison, Jennifer, and Constance had all attended Miss Lorrison's School of Charm and Scholarly Pursuits with Taylor. They had all been fast friends ever since. Alison was a year older than the others, and for that reason alone, she believed she was far more sophisticated.

She led the procession over to Taylor. Alison was tall, a bit ungainly, and had dark blond hair and hazel-colored eyes.

"Darling Taylor, you look beautiful tonight," she announced. "I do believe I look drab just standing next to you."

Taylor smiled. Alison called everyone darling. She believed it made her appear to be more sophisticated. "No one can make you look drab," she replied, knowing instinctively that was what Alison wanted to hear.

"I do look lovely, don't I? The gown is new," she went on to explain. "It cost Father a fortune. He's determined to get me married this season even if it bankrupts him."

Taylor found Alison's honesty refreshing. "I'm certain you could have your pick of any gentleman here."

"The only one I'm interested in won't give me a single glance," Alison confessed.

"She's done everything possible to gain his attention," Jennifer interjected. She reached up to pin a strand of her brown hair back into her coiled braid before adding, "She could try swooning in front of him, I suppose."

"He probably wouldn't catch her," Constance said. "Do leave your hair alone, Jennifer. You're making a mess of it. And put on your spectacles. Squinting makes wrinkles around the corners of your eyes."

Jennifer ignored Constance's suggestions. "Alison's father would have heart palpitations if that man did pursue her."

Constance nodded agreement. Her short, curly bob bounced in reaction. "He's quite the bad boy," she told Taylor.

"Boy? Darling, he's a man," Alison chided.

"A man with a black reputation," Constance countered. "Taylor, do I look all washed out wearing a pink gown? Jennifer said my red hair and freckles don't go at all well with any shade of pink, but I was so partial to this fabric . . ."

"You look beautiful," Taylor replied.

"He does have a black reputation," Alison admitted. "And that, you see, is what intrigues me about him."

"Melinda told me she'd heard he's taken a different woman to his bed every single night this past week alone," Constance interjected. "Can you imagine? He can have anyone he wants. He's very . . ."

"Seductive?" Alison suggested the description.

Constance immediately blushed. "I'll admit there is a certain raw appeal about him. He's so . . . huge. His eyes are simply divine. They're a dark, dark brown."

"Who are we talking about?" Taylor asked, her curiosity caught.

"We don't know his name yet," Alison explained. "But he's here tonight, and he isn't leaving until I get an introduction. There is something sinfully erotic about him." She paused to wave her fan in front of her face. "I declare he makes my heart skip."

Taylor suddenly noticed Jennifer was frowning at her and giving her what she could only conclude was a pitying look. "Is something the matter, Jennifer?" she asked.

"Oh, Taylor, it's so terribly brave of you to come here tonight."

Alison smacked Jennifer on the shoulder with the edge of her fan. "For God's sake, Jennifer, we said we wouldn't bring up her humiliation."

"Now you've done it," Constance snapped. "Shame on you for being so thoughtless. Taylor, is your heart breaking?"

"No. I really . . ."

She wasn't given time to say more. "Rumor has it that Jane's carrying his child," Jennifer whispered.

"The two were carrying on all the while he was courting you."

"Did you really need to bring that up?" Alison asked.

"She has a right to know," Jennifer argued.

"We didn't know," Constance interjected. "We would have told you, Taylor. We never would have let you marry such a scoundrel."

"I really don't want to talk . . ."

Once again Taylor was interrupted before she could finish her thought. "He's here, you know," Jennifer informed the group. "I saw Jane grab hold of his arm the minute Taylor walked in. She hasn't let go of him yet. William Merritt should be hung for his sins."

"I really don't want to talk about him," Taylor said.

"No, of course you don't," Alison agreed. "Mark my words, darling. The time will come when you'll realize how fortunate you were to be jilted."

"We shall stand by your side for the rest of the evening," Constance pledged. "If anyone tries to say anything thoughtless, I shall personally give him or her a setdown. You have my word, Taylor."

"Thank you," Taylor replied. "But I'm not so thin-skinned. You don't need to worry anyone's going to hurt my feelings. I can take care of myself."

"Yes, of course you can," Alison told her in a pitying tone of voice.

"Do you still have feelings for him?" Jennifer wanted to know.

"No. As a matter of fact I . . ."

"But of course she has feelings for him. She hates him," Constance decreed.

"No, I don't . . ." Taylor began again.

"Love and hate go hand in hand," Jennifer explained. "I believe she should hate all men in general and William Merritt in particular."

"I don't believe hating anyone will solve . . ."

"But of course you must hate him," Constance argued.

Taylor decided it was high time she gained control of the conversation and turned the topic. "I've written long letters to all of you with important news," she blurted out before she could be interrupted again.

"Whatever for?" Alison asked.

"News? What news?" Constance demanded.

Taylor shook her head. "You'll have to wait until tomorrow. You'll receive your letters by late afternoon."

"Tell us your news now," Jennifer insisted.

"You're being very mysterious," Constance remarked.

"I don't mean to be mysterious," Taylor replied. "Sometimes it's easier to write down what I want to say rather than . . ."

"Spill it out, Taylor," Alison demanded.

"You cannot leave us hanging like this," Constance interjected.

"Are you going away?" Jennifer asked. She turned to Constance. "People always write letters when they're going away."

Taylor was sorry she'd mentioned the letters. "It's a surprise," she insisted.

"Now you've got to tell us," Alison said. "You aren't leaving this ballroom until you do. I won't be able to sleep until I've heard this mysterious news."

Taylor shook her head. The look on Alison's face told her she wasn't going to let the matter drop. Constance inadvertently came to Taylor's rescue. She spotted Lady Catherine on the dance floor, recognized the sapphire necklace around her neck, and immediately demanded to know why she was wearing Taylor's jewelry.

Taylor took her time explaining her reasons for giving the jewels away.

Lucas watched her from across the ballroom. He was penned in by a crowd of men who took turns plying him with questions about life in America. He was amused by some of their obvious prejudices, irritated by others. The Englishmen all seemed to be fascinated by the Indians. Had Lucas killed many?

He patiently answered the less offensive questions but kept looking at his timepiece every other minute. He didn't particularly care if he was being rude or not. When midnight arrived, he was leaving. Lucas re-checked the time, noted he only had a few more minutes left, and then went back to answering the men. He was in the middle of explaining that his ranch was surrounded by mountains and that the Sioux and the Crow allowed him and his brothers to share their land when he spotted the son-of-a-bitch heir to the family fortune shrug off his wife's hand and head for Taylor. His new bride chased after him.

Taylor spotted him, too. She looked ready to bolt. Lucas watched her bend to lift the hem of her skirt, then suddenly let go and straighten up again. She had obviously decided not to run after all.

No one was going to know the panic she was feeling, not even her dearest friends. Taylor made that vow and smiled until her face felt brittle. *The humiliation.* She knew that was what everyone was calling the cancellation of her wedding. They all expected her to act humiliated, she supposed. Well, by God, they were going to be disappointed.

Alison was going on and on about something or other, but Taylor wasn't paying any attention. She didn't want to injure her friend's feelings, however, and so she pretended great interest. She nodded whenever Alison paused for air and kept right on smiling. Taylor could only hope she was telling an amusing story and not a tragic one.

They were getting closer. William was weaving his way around the couples on the dance floor. Jane was in hot pursuit of her husband.

Taylor might have been able to control her panic if she hadn't seen the expression on her cousin's face. Jane looked livid. When she was in a cheerful mood, she was a little malicious, but when she was angry . . . it was simply too chilling to think about.

Taylor thought she was going to be sick. Oh, Lord, she simply couldn't do it. Her noble intention to stand firm hadn't lasted more than a minute or two. She really was going to run. She had neither the strength nor the inclination to be civil to her cousin. Cousins, she silently corrected. Her ex-fiancé was related by marriage to her now.

Oh, yes, she was going to be sick all right.

Lucas saw the panic in her eyes, stopped his explanation about the Indians in midsentence, and pushed his way through the throng of men surrounding him. Both Morris and Hampton followed him as he headed across the ballroom.

"Taylor, what in heaven's name are you doing?" Alison demanded in an appalled tone of voice.

"She's taking great gulps of air," Constance said. She frowned over her own observation and leaned closer to Taylor in an attempt to understand her mysterious behavior.

"But why is she breathing like that?" Jennifer asked.

Taylor tried to calm herself. "I believe I should leave now," she began.

"You only just got here," Jennifer argued.

"Yes, but I really think I . . ."

"Dear heavens, he's coming over here."

Alison made the comment in a fluster and immediately set about straightening the sleeves of her gown.

Constance peeked around Alison, let out a gasp, and then turned back to Taylor. "Oh, wait until you meet him," she whispered. "Even though Mama has declared he's a sinfully bad man, I must admit he has the most adorable drawl."

"How would you know?" Jennifer asked.

"I heard him talking to Hampton," Constance explained.

"You were eavesdropping," Jennifer accused.

Constance nodded. "Yes," she admitted quite cheerfully.

Taylor was slowly backing away from her friends. She glanced over her shoulder to judge the distance to the entrance. Freedom, she decided, was a good thirty feet away. If she could just get to the steps, she could . . .

"Taylor, you simply must speak to the man," Alison insisted.

"Have you all gone crazy? I will not speak to him. Why, there isn't a thing adorable about William Merritt."

Taylor fairly shouted that statement of fact. Her friends all turned to look at her.

"William? No one mentioned William," Constance said.

"Do come back here, Taylor," Alison demanded.

"Oh, dear, William's on his way over, too," Jennifer announced in a low whisper. "No wonder Taylor's trying to sneak away."

"I'm not trying to sneak away," Taylor argued. It was a blatant lie, of course, but she'd go to her grave before admitting her cowardice. "I just want to avert a scene. If you'll excuse me, I . . ."

Constance grabbed hold of her arm to stop her from

41

leaving. "You can't sneak out," she whispered. "It would make you appear to be quite pitiful, Taylor. We can't have that. Simply ignore him. Alison, will you quit gawking at that man?"

"Someone really must introduce me," Alison insisted once again. She was violently swinging her fan in front of her face.

"Morris might introduce you," Jennifer suggested. She backed up a space so she wouldn't be injured by Alison's fan, then added, "Isn't he beautiful?"

She asked the question with a long, drawn-out sigh. Alison nodded agreement. "Men are handsome, darling, not beautiful, but I do believe this one is both. God, he's huge, isn't he? I fear I'm becoming fainthearted just looking at him."

Taylor was diligently trying to get Constance to unhand her. She finally managed to pull free and was just about to pick up her skirts again and run for her life when she happened to spot the man Alison and the others were carrying on about.

She froze. Her eyes widened just a fraction, and she thought she might have forgotten how to breathe, for she was suddenly, unexplainably, feeling terribly light-headed.

He was the most incredibly handsome man she had ever seen. He was a giant of a man, lean, yet muscular at the same time, with broad shoulders and dark, dark hair. His skin was bronzed in color, certainly achieved by spending long days out in the sun, and his eyes, dear God, his eyes were the most beguiling color. They were a deep, rich, chocolate brown. There were creases at the corners, wonderful little creases, probably caused from squinting against the sun.

He didn't look like the sort who laughed much. He didn't appear to be the kind of man you'd want to meet up with on a dark, deserted corner either or spend the rest of your life with . . . Oh, God, what had she done?

Taylor reached up and snatched Alison's fan out of her hand. Before her friend could protest, she began to furiously wave the thing in front of her face. Lord, but it had gone warm in here.

Wouldn't it be outrageous if she fainted at his feet? He'd probably step over her on his way to the doors. Taylor shook her head. She really had to get hold of her thoughts and her composure, she decided. She could feel herself blushing. How ridiculous, she thought. She had nothing to feel embarrassed about. It was the heat, she told herself. Why, it was as hot as purgatory now.

Was the giant walking toward her the one with the godawful reputation? Lord, she hoped not. Just as soon as she recovered her wits, Taylor was going to ask Constance why her mama didn't like him. She wished she'd paid more attention to the conversation. Hadn't Constance said he'd taken a different woman to his bed every night this past week? She'd ask Constance that question, too, along with at least a hundred more, for she suddenly wanted to know all about the mysterious stranger.

Dear God, it was a little late for questions, wasn't it? Heaven help her, she was losing her mind. She certainly wasn't thinking coherent thoughts now. It was probably all his fault. His gaze, after all, was fully directed on her. It was unnerving, penetrating. No wonder she was rattled. And so rudely undisciplined, she silently added. She couldn't stop staring at him. She wondered if her mouth were gaping open. She hoped it wasn't but doubted she could do anything about it even if it were. No matter, she told herself. The fan would hide most of her face.

Alison grabbed her fan back. Taylor felt as though

her gown had just been ripped off her. She felt exposed, but only for a second or two. Then she straightened her shoulders, slapped a smile on her face, and tried to remember how to act like a lady.

Oh, yes, he was handsome all right. She could barely catch her breath just looking at him. She wanted to sigh in appreciation. She didn't dare.

Taylor understood the reason behind her bizarre reaction to the man. He was her dream-come-true, for he reminded her of one of her mountain men. It was as though he'd stepped out of one of her dime novels. After reading so many stories about Davy Crockett and Daniel Boone, she had begun to think of both men as relatives from the past who belonged to her. There wasn't any harm in that romantic notion, was there? Surely no one else fantasized about the American frontiersmen the way she did. When she was younger, she constantly daydreamed about what life would have been like if she'd been married to one of those adventurous men. The Indians, or rather the savages as they were called in the stories, were reported to kill a man, then cut his scalp away to use as a trophy proving their prowess. Both Boone and Crockett had fought hundreds of Indians. Neither man had been scalped, however, and did in fact befriend the savages.

Taylor started shivering. The man scaring goosebumps on her arms wouldn't have any difficulty frightening the scalps off the Indians, she decided. Why, his stare was piercing enough to make her hair stand on end. He was a handsome devil, all right, but there was also an air of danger about him. And power, she thought. This one didn't look like he would be afraid of anything or be at all vulnerable to attack. From his appearance alone, she judged him to be more than capable of protecting his property.

And the babies, she thought. He would protect the babies.

Wasn't that all that really mattered? His reputation shouldn't concern her and neither should her bizarre reaction to him. For her purposes, he was more than adequate. He was perfect.

She let out a sigh. Her friends echoed the sound. They were obviously as mesmerized by the man as she was.

William and Lucas crossed the ballroom from different angles, yet they both reached Taylor at the same time. They stood no more than three feet apart. William was on her left side and Lucas was on her right.

William was the first to speak. His voice held a note of anger. "Taylor, I want a word in private with you."

"You aren't going anywhere alone with her," his wife snapped from behind.

Taylor ignored both William and Jane. Her head was tilted all the way back so she could keep her gaze firmly directed on the man who had stolen her every logical thought. She was desperately trying not to be afraid of him. He did have the most beautiful eyes.

"You're much taller than I remember."

The words came out in a bare whisper. Lucas smiled. Her voice appealed to him. It was throaty, soft, damned arousing.

"You're much prettier than I remember."

Constance was right. He did have an adorable drawl in his voice.

Chaos whirled around her. Everyone but Taylor and Lucas was suddenly talking at once. Constance and Jennifer were demanding to know when Taylor had met the stranger, Alison was begging for an introduction, William was arguing with his wife, and Hampton and Morris were loudly debating the possibility that Taylor might have already been introduced to the American, and how was that possible? Everyone knew Taylor had been in Scotland for the past several weeks, recovering from *the humiliation,* and when she was called back to London, she stayed cloistered with her ailing grandmother. When would she have had time to meet Lucas?

Taylor couldn't keep up with all the conversations going on around her. She was suddenly feeling quite exhilarated, however. The tightness inside her chest vanished. The chains binding her to England and to duty were being ripped away. She was going to be free. She knew that when she walked out of the ballroom, she would walk away from all the restrictions and responsibilities associated with England's rigid society.

She also knew she would never come back. She would never have to see her uncle Malcolm again, never have to look him in the eye and pretend she didn't know about the atrocity he'd committed, never ever have to speak a civil word to him. She would never have to suffer Jane's presence or cruelty again either, though that was certainly minor in comparison to her uncle's sins, and she would never again have to feel ashamed or humiliated.

Taylor let out another sigh. Freedom was just a few steps away.

"Is it almost midnight, sir?"

She blurted out her question, her eagerness sinfully evident. He gave her a quick nod in response. "We can leave now."

Everyone started pulling on her then. "Leave? Taylor, where is it you think you're going?" Constance demanded to know.

"Is she leaving with him?" Jennifer asked with a

wave of her hand in Lucas's direction. "She shouldn't do that, should she? What will people think?"

"Exactly when and where did you two meet?" Hampton asked.

"They couldn't have met before," Morris stubbornly insisted.

"You aren't going anywhere with him," William announced in a near shout so he'd be heard. He was so angry, the veins in the sides of his neck stood out. His complexion turned a splotchy, ugly red. "You're coming with me, Taylor. I demand a word in private with you. This blackguard you're lowering yourself to speak to is actually . . ."

Alison interrupted him. "Do be quiet, William. Taylor, darling, please introduce me to this gentleman."

William wasn't about to be deterred. He reached out to take hold of Taylor's arm. Lucas's command stopped him. It was whisper soft, yet chilling all the same.

"I wouldn't touch her if I were you."

He hadn't raised his voice, and his tone was actually quite mild, but the warning was there all the same, and William reacted as though Lucas had roared the command. He took a quick step back. It was probably an instinctive reaction, Taylor thought, but it was still quite telling. William was actually afraid of the man.

Jane let out a sharp gasp. "Keep Taylor here, William, while I go and fetch Father. He'll know what to do." She glared up at Lucas when she added, "My husband might be intimidated by you, but my father won't be. He's Taylor's guardian."

Lucas gave Jane as much attention as he would a gnat flying by. He showed absolutely no reaction to her remarks and didn't even bother to glance her way.

47

Taylor decided to follow his example. She refused to look at her cousin when she gave her denial. "Your father is not my guardian."

"He will be," Jane boasted. "Just as soon as the old lady dies. You'll be sorry then, Taylor. Father's going to lock you away before you can do or say anything further to disgrace us. Why, everyone knows you're in need of a keeper."

Morris and Hampton were the first two to rush to Taylor's defense. "You're the disgraceful one, Jane Merritt," Hampton fairly shouted. He lowered his voice when he added, "Haven't you wondered why neither you nor William has received any invitations to the affairs this season? You have both been marked off all the lists," he added with a nod.

"The only reason you were invited tonight is because you received the invite a good week before you eloped. You've done yourself in this time," Morris snapped. "Acting like a trollop with Taylor's fiancé. Tell me this. Are you really carrying William's child or did you make that up to trap him?"

"How dare you slander my character," Jane cried out. She slapped her husband on his shoulder to gain his attention. "William, aren't you going to defend my honor?"

Her husband didn't say a word. His full attention was focused on Taylor.

"Lady Taylor isn't mad or crazed, but you are if you believe she's done anything wrong. You're despicable, Jane. Oh, yes," Morris sputtered with indignation. "You and William deserve each other. I pray the two of you will get exactly what you deserve."

The war with words soon jumped to shouts, then shoves. Taylor found it impossible to keep up with who was giving what insults. Alison started pulling on her arm again, demanding her attention, and Constance was diligently poking her in the shoulder from behind with the plea that she please turn around and explain what was going on. Jennifer, the peacemaker in the crowd, was trying to get all of them to lower their voices.

Taylor became quite frazzled in no time at all. She turned to her left to tell William she had no intention of going anywhere with him but before she could get the words out of her mouth, Alison pulled on her arm again to gain her attention, and Taylor turned back to her. Constance wasn't about to be ignored, however, and once again prodded her from behind.

Taylor's head felt as though it were spinning. She glanced up at her escort to see how he was reacting to the fiasco and was quite astonished by the expression on his face.

The man looked bored. She wondered how he could remain so unaffected by the slander William was spewing about him. William was going on and on about his black character when Lucas reached into his pocket, pulled out his timepiece, and flipped open the latch to check the time.

Then William called Lucas a bastard. Alison, Jennifer, and Constance let out loud gasps, almost in perfect unison. Taylor waited for her escort to defend himself. A good fifteen seconds passed before she realized he wasn't going to do or say anything.

She suddenly became his champion. William repeated the blasphemous charge again. Taylor was outraged. She turned to Alison, snatched her fan out of her hand, then turned back to William. Before he had a glimmer of her intent, she smacked him across his face with the fan, then turned back to Alison.

"Thank you," she said as she handed the fan back to her friend.

Alison's mouth was gaping open. Taylor's shoulders

slumped. She detested making a scene, for it really wasn't ladylike, but there came a time when proper behavior had to be set aside.

William was slow to understand that Taylor had reached her limit. "If you'll only listen to me," he demanded. "You'll realize I speak the truth. He's nothing but a . . ."

Taylor grabbed Alison's fan again. She turned to confront William once again.

"If you say one more slanderous word, I swear I'll poke your eye out."

"Taylor, whatever has come over you?" Alison whispered.

Taylor tossed the fan in her friend's direction. She turned her gaze to her escort.

"May we please leave, sir?"

She sounded desperate. She didn't care. Lucas smiled in reaction. "Yes," he answered. "It's past midnight."

She let out a long sigh. Lucas nodded to Morris and Hampton, then started for the entrance. He passed Taylor, didn't pause, but clasped hold of her hand and continued right along. His stride was long, purposeful. She didn't resist. She turned around and let herself be pulled along, and Lord, she was actually smiling now.

Hampton's shout made Lucas stop on the top step. "Will she be safe with you?"

He should have been insulted by the question. Yet the concern he heard in Hampton's voice overrode his initial irritation. It was a logical question, he decided, given the fact that the Englishman didn't know him well at all.

He turned around to give his answer. "Yes, she'll be safe."

Alison ran forward to shout her plea next. "Taylor,

before you leave, won't you please introduce me to the gentleman?"

"Yes, of course I'll introduce you," Taylor agreed. "He's . . ."

Her mind went blank. Dear God, she couldn't remember his name. Panic grabbed hold. Taylor didn't know if she were going to burst into laughter or dissolve into tears. Maybe Jane was right after all. Maybe she was crazed and in need of a keeper.

She opened her mouth to answer. No words came out.

"Well?" Alison demanded. She put her hands on her hips and frowned with impatience. "Who is he?"

"Yes," Constance blurted out. "Who is he?"

Taylor looked up at her escort, hoping he might come to her rescue. He didn't say a word, however. He simply stared down at her and waited to see what she would do.

Taylor was mortified. Why couldn't she remember his name? She took a deep breath, shook her head over her own sorry behavior, and then turned back to her audience.

She couldn't remember who he was, but she at least remembered what he was.

"He's my husband."

2

Truth is truth to the end of reckoning.
—William Shakespeare,
Measure for Measure

They didn't take the news at all well. Alison, Jennifer, and Constance were too astonished to say a word, so they took turns screaming instead. Hampton and Morris were both obviously thrilled with the announcement. They cheered in unison. Jane bellowed a foul, unrepeatable blasphemy, which was only partially drowned out by William's immediate roar of denial.

Lucas ignored the chaos. He accepted Taylor's cloak from the butler, casually draped it around her shoulders, then caught hold of her hand again and went outside. She had to run to keep up with him. She didn't even have time to wave farewell to her friends. With her free hand, she grabbed hold of the hem of her gown so she wouldn't trip going down the stone steps.

He didn't slow his pace until they reached the circle

drive. He stopped then, and after motioning to the driver to bring the carriage forward, he let go of her hand and half turned to look down at her.

She immediately set about straightening her appearance. She smoothed her hair back over her shoulders, readjusted her cloak, then reached into her pocket to get her gloves.

Her hands were shaking. Lucas noticed she had a difficult time getting her gloves on. She was obviously flustered, perhaps even a little afraid. He wondered if this was due to the way her friends and enemies reacted to her announcement or if he were in some way responsible. He considered asking her why she was trembling, then discarded the idea. She probably wouldn't like knowing he was aware of her discomfort.

In truth, he didn't know what to make of her. She was such a dainty, feminine thing, yet certainly a tone high-strung. She blushed just like a schoolgirl and couldn't look him in the eye. Her shyness amused him. He tried to picture her in the wilderness of Montana Territory and almost laughed out loud. Lady Taylor wouldn't last five minutes. He knew he was making a snap judgment based solely upon appearance. Still, he didn't think he was wrong. She looked as fragile and as exquisite as a piece of fine porcelain, an object to be admired from a distance but certainly not to be handled. Porcelain would easily shatter, and from his initial observation of the piece of fluff standing next to him, so would she. No, she couldn't possibly survive in the wild, and thank God, she would never have to be put to the test.

The sudden memory of Taylor using that ridiculous paper fan as a weapon to slap Merritt flashed into Lucas's mind. She certainly hadn't been timid then. Lucas frowned over the inconsistency.

Taylor finally gained enough courage to look up at him. She could feel herself blushing and wished to God she wasn't so transparent. The man had to believe she was a twit. God only knew she was feeling like one. She was determined to apologize to him no matter how embarrassing it was. She would have to admit she didn't remember his name, unfortunately.

Taylor caught him frowning down at her and immediately forgot all about apologies. She assumed he was irritated because she'd blurted out their secret. She felt guilty enough without his censure.

"Please don't be annoyed with me, sir. I know I shouldn't have told everyone we were married, but I was simply too flustered to think straight. William was saying such horrible things about you, and I kept waiting for you to defend yourself. I realize you've been trained from a very early age to be a gentleman at all times, but still, there are some situations where manners should be set aside. You really should learn to stand up for yourself. I believe protecting one's honor is more important than being gallant. Don't you?"

She waited a full minute for him to answer her. He remained stubbornly silent. She guessed that he didn't agree with her. She let out a little sigh to cover her nervousness. "Do think about what I just said. I believe in time you'll realize my suggestion has merit."

She had rendered him speechless. Lucas was simply too astonished to say anything. Never in his life had he ever been mistaken for a gentleman. And never had anyone ever tried to defend his honor. It was amusing and humbling. It was obvious to him from her earnest expression that she meant every word she'd said, and hell, should he set her straight now or wait?

The driver had finally negotiated the carriage

through the clutter of vehicles lining the drive and the street beyond. It was still rocking to a stop when Lucas turned to open the door for Taylor. William's bellow and Taylor's whispered exclamation made him pause.

"Taylor, wait up."

"Oh, dear, now what does he want?"

She instinctively turned to look up at the steps. William was racing toward her, taking the stairs two at a time in his haste to get to her.

Lucas's patience was wearing thin. "Get inside the carriage, Taylor," he ordered. His tone was filled with irritation. "I'll take care of him."

She ignored his command. "I really do wish he'd leave me alone, and I fully intend to tell him to do just that. You can't fight my battles for me, sir. I have to fight my own. Do you know I almost married him?" She paused to add a dramatic shiver, then continued on. "Can you imagine? I thank God almost hourly I escaped such a tragedy."

Lucas turned to her. He smiled when he saw the disgruntled expression on her face. "Hourly?" he repeated.

"Hourly," she confirmed with a nod.

William finally reached the bottom step. "Do remember my suggestion to stand up for yourself," Taylor whispered to Lucas.

"You aren't playing fair, Taylor," William began. He stopped no more than a foot or two away from her. "You haven't given me an opportunity to explain why I had to marry Jane. You owe me that much. After all the time I spent courting you . . ."

"I don't owe you anything, William. Go away and leave me alone. I have nothing more to say to you."

He acted as though he hadn't heard her. "We can go on like before. You'll see. I can make you forget I'm married."

Her gasp of outrage would have knocked her over if she hadn't grabbed hold of Lucas's arm. Her dramatic reaction made him want to laugh, but he didn't dare. He kept his gaze on Merritt when he spoke to Taylor. "I'll be happy to finish this discussion for you. Just say the word."

She shook her head.

"Tomorrow I'll call on you, early in the morning before Jane wakes up," William continued matter-of-factly. "You and I will find someplace quiet where we can talk. I have to make you understand. I know I hurt you. Still, that certainly wasn't sufficient reason for you to lie about getting married. Whatever were you thinking to make up such an outrageous tale?"

Taylor was too shocked by what William had just suggested to do more than glare at him. Good God, what had she ever seen in him? How had she ever believed he was attractive? His dark hair and green eyes no longer appealed to her. She used to find him a charmer. Now she thought of him as a smooth-talking devil. Lord, what an idiot she'd been. There wasn't anything attractive about William Merritt. He disgusted her, for he lacked all of the qualities she most valued: honor, integrity, and loyalty.

"You dare suggest I would continue associating with you after . . . after . . ." She was too indignant to go on. She had no wish to make a scene. Besides, nothing she could say would make him understand the grave insult he'd just given her. Did he really believe she would ever consider becoming his mistress?

The thought made her stomach turn. She could feel her face burning. Taylor shook her head, then turned around and reached for the door latch to the carriage. Lucas beat her to the task. He grabbed hold of her elbow to steady her, assisted her inside, and then started to get inside with her.

William took a step forward. "You shouldn't let him escort you home," he shouted so she would be certain to hear. "He's a bastard, you know, with a reputation as black as the devil's."

Taylor's temper ignited. She shoved the door wider. It would have slammed into Lucas's side if he hadn't reached out to hold it steady. He didn't want it to swing back into her face.

"You will not talk about my husband with such disrespect. Get out of my sight, William, and never dare speak to me again. You're a vile man, and I want nothing more to do with you."

After giving the cur what she considered a proper blistering, Taylor grabbed hold of the handle and pulled the door closed.

Lucas could hear her muttering. William was proving to be as dense as a mule. He refused to believe the truth. Lucas leaned against the side of the carriage, folded his arms across his chest, and simply waited to see what he would do next.

"You're overly distraught, Taylor. I understand how you feel. You think I abandoned you and that's why you lied about being married. First thing tomorrow morning, we'll have our talk. Then you'll forgive me."

Taylor gave up. She threw her hands up in vexation, then reached through the window to poke Lucas in the shoulder.

"Please get inside. I would like to leave now."

"Isn't it my turn yet?" Lucas asked. "I'm sure I could convince him."

William glared at Lucas. Lucas smiled back.

"I would rather you didn't get involved, sir," she called through the window.

"I'm already involved now that you're my wife, Taylor."

William let out a roar very like a wounded animal.

Taylor thought the squeal he made sounded like an injured pig. It was grating on the ears and most unpleasant.

The obtuse man had finally caught on to the truth, however. "You actually married him? Are you crazy? Don't you realize what you've done?"

Taylor pushed the door open again. She leaned out, intent on giving William one final blistering, but the look on her escort's face suggested she keep silent. His eyes had gone . . . cold. Taylor thought he probably wanted to avert a scene, and couples were already gathering on the steps, silently watching William make a fool of himself.

Hampton and Morris came running down the steps. Taylor forced a smile for their benefit and then sat back.

"Couldn't we please leave now?" she whispered, hoping her escort would hear her.

"Yes," Lucas agreed. He turned to get inside, but William's next words changed his mind.

"Good riddance to the both of you. How does it feel knowing I had her first, brother? You're getting my leftovers. She's fit only for a savage like you," he shouted.

Taylor was appalled by the slander. Then she saw her escort's expression. She became instantly frightened. God help her, she started shivering. She'd never seen anyone that angry before. He looked furious enough to kill someone. He'd turned into a barbarian right before her eyes.

"Now it's my turn."

She didn't like the sound of that. She vigorously shook her head, but Lucas ignored her.

William realized he'd gone too far when he saw the expression on Lucas's face. He instinctively stepped back, then turned to his left and then his right, looking for a means of escape. There wasn't any. Hampton, his face as white as flour, and Morris, his face as red as fire, deliberately blocked him on both sides. Neither man was going to let William go anywhere. They'd heard what he'd said about Taylor, and both men were still reeling with outrage.

Lucas towered over his half brother. He reached out, grabbed hold of William by his neck with one hand, half lifted him off the ground, and then slammed his fist into his face.

He continued to hold him up in the air when he spoke to him. "If you ever repeat such slander again, I'll come back here and kill you."

After giving the dark promise, he tossed him onto the curb. William collapsed to the ground with a loud thud.

Lucas smiled at Morris and Hampton. His voice was quite mild when he said, "You'll be sure to let me know if he ever says anything uncomplimentary about my wife, won't you, boys?"

"Yes, of course we will," Morris fervently promised.

Hampton nodded. He was fully occupied watching William struggle to his knees.

Lucas got into the carriage, pulled the door closed, and leaned back against the seat across from Taylor. He was smiling with satisfaction.

They were finally on their way. Taylor tried to squeeze herself into the opposite corner to put as much distance as possible between the two of them. It was a ludicrous goal, given the small dimensions inside the carriage and the large size of her escort, but Taylor wasn't thinking very logically at the moment. She was too busy fighting her panic. She took a couple of deep breaths in a bid to calm herself. It didn't help much, but she wanted to hide her nervousness from him. She did have her pride, after all.

"A gentleman doesn't settle disputes with his fists," she dictated.

She waited a long minute for him to offer his apology. He didn't say a word. She decided to prod him. "I do believe you broke William's nose. Have you nothing to say about that, sir?"

"God, it felt good."

"I beg your pardon?" she asked.

Lucas watched as she wrung her hands together with such agitation, she actually twisted her gloves off. He watched her for a long moment, then repeated his remark. "I said, it felt good. You wouldn't want me to lie to you, would you?"

"No, of course I wouldn't want you to lie to me. You aren't at all sorry?"

"No. I've wanted to hit him for a long while."

"Yes, but once the spontaneous, uncontrolled action was . . . finished, and you've had time to consider all the ramifications of such ungentlemanly conduct, haven't you concluded . . ."

She was going to ask him to admit he had a little regret for acting like a barbarian, but he never gave her time to finish her question.

"Wishes do come true," he drawled out. "That is my conclusion."

She let out a loud sigh. He decided to change the subject. "You couldn't remember my name, could you?"

There was a vast amount of amusement in his voice. She couldn't see his face now, for it was quite dark inside the carriage, but she strongly suspected he was smiling.

One day she, too, might find some humor in this situation. She didn't now, however, and furthermore she was appalled by the entire evening. Her own forgetfulness was at the top of her list of horrors to live down. Watching William get knocked to the ground came in second. She was feeling frightened again, and all because she was all alone with this man. Good God, she was married to a complete stranger.

"I'm not usually so forgetful," she said. "It's true, I couldn't remember your name, but that was only because I was flustered."

"What made you tell them . . ."

She didn't let him finish his question. "You are my husband, like it or not."

"I'm your legal guardian," he amended, for he liked the sound of that much better.

She shrugged. "You married me in order to become my guardian. That was part of the agreement, remember?"

He let out a sigh. "I remember."

He sounded irritated to her. She could only conclude he wasn't very happy about his circumstances. She tried not to take offense. She knew he didn't want to be married, her grandmother had told her so. It was, therefore, ridiculous for her to have hurt feelings. Why, she barely knew the man. Besides, she was still too busy battling her fear of the giant. She didn't have time for other worries.

How had she ever thought he was a gentleman? Lord, she'd instructed him to learn how to stand up for himself. Taylor could feel herself blushing. She was suddenly quite thankful it was so dark inside the vehicle.

Confront the fear, she thought. A free woman could do that, couldn't she?

She cleared her throat. "When you first spoke to William Merritt, the look in your eyes held my attention. You made me . . ."

"I made you what?" he asked, wondering over her sudden timidity.

61

"Worry," she blurted out. She couldn't bring herself to admit she'd been afraid. "I know he besmirched my character and that is why you struck him, but I got the feeling you disliked him before he said those unpleasant things about me. Is that true? Did you dislike him before . . ."

"I hate the son of a bitch."

He couldn't be more blunt than that, she supposed. She found herself smiling and couldn't imagine why. Her worry was making her daft, she supposed. "Is that the reason you married me? Were you thinking to get even with your brother for his past sins?"

"No," he answered. "I needed the money. Your grandmother made me an offer I couldn't walk away from. Getting even was an added incentive. Taylor, we probably should discuss how this arrangement is going to work. There hasn't been time until now."

"There isn't anything to discuss. I'll keep my end of the bargain. You needn't worry about that. I know you didn't want to get married. And that, you see, is one of the many reasons why my grandmother found you so appealing."

He didn't see. "You chose me because I didn't want to get married?"

"Yes." She didn't elaborate.

"That doesn't make sense, Taylor."

"It makes sense to me," she argued. "I wanted to be free, and being married to you would insure that goal. I certainly didn't want to get married. But there was Uncle Malcolm just waiting to take over, and Madam and I both knew that when she died, he would force me to marry someone he chose. I now have legal protection against my uncle," she added with a nod. "Because I carry your name. What is it, by the way?"

"Ross," he answered. "Lucas Ross."

She still didn't remember ever having heard the

PRINCE CHARMING

name before. She wasn't about to admit that truth,
however. He was bound to think she was a complete
imbecile. "Yes, of course. Lucas Ross. I remember
now," she blatantly lied. "It's a very . . . American
name, isn't it?"

He didn't have the faintest idea what she meant by
that comment. The entire situation was ludicrous to
him. He was both exasperated and amused by his
bride. God, he was actually married to the woman,
and now that he thought about it, he didn't know a
damned thing about her. Except that she was an
incredibly good-looking woman. And that, he told
himself, shouldn't matter to him at all.

"In this day and age, no woman can be forced to
marry against her will," he remarked.

She let out a rather unladylike snort. "Perhaps in
America that is true, but not in England," she replied.
"And certainly not when estates and factories and
trusts are at issue. There are other circumstances you
don't know about and really never have any need to
know, sir. Suffice it to say that Madam chose you
because she knew you would complete your end of the
bargain and then go away. Once we get to Boston, I
shall be quite all right. You aren't having second
thoughts, are you?"

He could hear the concern in her voice. "No," he
answered. "I haven't changed my mind."

"Good." She drew the word out. Lucas didn't know
what to make of her. Hell, he didn't think she was old
enough to even be called a woman. She was so young,
so innocent looking. It was his duty to make certain
she arrived in Boston safe and sound, hand her over to
her legal advisors there, and then leave her.

The plan sounded just fine to him. "Are there
people besides your legal advisors who will take over
your care?"

"Take over my care? I'm capable of taking care of myself, Mr. Ross."

She sounded incensed. Lucas smiled. He had obviously pricked her temper with his poorly phrased question. He hadn't heard any fear in her outraged reaction, however, and filed that bit of information away for future use. When Taylor was angry, she forgot to be afraid.

And she was afraid all right, afraid of him. From the moment she had spotted him walking toward her in the ballroom, she'd become as frightened as a trapped rabbit. Yet hadn't he spotted relief as well? That didn't make any sense. How could she be frightened and relieved at the same time.

"I meant to ask you if you had relatives living in Boston," he said.

"Yes, I do," she answered. She deliberately failed to add the fact that the relatives in question were only two years old. He didn't need to know that particular.

"Good."

He sounded relieved. She tried not to become irritated. "Do women in America need to be taken care of like children?"

"Some do," he supposed.

"I don't," she announced. "I'm very self-sufficient. However, aside from relatives and financial advisors waiting for me, there are also a number of other bankers eager to help make my adjustment to Boston society easier. I'm certain someone has already found me suitable lodging. Where is your home, sir?"

"Don't call me sir. My name's Lucas."

"My name's Taylor." Oh, God, he already knew that. "I mean to say you have my permission to call me Taylor. You have a ranch somewhere in the wilderness, don't you?"

She was sounding worried again. Lucas wanted to put her at ease but couldn't figure out how he was ever going to accomplish that goal. She was as skittish as a young colt. The journey to America was going to take an eternity, he decided, if Taylor continued to act so timid around him.

"Didn't your grandmother fill you in on the particulars?"

"No," she answered. "There wasn't time. I understand she spent a good deal of time with you. You visited with her on many occasions before she decided to ask you to marry me. Isn't that right?"

"Yes."

"I only arrived back from Scotland this afternoon. You were there, waiting, and Madam said the minister was late for another engagement. She would have fretted if I had plied her with questions."

"So you married me without knowing anything at all about me?"

"Madam said you were acceptable," Taylor replied. "You don't know much about me either, unless Madam told you about my background, but since we won't be seeing one another once we reach Boston, it really doesn't matter, does it?"

"No," he answered. "I suppose it doesn't." He decided to answer her earlier question then. "I have a ranch in an area called Montana Territory, near the edge of the valley. It's isolated, sparsely populated now that the gold rush is over, and the only town around is just two streets wide and long. You would hate it."

"Why would you think I'd hate it?" she asked.

"The only society there is the Sunday gathering in front of the general store for the reading of the newspaper from Rosewood. There aren't any parties or balls. Survival's a lot more important there than society."

"And that is what appeals to you?" He didn't answer her. "What is the name of the town?"

"Redemption."

It sounded wonderful to her. "Could a person get lost there? Is there enough space to walk for a full day and never see another soul?"

If he thought her question odd, he didn't say. The carriage rocked to a stop near the street leading to the loading docks. The ship they would board was called the *Emerald,* a two-ton paddle wheel steamer moored in the center of the river. A small steam tender would convey the passengers to the ship.

Taylor was suddenly anxious to be on her way. It was well past one o'clock in the morning, yet the streets and pavement were teeming with activity. Their carriage was hindered from progressing any further by all the wagons, mail carts, and carriages ahead of them being unloaded of their letters, packages, and passengers.

"Are our suitcases already on board?" she asked. "Or must we find them in this clutter?"

"They're already in our stateroom."

"Our stateroom? Don't we have separate quarters, sir?"

She was trying hard not to panic again. Lucas wasn't paying any attention to her now, and that was a blessing, she thought. She knew she'd gone pale. She felt faint. Did the man expect to share her bed? Heavens, she hadn't considered that obscene possibility.

Lucas unlatched the door, pulled the drape back, and then turned to her.

"Your grandmother insisted the log show we shared the same quarters, Taylor. She wanted only one reservation written down. Feel like walking the rest of the way?"

She felt like running. She nodded instead. He got out of the vehicle, then turned to assist her. She left her cloak behind. He reached behind her to get the garment, saw her gloves were on the floor, and collected those as well, then turned to help her put her cloak on. Taylor seemed surprised she wasn't wearing her gloves and hastily put them in her pocket. She knew he was being extremely considerate with her, and that fact made her feel better. Perhaps he wasn't such a barbarian after all.

"Why didn't I notice how tall you were?"

She hadn't realized she'd asked the question until the words were out of her mouth and she couldn't take them back.

"You were standing on the step next to your grandmother's bed. I wasn't."

She barely heard his explanation. She was thoroughly occupied staring at him. He had a wonderful smile. And beautiful white teeth, she couldn't help but notice. Heavens, he even had a dimple in the side of his cheek. If that wasn't appealing, she didn't know what was. She let out a little sigh over her errant thoughts.

He glanced down, caught her staring up at him, and wondered what had come over her. She was blushing. She was such an innocent, he thought. Taylor looked mesmerized, almost dazed. What in thunder was the matter with her?

"What are you thinking about?" he asked.

"You're very handsome," she blurted out. She immediately regretted telling him the truth. He looked exasperated with her. Her face felt as though it were burning. God, she wished she were more worldly, more sophisticated. "Of course, I'm a horrible judge of men," she hastily added. "You've probably figured that out by now."

"Why's that?"

Now she was exasperated. "I was going to marry William," she reminded him.

He shrugged. She didn't know what that was supposed to mean. "I should hate all men, I suppose."

He laughed. "You're too young to hate anyone."

"How old are you?" she asked.

"Old enough to hate the world."

He was through discussing the matter. Lucas grabbed hold of her hand and started walking. She had to run to keep pace. Fortunately, the crowd swelled near the corner, and he was forced to slow down.

He had a firm grip on her hand. Taylor felt safe. It was an interesting feeling, overwhelmingly pleasant, actually, for she hadn't felt safe in such a long time. Things were looking much, much brighter.

They threaded their way through the chaos. The wharf was ablaze with light and activity. Carts piled high with trunks and suitcases stood unattended in the center of the street. Vendors shouted their prices and waved their wares as they pushed their way around the obstacles, while couples huddled together in a waiting line outside the ticketing office. Pickpockets darted in and out of the crowd, some as young as eight, others as old as eighty, but no one got within spitting distance of Taylor. Lucas wouldn't allow that. Men did gawk. They didn't touch. She noticed several gentlemen staring at her and believed her formal attire was drawing all the attention. With her free hand, she pulled the dark cape close and held the edges together against her chest.

Lucas noticed the action. "Are you getting cold?"

She shook her head. "I'm trying not to draw attention," she explained. "I'm not dressed appropriately for travel," she added when he continued to look down at her.

It wouldn't have mattered what she wore, Lucas decided. She couldn't change what she looked like. Her curly hair cascaded down her back. The color, as pure a gold as a stalk of prairie wheat, was like a beacon to anyone who happened to glance their way. Taylor was of medium height, yet she held herself like a tall, regal princess. There was a definite sensuality in her walk, too, Lucas had noticed that right away, and those were just a few of the hundred or so reasons why he didn't believe it was possible for her not to draw attention to herself. She was damned beautiful, and when she looked directly at a man with those big blue eyes, he might as well give up trying to do anything but stare back. Even if Taylor were dressed in beggar's britches and an oversized man's shirt, she would still attract notice and lustful stares.

He didn't like the attention she was getting any more than she did. He felt possessive and couldn't understand why. His reaction to her didn't make any sense, yet the need to protect her fairly overwhelmed him. Hell, he barely knew her. Yet she belonged to him. She was his wife now. And what in God's name was he going to do about that?

He was glaring down at her. His moods, she decided, were as contrary and unpredictable as the weather.

"I should have changed my gown after the ball," she announced for lack of anything better to say.

"It wouldn't have helped."

He sounded surly. He was still frowning something fierce, though Taylor was happy to notice the focus of his displeasure now seemed to be centered on a group of young men lounging against the metal hitching posts.

She didn't waste time speculating about his sudden change in mood, however, because they turned the corner then and she spotted the *Emerald* in the distance. Her breath caught in the back of her throat. The ship was a magnificent sight. The moon cast a golden glow upon the mighty vessel, making it appear mystical in size. White frothing caps from the churning waves of the Mersey slapped against the sides but the ship didn't appear to move at all. Why, the *Emerald* looked as sturdy as a mountain and as welcoming as a preacher on Sunday morning.

Taylor was awed by the sight. She came to a dead stop and stared in fascination. "Isn't it beautiful, Mr. Ross?"

The wonder in her voice made him feel like smiling. He looked at the ship, then turned back to her. "Yes, she is beautiful," he agreed.

"She must weigh at least five thousand tons."

"Not quite two," he corrected. "We aren't in church, Taylor. You don't have to whisper."

She hadn't realized she'd been whispering; she laughed over her own behavior. "She's very majestic looking, isn't she?" she remarked in a louder tone of voice.

Lucas didn't want to dampen her enthusiasm. He had sailed on larger, more impressive ships, but the look of pleasure he saw on her face made him keep that bit of information to himself.

Taylor was turning out to be a bit of a puzzle. He knew she came from an extremely wealthy family and, therefore, he assumed she'd had every advantage. Yet now she acted as though this were her first journey

70

into the big city. She wasn't a country farm girl, but damned if she weren't acting like one.

She caught him staring down at her. "Am I gawking, Mr. Ross?"

"Just a little."

She smiled. "I fear I'm not very sophisticated," she admitted.

"Have you never left England before?"

"I've gone to Scotland many, many times," she replied. "But I've never gone on the ocean. I'm looking forward to the experience."

"Let's hope you don't get seasick."

"Oh, I won't. I'm a very strong woman," Taylor boasted. "I never get sick."

He gave her a look that suggested he didn't believe her. She decided to turn the topic. "My grandfather Taylor and his brother-in-law, Andrew, sailed on the original *Emerald*. Andrew was too young to remember the adventure, but Grandfather was full of stories about life aboard ship and his friendship with the notorious nearsighted pirate named Black Harry. Have you ever heard of him, Mr. Ross?"

Lucas shook his head. "Do your grandfather and your uncle know you're sailing on yet another *Emerald?*"

"I told Uncle Andrew, and he gave his blessing. Grandfather Taylor died over ten years ago, but in my heart I'm certain he knows. I believe he watches out for me. You may laugh, if you're inclined, but I think of him as my protector. He won't let anything happen to me."

He was married to a crazy woman. Lucas didn't know what to say in response to such foolish beliefs. He was a realist. She obviously wasn't. Such naïveté would get her killed in the wilderness. But she wasn't going to Montana Territory, he reminded himself. She was going to Boston. It was civilized there and somewhat safe.

Still, to his way of thinking, she needed a live protector, not a ghost. "Did you say your uncle Andrew knows? Does that mean he's alive?"

"He's very much alive," she replied. "He lives in the Highlands of Scotland. He's considered the black sheep of the family," she added with a good deal of pride in her voice. "Madam often worried I would become overly influenced by her younger brother."

They were hemmed in by traffic circling the corner now, and since it was impossible for them to go any further until the mail carts were unloaded, Lucas had an excuse for continuing the conversation. He was becoming fascinated by his bride. She was extremely open about her family and her past. Her honesty was refreshing. He was used to guarding every word he said. The less people knew about him and his family, the better off everyone would be. Taylor appeared to believe differently. She told her every thought, or so it seemed to him.

"Why did your grandmother worry you'd be influenced by her brother?"

"Why? Because he's peculiar," she answered.

"I see," Lucas replied for lack of anything better to say.

"My great-uncle is a wonderful teacher, and he taught me many valuable lessons."

"Such as?"

"He taught me how to play the piano in grand style."

He didn't laugh. "I suppose that will come in handy in the chamber rooms of Boston."

He sounded a little condescending to her. "He also taught me all about guns and rifles, Mr. Ross. Uncle

Andrew is a respected collector. If I were going to live on the frontier, I would be able to take care of myself," she added. "He trained me well, sir. And so, you see, his lessons gave me both polish and practicality."

"Could you shoot a man?"

She hesitated a long minute before answering. "I suppose I could," she said. "It would depend."

"Depend on what?" He couldn't help smiling. He couldn't imagine her holding a gun, let alone firing the thing.

She thought he was making fun of her. Why else would he be smiling? Her spine stiffened in reaction to her own conclusion.

Her voice was full of authority when she explained her position. "It would depend upon the circumstances. If I were protecting someone I loved, I most certainly could injure someone. I wouldn't want to," she hastily added. "But I would. What about you?" she asked then. "Could you take another man's life?"

He didn't hesitate in giving his answer. "Without blinking an eye."

It wasn't what he said as much as how he said it that made Taylor start worrying. They might be discussing the weather, so matter-of-fact was his attitude. It was unnerving. She couldn't seem to stop herself from asking, "Have you killed before?"

He rolled his eyes heavenward. "I was in the war against the South, Taylor. Of course I killed."

"For duty," she said, relieved. "I read all about the conflict between the States."

"So you were named after your grandfather."

It was apparent he wanted to change the subject. She was happy to accommodate him. "Yes."

He nodded, dismissed the topic, then tightened his hold on her hand and started walking again. He shoved his way through the crowd. She kept trying to

73

watch where she was going and to keep her gaze on the ship at the same time. She stumbled twice. Lucas noticed the second time. He slowed down then, and when the crowd became too pressing, he put his arm around her shoulders and pulled her into his side.

It wasn't until they were standing side by side in the center of the throng of passengers inside the steam tender and on their way to the *Emerald* that the magnitude of what she was doing hit her full force. She should have been terrified. She usually worried over a plan of action until it became as worn as an old rosary bead, but she didn't have a single qualm or a second thought this time. Madam had suggested the marriage and Taylor had gone right along with the idea. What was done was done.

She was content. She wasn't saddened or filled with regrets because she was leaving her homeland. She wouldn't even look back toward the shore as some of the other young ladies were doing. One woman was dabbing at the corners of her eyes with her handkerchief. Another was openly weeping. Taylor's reaction was just the opposite. She felt like laughing, her joy barely contained. She was overwhelmed by the rightness of what she was doing. Lucas still had his arm around her shoulders. She moved closer, trying to gain a little more of his warmth. She wanted to rest her head on his shoulder. She felt that safe with her escort; she couldn't bring herself to think of him as her husband yet, and it really didn't matter anyway she supposed, since they would soon part company.

Taylor thought about the babies. Soon she would be able to hold them again. She wondered if she would recognize them. When last she'd seen them, they weren't even crawling. Now they must be walking and talking, and Lord, she could barely contain her excitement. She closed her eyes and said a prayer of thanksgiving because she was finally on her way, and then she said another prayer in anticipation of the new life she was about to begin.

She would collect the little girls as soon as she reached Boston, and then she would take them to safety. She would hide them where Uncle Malcolm would never think to look.

A glimmer of an idea came into her mind. Redemption. My, but she liked the sound of that. Could it be the sanctuary she was looking for? She let out a little sigh. Redemption.

3

Sweet mercy is nobility's true badge.
—William Shakespeare,
Titus Andronicus

*L*ady Victoria Helmit was making a muck out of trying to kill herself.

She shouldn't have been surprised, for God only knew she had certainly made a muck out of her life, just as her parents had predicted she would. Oh, if they could only see her now. They'd have a good laugh all right, then purse their lips in satisfaction. Their wayward, no-account daughter was fulfilling their every expectation. She couldn't even stop crying long enough to get a good foothold and climb over the railing so she could hurl herself into the ocean. Victoria was everything they said she was and more. She was also proving to be a coward.

To outsiders, she appeared to be a woman who had it all. In appearance, she'd obviously been blessed by the gods. She was strikingly pretty, with deep auburn-colored hair and eyes as brilliant and as green as

Ireland's spring grass. Her coloring came from her
mother's side of the family. Grandmother Aisley
hailed from County Clare. Victoria's high cheekbones
and patrician features also came from her mother's
side. Her grandfather had been born and raised in a
small province in the north of France. Since Grandmother's relatives couldn't even speak the French-
man's name without giving into a round of lusty, loud
vulgarities, and since Grandfather's family despised
the no-good, never-could-hold-their-drink Irish with
just as much intensity, when the two mismatched
lovers married, they settled in England on what they
called neutral ground.

While her grandparents were alive, Victoria was
doted upon. Her grandfather loved to boast she'd
inherited her flair for drama and her love of Shakespeare from him, and her grandmother was just as
happy to claim she'd gotten her quick temper and her
passionate nature from her.

Victoria wasn't the apple of her parents' eyes,
however. They wouldn't have thrown her out on the
streets if that had been the case. She had shamed and
disgraced them. They told her they were disgusted and
repelled by the very sight of her. They called her every
vile name they could think of, but the one that stuck
in her mind and played over and over again in her
memory was the claim that she had been, and always
would be, a fool.

They were right about that. She was a fool. Victoria
acknowledged the truth with a low, keening sob. She
immediately stopped herself from making another
sound and hurriedly looked to her left and then her
right to make certain she was still all alone. It was past
three o'clock in the morning. The other passengers
aboard the *Emerald* were fast asleep, and the crew was
obviously occupied elsewhere.

It was now or never. The *Emerald* had been at sea for three nights now. The water wouldn't get any deeper, and if she was going to get the deed done, she believed this was the perfect opportunity, for she was all alone.

She was mistaken in that belief. Lucas stood on the other side of the staircase and watched her. He couldn't figure out what in God's name the daft woman was trying to do.

Then he heard another sound. It was silk brushing against silk. He turned and spotted Taylor making her way up the stairs. She couldn't see him, and he didn't let her know he was there, watching her from the shadows. He wanted to find out what in thunder she was up to, strolling up on deck in the middle of the night.

The sobbing woman drew his attention again. She was struggling to move a heavy crate across the deck.

Victoria was weak from crying. It seemed to take her forever to move the crate over to the railing. Her feet felt like lead. She finally made it to the top of the crate and then latched onto the railing. She was poised to leap over the side if she could get one leg high enough. Her hands were tightly gripping the rail now and her white petticoats were waving about her like a flag in surrender. She stood there for only a second or two and yet it seemed an eternity to her. She was openly sobbing now with terror and defeat. Dear God, she couldn't do it. She simply couldn't do it.

She climbed down off the crate, then collapsed to the floor and wept without restraint. What was she going to do? What in God's name was she going to do?

"Pray forgive me for intruding on your privacy, but I would like to be of assistance if I may. Are you going to be all right?"

The question came in a whisper. Victoria squinted

against the darkness while she vehemently shook her head.

Taylor took a step forward into the light provided by the half-moon. She folded her hands in front of her and tried to act as calm as possible. She didn't want to frighten the young woman into doing anything drastic, because Taylor wasn't close enough to stop her if she tried again to jump over the side.

She watched as the woman mopped the tears away from her face with the backs of her hands. She took several deep breaths, obviously trying to regain a little of her composure. She was shaking from head to foot. The sadness Taylor saw in her eyes was heartbreaking. Taylor had never seen anyone this desolate, except her sister, Marian, she reminded herself. Marian had looked this defeated the morning she'd warned Taylor what Uncle Malcolm might try to do to her.

Taylor forced herself to block the image. "What in heaven's name were you thinking to do?" she asked.

"To be or not to be."

Taylor was certain she hadn't heard correctly. "I beg your pardon?"

"To be or not to be," Victoria repeated angrily. "That is what I was contemplating."

"You quote Shakespeare to me now?" Was the woman demented?

Victoria's anger over being interrupted vanished as quickly as it had come. She was exhausted now, defeated. "Quoting Shakespeare seemed appropriate," she whispered. Her voice was empty of all emotion when she continued. "I don't want to be any longer, you see, but I can't seem to gather enough courage to end my life. Please go away. I want to be left alone."

"I won't leave you alone," Taylor argued. "Tell me what I can do to help you."

"Assist me over the side."

"Stop talking like that." Her voice was sharper than she intended. She shook her head over her own lack of discipline. The woman needed help now, not a lecture. She took another step forward. "I didn't mean to raise my voice to you. Please accept my apology. I don't believe you really want to jump," she added in a rush. "You already made the decision not to end your life. I was about to stop you when you climbed down from the rail. You gave me quite a start, I'll admit. Turning the corner and seeing you perched up there so precariously." Taylor shivered with the memory. She rubbed the chill from her arms. "What is your name?"

"Victoria."

"Victoria's a lovely name," Taylor remarked. She couldn't think of anything better to say. She wanted to grab the woman by her shoulders and shake some sense into her. She didn't succumb to her urge, however, but would reason with her instead. "Please tell me what's wrong. I would like to help you."

Victoria pressed her back against the rail when Taylor took another step toward her. She looked like a cornered animal, waiting for the kill. Her eyes were wide with terror, and she gripped her hands together with such force, her arms began to shake.

"No one can help me."

"I cannot know if I can help you or not until you explain your circumstances."

"If you knew . . . you would turn your back on me and run," Victoria predicted.

"I doubt that," Taylor replied. "Please trust me enough to tell me what's wrong."

Victoria buried her face in her hands and began sobbing again. Taylor couldn't stand to witness her pain a moment longer. She rushed forward until she stood directly in front of her and then put her hand out.

"All you have to do is take hold, Victoria. I'll do the rest."

Victoria stared up at Taylor a long while, trying to make up her mind. And then, just when Taylor became convinced her offer of friendship was going to be rejected, Victoria surprised her. She slowly, timidly reached up to take hold of her hand.

Taylor assisted her to her feet, then put her arm around Victoria's shoulders with the thought of leading her away from the railing. She wanted to put as much distance between the ocean and the distraught woman as possible, an unrealistic feat, given the fact that they were surrounded on all sides by water.

Victoria was so desperate for a touch of human kindness and a tender, nonaccusatory word of comfort, she literally threw herself into Taylor's arms, very nearly knocking the two of them over. Taylor quickly recovered her balance. Victoria was weeping uncontrollably against her shoulder. She was an inch or two taller than Taylor, and consoling the woman proved to be a little awkward, though certainly not impossible. Taylor patted her in what she hoped was a soothing motion. She didn't try to do anything more to calm her. Victoria obviously needed to cry. In Taylor's mind, weeping could very well be the first step toward healing. Marian never cried, and Taylor thought that perhaps that was one of the many reasons she'd become such a brittle, hard woman.

It didn't take long for Victoria's sobs to unnerve Taylor. She tried to remain dispassionate, yet found she couldn't remain unaffected by such heartbreaking agony, and within minutes, tears were blurring her own vision.

Victoria was rambling incoherent words and phrases mixed with a good number of quotes from Shakespeare's tragedies, but when she confessed she had trusted the man, had really loved him and believed with all her heart that he would marry her, Taylor thought she finally understood the reason behind her desolation.

She was pregnant.

Taylor got good and mad. "Dear God, is that all?" she cried out. "You're going to have a baby, aren't you? I thought you'd committed some atrocious crime."

"It is atrocious," Victoria wailed.

Taylor let out a loud, unladylike snort. "No," she contradicted. "Murdering the man who lied to you and took advantage of your innocence would be atrocious," she told her. She paused to sigh. "Then again, perhaps that wouldn't have been so atrocious after all."

"My life is over."

Taylor forced herself to get her temper under control. The poor woman had probably had quite enough accusations thrown her way. She tried to think of something positive to say to her. It took her a few minutes to come up with something.

"The life you led is over, yes, but now you'll simply start another one. Come and sit down and compose yourself."

Victoria was limp and drained from weeping. Taylor led her over to a bench set against the wall adjacent to the strolling deck.

Victoria sat down, adjusted her skirts, and then folded her hands together in her lap. Her head was bowed in dejection.

Lucas, glad that the immediate threat was over,

moved further into the shadows where he could still watch but wouldn't disturb their privacy.

Taylor was too agitated to sit. She paced back and forth in front of Victoria while she worried the problem over in her mind.

"Do you still love this man?"

"No." Her answer was emphatic.

Taylor nodded. "Good," she announced. "He isn't worth loving," she added. "Do you have relatives who will give you shelter in America?"

"No. I hadn't planned on getting there. I used up all my money to purchase a berth. The only reason I carried along my clothes was because my father threw them out on the pavement."

"Your parents threw you out?" Taylor was appalled.

Victoria nodded. "I cannot blame them. I have been a disappointment."

"I can certainly blame them," Taylor argued. "They are your parents. They should have stood by you. My grandmother would have stood by me."

"If she were alive, my grandmother would have stood by me as well," Victoria said.

"What about the man responsible for your condition? Does he know you're carrying his child?"

"Yes."

"And?" Taylor prodded when she didn't continue.

"He doesn't wish to become involved."

"It's a bit late for that decision, isn't it?"

"He wanted to marry Lady Margaret Kingsworth. She has a large dowry."

Taylor's curiosity was captured. She knew Lady Margaret and wondered who the scoundrel was.

"Who is the man . . ."

"I will never say his name." She fairly shouted her denial.

Taylor hurried to soothe her. "I won't ever ask you again," she promised. "You're certain you don't still love him?"

"I can't imagine what I ever saw in him now. I should have heeded William's advice, for he wrote, 'Love moderately; long love doth so; too swift arrives as tardy as too slow.' "

Lord, she was quoting Shakespeare again. And crying. Taylor tried to hold onto her patience. It was a most difficult task. "The past is the past, Victoria. You cannot undo what has already been done. You must look to the future now."

"I believed with all my heart he would marry me."

"Many a good hanging prevents a bad marriage," Taylor said, turning Shakespeare's words back on the distraught woman.

Victoria found her first smile. "I do believe I would like to see him hang for his lies to me. Still, I was a willing . . . participant."

"You were naive and he took full advantage. The man's a snake."

"I was equally responsible for my mistake."

Taylor couldn't help but admire the woman because she took responsibility for her actions. She didn't blame anyone else, not even the pig who seduced her. She was about to tell her she admired her when Victoria asked her who she was.

"What is your name?"

"Taylor."

"Taylor? The Lady Taylor?"

"You've heard of me?"

"Oh, yes, everyone has heard of you, milady."

"Why?" Taylor asked.

"The humiliation . . . oh, dear, I shouldn't have mentioned such an indelicate topic."

Taylor's shoulders slumped. Did everyone in En-

gland know about her disgrace? "It wasn't a humiliation. It was a blessing as far as I'm concerned." Lord,
how many times had she said those words while in
London? At least a hundred times, she thought.

"Do you still love him?" Victoria asked.

"I never did love him," Taylor admitted. "I realize
that now. I married his brother," she added with a
nod when Victoria looked so surprised. "I don't love
him either," she confessed. "But I will admit I am
becoming attracted to him. Still, he is a man and,
therefore, probably a scoundrel. Most of them are. My
husband is honorable though. I've already noticed
that attribute."

"Perhaps you will eventually fall in love with him,"
Victoria suggested.

What an awful thought, given that Lucas would be
leaving her the minute they reached Boston. "Perhaps," she said aloud so that Victoria would believe
she'd offered a viable hope.

Taylor went over and sat down next to her new
friend. She gently turned the topic around to
Victoria's delicate condition.

"You made an important decision tonight."

"I did? What was that?"

"To live," Taylor answered. "The rest is going to be
easy. I promise you."

Victoria didn't understand. Taylor said she would
explain what she meant later. She asked Victoria what
she thought she most wanted to accomplish with her
life. What were her hopes and her dreams? If she
could have anything in the world, what would she
want?

Victoria answered her questions. She talked for
almost two hours. Taylor did most of the listening.
Discussing her fears helped lessen them in Victoria's
mind. The unknown terrified her, she admitted. And

being alone. That terrified her most of all. Taylor understood far better than Victoria thought she would. Being alone . . . and responsible for two children was terrifying for her, but she would do whatever she had to do to keep the twins safe. And, she had a feeling Victoria would be just as protective of her own little one.

"You have to get used to the idea first," Taylor said.

"What idea?" Victoria asked.

"Being a mother," Taylor explained. "I wager before long you'll love your baby with all your heart."

"I haven't really thought about the baby. I've been too busy feeling sorry for myself."

Taylor patted her hand. "You'd been betrayed. It was only natural for you to feel sorry for yourself."

Victoria let out a loud yawn, apologized for her unladylike action, and then said, "The wind has certainly picked up. Captain said a storm's brewing."

A sudden gust of wind swept across the deck. Victoria started shivering. Taylor didn't notice the chill in the air until Victoria mentioned it. Then she also started shivering.

"We'd better go back to our cabins," she suggested.

"Yes," Victoria agreed. She stood up, then turned to Taylor. "Thank you for listening to me. You've been very kind, milady."

Taylor was at a loss as to what to say in response. She wasn't at all comfortable receiving compliments. They'd been so far and few in her life. She had seldom received outright praise for any of her actions. Madam expected certain behavior, and Taylor only heard when she had disappointed her grandmother.

Victoria seemed to be waiting for her to do or say something, however, and so Taylor simply gave her a nod of acceptance. Then she cleared her throat. In a no-nonsense tone of voice very much like her grandmother's, she said, "Tomorrow I would like for you to meet me in the ship's library at two o'clock. In the last few days I've noticed that room is usually deserted at that time of day and we should have plenty of privacy while we formulate our plans."

"We will?"

"I believe so."

"What plans, milady?"

Taylor was surprised by the question. "Why, plans for your future of course," she explained. "Did you think I would pat you on your back in sympathy and then walk away?"

"I didn't know what to think, milady."

"Do quit calling me your lady. In America, titles have no significance whatsoever."

"Are you certain?"

"Oh, yes. I read it in a book, so it must be true."

Victoria nodded. "Are you really going to help me?"

"How could I not?"

Lord, she started crying again. Taylor didn't want to go through another round of weeping and consoling. "Please stop that," she pleaded. "You're going to wear yourself out. I cannot believe you thought I would abandon you. Shame on you, Victoria."

"I don't want to be a burden or suggest that you . . ."

Taylor took hold of Victoria's arm and led her over to the staircase. "Of course you don't want to be a burden. You won't be, I promise. I have a terrible habit," she confessed then. "I seem to believe I know what's best for everyone around me."

"I don't believe knowing what's best for someone else is a terrible habit," Victoria replied.

"Not just someone else," Taylor corrected. "Everyone else. And yes, it is a terrible flaw. Madam calls it my affliction. She says I shouldn't interfere and it's quite arrogant of me to think I can make a difference in anyone else's life. Very arrogant indeed. Those were her very words to me time and again. I fear she's right. I give you my word I won't force you to do anything you don't want to do, Victoria. But I do insist on helping you."

"Thank you, Taylor."

"We'll talk again tomorrow after you've had a good night's sleep and aren't so tired."

"I would be most appreciative of your counsel." Victoria paused a moment before continuing. "Are you able to know what's best for you all the time?"

Taylor's shoulders slumped. "That's the rub in this affliction I'm cursed with," she explained. "I never seem to know what's best for me. Just everyone else."

The bewilderment in Taylor's voice made Victoria smile. "Perhaps I'll know what's best for you."

Taylor smiled back. "Perhaps you will."

Because the staircase was only wide enough to accommodate one person at a time, Taylor motioned for Victoria to take the lead. "I'll walk with you to your cabin door so I'll know where to find you."

Victoria paused on the bottom step. Her expression was solemn when she turned to look up at Taylor. "Are we going to be friends?"

Taylor didn't hesitate in giving her answer. "I believe we already are."

The commitment was made. Taylor knew full well what she was taking on. She didn't blanch over the responsibility she'd just taken upon herself. She would take care of Victoria until she was strong enough and able enough to take care of herself. And the baby, Taylor silently added. She mustn't forget about the baby.

Friends helped friends, yes, but there was more to

Taylor's promise than that. Much, much more. Children, all children, should be cherished and protected from harm by every able adult. It wasn't a rule; it was a sacred commandment in Taylor's estimation, and she would do whatever it took to ensure Victoria's and her baby's safety . . .

No matter what the cost. It wasn't a choice. It was her duty.

Her noble intentions were going to die with her. She wasn't going to be able to help anyone, least of all herself. The ship was going down, and there wasn't a thing she could do about it. She was convinced it was only a matter of minutes before everyone was sleeping on the bottom of the ocean. Taylor would have knelt on the floor and said her prayers for forgiveness to her Maker for all the mean things she had ever thought about anyone, except her uncle Malcolm, of course. She believed that if she really was contrite about being so arrogant and bossy, she might be able to sneak into heaven, but kneeling anywhere was simply impossible with the hurricane-force winds knocking the little ship around and around. She wedged herself into the corner of the bed and pressed her shoulders against the wall. She really tried not to be afraid, but Lord it was an impossible task. Perhaps it wouldn't have been so horrible if it weren't the middle of the night and so pitch black inside the cabin. Taylor hated the darkness, but she didn't dare try to relight the lamp for fear she might accidentally set the walls on fire. And so she sat in the dark with her eyes squeezed shut and her arms clutched around a pillow, listening as her trunks slammed against one wall and then another. She fought her terror and her panic with prayers and pleas to her Maker while she waited for the end.

What was going to happen to her sister's babies?

The twins needed a mother. She couldn't even imagine what would become of the little ones. And Victoria . . . What would happen if she survived and Taylor didn't? She'd promised to help her new friend, and how would Victoria survive without any money or family in America?

Oh, God, there was so much she wanted to do. It wasn't fair to die like this. She let out a loud sob and gave in to her tears. No one, not even a bossy, arrogant, think-she-knows-everything young lady should have to die like this. She didn't want to die all alone. She wanted company.

And most of all, she wanted Madam.

The door opened with a bang. Taylor jumped a foot. Mr. Ross stood in the entrance. He all but filled up the entire doorway. She could see him clearly, for the light from the lamp perched in the leather holder high up on the hallway wall shown brightly all around him.

She'd never been so happy to see anyone in all her life. He looked like a god to her. Or a prince. He was drenched from head to foot. His dark hair hung down over his forehead and his white shirt and black pants were molded to his body. The bulge of muscle in his upper arms and his thighs made him look invincible to her. He was like a mighty warrior from the past, this princely giant she was married to, and Taylor found herself calmed by his mere presence. He was such a commanding figure, and the casual ease in his every movement, so graceful for such a huge man, actually captivated and soothed her.

Lucas Ross couldn't have been more appealing to her if he'd been dressed in elegant, regal robes.

"Hell of a wind kicking up." He made the remark in a casual tone of voice and took another step inside. "I'm soaked through." He turned then, tossed his wet bedroll into the corner of the stateroom next to his satchels, then shook his head very like a dog would do to rid himself of the rain. Drops of water flew outward in an arch.

He smiled at Taylor. One look at her face told him she was terrified. He noticed the tears coursing down her face. Her eyes were as wide as saucers. Her gaze was centered on him, but he didn't think the terror he saw in her expression was because he'd entered the cabin in the middle of the night. He used the cabin to house his clothes and came and went several times during the day. No, he wasn't responsible for her tears. The storm was causing her panic.

He couldn't fault her reaction. In truth, he felt the way she looked. He'd been in storms before but nothing as violent as this one. They were in real jeopardy of going down.

He wasn't about to share his opinion about their dire circumstances with Taylor, however. The last thing he wanted or needed was a hysterical woman on his hands, and for that reason, he forced himself to move slowly, to act as though he had all the time in the world. He was as nonchalant as possible. He even whistled.

She shifted in the bed when the ship tilted again.

"Do you prefer sitting in the dark?"

It took her a full minute to find her voice. "No," she whispered. She moved back so she was once again visible to him in the beam of light from the hallway. "But I was concerned I would set the cabin on fire if I tried to relight the lamp."

Lucas turned to go back outside. "Where are you going, Mr. Ross?"

Panic made her tone sharp and her words tremble. She couldn't seem to calm down. She didn't want him to know how afraid she was. He might think she was a coward. It really was laughable, she supposed, worrying about his opinion of her now, just minutes before they were both surely going to die, but foolish as it was, she still tried to hide her fear. He didn't know her very well, and she didn't want him to go to his watery grave believing he'd married a weakling.

"I'm just getting the lantern from the hallway," he called out.

He was already back inside the cabin by the time he finished his explanation. She watched him shut the door, then walk over to the opposite side of the room and tie the lantern to the metal hook protruding from the wall. One of her trunks went sailing past him while he was securing the base of the lamp to the stand. The ship took a perilous dive then. Taylor pressed her back against the wall, dug her heels into the sheets, and tried to maintain her balance. She was still tossed to the side. Lucas hadn't budged. His balance was impressive. So was his attitude, she decided. He didn't seem to be at all concerned about their perilous situation.

She felt it necessary to point out the obvious. "We're in the middle of a hurricane, sir. I believe it's only a matter of time before the ship goes down."

Lucas shrugged, pretending indifference. He took his time removing his shirt. He sidestepped the trunk, shoved it into the corner, then sat down on top of it so he could remove his shoes.

"Aren't you worried, Mr. Ross?"

"It's just a little high wind, Taylor. It's too early in the season for a hurricane. It should blow over in a couple of hours."

He gave the lie without batting an eye. She was watching him closely, looking for the least little sign of concern.

She didn't find any. "You aren't at all concerned,

Mr. Ross?" She didn't give him time to answer. "Have you been in other storms like this one?"

"Lots of them," he lied.

"Well then." Her sigh was long and filled with relief. She even managed a smile.

She was feeling much better now, almost safe. Then he inadvertently went and ruined her near recovery. He took his pants off.

She squeezed her eyes shut. "Mr. Ross, whatever are you thinking?"

She fairly shouted the question. He lost his patience with her. "Will you quit calling me Mr. Ross?"

He'd snapped his demand back at her. She was astonished by his show of temper. "If you wish," she replied. She kept her eyes closed. She heard him mutter something under his breath but couldn't make out the words. It was probably a blasphemy, she supposed with a frown she sincerely hoped he would notice.

Lucas stripped out of the rest of his clothes and walked over to his suitcase to get fresh, dry pants. He normally slept in the nude, but because he'd been sleeping up on deck, he had, of course, kept his clothes on. He was going to have to wear pants tonight as well, he knew, and all because this young lady he was saddled with was acting so damned squeamish and prim.

God save him from virgins, he thought. She was probably going to have heart failure when she realized he had every intention of sharing the bed with her.

He didn't have any intention of touching her, however. Being intimate with his bride would only complicate their financial arrangement. The last thing he wanted or needed was a wife, and he knew that if he touched her, he would feel honor bound to stay married. He'd just as soon be hanged. Or put back in prison.

His mind was filled with thoughts about the horrors associated with marriage, and for that reason he didn't notice the ship had tilted again. The trunk slammed into his right foot. He muttered an expletive, shook himself out of his dour thoughts, and put his pants on.

Taylor watched him. She was mesmerized by his physique, and since she was certain he wasn't aware she was looking at him, she barely blushed at all over what she was seeing.

Lucas Ross was as sleek as a panther. The splay of muscle in the backs of his thighs and shoulders seemed to roll with each movement he made. His skin was bronzed in color, no doubt by the sun. His waist was narrow, his shoulders were incredibly wide, and heavens, he really was a fine specimen of male perfection. If she'd been the faint-hearted sort, she was certain she would have swooned by now. In her opinion, he was magnificent.

She found herself wishing he would turn around. Lucas didn't accommodate her. He buttoned up his pants and walked over to the side of the bed. His chest was covered with a thick mat of dark hair. It tapered to a vee at his waist.

The ship suddenly lurched again. Taylor was so mesmerized by the sight of her husband, she forgot to brace herself. She went flying. He caught her in his arms just as she was about to be pitched to the floor.

Her reaction surprised him. She laughed. He hoped to God she wasn't getting hysterical on him.

"What's so amusing?"

She shrugged. His skin was warm to her touch. She noticed that when she wrapped her arms around his neck. The ship rocked again. It was an excuse she had been waiting for. She put her head on his shoulder and held tight.

"You aren't going to go back up on deck, are you? You'll only get wet again."

"I'm not going back up on deck."

She didn't loosen her hold. She wasn't about to let him get away. Being alone was too frightening. Lucas had become her safe haven against the storm.

"You can't sleep on the floor," she blurted out. "The trunks will drive you to distraction, flying about the way they are."

"What do you suggest?"

"You'll have to sleep with me."

He almost dropped her. She leaned back and looked up at him. Damn but she had the prettiest eyes he'd ever seen. And mouth. A man could get lost staring into those blue eyes and thinking about what he would want her to do to him with those sweet sexy lips.

"I'll sleep under the covers and you may sleep on top," she rushed out. The look on his face confused her. She didn't want him to think she was being brazen, just practical.

"It's a sound solution," she announced with a nod. "And very civilized."

He tossed her into the middle of the bed. Taylor realized her nightgown was bunched up around her knees. She hurried to straighten her gown and get under the sheets. While he stood there watching her with his hands on his hips and a strange, indefinable look on his face, she squeezed herself up against the wall, fluffed her pillow behind her head, and closed her eyes.

Lucas was too tired to figure out why Taylor wasn't acting frightened by him any longer. He fully intended to take advantage of his temporary good fortune. He would get into bed before she changed her mind. He went over to the lantern, turned the flame down, shoved a trunk out of his path, and then walked back over to the bed.

She tried to stay on her side, but the rocking of the ship made that extremely difficult. She didn't have enough bulk to keep her still or an anchor to hold onto, and Lucas had only just stretched out on his back when he found her plastered up against his left side. She apologized profusely, then scooted back to the wall.

She kept coming back. Each time the ship rocked she slammed into his side. He suspected she'd be black and blue by morning. Each time she hit him, she groaned. The moans soon became a prelude to her pleas for forgiveness.

It was like sleeping with a fish. Lucas's patience was quickly worn out. He rolled to his side, threw his arm around her waist and his thigh over her legs, and pulled her up close to him.

She didn't protest. She was, in fact, thankful for the anchor. She reached up to nudge his head out of her way, then lifted her hair back from where he'd trapped it with his shoulder. She pushed the thick curls to the other side of her neck. She should have braided her hair before going to bed, she supposed, but it had seemed silly to do such an ordinary chore when death was behind the next wave. As soon as the storm had begun, she'd hurried down to Victoria's cabin to make certain she was all right, and by the time she'd made it back to her own room, she could barely walk a straight line.

Everything was going to be all right. Taylor let out a loud yawn. Odd, but she wasn't at all afraid now. The warmth from her husband's body soothed her, and it only took a few minutes for her to completely relax.

"Mr. Ross?"

He didn't answer her. "Lucas?"

"Yes?"

He sounded surly. She pretended not to notice. "Are you sleepy?"

"Yes."

She folded her arms across her chest, being careful not to touch his arm.

"Isn't it odd neither one of us has become seasick?"

"Go to sleep, Taylor."

A full minute passed before she spoke again. Lucas thought she was going to cooperate. He was wrong. "I'm very weary," she whispered. "But not at all sleepy. Isn't that odd?"

He didn't answer her. "Perhaps, if you talked to me, I might become sleepy."

"Why would my talking make you sleepy?"

"You might be boring."

He grinned. She said the damnedest things. "Fine, I'll talk you to sleep. Do you have any particular topic in mind?"

"Tell me about Redemption."

He was surprised she remembered the name of his town. He couldn't imagine why she would be interested enough to hear anything more about the desolate place.

"I already told you all about Redemption. You'd hate it. Why don't you think about all the parties you'll attend in Boston. That should put you to sleep. God knows it would me."

Parties were the last thing she wanted to think about. She hated formal affairs, and the thought that she would never again have to attend an artificial

97

gathering filled with pompous, self-opinionated bigots made her smile. She knew Lucas believed she wanted to be part of Boston's society, and she saw no reason to dissuade him. She supposed most young ladies would like all the frivolity. She wasn't like most, however. Maybe she really was almost as peculiar as her great-uncle Andrew, as Madam had proclaimed on more than one occasion.

"You don't hate Redemption, do you?"

"I'm starting to," he answered with a yawn. "It's already getting crowded and growing every day. I'll be glad to leave."

"Leave? Why would you leave?"

"I don't like crowds."

"Aren't your brothers there?"

"The ranch is a day's ride away from the town."

"Well then?"

He let out a loud sigh. She really wasn't going to stop nagging him until she had her answers. Lucas gritted his teeth in frustration. She poked him in the shoulder. "Do you actually plan to abandon your brothers?"

"Jordan and Douglas have enough cattle and horses now. They don't need me any longer. I'll help Kelsey, the youngest, get settled, then I'll leave. They'll do just fine."

She believed his attitude was callous and cold, but she kept her opinion to herself. She didn't want to alienate him. Besides, she wanted answers, not an argument.

"Where will you go?" she asked.

"Hunting."

"Hunting for what?" she asked.

"A man."

She hadn't expected that answer. She thought he

would tell her he wanted to hunt for gold or silver. Even though the rush was officially over, she'd read there were still reports of veins located further west. But hunting for a man?

"And when you find him?"

Lucas didn't answer her for a long while. He wasn't about to tell her the truth, that he had every intention of killing the bastard. He didn't think her delicate nature could handle knowing exactly what was on his mind, and so he simply said, "I'm going to finish what he started."

"Is he an evil man?"

"Yes."

She thought about that for several minutes. The differences between the two of them were startlingly clear to her. She was running away from evil; Lucas was going to confront it. Was he a man of courage or was he letting vengeance rule his life?

She decided to find out. "Was he . . ."

He cut her off. "When I'm finished, I'll go back to the mountains, where a man can't be hemmed in."

She took the hint. Mr. Ross obviously wanted to end the discussion. She decided to let him have his way. She was a patient woman. She could wait to find out all the particulars.

"Madam told me you were born in Kentucky."

"Yes."

"But you fought on the side of the North?"

"Yes," he answered. "I moved North a long, long time ago."

"Before Montana Territory?"

"Yes."

"Did you believe in the war?"

"I believed every man in America has a right to freedom."

"And every woman and child," she interjected. "They should have the same rights. No man should have the power to own another . . . isn't that right?"

"Yes."

"You said you were eventually going back to the mountains. You want to be completely free, is that it? To go where the wind takes you."

"Yes."

"Won't you get lonely?"

"No."

"You're very antisocial."

He couldn't help but smile. She sounded as though she felt sorry for him. "You don't have to pity me, Taylor. I don't want a family."

Too late, she almost blurted out. He had a family, and it didn't matter to her that he might not want one. The babies came first. They were too young to fend for themselves. "And so you'll turn your back on . . . everyone?" *Me,* she silently added. *You'll turn your back on me.* Lord, what would she do if she needed him? How would she and the twins and Victoria and her baby ever get along?

Taylor's burst of panic was short-lived. She calmed herself almost immediately. She would do just fine. She hadn't planned on needing or wanting Lucas Ross in her life. It was ridiculous to feel even a bit of nervousness. She was an independent woman of means.

When she first heard the news of George's death and knew she was going to go to Boston to take on the responsibility of raising her nieces, she thought she would find a small city somewhere out West and take the little ones there. She would hire a housekeeper, and when the girls were older, she would make certain they had the finest tutors in America so they would be properly educated. Why, there might even be an acceptable school they could attend. The children were going to have every advantage, but more important, they would be safe from harm. Taylor wanted to make certain her uncle Malcolm never found them.

She was now reevaluating her decision. Every city in America had access to the telegraphs . . . and trains. They could easily be found in a city such as St. Louis or even Kansas City. Neither place was far enough away or difficult enough to get to should her uncle decide to send someone after her.

She let out a little sigh. Her voice was a bare whisper when she spoke. "Have you ever had a fear so unreasonable, it consumed you?"

She didn't wait for him to answer her. "I remember once, when I was a little girl, being unreasonably afraid of a falcon my father brought home. It wasn't enough that the predator was in a cage. I couldn't even stay inside the barn. Then the yard wasn't acceptable either. I ended up hiding in my room."

Lucas was curious by what he considered a damned odd reaction. "Why do you think you were so afraid?"

"My uncle Malcolm told me the falcon liked blue eyes. I still get the shivers when I think about what he told me. Have you ever noticed how sharp a falcon's claws are?"

"Your uncle had a cruel sense of humor."

"I was afraid of my uncle as well as the falcon," she confessed in another whisper.

"Was it unreasonable, too?"

"No. I was right to fear him. It's easy to find someone in a city, isn't it? Now that the telegraph has become so fashionable, and trains run almost everywhere, it is awfully easy to find someone . . . if you're looking. Isn't it?"

"Yes," he answered. "Why do you ask?"

She didn't want to tell him the truth. Perhaps she

was being overly anxious. Surely once Uncle Malcolm received his mother's money, he wouldn't think twice about her or the twins. He wouldn't have any reason to come after her.

And yet she knew he would.

"I'm being foolish," she told Lucas.

"What other unreasonable fears did you have?"

"I used to bolt my bedroom door every night for fear someone would come inside while I was asleep."

"That doesn't sound unreasonable to me."

"Maybe it wasn't," she agreed. "But I also pushed the heavy oak dresser in front of the door as an added barrier."

"Who did you think would come inside while you slept? Somebody or anybody?"

"Just somebody." She changed the subject before he had time to question her further. "If you go back to your mountains . . ."

"Not if, Taylor, when," he corrected.

"What happens if your brothers need you?"

"They'll know where to look. It would only take a month or two of searching."

"I'm sure they'll find that comforting news indeed in the event of an emergency."

"They'll do just fine," he stubbornly insisted.

"I certainly wouldn't come looking for you."

"I didn't think you would."

She snorted. He smiled. The little woman had a temper. She kept trying to hide it from him, but she wasn't doing a very good job. She had a death grip on his arm. Her nails were digging into his skin. He doubted she realized what she was doing. He wondered why she was so outraged on his brothers' behalf. She acted as though he really were abandoning his family. She just didn't understand. He had made a bargain with his brothers when they had asked him for help, and he'd done everything he promised he would do. Hell, he'd done more than enough.

How could she know what his life was like? She'd been pampered and protected all her life. She certainly had never done without. She couldn't imagine what it had been like locked in a two-by-four cell without windows but with plenty of rats and screams of death all around him.

Lucas wasn't going to try to make her understand how he felt or why. He never talked about the war and he wasn't going to start now. Her opinion of him wasn't important.

Lucas recognized the lie immediately. For some reason, her opinion of him did matter. He couldn't imagine why and knew he wasn't making a lick of sense. He was tired, that was all. Fatigue was making it difficult to think straight. The storm was still raging with just as much intensity, and he wouldn't have been surprised to hear the warning bell ring alerting the passengers to abandon ship.

He wasn't going to worry over things he couldn't do anything about. If the ship went down, he'd grab Taylor and swim for the nearest shore or die trying.

He couldn't do anything about Taylor's nearness either. She was so wonderfully soft and silky. She smelled good, too. Like roses. Her smooth, kissable skin could drive a man to distraction, and all he really wanted to do was bury his face in the crook of her neck and fall asleep inhaling her fragrance.

He was lying again. He wanted to make love to her, to bury himself inside . . .

"Do your brothers realize you're going to desert them?"

He was thankful for the interruption. His thoughts

103

were about to get him into trouble. He didn't mind that her question was actually insulting. She just didn't understand. Until she had called Jordan, Douglas, and Kelsey his family, he really hadn't considered them kin. They were just half brothers. Lucas had been alone for so long now, the notion of family was altogether foreign to him.

"You sound outraged," he remarked with a loud yawn.

"I believe I am a little outraged," she responded. "I realize your brothers and their problems shouldn't be my concern, but—"

He didn't let her finish. "You're right. They aren't your concern. Go to sleep."

"Are we finished discussing family responsibilities then?"

He ignored her question, letting his silence be all the answer she was going to get.

There was a bright side to the odd turn in the conversation, however. Taylor was so caught up in her outrage over what she considered to be disloyal family conduct on his part, she didn't have time or room to be worried about their situation any longer, and he supposed that was all good and well. His hide could withstand a few insults, especially if it kept her from being afraid. He didn't want her to think about drowning or dwell on the possibility. God only knew he had enough concern inside him for the two of them. He was beginning to wonder how much more battering the ship could take before being torn apart.

"Taylor, can you swim?"

"Yes. Why do you ask?"

"Just wondered."

"Can you?"

"Yeah."

A minute passed before she understood the motive

behind his question. "Could you swim all the way to Boston?" she asked.

No one could. They were still a good two days away from port, perhaps even more, if the ship had been thrown off course by the high winds and relentless waves. "Sure I could," he answered without even a hint of laughter in his voice. He hoped his lie would help keep her fears at bay.

"Mr. Ross?"

God, he hated it when she called him that. "What now?"

"I'm really not that gullible," she said.

He smiled in the darkness. She let out a loud, lusty yawn. "I wonder if I'll sleep through drowning."

"We won't drown."

"No," she agreed. "We won't."

Several minutes passed in silence. Lucas thought she had finally fallen asleep. He couldn't stop himself from moving just a little bit closer to her. His head dropped to rest in the crook of her neck. He closed his eyes and tried for a long while to block his lustful thoughts. His discipline deserted him. He knew he should turn away from her. He couldn't. He should have been able to control his fantasies, damn it all. She was beguiling, yes, with those magical eyes and enchanting mouth and it was only a normal, healthy reaction on his part to get hard and want her. He was in bed with her, after all, and all she was wearing was a thin white nightgown. In the dark, wasn't one woman as good as another? Of course, he told himself. Taylor wasn't anything special.

And if that wasn't a lie, he didn't know what was. There wasn't a thing ordinary about Taylor. Lucas gritted his teeth and forced himself to roll away from her. He blocked her from being tossed about with his back, closed his eyes, and willed himself to go to sleep.

She wondered what he was thinking about. He'd abruptly turned away. The storm probably had him nervous, she thought. His arrogance and his pride wouldn't let him admit he was worried, however, and how like a man to let his ego rule his reactions, even in a crisis. Men were a confusing lot. She didn't think the way most men thought things through was very complex. At least Lucas Ross didn't seem overly complex to her. What you saw was what there was. He seemed . . . genuine. He was a little blunt with his honesty, and heavens, wasn't that an endearing quality? She might not agree with some of his opinions . . . going off to the mountains and leaving his family to fend for themselves didn't seem like a very brotherly thing to do, but she found she had to admire him because he'd been very open about his intentions.

Lucas didn't seem the sort to have hidden motives. That possibility appealed to her more than anything else about him. There was also the fact that he wanted to become a mountain man. She couldn't fault his goal. If she'd been a man without responsibilities, she would have done the same thing. She wondered if he'd read any of the stories about Daniel Boone or Davy Crockett.

It was a pity really. A man should be able to follow his dream. And so should a woman. Still, Lucas wasn't going to be able to live in the mountains all alone, at least not for a long, long time . . . until the babies were old enough and able enough to take care of themselves.

She was going to Redemption. The decision sort of snuck up on her, she supposed. In her heart she knew it was the right thing. The secluded little town was perfect for her and the twins. If Victoria wanted to come with her, Taylor would welcome her.

There was only one wrinkle in her plan. It was galling to admit, but since it was the dead of night and she would probably sink to the bottom of the ocean before morning light, she supposed she could admit her vulnerability.

She needed Lucas Ross.

4

The course of true love never did run smooth.
— William Shakespeare,
Midsummer Night's Dream

*H*e couldn't wait to get away from her. The physical attraction he felt for her hadn't diminished over the length of the voyage. During the night when the storm had seemed most threatening, he awakened on top of Taylor, nuzzling the side of her neck. He didn't have any idea how he'd gotten there. He only knew he wanted her with an intensity he'd never experienced before. In his sleep, his defenses had been weakened, and surely that was why he instinctively reached for her to satisfy his hunger. Wanting her wasn't just painful. It also scared the hell out of him. Thank God, he'd awakened when he did, before he'd stripped her of her gown and scared the hell out of her. Luckily, Taylor never had an inkling of her own danger. She was so exhausted, she slept through his unplanned attack. It was only when he became aware of what he was doing and summoned enough discipline to roll away from her that she woke up. Damned if she didn't follow him across the bed. She brazenly cuddled up against him and went back to sleep. The woman was entirely too trusting for her own good. Still, he was her husband, even if it was in name only and for a short duration, and she really should feel safe with him. It was his duty to protect her, not ravish her.

Lucas spent the remainder of the journey crossing the ocean battling his lust. By the time they disembarked in Boston, he was feeling like an ogre and a lecher. Only his discipline kept him from acting like one. Taylor wanted him to continue to sleep in their stateroom every night, even after the storm had worn itself out. She hadn't come right out and asked, of course. No, she danced around the issue for almost an hour, making what he decided was the most illogical argument he'd ever heard, and when she was finished explaining her position on the matter, her conclusion was that they should continue their companionable sleeping arrangement for his sake. She had the gall to add that she was actually doing him an enormous favor.

He translated her rambling dissertation to mean she was afraid to be alone but was too stubborn to admit it. The storm had obviously spooked her. She felt safe with him, and although that was a compliment of sorts, it was also damned ironic, he decided, because if she had any idea what he was constantly thinking about, she would be terrified of him.

The last night on board the *Emerald* was the most difficult. He waited until he was certain she had already gone to sleep, then came into the stateroom as quietly as possible. He'd been sleeping on his bedroll on the floor. It wasn't uncomfortable. Over the years of living outdoors, he'd learned to sleep anywhere. No, the hard floor wasn't the problem. Taylor was. He found her sitting in a chair, wearing a white night-gown and wrapper and a pair of white slippers with ridiculous little satin bows on them. She was brushing her hair. And humming. It was hypnotic. Lucas stood there staring at her for a long minute. She smiled in greeting. He frowned in response. Then he turned around to leave. He wanted to run. He walked instead.

"Where are you going?" she called out. She hurriedly put her brush down on the trunk next to her chair and stood up.

He didn't turn around when he answered her. "Up on deck."

"Please don't leave. I need to talk to you."

He reached for the doorknob. "Go to sleep, Taylor. We'll talk tomorrow."

"But I wish to talk to you now."

He gritted his teeth in frustration. There didn't seem to be any way out of the torture. He was going to have to look at her again, see her in that paper-thin robe and gown and pretend he wasn't at all affected.

He was already beginning to imagine what was underneath. "Hell."

"I beg your pardon?"

Lucas turned around. He folded his arms across his chest and leaned back against the door. Then he let out a loud sigh. It was forceful enough to rock the ship.

"What do you want to talk about?"

"Us," she blurted out.

He raised an eyebrow. She forced a smile. She was desperately trying not to be intimidated by his gruff manner. She didn't want to argue with him. In truth, she hated confrontations of any kind. She was and always had been a peacemaker. She used to tell Madam she wished everyone would get along. Her grandmother informed her the wish was unattainable.

Now that Taylor was an adult, she set more attainable goals, and right now all she wanted was for Lucas to get along with her.

"Have I done or said something to upset you?" she asked.

"No."

She tried to act composed. She certainly didn't want him to think the topic distressed her. "You're certain?"

"I'm certain."

She didn't believe him. "You've spent most of the voyage avoiding me. We haven't had a single conversation that lasted more than five minutes, and I cannot help but wonder if I said something . . ."

He cut her off in midsentence. "It's late, Taylor. Go to sleep. Tomorrow we'll . . ."

She interrupted him. "We leave the ship tomorrow. We have to discuss our plans before then. I don't wish to talk about such a private matter in front of strangers."

She was wringing her hands together in obvious agitation. Her face was getting flushed, too. Lucas felt guilty as hell because he knew he was the cause of her distress. She was right, of course. He had been avoiding her. He had done everything possible to distance himself from her. He wasn't about to explain why. The truth would only make her more uncomfortable around him.

He was being noble, a first in his estimation, and she was never going to know about it. Lucas pulled away from the door, crossed the stateroom, and sat down in the chair Taylor had only just vacated. He stretched his long legs out, leaned back, and stared at her.

Taylor went over to the side of the bed, sat down, and folded her hands in her lap. She never took her gaze off him. She was determined to get some answers, even if it took her all night. She believed she was being quite noble, a first in her opinion, for she was determined to confront Lucas Ross, even if a full-blown argument resulted. She was getting sick to her stomach just thinking about the possibility.

His beautiful, untouchable wife looked miserable. His guilt increased tenfold. He decided to give her only a half-truth. "I have been avoiding you as much as possible," he admitted. *And it has been one hell of a challenge,* he silently added. They were on a ship, for God's sake, and the *Emerald* seemed to have gotten smaller and smaller since they left England. "It's been difficult," he added with a nod.

"It has?"

"Yes."

"Why?"

"Look, Taylor. I gave your grandmother a promise to look out for you. I've been trying to make certain you were all right and that no one bothered you, yet at the same time trying to maintain my distance. Hell, yes, it's been difficult."

She looked bewildered. She threaded her hands through her hair. He wanted to tell her to quit doing that. It was provocative, arousing. She was an enchantress, all right, and didn't even know it. Lucas felt he was approaching sainthood.

"You still haven't explained why you felt the need to avoid me," she reminded him.

She was like a bear after honey. She wasn't going to give up. He decided he only had one alternative left. He would lie to her. "I didn't want you to become attached to me."

He was back to feeling proud of himself. He'd told the lie without laughing.

She was frowning at him. "Are you serious or are you jesting with me?" She didn't give him time to answer her. "I happen to be your wife," she reminded him in a near shout.

Damned if she didn't thread her fingers through her hair again. He could almost feel the silky texture running through his fingers, could almost smell the fragrance, could almost . . .

He closed his eyes so he wouldn't have to look at her. He was thoroughly disgusted with himself. He had the discipline of a goat.

"Please forgive me for raising my voice," she said. She took a deep breath, relaxed her shoulders, and forced herself to relax. She knew she wouldn't accomplish anything if she didn't control her temper. Getting straight answers out of Lucas Ross was proving to be a most difficult challenge. It was also maddening and infuriating. The man wasn't making any sense. She didn't think he'd appreciate hearing that opinion, however, and so she decided to take a different approach. She'd use diplomacy.

"I know you didn't wish to be married."

"I'd rather be hanged."

She should have been insulted or, at the very least, pricked by his attitude. She had just the opposite reaction. His honesty was refreshing and humorous to her. She didn't laugh, but she couldn't quite hide her smile.

He opened his eyes and looked at her to see how she was reacting to his bluntness. Her smile took him by surprise. He found himself smiling back.

"We're in one hell of a mess, aren't we?"

"I'm not certain I understand what you mean."

He wasn't inclined to explain. He leaned forward in his chair and reached down to take his shoes off. His socks came next. Then he stood up and began to unbutton his shirt. He let out a loud yawn. It was a non-too-subtle hint he was tired.

Taylor didn't say another word. She continued to sit on the side of the bed and watch her husband. Lord, he was a frustration to her. She wondered if Madam had realized how contrary Lucas could be and how stubborn. Her grandmother had told her she'd researched the topic of Lucas Ross quite thoroughly and that she had had several long discussions with the man. Taylor was certain Lucas answered all of Madam's questions. Knowing how her grandmother usually operated, Taylor supposed the interviews were thinly veiled interrogations. Oh, yes, she was certain her grandmother got every one of her questions answered. Taylor let out a loud sigh. She wished she had inherited that trait from Madam. Being a bit of a bully every now and then did have merit.

Lucas wasn't paying any attention to his bride. He removed his shirt, unrolled his bedding, doused the light, and then stretched out on top of the blankets. His makeshift bed was all the way across the room. Even when he went to sleep, he put as much distance between them as possible. Waking up on top of Taylor had been a close call. He wasn't about to let anything like that happen again.

Taylor gave up trying to talk to him. She stood up, removed her robe, and then got into bed. She fluffed her pillows and adjusted her covers until all the wrinkles were out, and when she was finally comfortable, she called out, "Good night, Mr. Ross."

She knew full well he hated it when she called him Mr. Ross and that's exactly why she'd done it. She was obviously angry with him. She was muttering under her breath and making enough racket punching her pillows to let him know she was upset.

The little woman was as transparent as air. She apparently never learned the art of hiding her feelings. With her beauty and her innocence, she'd be easy pickings for every gold digger in Boston. Lucas's mood quickly soured. The thought of Taylor with any other man bothered the hell out of him. What in thunder was the matter with him? Why did he care who she ended up with once their marriage was legally dissolved?

"Are you asleep?" Taylor whispered the question in the darkness and waited for a response.

He didn't answer her. She wasn't deterred. She simply asked the question again in a much louder tone of voice.

He gave up the pretense. "What is it?"

She rolled onto her side and tried to find him in the darkness. "I just thought I would remind you about our appointment with the bankers. I'll set the time once we get to the hotel. You'll have to stay long enough to talk to them."

"I will."

"It could mean staying in Boston an extra day or two."

"I know."

She didn't say another word for a long while. Just when Lucas was certain she'd fallen asleep, she whispered his name.

"What now?"

She ignored the irritation she heard in his voice. "You gave up your future for me. It was a noble sacrifice."

"It wasn't noble, Taylor."

She didn't argue with him. "Will you promise me something?"

"Will you let me sleep if I do?"

"Yes," she agreed.

"All right. What do you want me to promise?"

"You won't leave without saying good-bye."

The worry in her voice was quite apparent to him. "I promise. I won't go anywhere without saying good-bye."

"Thank you."

Taylor closed her eyes and said her nightly prayers. Lucas closed his eyes and tried to block all the lustful thoughts about his bride raging through his mind. He decided to list all the reasons why he never wanted to be married. First, and most important, was his freedom, he reminded himself. He was a wanderer, not a family man. A wife was a rope around his neck. She was a complication he neither wanted nor needed.

A sudden thought interrupted his concentration. She'd told him he'd given up his future. Since he had no intention of ever marrying anyone once Taylor was out of his life, her praise was ill-placed. He hadn't been noble marrying her. He'd done it for money so that he could buy Kelsey's freedom.

What had Taylor's motive been? He remembered being surprised and curious their last night in London when he'd watched Taylor remove her jewelry and give it away. Was she so wealthy she could replace the gems without a concern for cost?

Something wasn't quite right about his conclusions and her motives. Lucas had spent enough time with Taylor to learn a few things about her. The way she treated her clothing, with such care and attention when she was folding the gowns and putting them back in her trunk, told him she was used to doing for herself. She hadn't insisted on bringing along a lady's maid. He wouldn't have allowed servants, of course, but damn it all, she hadn't asked.

The *Emerald* offered a butler service. Taylor hadn't

taken advantage of the service. She hadn't let anyone clean the stateroom either but had seen to the task herself. For a rich, pampered woman, her behavior was confusing.

"Taylor?"

"Yes?"

"In London, that last night, why did you give your necklace to that young girl?"

What an odd thing for him to be thinking about now, she thought. She stifled a yawn before she answered. "It gave her pleasure to have it."

He wouldn't accept that half answer. "And?" he prodded.

"I knew I wouldn't be needing it."

Lucas frowned over her explanation a long minute. "They don't wear expensive necklaces in Boston?"

"I imagine some do."

The tables had been neatly turned on him. Lucas found it frustrating not to be able to get a straight answer out of her. He wasn't going to give up. "Your grandmother told me the marriage would protect your inheritance from your uncle."

"Yes, that's true. What else did Madam tell you?"

"To watch out for you."

"I can watch out for myself."

She sounded indignant. Lucas smiled. How like an innocent to think she could take on the world and all the evil associated with it.

He stacked his hands behind his head and stared up at the ceiling while he gathered his thoughts. "But the inheritance isn't the only reason why you married me, is it?"

"Madam worked hard to accumulate her wealth. She didn't want to see it squandered away. I feel the same way."

"Then why did you give your necklace away? I assume it was valuable. Those were real gems, weren't they?"

"Yes."

"Then why . . ."

"I have already explained," she insisted. "I don't need such trinkets any longer."

They were right back where they had started. Lucas grudgingly admitted Taylor was every bit as good as he was when it came to giving only evasive answers.

"I still want to know—"

She cut him off. "I'm very tired, Mr. Ross. Do let me sleep." She rolled over to face the wall. She closed her eyes and let out a loud, thoroughly forced yawn.

She prayed Lucas would take the hint. She wanted him to quit his inquisition and go to sleep. He would have to know about the babies, of course, but in Taylor's mind, later was better than sooner. She didn't see any reason to enlighten him just yet. He'd already proven to be a little stubborn, and she knew that if he found out she planned to follow him to Redemption, he might try to stop her. Taylor let out a sigh. Of course he would stop her. He would have noble reasons, too. In his opinion, she belonged in the parlors of Boston, sipping tea and acting like a silly chit. She certainly didn't belong in Redemption. Hadn't he said she'd hate it?

Taylor's thoughts were all but forgotten when she felt the covers being pulled back. She rolled onto her back and let out a little gasp of surprise. Lucas was towering over her. It was dark inside the stateroom, but she could still see the frown on his face.

"What are you doing?" she asked.

He sat down. She tried to get out of his way. Her nightgown was trapped under his thigh and she tried to pull the thing free, but Lucas turned her attention again when he put his hands on her shoulders.

"Look at me," he commanded.

His voice was gruff, filled with irritation. She let him see how disgruntled she was. "Do you know, Mr. Ross, you become irritated at the drop of a hat."

"I want you to answer a question for me."

"All right. What is it?"

"Why did you marry me?"

She couldn't look him in the eye when she answered him. Her full attention was centered on his throat. "To protect my inheritance."

"And?" he prodded.

She sighed. He was like a cat after a ball of yarn. He wasn't going to give up until he had all his questions answered. "To prevent Uncle Malcolm from marrying me to the first rake he spotted."

Lucas shook his head. There was still more than she was telling. He was sure of it. "And what other reason did you have?"

"I married you for the greater good. There, I've told you all you need to know."

"What greater good?"

She shook her head. "You shouldn't be sitting on my bed," she announced with as much indignation as she could muster. "It isn't appropriate. I sleep under the covers. You sleep on top, remember?"

"We're married," he snapped. "Anything's appropriate."

She opened her mouth to say something, then promptly shut it again. Her mind emptied of every thought. She stared up at him and simply waited to see what he would do.

She wasn't afraid of him. The second she remembered that important fact, she started breathing again.

She didn't have any idea how long they stared at each other. It seemed an eternity to her. Lucas seemed to be making his mind up about something important, and from the frown on his face, whatever he was considering wasn't very pleasant.

"You're my wife, Taylor."

She didn't like the sound of that. "Are you telling me you wish to exercise your . . . rights as my husband?"

She could barely get the question out. She looked appalled by the very idea. Her reaction chafed. He suddenly wanted to throttle her and kiss her at the same time.

Lucas suddenly realized his mistake. He'd gotten too close to her. He could feel the warmth of her skin beneath his hands and all he could think about was touching her. He wanted to taste her, devour her. One kiss, he told himself, just one kiss. Then he would be satisfied.

Hell, he was lying to himself again. He didn't want one kiss. He wanted it all. "No, I don't want to exercise my rights as your husband."

He sounded angry. Taylor couldn't help but be stung by his attitude. He didn't have to look so horrified by the mere idea. She knew she should be feeling relief. She wasn't though. Although she wasn't ready or willing to give herself to Lucas Ross, she still wanted him to find her a little desirable. Every wife wanted her husband to think she was attractive, didn't she? Taylor was honest enough to admit she wanted Lucas to think she was at least pretty.

He, however, acted repulsed by the very thought of touching her.

It was ridiculous for her to have hurt feelings. Yet she was devastated. She was just tired, she decided.

Surely that was the reason his rejection made her feel so inadequate.

Yes, she was overly sensitive tonight, and Lucas Ross was an insensitive lout. "Some men find me attractive."

She hadn't meant to blurt that thought out loud. She let out a sigh. "At least I think they do. You don't like me very much, do you, Lucas?"

"I like you just fine," he replied.

She didn't look like she believed him. He could tell from her expression he'd hurt her feelings. He decided to try to make her understand his position.

"Do you know why I won't touch you?"

"Yes," she answered. "It's quite simple for anyone to understand. You don't want me. An imbecile could figure it out."

"I didn't say I didn't want you."

"Yes, you did."

"I do want you."

Her eyes widened in surprise. Then she shook her head at him. The conversation had taken a bizarre twist. He decided he might as well finish what he started.

"Hell, yes, I want you," he muttered. Then he qualified his answer. "I just don't want to be married to you."

"You can't have it both ways, Lucas."

"What is that supposed to mean?"

She wasn't certain. But she was beginning to feel better now that he acknowledged he was attracted to her.

Then she realized the veiled insult he'd given her. "Do I have a sign on my forehead asking to be insulted?" she snapped. "Honest to heaven, first William Merritt insults me by suggesting I become his mistress and now you insult me by saying you want to . . . you know, but you don't want to be married. Well?" she demanded.

He was going to answer her question, and while he was at it, he'd tell her he didn't like being lumped into any category with that son-of-a-bitch Merritt. She distracted him before he could defend himself. She touched him.

A lock of his hair had fallen forward to rest on his forehead. It was driving her to distraction. Without a thought as to what she was doing, she pushed his hand away from her shoulder and reached up to brush the hair back where it belonged.

He jerked back, acting very like she'd just struck him. She was immediately embarrassed by her boldness.

"Madam says men would rut with a rock if it were possible." The outrageous statement gained his full attention. "And do you know why?" she asked.

He told himself not to ask. He knew he wasn't going to like the answer. Curiosity won out, however. "No, why?"

"Men don't think with their heads but with their . . ."

He stopped her from finishing her explanation. His hand covered her mouth. "For the love of God, Taylor. You will not talk like that."

"I was just telling you what Madam explained to me about men," Taylor whispered the second Lucas removed his hand. "It's true, isn't it? Lust is always uppermost in every man's mind."

"Not all men are like that."

"Are you?"

He gave her a scorching look. Then he braced his hands on either side of her face and slowly leaned forward. "No, I'm not. I want you to understand something, Taylor. You've been one hell of a distraction to me, but I won't ever settle down. No matter how enticing the thought might be."

"Is that why you're sitting on my bed in the middle of the night lecturing me? You want me to know you won't settle down? I believe you've already made that perfectly clear, Lucas."

"I also wanted you to know you're safe with me. Even though I'm attracted to you, I won't take advantage of our circumstances."

"You'll be honorable."

"Yes."

She nodded. Lucas was getting all riled up. His voice had turned gritty and his expression was hard, angry.

She decided to try to lighten his mood. "I don't want you to worry about me," she told him.

He shook his head. "I'm not worried."

"I believe I can put your mind at ease about this attraction and our close quarters."

"How?"

"Ask me if I want you to touch me."

"Do you?"

"I'd rather be hanged."

He was startled, but only for a second or two, and then he broke into a wide smile. She'd sounded sincere, yet the sparkle in her eyes told him she was jesting with him. He was beginning to like the way she turned his words back on him. She was being sassy and clever.

"Are you mocking me?"

She gave him that wide-eyed stare he found intoxicating and damned if she wasn't becoming impossible to resist.

"Yes."

He laughed. His sour mood evaporated. He shook his head at her, then leaned down to place a chaste kiss on her forehead.

He kissed the bridge of her nose next. He was treating her like a child he was tucking into bed for the night. Taylor was having none of that. Her curiosity to find out what it would feel like to be properly kissed by Lucas suddenly overrode all caution. Before she could stop herself, she clasped the sides of his face with her hands and leaned up. Her mouth brushed against his. It was a featherlight touch, over within the space of a heartbeat, and in her estimation, it was really very nice. She liked the feel of his rough skin against her fingers. Lucas needed a shave, but the day's shadow of a beard made him look extremely rugged.

Taylor was content. Her curiosity had been satisfied. She let go of him and fell back against the pillows.

He followed her. He clasped her chin with one hand and forced her to look up at him. "What the hell did you do that for?"

She hurried to placate him. "It was just a kiss, Lucas."

He shook his head. "No, Taylor. This is a kiss."

His mouth came down hard on top of hers. He took absolute possession. She opened her mouth to protest. He took immediate advantage. His tongue swept inside to mate with hers. Taylor was stunned. She didn't know if she wanted to push him away or pull him closer, and what in God's name was his tongue doing inside her mouth? She'd never heard of anyone kissing that way. It was too intimate, too consuming. Heaven help her, she liked it. Her hands found their way around his neck. She clung to him while he gently ravished her. She couldn't remain passive for long, however. She started kissing him back. Her tongue rubbed against him, slowly at first, then more boldly. The kiss turned carnal. The heat burning between them was as arousing as the mingling of their scents.

He couldn't seem to get enough of her. He could feel her breasts pressing against his chest through the thin material of her gown. It drove him crazy. He pulled her even closer, cupped his hands behind her neck and angled her head to one side so his tongue could make deeper penetration. His mouth slanted over hers again and again. He shook with his desire. She tasted so good, so sweet, and the little whimpers she made in the back of her throat destroyed his control.

He never wanted to stop. The realization jarred him back to reality. Lucas ended the kiss abruptly. Getting her to let go of him took a little longer. He had to pull her hands away and gently push her back against the bed.

He was out of breath. She didn't think she was breathing at all. Lucas had overwhelmed her. She could still taste him on her lips, still feel the heat of his mouth as he devoured hers.

The kiss had gotten completely out of hand in a matter of seconds. His heart was still hammering thunderously inside his chest. Passion was slow to ebb. She wasn't helping matters. Her eyes were misty and her rosy lips were still swollen from his touch. She looked bemused and too damned touchable.

"You're dangerous, lady."

His frustration made his voice thick with anger. Lucas stood up; grabbed his boots, shirt, and bedroll; and stormed out of the room. He wasn't about to take any chances. He was on edge now, aching with the need to plant himself solidly inside her, and since he couldn't do what he most wanted to do, he was determined to get the hell away from her.

He went looking for a bucket of cold water to pour over his head.

As soon as the door closed behind him, Taylor burst into tears. She started shaking from head to foot.

She was thoroughly ashamed of herself. Whatever had she been thinking of to taunt him for a kiss? She shook her head over her own sinful conduct. She'd been playing with fire, she told herself. She knew better now. She certainly couldn't continue on with this attraction. It would be too easy for her to lose sight of her goals.

Taylor no longer trusted her own judgment. She believed she was in love with William Merritt, and Lord, hadn't she been a complete fool then? Lucas might be different, but he was still a man and therefore not to be trusted in matters of love and commitment.

At least he had been honest with her from the beginning. He had told her he didn't want or need her. And how had she repaid his honesty? By throwing herself at him.

She was mortified. If she didn't know better, she'd think she was beginning to act like a wife. No wonder he went running for safety.

Taylor let out a loud groan, rolled over, and pulled the covers up. She vowed to apologize to Lucas first thing in the morning and promise him he wouldn't have to deal with her curiosity again. She fell asleep minutes later. She dreamed about him.

He had nightmares about her. He woke up in a cold sweat. Remnants of the godawful dream still lingered in his mind. Taylor was trapped inside a cave. He went in after her, but just as he was reaching for her, the walls and the ceiling came crashing down around the two of them. Air suddenly turned into dirt. They couldn't breathe, couldn't move. He was desperate to get her out before she died . . . like the others.

In his sleep, Lucas's mind blended two nightmares together. One was real, the other imaginary. The others who had magically appeared in the cave with Taylor were soldiers he had known and befriended, comrades, who had been led, just as he'd been led, into a deadly trap by their own superior officer. Major John Caulder sold out what was left of his unit to save his own hide. Cowardice wasn't his only motive, however. Greed was also involved. Like Judas, his treachery was richly rewarded and for an amount far greater than thirty pieces of silver. Caulder personally confiscated a large share of a shipment of gold he was supposed to be protecting.

Lucas was the only man who survived, though only because the renegades told Caulder they were certain all nine men were dead. The major was a worrier, however. It wasn't enough that a bullet had been shot into each man's back. He wanted to be certain no one was still breathing. He had his career to protect, to say nothing of his neck, and he didn't want anything to mar his brilliant, blemish-free military record.

No, he wasn't about to take any chances. He didn't want anyone sniffing out the truth after the war was over. And so he did what any meticulous man would do. He buried the evidence.

The shout of rage building in the back of Lucas's throat woke him up. Sweat was pouring down from his brow and he was gasping for air. His mind was quick to clear, and with it his rage, but he still spent several minutes pacing the deck until the tightness inside his chest eased up.

He was accustomed to having nightmares about the

war. Finding Taylor in the middle of his dream was another matter altogether. How in God's name had that happened? He wasn't worried about her. He knew she was all right, yet even though he was certain she was sound asleep down in their stateroom, he needed to look in on her just to make certain.

She didn't stir when he walked into the room. She was sleeping on her back with her hair spread out like a golden halo all around her head. She looked angelic, serene, peaceful. She was probably dreaming about afternoon teas and handsome suitors. Damn but he almost envied her. Demons always filled his dreams. He and Taylor were complete opposites in every way imaginable, and perhaps that was why he was drawn to her. She represented warmth and sunlight to a man who'd been denied both for long, long years.

Lucas stood by the side of the bed and stared down at her for several minutes. He couldn't seem to make himself leave. He knew she would be disgusted by the very sight of him if she knew about his background. In the name of war and honor, he had done unspeakable things in order to survive.

He shook his head. He didn't want to fight the temptation any longer. The lure of her innocence and her purity was too powerful to turn his back on. He didn't even try. He sat down, took off his boots and his socks, and then stretched out next to her. She scooted closer to him. He rolled onto his side and pulled her into his arms. He buried his face in the crook of her neck and closed his eyes.

He was sound asleep a minute later.

God proved merciful. The demons left him alone.

5

Words without thoughts never to heaven go.
—William Shakespeare,
Hamlet

*P*romptness wasn't one of Taylor's attributes. Lucas waited for well over an hour for her to join him up on deck. He had plenty of time to think about the night before. Whatever had possessed him to get in bed with her? What weakness drove him to take her into his arms and hold her close? He didn't ever remember sleeping so soundly or so peacefully. It was galling. And damned confusing to him. He let out a sigh then. Thank God he awakened when he did. He remembered being sprawled on top of her sweet, warm, soft body and immediately forced himself to stop thinking about it. She hadn't awakened and that was all that mattered.

He wanted to get going. He ran out of patience and was just about to go down below and drag her off the ship when she came hurrying up the stairs.

She looked flustered, worried, and lovely. She wore

a pale pink dress that had tiny white threads embroidered into rose buds along the high, square-necked bodice. The color of the gown complemented her skin, and Lucas thought she was probably the most feminine thing he'd ever seen.

He let out a sigh that sounded very like a growl of a bear and frowned at her.

She smiled back. She assumed her tardiness was the reason behind his irritation. She apologized for making him wait, all the while looking around the deck for Victoria. Her friend was nowhere to be found. Since most of the passengers had already left the ship, Taylor decided Victoria must be waiting for them wherever the luggage had been deposited. She'd already gone to Victoria's cabin to make certain she wasn't waiting for her there, but the cabin was empty.

"I'm very anxious to step on American ground," she remarked.

"Could have fooled me," he replied. He latched onto her arm and turned to leave.

The remark he'd just made was an obvious jab because she'd made him wait. Taylor ignored his sarcasm and turned her attention to the harbor.

At first glance, the city skyline reminded her of London, though on a larger scale. She noticed almost immediately one primary difference between the two cities, however. London always had a gray film looming over her buildings. The sky above Boston was pristine clean, or so it seemed to her.

Taylor didn't say another word to Lucas until they reached the luggage carts. She was so overwhelmed by the sights and sounds of her new homeland, she could barely form a coherent thought. She wanted to close her eyes and listen to all the vastly different accents and try to guess the name of the country each had come from. So many different foreign languages soon blended together, however, and she gave up her game. She tried then to look everywhere at once. There was so much to see and to explore, so much . . .

"Taylor, will you pay attention to what I'm telling you?"

She finally looked up at him. "Isn't it wonderful, Lucas?"

The wonder in her voice made him smile. "Boston?"

"America," she qualified.

He nodded. "You've yet to see America," he told her. "But you'll like living in Boston. It's very cosmopolitan," he added. "Very much like London."

"I already like Boston, but I don't want it to be anything like London."

After making that statement, she turned her attention to the chaos surrounding her. Lucas stared down at her for several minutes. When he realized what he was doing, he became disgusted with himself. He was acting like a besotted farm boy, but damn it all, it was her fault.

She was an enchantress all right. He was certain she was deliberately enticing him with that come-and-kiss-me smile of hers. The way she brushed her fingers through her hair and tossed her head back was a definite provocation meant to attract him. Even the way she looked up at him with those magical blue eyes and that trusting look on her face was meant to capture his full attention.

"Shouldn't we collect our luggage?"

Her question interrupted his thoughts. Lucas forced himself back to the business at hand.

"Stay right here," he ordered. "I'll be back in a minute."

Taylor only had enough time to nod before he walked away. She had the luggage tickets clutched in her hand. Lucas had secured reservations at the Hamilton House just outside of Boston proper, per Madam's explicit instructions. It was one of the best hotels in America, certainly on a par with the States Hotel, though on a smaller scale. Madam had read all the literature on both establishments and had declared that Hamilton House was a bit more exclusive. She told Lucas the States Hotel catered to too many businessmen, and she didn't want her granddaughter mingling with what she called the ordinary working man. Lucas didn't argue. He would deposit Taylor wherever her grandmother wanted her deposited, spend one or two more nights in the city, depending upon the bankers' meetings, and then head for home.

He returned to Taylor with a clerk from Hamilton House a few minutes later. He was in the nick of time. Taylor was in the process of handing over their luggage tickets to a man who had convinced her he was a representative of the hotel and would take care of the baggage.

Lucas snatched the tickets out of the thief's hands and sent him running. Taylor was appalled by what she deemed rude and certainly improper conduct. When she noticed the man Lucas handed the tickets to was wearing a hotel badge on his hat and the man she'd almost given her possessions to hadn't been wearing any such credentials, she became horrified by her own naïveté.

"He would have stolen our luggage."

Lucas nodded. Taylor wasn't about to let the matter drop. She lifted the hem of her skirt and went running after the thief. Lucas grabbed her before she got lost in the crowd.

"Where in God's name do you think you're going?"

"To catch the scoundrel," she explained in a near shout. "Someone should alert the authorities."

Lucas let her see his exasperation. He anchored her to his side and turned toward the line of public vehicles.

"Aren't you going to do something?" she demanded.

"He's gone, Taylor. We'd never find him in this crowd."

"I remember his face," she boasted.

Lucas didn't laugh. She sounded so damned earnest. "What would you do if you caught up with him?"

She hadn't thought that far ahead. She considered the matter for a minute or two, then shrugged. "I would hold onto him while I shouted for assistance."

He rolled his eyes heavenward. She was beginning to see the folly in her plan but would go to her grave before admitting her foolishness.

"What would happen if he didn't stand there peacefully while you did your shouting, Taylor?"

"I suppose I'd have to pound him."

It was an empty boast, and they both knew it. "I think you should begin to think about consequences," Lucas remarked.

He was barely paying her any attention now. They reached the vehicles. He stopped to give their destination to the driver.

Taylor was trying to get him to unhand her. He finally noticed what she was doing when he turned to open the door to the conveyance for her.

"Get in."

"We can't leave just yet. I'm waiting for my friend. She's going to ride to the hotel with us. You'll have to be patient, Lucas. I was supposed to meet her by the luggage. Excuse me for one minute while I go look for her."

"You'll never find her in this crush."

"There she is," Taylor cried out. She called Victoria's name, but her friend didn't hear her. Taylor couldn't get Lucas to unhand her long enough to go after her friend, and so she gave the errand to him.

"Do go and fetch Victoria."

Lucas let go of her. He turned to look at the crowd. "Who is Victoria?"

He was talking to air. The second he unhanded her, she took off. Lucas muttered an expletive and went chasing after her. Because he was so much bigger than she was, he couldn't slip through the crowd as easily as she could. He resorted to shoving several men out of his path. He caught up with Taylor just as she came to a stop behind a red-headed woman.

"Victoria, do turn around," Taylor requested.

Her friend was obviously taken by surprise. She jumped a good foot and then whirled around. The relief on her face was pronounced, and there were tears in her eyes.

"Oh, I'm so happy to see you, Taylor. I thought you'd left me behind. I couldn't remember where we had agreed to meet," she added in a rush.

Victoria tried to hide her panic. In truth, she'd been terrified. She felt ill now. Her stomach was queasy, and she thought she was going to be sick. Dear God, she didn't know what she was going to do. She wanted to weep with relief because Taylor hadn't left her behind but knew such undignified behavior wouldn't be at all appropriate.

Taylor could see how distressed her friend was. She hurried to soothe her. "I also became confused about our meeting place," she said. "I thought we were supposed to meet on deck where the luggage was being stacked for transfer. It doesn't matter," she hastily added. "I would never have left you. Besides, if something had happened and we hadn't found each other, you knew the name of the hotel. You could have gotten there on your own."

Victoria nodded. She was too embarrassed to admit she didn't even have sufficient funds to pay the driver. She would have had to walk to Hamilton House. Still, Taylor was right. Victoria felt she was resourceful enough to find a way. She just wished she wasn't so emotional. The past week had been a test of endurance for her, what with all the changes in her life and her body, and she seemed to cry almost hourly.

"I'm not usually so emotional, milady," she announced.

And then she burst into tears. Taylor pulled a lacy handkerchief out of the cuff of her sleeve, handed it to Victoria, and then took hold of her hand. She turned to Lucas and quickly made the introductions.

"Victoria is a dear friend of mine," she informed him.

"Why is she crying?"

Taylor frowned at Lucas for bringing up the topic. Victoria was valiantly trying to control herself. "She's had a difficult time of it," she explained. "She's in mourning."

"I am?" Victoria asked in a whisper.

Taylor nodded. "Yes, you are."

She turned back to Lucas. "She's mourning the death of her beloved husband."

He didn't ask any questions. He knew very well who she was. He still remembered well every word the two women had exchanged the night Taylor had come to Victoria's assistance. He'd been about to haul the crazy woman down off that warped crate and ask her what the hell was the matter with her when Taylor intervened. And so he'd stayed in the shadows. He wasn't deliberately eavesdropping. He was simply making certain Taylor stayed safe. He was keeping his part of the bargain he'd made with her grandmother. Hearing that Victoria was pregnant and unmarried had struck a chord with him. He felt pity for her, of course, as well as a little compassion. She wasn't going to have an easy time of it. His own mother hadn't.

Lucas couldn't help but admire Taylor because she was looking out for the woman. "Are you going to help Victoria get settled in Boston?" he asked.

"That is my intention," she answered.

He smiled. She didn't know what to make of that reaction. And so she simply smiled back.

"Shouldn't we get going? All the vehicles will be taken up, sir."

He was in full agreement. He suddenly wanted to get to their destination, too. He grabbed hold of Taylor's left hand and Victoria's right hand and strode toward the vehicles. Victoria's flower-laden bonnet was in jeopardy of flying off her head, so fast was his pace. She put her left hand on top of her head to anchor her hat in place.

Taylor was trying not to trip on her skirt. "We aren't running from a fire, Mr. Ross," she called out.

He slowed down. He gave the driver their destination, then opened the door and turned to Victoria.

"Has your luggage been sent on?"

"Taylor had my tickets," Victoria answered.

She was talking to the ground. She kept her gaze downcast while she answered him. She was a timid thing, and he found himself wondering how in God's name she was going to survive with only Taylor looking after her. He decided he would take the bankers aside and have a talk with them. Since the trust fund they held in their bank was quite substantial and they were certainly making a nice, tidy profit from the investments, Lucas felt certain they would be happy to look out for Taylor and Victoria. Also, Taylor supposedly had relatives living in Boston. Surely one or two of her family members would watch out for his wife and her friend.

His wife. Lucas shook his head in amazement. If someone had told him six months ago that he would be married, he would have had a good laugh. Then he probably would have punched the prophet in his face for suggesting the blasphemy.

"We're ready, Mr. Ross."

Taylor nudged Lucas in his side to get him moving. She wanted to tell him to wipe that frown off his face as well. Like it or not, Victoria was going with them. Taylor assumed the irritation was due to the addition of another passenger. Lucas obviously didn't like to have his plans altered. She wondered how he was going to feel about having his future altered and immediately decided he wouldn't like that much either. She knew he'd be difficult; she prayed he wouldn't be impossible.

Lucas turned to Victoria and smiled at her. She felt it necessary to remove her bonnet before she got inside the carriage. He was being extremely patient with her friend, Taylor was quick to notice. He treated her like a piece of fine china that might shatter if he weren't careful. Why, he was ridiculously gentle assisting her inside the vehicle. He even held her bonnet for her while she adjusted her skirts just so. When she was settled to her satisfaction, Lucas finally turned to Taylor. He all but tossed her inside.

She wanted to sit next to her friend. Lucas had other ideas. By the time she'd straightened up in the seat he'd thrown her in, he was sitting beside her, squeezing her with his bulk into the corner. She couldn't go anywhere.

She gave him a good frown to let him know what she thought about his high-handed behavior, then realized she shouldn't have bothered. Lucas wasn't paying any attention to her. He was staring out the window, lost in thought.

Victoria drew her attention. "Look, Taylor. There's Morrison's Coffee House. We have one just like it in London." Her voice was laced with excitement. "And there's Tyler's Bootery. Why, he's famous in England."

Taylor leaned forward to look out the window. "There seem to be many English stores here," she remarked. "It's disappointing, isn't it?"

"Why is it disappointing?" Lucas asked, drawn into the conversation by Taylor's odd remark.

She didn't want to tell him the truth, that she didn't want anything in America to remind her of England. He wouldn't understand. She gave him a half answer.

"I just want everything to be different."

"Oh, most of the shops are different," Victoria announced. "It's going to take some getting used to, isn't it? America seems so grand."

Taylor nodded. She tried to pay attention to what Victoria was saying, but her mind kept wandering. Excitement was quick to build inside her. She could barely sit still in her seat. Her thoughts were on the babies. They were here . . . in this wonderful city, and just as soon as her business was concluded with the bankers and Lucas was on his way back to Redemption, she would go and collect the twins and their nanny, dear Mrs. Bartlesmith. They would all have to spend at least a week in Boston while Taylor hired the help she would need and bought whatever clothes the little ones needed for the coming season.

She wished she could see her nieces now. If she were clever, Lucas would never know she'd left. Just for an hour, she told herself. She would hire a vehicle and be back at the hotel before she was even missed.

Mrs. Bartlesmith would be happy for the company. Taylor would explain her plans and offer to hire someone to help with the packing. In her excitement, she reached over and grabbed hold of Lucas's hand.

He was startled by the show of affection. He saw the look of joy on her face and found himself smiling over her enthusiasm.

"Boston certainly appeals to you," he remarked.

"It appears to be quite nice."

She didn't sound overly enthusiastic about the city. Yet her expression told him she was excited about something. He was curious to find out what it was. Then he decided she was probably thinking about the coming reunion with her relatives and her friends, and perhaps she was considering where she was going to live. She would probably choose the Hill, where all the rich and influential resided. She'd fit right in. She'd like it, too. Lucas was sure of it.

Victoria kept up a steady stream of comments about the city. Taylor occasionally nodded, but it soon became evident she was preoccupied.

Lucas finally nudged her to get her attention. "Tell me what you're thinking about."

"My relatives," she answered.

He smiled. "I thought so."

"And . . ."

"Yes?"

She let out a sigh. "I was also thinking about the greater good."

He didn't understand what she meant. Neither did Victoria. "Is Boston the greater good?" her friend asked.

Taylor shook her head. She started to say something more, but her attention was turned then, for she suddenly realized she was holding onto Lucas's hand. She immediately let go.

"Pray forgive me for being forward," she said.

He shook his head in exasperation. She turned to look out the window again before he could respond to the ridiculous apology. Victoria looked astonished by Taylor's comment. She stared at her friend for a long minute, obviously waiting for her to say something, and when Taylor remained silent, she turned her attention to Lucas. He thought about giving her some sort of explanation, then changed his mind.

"The sun's going down."

Taylor made the announcement. She sounded disheartened. "It will be dark in another half hour," Lucas guessed. "Does that bother you?"

"Yes."

"Why?"

"I wanted to go and see my relatives," she explained. "I'll have to wait until tomorrow."

"People do go out at night," Lucas said.

"They'll be asleep."

Taylor didn't elaborate. She turned back to look out the window. Lucas assumed the relatives in question were old and feeble. Who else would go to bed so early in the evening.

Victoria's attention went back and forth between Lucas and Taylor. She wanted to ask why they were both acting so formal with each other. She supposed that wouldn't be very polite, however, and finally let the matter drop. They rode the rest of the way in silence and arrived at their destination a few minutes later.

At first glance, the Hamilton House was a severe disappointment. While Lucas paid the driver, Victoria and Taylor stood on the sidewalk and stared up at the huge, gray granite building. Victoria whispered it looked quite dreary. Taylor was more emphatic. She declared it was as ugly as sin.

For some reason, Lucas found her opinion amusing. He told her to lower her voice, but he gave the order with a grin. She didn't know what to make of that. She noticed he was once again being very solicitous toward Victoria. She wasn't jealous, however. She was pleased. Lucas was proving he could be a gentleman when he put his mind to the chore.

Victoria was taking forever to put on her bonnet. It took her three attempts to tie the satin strings into a perfect bow. Taylor wanted to take over the task for her, so impatient was she to get moving. Lucas acted as though he had all the time in the world. He simply stood there with his hands clasped behind his back, waiting for Victoria to finish. Then he offered his arm to her. Victoria took hold and smiled sweetly up at him.

They left her standing on the sidewalk. She followed the pair inside. Since Lucas was watching out for Victoria, Taylor felt free to explore the ground floor. It was filled with retail shops, and in the very center of the area was another set of double doors leading to the hotel's reception area. There was a large crowd of men smoking in front of the entrance. Most were dressed in business suits, though there were a few garbed in buckskin jackets. Several of the men openly gawked at her in a way that made Taylor feel decidedly uneasy. She held her head high as she hurried through the entrance the doorman held open for her.

Lucas suddenly seemed to remember he had a wife. He turned, grabbed hold of her hand, and pulled her close to his side. She didn't understand what had come over him. One minute he was smiling down at Victoria and the next he was frowning at everyone who looked their way. Victoria seemed to understand, if her smile was any indication, and Taylor thought her friend might actually burst into laughter so amusing did she seem to find Lucas's conduct.

Taylor decided to ignore her husband until he got over his sour mood. Both she and Victoria changed their opinion of the hotel. The owners had obviously decided to spend their money on the inside. It was, as Taylor whispered to her friend, grand. The floor was black and white marble squares, and circling the gigantic foyer were magnificent white pillars.

Everything was sparkling clean. The lounges in the spacious hall were covered with buffalo skins. Taylor wanted to go across the room and touch one.

Victoria drew her attention with her remark. "Do you notice there aren't any ladies here?" she whispered.

"I did notice," Taylor replied.

"There's a separate entrance for ladies traveling alone," Lucas explained. "But since you're with me, it's all right for you to be here. Wait by the luggage while I sign in and get a room for Victoria."

Lucas underscored his order by adding what he obviously considered a meaningful frown at Taylor and then walked away.

The luggage was easy to spot. It was a pyramid of baggage really and stacked in the center of the hall.

Taylor was a bit overwhelmed by the chaos surrounding her. There were at least two hundred gentlemen coming and going, more reading the daily papers on the settees, and large groups of men standing around talking to one another. The noise made conversation difficult.

Victoria had to ask Taylor her question twice before she heard her. "What if all the rooms are full?"

"Then you'll stay with me."

"But what about your husband?"

"Oh, I'm certain he'll get his own room."

"But you're married."

"Yes," Taylor agreed. She patted Victoria's hand. "In your delicate condition, you shouldn't be worrying about inconsequential matters. I think you should sit down. You look weary to me. Let's try out the buffalo lounges."

Victoria nodded agreement. She pinched her cheeks for color, hoping to hide her fatigue, and followed Taylor over to an empty lounge.

The two women sat side by side. Taylor stroked the animal skin with her fingertips and smiled at her friend. "We can now boast that we sat on a buffalo."

Victoria gave her a weak smile. She folded her hands in her lap and stared down at the floor.

"You're worrying, aren't you?"

"Yes," Victoria admitted. "I'm thinking you shouldn't have told your husband I was married. If we keep to the lie, I'm bound to run into people I know in Boston who have moved here from London . . ."

She didn't go on. Taylor immediately felt guilty. "I shouldn't have made up the lie, and I apologize for putting you in an awkward position. If I tell you something, do you promise not to say a word in front of Mr. Ross?"

"Yes."

"I don't have any intention of living in Boston. You don't have to stay here either, Victoria. There are at least a dozen other cities to consider."

Victoria's eyes widened. "But I heard your husband mention . . ."

"Oh, he thinks I'm staying in Boston, and it's best he doesn't know the truth just yet."

"I don't understand. Won't he notice if you leave?"

"It's complicated," Taylor told her. "Tomorrow morning, after you've had a good night's rest, we'll sit down and have a long talk. It's going to be all right. I promise you. Heavens, I'm so excited to be in Boston, I can barely sit still."

A beautiful marble statue of a Greek warrior holding a disc caught her eye. It was at least nine feet tall. Taylor stood up, told Victoria she would be right back, and then crossed the hall to have a closer look.

One gentleman after another tried to catch her attention by calling out a greeting. Taylor ignored the men, yet by the time she reached the impressive statue, she found herself surrounded by strangers wishing to engage her in conversation.

They were all Americans, and for that reason alone, Taylor found it impossible to maintain her haughty facade. She was smiling in no time at all. The Americans were very open and friendly, just as she'd read they would be. One gentleman said howdy to her instead of hello and with the most wonderful accent she'd ever heard. She was enchanted. She soon forgot all about proper etiquette. She introduced herself, explained she had just arrived from London, England, and then asked each man to tell her where he lived. Everyone tried to answer her at once. One, she learned, lived in the heart of Boston and was at the hotel for a business meeting. He sounded as though he were pinching his nose shut when he spoke. Another gentleman resided in the valley of Ohio, two were from Missouri, and three, cousins she discovered, lived in the state of Texas. Their accents were outrageously divine.

A spirited conversation ensued. Each man was trying to outdo the others with tall tales about his home. Taylor was having trouble controlling her laughter. They were such delightful, good-hearted men. They were proud of their homeland and obviously wanted her to love America as much as they did.

She wanted Victoria to meet her new friends and was about to suggest they follow her across the hall when the attitude of the group suddenly changed. They were laughing and jesting one minute and looking as though they'd lost their best friend the next. Several were frowning enough to make her think they were extremely worried about something. The men standing directly in front of her weren't looking at her any longer. They were intently staring at something above her head. The gentleman from Boston, she noticed, was even backing away.

The silence was heavy with expectation. Taylor had a feeling she knew what, or rather who, had caused the radical change in the men's behavior. She slowly turned around to find out if her guess proved accurate.

She was right on target. Lucas was standing directly behind her. She'd half-expected him to be there. The expression on his face was a surprise, however. It was frightening enough to make an ordinary woman's hair stand on end. Lord, he was intimidating. No wonder the gentlemen weren't laughing any longer. Lucas was looking as though he wanted to shoot a couple of them.

Why, he even made her feel a bit nervous. She certainly wasn't intimidated or afraid, she hastily reminded herself, just . . . nervous. She decided to catch the cat by his tail. She knew he was irritated because he'd had to look for her in the crowd, and so she simply turned the table around on him.

She folded her hands together, plastered a smile on her face, and then said, "Here you are at last, Mr. Ross. I've been waiting to introduce you to my new friends."

He wasn't going to let her get away with her clever

ploy. He shook his head at her. "Taylor, I specifically remember telling you to wait by the luggage. If . . ."

She wasn't going to listen to a lecture. She broke his concentration by simply reaching out and taking hold of his hand. She turned around to face their audience then so that she could introduce her husband, but the eldest of the Texans spoke before she could.

"This little filly belong to you?" He directed his inquiry to Lucas and in such a slow drawl it seemed to take him a full minute to get the question finished.

Taylor wasn't certain if she should be insulted or not. She opened her mouth to ask the Texan if women were often referred to as horses in America, but she never got the question out. Lucas put his hands on her shoulders and squeezed.

The message was distinct. She was supposed to keep quiet. Taylor decided to act subservient for the time being. God help Lucas Ross when they were alone. She would give him a piece of her mind then, she thought to herself, for being so high-handed in public. She pictured herself giving him a sound kick, and even though she knew she'd never do such an unladylike thing, the fantasy still made her smile.

"She's my wife." Lucas made the announcement with a good deal of possessiveness in his voice. Odd, but he didn't grimace when he said the word *wife*. In truth, it sounded almost pleasant to him. Almost.

"She ain't wearing a ring." Another Texan made that remark and was staring at Taylor suspiciously. He was acting as though Lucas and she were trying to play some clever trick on him. His attitude didn't make a bit of sense to Taylor.

"Ring or not, she's still Mrs. Ross," Lucas said.

"Ross? Well now, she didn't call herself Ross," the first Texan pointed out.

Taylor's eyes widened. She almost laughed over her own error. "I forgot," she blurted out. "We are newly married," she hastily added.

They didn't look like they believed her. She let out a sigh, shrugged away from Lucas, and then moved to his side. She kept her gaze on her audience.

"Gentlemen, I would like you to meet my husband, Mr. Lucas Ross."

What happened next so surprised Taylor, she couldn't hide her astonishment. The eldest of the Texans squinted at Lucas and then whispered in what could only be interpreted as awe, "The Lucas Ross from Montana Territory?"

Lucas gave a quick nod. Then he started to back away. Taylor looked up and saw his expression had changed dramatically. He looked wary now and horribly uncomfortable. She was intrigued by the change in him. She felt the sudden need to save him, yet couldn't imagine what exactly she was saving him from.

"*The* Lucas Ross?" The gentleman from the valley in Ohio asked the question in a stammer of disbelief.

Lucas sighed. "Yes."

Taylor didn't think grown men were given to gasping, but these men did. She was all but forgotten from that moment on. The men surged forward. She got out of their way in the nick of time, for she would surely have been flattened against the statue by the eager crowd if she hadn't moved quickly. The men surrounded Lucas on all sides. Everyone was talking at once. They wanted to shake his hand and pound him on his back.

The Texans were the most effusive in their admiration. "If that don't beat all," the eldest of the cousins kept repeating.

Word that Lucas Ross was in the lobby of the

Hamilton House spread like free whiskey, and within minutes, most of the gentlemen inside the lobby had joined the group of adoring fans. They all wanted to meet the legend.

Taylor was flabbergasted. She heard the words *hero* and *legend* over and over again, and because the gentleman from Boston mentioned the war when he gave his praise, she naturally assumed Lucas had won his reputation during the time of the dispute between the North and the South. She was familiar with both the cause and the outcome of the war, of course. She'd read everything she could get her hands on about the division of the country. Odd, she didn't remember reading anything about Lucas Ross.

Taylor stood there watching Lucas and his enthusiastic admirers for a good fifteen minutes. Her husband was easy to keep track of, as he was the tallest man in the lobby. He was keeping his eye on her as well, she noticed, for every now and then he would glance over to make certain she was still there.

He didn't look very happy about all the attention he was receiving. He didn't like anyone standing behind his back either. Taylor came to that conclusion when she noticed how he slowly negotiated his way over to stand directly in front of the marble statue. He seemed determined to protect his back, just like all the famous gunfighters liked to do, or so Taylor had read in one of her countless dime novels.

One thought jumped to another. Good God, was Lucas a gunfighter? Is that how he gained his reputation? Taylor discarded the notion the second it popped into her mind. No, of course he wasn't. He was temperamental and surly natured, but he wasn't a killer. Taylor's conclusions weren't based solely on instinct. Madam had done a thorough investigation into Lucas's background, and although she hadn't had the time or the inclination to share the information she'd gathered with her granddaughter, Taylor knew in her heart that her grandmother would never have insisted she marry the man if he hadn't proven to be honorable and courageous and noble.

There was also the undisputed fact that all gunfighters went looking for trouble. The stories she'd read about Ornery Eddie of Wolkum Junction had confirmed that truth. Eddie always wanted to fight. According to the tales, the gunfighter prided himself on the fact that he would always shoot someone dead within ten minutes after arriving in a new town. Oh, yes, gunfighters went looking for trouble. Ornery Eddie was just one example of that rule, but there were at least a hundred others written down in the dime novels.

Lucas was the complete opposite in attitude. He wanted solitude and wide-open spaces. She remembered he'd been quite specific when he told her he no longer liked living in Redemption because the two-block-wide town was becoming too crowded. He hated being penned in.

He apparently hated crowds, too. His expression told her so. The look he was now giving her indicated he somehow held her responsible for making him the center of attention.

She didn't want to accept the blame. She hadn't had anything to do with making him a legend. No, of course she hadn't. If the man had bothered to mention he was such a celebrity, she wouldn't have introduced him.

His discomfort was all his own fault. She still felt guilty. She was going to have to save him anyway. She let out a sigh, then nudged her way through the throng of men. When she reached Lucas, she took hold of his hand. In a rather loud voice, she announced that they were going to be late for an important meeting if they didn't leave immediately.

"You shouldn't be going to meetings on your honeymoon," one of the Texans declared in his slow drawl.

"They're newly married?" A gentleman she hadn't met before asked the question.

Someone in the crowd shouted, "If that don't beat all." Because Taylor had already heard that colorful, but illogical remark before, she assumed it was some sort of popular American slang. She filed the saying away for future use.

"He got himself hitched all right," another said.

A round of hearty congratulations followed the confirmation. There was more pounding on Lucas's back, though one eager gentleman's aim was off and he accidentally whacked Taylor squarely between her shoulder blades. She was kept from being thrown forward by her husband. He tightened his hold on her, frowned at the offender, and started to edge his way through the crowd.

The men finally let them alone. Lucas had dragged Taylor halfway across the lobby before she protested. "You may lessen your hold on me, sir, and do quit frowning. People will think we aren't happily married."

Lucas ignored both suggestions. Taylor looked up at him and matched his frown. She decided to give exactly what she was getting. "You're a very moody individual," she announced in a low whisper so her criticism wouldn't be overheard.

"I didn't used to be," he responded.

"Do you mean to say you used to be pleasant?"

"Yes."

She almost snorted with disbelief but stopped herself in time. "When?" she asked.

"When I wasn't married."

She tried not to take offense. "You're blaming me for the chaos back there, aren't you?" She didn't give him time to answer. "I wouldn't have introduced you to those gentlemen if you'd told me you were such a popular fellow."

"Why were you talking to them?" he asked.

"Excuse me?"

He let out a sigh. "Taylor, didn't your grandmother tell you it's dangerous to talk to strangers?"

He asked the question in a low growl. "I was perfectly safe," she announced. "No one would dare accost me in the middle of the hotel lobby."

"Oh? And why is that?"

He was fully prepared to hear her answer, then give her a good lecture on her naïveté. Hell, the lobby was so crowded, anyone could have grabbed hold of her and dragged her outside without being noticed. Didn't she know about the dangers inherent in the cities? Obviously not, he thought. Well, by God, he would make her understand.

Taylor was staring up at him with that wide-eyed, innocent stare. He wanted to shake some sense into her. He decided to scare her instead.

"Explain why no one would dare accost you," he ordered in a voice he thought sounded downright mean.

She stared him right in the eye when she gave him her answer. "You wouldn't let them."

The bluster went right out of him. Her answer, given so quickly and in such a matter-of-fact tone of voice, sliced right through his frustration and reached his heart. He was at a loss for words. The compliment shocked him. She was too trusting, he thought, and how could she have such faith in him? It was downright humbling.

"You're right I wouldn't let anyone touch you," he heard himself mutter.

She smiled. He glared. Lucas suddenly felt an overwhelming urge to kiss her.

Her next remark changed his inclination. "I happen to know for a fact that a woman can travel alone throughout this magnificent country and never have the fear she'll be bothered by a stranger."

He was back to wanting to shake some sense into her. "Taylor . . ." he began as a prelude to his lecture addressing her ridiculous opinions.

"I read it in a book, so it has to be true. Mrs. Livingston's journal of her travels through America was quite informative. She was never accosted."

"Was she old and wrinkled?"

"What difference does that make?"

He stared down into those incredible blue eyes for a long minute. "It makes a big difference," he snapped.

She decided to end the discussion by having the last word. "Please quit worrying. I assure you I will not be accosted by strangers."

"What about husbands?"

6

They do not love who show their love.
— William Shakespeare,
Two Gentlemen of Verona

*T*he man had a warped sense of humor. It took Taylor a minute to understand what he was suggesting. She didn't get angry. Just irritated.

"I don't have any fear of being accosted by you, Mr. Ross. Should I?"

"Taylor . . ."

He said her name in a warning tone of voice. "Yes?" she replied.

"I'll be right back. Don't wander."

He squeezed her shoulders until she gave her agreement. Then he went back over to the front desk. She watched as he handed a key to one of the hotel's staff. He leaned forward and spoke to the man, then turned around and walked back to her.

"We're staying in the same room."

Her eyes widened. Mr. Ross didn't look at all happy

about the arrangement. She shook her head. "You weren't able to secure a room of your own?"

"I gave it back."

"Why?"

"Because you draw a crowd."

"What's that supposed to mean?"

"Never mind. We're married now and we've already slept in the same bed."

"But Mr. Ross . . ."

"Don't argue with me."

He grabbed hold of her hand and turned to walk over to her friend. He kept right on frowning until he reached Victoria. He smiled at her. He let go of Taylor and assisted Victoria to her feet.

"Shall we go upstairs and get you settled in your room?" he asked, his voice every bit as pleasant as a summer's breeze.

"Then you were able to secure a room for me?" Victoria asked. "There were so many gentlemen in the lobby I thought all the rooms must surely be taken."

The worried expression on her face told Taylor she'd obviously been sitting there fretting about their sleeping arrangements. Taylor felt terrible. Her new friend wouldn't have worried if she'd stayed by her side to soothe her fears. In her delicate condition, she shouldn't be worrying about anything. Expectant mothers needed a tranquil environment. They needed rest, too. Poor Victoria looked exhausted.

Taylor stepped forward to apologize. "I've been very thoughtless," she said. "I should have stayed with you. I'm sorry, Victoria."

"I was quite all right," Victoria replied, embarrassed over the attention she was getting. "Several gentlemen tried to keep me company, but I sent them on their way. Will you tell me what was going on over there? Why were all those men cheering?"

"The porter's waiting," Lucas announced. "Taylor will explain later. Shall we go upstairs?"

His impatience was apparent. He glanced back over his shoulder several times on the way up the stairs to the gallery level of the hotel, and Taylor thought he was anxious to get away from his admirers.

Their rooms were on the fourth floor. Victoria's bedroom was at one end of a long, winding corridor, and Lucas and Taylor's room was at the opposite end. Lucas left Taylor to help Victoria with her unpacking and went with the porter down to their rooms to see to the deposit of their luggage. The trunks would be left in storage in the hotel's basement for safekeeping until they departed.

Victoria's room had been painted a pale lemon yellow that Taylor declared was very soothing on the eyes. It wasn't a large room, but it was elegantly appointed. The furniture was a dark, polished cherry wood. Taylor couldn't resist trailing her fingers over the exquisite detail on the front of the wardrobe. The craftsman must have spent months carving the delicate design of leaves on the front of both the dresser and the wardrobe.

While she hung up Victoria's dresses, her friend went to look out the window.

"I didn't realize how sophisticated Boston was," she remarked. "It's every bit as modern as London, isn't it?"

"I suppose it is," Taylor agreed. "There's a laundry downstairs, Victoria. If you need anything washed and pressed, the hotel staff boasts they will have it back to you in less than a day. Madam told me in the literature she read that most of the better hotels have steam laundries attached and that businessmen never have to bring more than a single shirt when they travel. And do you know why?" she asked. "The linen is washed in a machine that actually churns. It's moved about by steam, you see, and wrung out by a strange method called centrifugal force. The shirts are dried by currents of hot air. God's truth, they can be washed, dried, and ironed in just a few minutes. Isn't that amazing?"

Victoria didn't answer her. Taylor had been so occupied unpacking her friend's clothing, she hadn't noticed how withdrawn Victoria had become. When she didn't get an answer or a comment about the marvel of steam laundries, she turned to look at her friend. Victoria was sitting on the side of her double bed. Her hands were folded in her lap and her head was bent so low, her chin was all but touching her chest. She looked dejected and horribly sad.

Taylor immediately stopped what she was doing and went over to stand in front of her friend.

"Is something worrying you?" she asked.

"No."

She gave her answer in a soft whisper. She sounded pathetic. Taylor frowned with concern. Something was definitely wrong all right, and she was determined to find out what it was.

"Are you ill?" she asked, her worry obvious in her voice.

"No."

Taylor stared down at her friend for a long minute. She wanted Victoria to tell her what was wrong. She didn't want to nag the problem out of her. Well-bred young ladies didn't pry, and they never, ever nagged. It was, in Madam's estimation, the eleventh commandment.

"Would you like to rest before dining?"

"I suppose I would."

"Are you hungry now?"

"I suppose I am."

Taylor held onto her patience. She sat down on the side of the bed next to Victoria, then folded her hands in her lap and simply waited for her friend to tell her what was bothering her.

She was thoroughly confused by Victoria's sudden bout of timidity. They had spent a good deal of time together on the ship, almost every afternoon in fact. While the more seasoned travelers huddled around the funnel to smoke and share stories about their past voyages or played chess and backgammon in the gaming salon and the younger, more energetic men played rowdy games of shuffleboard up on deck to pass the time, she and Victoria stayed closeted inside the ship's library and talked about every subject known to man. They solved most of the world's considerable problems and a few of their own. Victoria told Taylor all about her family, a little about the man who had betrayed her, though she stubbornly insisted on never revealing his name, and she also talked about her dreams and her hopes. Taylor never talked about herself. She did, however, tell Victoria dozens of stories she'd read about the American wilderness. The only hope she admitted to harboring was that she might one day meet a real mountain man.

Because of the storms, the voyage had taken longer than anticipated. They were on the ship a full twelve days, and in all that time, Victoria hadn't ever been shy or reserved with her. Taylor believed her friend had confided all her secrets. This sudden change in her disposition worried her. Perhaps there was one more secret that needed telling.

Long minutes passed in silence. Taylor decided then she'd waited long enough. Victoria looked miserable. Taylor reached over and patted her hand. She was determined to get to the heart of the problem so she could help her solve it.

"Is there something more you haven't told me? Something that has you fretting now?"

"No."

Taylor let out a loud sigh. "You're going to make me do it, aren't you?" she announced in a dramatic tone of voice.

Victoria finally looked at her. Taylor noticed she had tears in her eyes.

"Do what?" Victoria asked, intrigued by Taylor's remark in spite of her misery.

"You're going to make me nag you until you tell me what's bothering you."

Victoria managed a weak smile. Taylor sounded pitiful. "I take it you don't like to nag," she replied. The smile had moved into her voice.

"I love to nag," Taylor confessed. "I just know I shouldn't. Now tell me what the problem is, please. I want to help."

Victoria burst into tears. " 'A heavy heart bears not a nimble tongue,' " she whispered.

Taylor rolled her eyes heavenward. Victoria didn't notice her exasperation. She was fully occupied staring down at her hands.

She was quoting Shakespeare again. It seemed to be a peculiar trait of hers, Taylor decided, because whenever she became upset, she hid behind the famous playwright's poetic words.

"In other words, you're having difficulty telling me what's wrong," Taylor interpreted. "Is that right?"

Victoria nodded.

"Just spill it out. We cannot solve this problem until you name it."

"I can't pay for this lodging."

"Well, of course, you can't pay," Taylor replied. "I realize that. I'm going to . . ."

Victoria interrupted her before she could finish her

sentence. "I feel like a pauper. Back home I could buy anything I wanted. My parents had accounts with all the fashionable establishments in London. Oh, God, I am a pauper."

She wailed out the last of her worry. Taylor patted her hand sympathetically. Then she stood up and began to pace around the room. She considered the problem for several minutes before coming up with what she believed was a sound solution.

"You will only be a pauper until tomorrow."

Her statement gained Victoria's full attention. She mopped at the corners of her eyes with the handkerchief Taylor handed her and then demanded to know what in heaven's name she meant by that odd remark.

"How can I be a pauper today and not tomorrow?"

"Madam used to tell me that the best way to understand how someone feels is to try to put yourself in the other person's shoes. I know I wouldn't like to be . . ."

"Pregnant?" Victoria supplied.

She was nodding before Taylor could answer, so certain was she of her friend's conclusion.

Taylor surprised her by shaking her head. "That isn't what I was going to say," she explained. "But as a matter of fact, I would very much like to be pregnant some day. If you think about it, in a different light, of course, and put aside just for the moment all the reasons why you wish you weren't carrying . . ."

"Yes?" Victoria asked when Taylor hesitated.

It was difficult for Taylor to put into words the emotions she was feeling. "It's a blessing," she finally blurted out. "And a miracle. It truly is. You have a precious life growing inside you. Think about that, Victoria. An innocent new life. I envy you."

Victoria's hand went to rest on her stomach. "I've never even held a baby in my arms," she confessed.

"You're going to be a wonderful mother," Taylor predicted.

"It's easy enough for you to talk about wanting to be pregnant. You're married and . . . why do you think I'll be a wonderful mother?"

"Because you're kind and loving and thoughtful."

Victoria started to blush. "Enough flattery," she demanded. "You'll fill my head with pride and then I won't be fit to live with."

Taylor smiled. She was pleased to see her friend was in a more cheerful frame of mind. She decided to change the subject back to the issue of finances.

"What I was going to say a minute ago is this," she began again. "I know I wouldn't like to feel like a pauper, and so, tomorrow, when I meet with Madam's bankers, I'll transfer funds into an account for you. By early afternoon, you'll be a completely independent woman."

Victoria was shaking her head before Taylor finished explaining her plan of action. "I cannot accept charity. It wouldn't be right," she protested vehemently.

Tears were already welling up in her eyes again. How she could laugh one minute and cry the next was a mystery to Taylor. She thought that perhaps her friend's delicate condition made her more emotional. If that were true, it was only a temporary condition. Taylor had been raised never to show her feelings. It wasn't considered ladylike to laugh loudly in public, and weeping was always frowned upon, regardless of the circumstances. Dealing with someone who constantly broke that sacred rule was difficult. "I did promise I would help you," she reminded her friend.

"And you have helped," Victoria insisted. "You've been a very good friend to me."

Now she was being stubborn. Taylor decided to convince her by quoting from Shakespeare. She seemed to hold great store in his clever words. The problem, however, was that she couldn't think of a single phrase to use. And so she simply made one up. Perhaps Victoria was too distraught to notice.

"It is far better to receive than to decline," she announced with a good deal of authority in her voice. "Shakespeare," she added with a nod when Victoria gave her a quizzical look.

"He never said that."

So much for her clever ploy. "He would have if he'd lived long enough," Taylor said.

Victoria shook her head again. She let out an inelegant snort, too. Taylor immediately tried a different approach. "The money is for the baby," she said. She felt certain her friend wouldn't be able to argue that point.

"I'll find work. I'm strong and quite resourceful."

"And pregnant," Taylor reminded her. "I cannot let you do anything that would jeopardize the baby." She raised one hand when it appeared to her that Victoria was going to argue. "I know you wouldn't deliberately do anything to injure your daughter, but if you work long hours every day you'll surely exhaust yourself. You need lots of rest and so does the baby. No, Victoria, I won't hear of it. You're taking the money. Madam would want you to have it."

Victoria stared up at Taylor for a long while before saying another word. Her mind was racing from one thought to another. She was stunned by her friend's generosity. Yet she was confused as well. She had never met anyone quite like Taylor. She was caring and compassionate and kind. She was, in Victoria's estimation, an angel who had come down from heaven in the moment of Victoria's greatest need and had taken her under her wing.

But she was also human, Victoria reminded herself, and it suddenly occurred to her that she actually knew very little about her friend and benefactor.

"We spent hours and hours together on the ship, didn't we?"

Taylor was confused by the turn in the topic. "Yes," she agreed. "We did."

"I told you everything about myself, didn't I?"

Taylor nodded. "What does—"

Victoria interrupted her. "I was very self-concerned during the voyage," she admitted. "And because I was so consumed with my own problems, I never noticed, until now, how little you told me about yourself. It has just struck me how secretive you've been."

"Not secretive," Taylor corrected. "Just . . . private."

"Are we not friends?"

"Of course we are."

"'A friend should bear his friend's infirmities.'"

"Why do you quote Shakespeare whenever you're upset?" Taylor asked.

Victoria shrugged. "He was a comfort to me growing up," she explained. "I could forget my problems when I immersed myself in one of his plays. There were times when it was very . . . difficult at home. You do the same thing, Taylor."

"I don't."

Victoria smiled. "All those stories about Daniel Boone and Davy Crockett. They were your friends. You didn't have an easy time of it growing up, did you?"

Taylor shook her head. "Are you deliberately changing the topic, Victoria?"

"Do you trust me?"

Taylor only hesitated a second or two before answering. "Yes."

"Then why do I feel . . ."

"Feel what?"

"Left out."

Taylor's shoulders slumped. She walked back over to the bed and sat down next to her friend again. "I'm sorry you feel that way," she said. "It's just that . . . it's very difficult for me to talk about myself or my family in any way that isn't superficial."

"Because of the way you were raised?"

"Perhaps," Taylor answered.

Victoria let out a sigh. "Friends share confidences," she said. "You've never shared any confidences or worries with me. Don't you have any?"

Taylor almost laughed, so ludicrous was the question to her. "Oh, yes, I have worries," she admitted. "Too many to count."

Victoria reached over to take hold of her hand. "Am I one of your worries?"

"You aren't a worry," Taylor assured her. "I was in dire need of a friend and suddenly there you were. It was almost . . . mystical. Heavens, I'm being very dramatic, aren't I?"

Victoria smiled. "I was thinking the angels sent you to me," she admitted. "Illogical though it may seem, it is the only answer I can come up with. You did appear out of nowhere and save me from disaster."

Taylor was becoming uncomfortable with the praise she was receiving. She hurried to turn the topic around.

"About the money," she began again. "We really should get this issue settled now."

"I want to ask you a question first."

"Yes?"

"Would you take money from me? Be completely honest, Taylor. Would you?"

"I would do anything to protect the babies. Anything."

Her voice radiated with conviction. And still Victoria's pride wasn't completely soothed. "You aren't just telling me what you think I want to hear, are you? You would really accept charity?"

"I would demand charity if I had to," Taylor told her. She let out a weary sigh and threaded her fingers through her hair in an act of frustration. "Dear God, Victoria, I've already done things I never would have thought possible. I married a complete stranger just to . . ."

"You what?"

Taylor stood up and began to pace while she collected her thoughts. "It's a long story," she said at last. "I'll explain everything to you tomorrow. I promise. For now, please accept the fact that you have one very special reason to stay healthy and do whatever it takes to survive in this confusing world, and I have two very special reasons. I'm too weary now to go into details, and I know you have to be just as exhausted. Let's have a quiet supper and go to bed early tonight. I'll answer all your questions after I meet with the bankers. All right?"

Victoria's mouth had dropped open when Taylor admitted marrying a complete stranger. She was, in fact, rendered speechless. No wonder she called him Mr. Ross all the time. It was starting to make sense to Victoria now. The reason behind the marriage remained a mystery, however, and she found she was already becoming impatient for tomorrow to arrive.

She finally found her voice. "Yes, we'll wait until

tomorrow to have our talk. Just answer one more question for me now, please."

"All right," Taylor agreed.

"Do you ever get scared? I know it's a foolish question. I was just curious," Victoria blurted out when she saw Taylor's expression. Her friend looked incredibly sad. "You radiate such confidence all the time. In truth, you're a comfort to me. I always feel you'll know exactly what to do . . . even twenty years from now."

Taylor suddenly felt overwhelmed with fatigue. Her nerves felt frayed and she wanted more than anything to be able to let her guard down, if only for a minute or two.

She gave in to the urge. "Scared? Oh, yes, I get scared. Sometimes I'm so afraid inside I shake with it."

Her voice trembled with emotion when she gave her confession. Sharing the confidence had been difficult for her. Victoria immediately felt guilty because she'd broached the topic.

"You are right," she announced then. "We are both very tired. We'll wait until tomorrow to have our talk."

Taylor gave an abrupt nod. "And the money?" she asked.

"I will be happy for your assistance."

"Thank you."

"It is I who should be thanking you," Victoria said. She stood up and smiled at her friend. She wanted to try to lighten her mood, for Taylor was looking as though she had all the burdens of the world on her slender shoulders.

"Tell me another story about Daniel Boone," she requested.

Taylor was thrilled by the request. She immediately launched into one of her favorite tales about the mountain man. That story led to another and another, and only when her stomach started protesting did she realize how late the hour was.

"Mr. Ross is probably pacing the floor waiting for me," she announced. "Tomorrow I insist upon giving Davy Crockett equal time," she added with a smile. "He also was quite a gallant figure."

"Yes," Victoria agreed. "And when you're finished, I shall recite my favorite verse from one of William's most famous plays."

Taylor laughed. "I believe we are both quite peculiar," she remarked. "You must be famished. I know I am. Your baby must have immediate nourishment. I don't believe I'll even take the time to change my dress. I'll just run along down to my room and collect Mr. Ross."

She started for the door, but Victoria stopped her with a casually given remark.

"When we were talking about finances, you said you would do anything to protect the babies. Do you remember?"

Taylor turned around. "Yes, I remember."

"I'm pretty certain I'm only going to have one baby. I can't imagine having two," she added with a bit of laughter in her voice. "And twins don't run in my family."

Taylor smiled. "They run in mine."

"Oh?"

"Georgie and Allie," Taylor said then. "They're twins."

"Who do they belong to?"

"Me."

Victoria looked stunned. She had to sit down before her knees gave out on her. "Yours?" she whispered.

"Yes," Taylor answered.

"You have two babies?" Victoria asked. She couldn't seem to take it in.

Taylor smiled. A knock sounded at the door, interrupting the conversation. Neither Taylor nor Victoria moved. "What I've just told you must remain in confidence a little longer. I'll explain why tomorrow."

She waited for her friend to agree before turning around to answer the door.

"Does Mr. Ross know about the twins?"

"Not yet."

"Good heavens."

"Exactly."

"Are they his?"

Taylor continued on. She reached for the doorknob before answering. "They will be," she called out. "If I need him to help keep them safe," she qualified.

She opened the door and found Lucas standing in the entrance. He looked impatient, irritated, and completely wonderful to her. She couldn't seem to get used to his size, she realized once again. The man towered over her, even when he was leaning against the frame of the doorway in such a relaxed stance, obviously meant to suggest he'd been waiting a good long while for her to open the door.

His frown didn't bother her much. She was too busy noticing all the differences about him. He'd changed into a black jacket and black pants. The white shirt he wore underneath was sparkling clean and starched stiff, indicating to her that he'd taken advantage of the hotel's amazing laundry facilities. The whiteness of the shirt made his skin look all the more bronzed.

She gave him a thorough once-over before looking into his eyes. His shoes were newly polished, his pants were definitely too snug, his shoulders seemed to have grown wider in the hour or so they'd been apart, and his hair was still damp, indicating he'd taken a bath. He smelled just as wonderful as he looked.

She let out a little sigh. Then she finally settled her gaze on his eyes. She decided the color was his finest feature. His eyes were such a dark, velvety brown, with a hint of gold in them. When he smiled, his eyes seemed to shine.

He was going to make a wonderful father. Lord, how she hoped he would come to love the babies. What if he didn't or couldn't? It was a chilling possibility.

Lucas was thoroughly exasperated with Taylor. He was about to ask her if she was finished with her inspection and didn't she realize wives shouldn't be looking at their husbands with such blatant curiosity, but something in her eyes stopped him from making any sarcastic remarks.

The smile was gone. She looked somber now, but there was something more he couldn't quite put his finger on. Just as strange was his own reaction. He suddenly felt like taking her into his arms and telling her everything was going to be all right.

He wanted to protect her from harm. He wanted to keep her safe.

He wanted to grow old with her.

The appalling thought popped into his mind before he could stop it. Lucas could feel the noose tightening around his neck. Damned if he would spend the rest of his life with her. He straightened away from the door frame and all but glared at the woman trying to turn his life upside down.

Taylor's manner also changed. She gathered her composure and forced a smile for her surly husband's benefit.

She seemed to have just noticed his irritation.

"Why are you frowning?" she asked. "Did you receive bad news?"

"No."

"You won't digest your food properly if you're irritated while you eat, sir. I suggest you rid yourself of your unpleasant mood with all possible haste."

He felt like throttling her. "Taylor, do you know what time it is?"

She shook her head. "I've been waiting over two hours," he told her.

"You have?"

"Yes," he snapped out. "What in thunder's taking you so long?"

She lifted her shoulders in a shrug. She continued to stare into his eyes when she asked, "Have you been waiting long?"

Hadn't he just told her he had? What was the matter with her? He expected an immediate apology. Yet she was staring up at him with a look that suggested she wasn't even paying attention to the conversation. Her mind was obviously somewhere else.

Lucas decided he wanted her full attention. By God, he wanted an apology, too. And just as soon as she finished being contrite, he'd tell her how much he detested waiting on anyone for anything and that she'd best learn to be prompt from this moment on.

"Mr. Ross?"

"Yes?" he answered in a hard, downright mean voice. She knew damned good and well he hated being called Mr. Ross and yet she persisted with the formal address. He'd go to his grave before reminding her once again to call him Lucas.

She didn't say another word for a full minute. He decided she was trying to find the right words to apologize. She probably didn't like admitting she was in error, and since he'd never ever apologized to anyone in all his days, he found himself sympathetic. He decided to make it easy for her.

"You're sorry, right?"

"Excuse me?"

"You're sorry you made me wait. Don't let it happen again. If you're finished unpacking, we'll go to supper now. I'm starved and I have a meeting I don't want to miss in an hour."

She didn't know what he was rambling on and on about. Her mind was fully occupied with the question she realized she needed to ask him. Heavens, why hadn't she asked him before? She immediately excused her own stupidity by telling herself she'd been too occupied with other matters. Besides, Madam had certainly asked him, or at least Taylor hoped she had.

The second he quit talking, she blurted out his name.

"Yes?" he said, thinking she was about to add a word or two to the apology he'd very nicely made for her.

"Do you like children?"

7

Brevity is the soul of wit.
—William Shakespeare,
Hamlet

"**N**ot particularly."

She looked crushed. He didn't know why she'd react like that. She wasn't the one having the baby. Victoria was.

"Why don't you like children?" she demanded to know.

Lucas was having trouble holding onto his patience. His sigh was loud. Then he shook his head at her, motioned her out of his way, and walked past her over to where Victoria was standing. In a gentle tone of voice, he asked her if she were ready to accompany him to the dining room.

He was being extremely solicitous. "There are two dining areas in the hotel," he explained. "The Ladies Ordinary is for families and their guests. The other is for businessmen only. I hear the food is quite good in both rooms. Shall we go?"

Victoria blushed over the attention he was giving her. She took hold of his arm and let him escort her out into the hallway. Taylor followed along after snatching up the room key and making certain Victoria's door was firmly locked.

Supper was a chaotic affair. Taylor didn't eat much of the seven-course meal, for she was too busy watching all the Americans coming and going. The dining room was as busy as a train station, with the swinging door from the salon in constant motion. It was extremely noisy, too. The Americans, she noticed, had a rather peculiar habit of gulping down their food with amazing speed. Taylor felt very much like a country girl at her first fair. She tried to watch everyone at the same time. It was both exciting and wearisome.

Everyone proved to be extremely friendly. Men she didn't even know greeted her warmly and tried to engage her in conversation. Lucas put a stop to that, however, with well-placed glares at the more effervescent strangers. He ran into two acquaintances who engaged him in a long conversation, and astonishing as it seemed to Taylor, she also bumped into a cousin of a cousin from London. She took the interruptions all in stride. Victoria didn't. She paled considerably when a young woman from New York greeted her with the reminder that they had met at the Smithers ball the year before. She wanted to know how long Victoria would be staying in Boston, and before she was given an answer, she insisted they get together soon so that when she returned to London she could call upon Victoria's dear parents and tell them all about her encounter with their daughter.

Victoria was very withdrawn on the way back to her room. Taylor assumed she was simply exhausted and in need of a good night's sleep. Both she and Lucas accompanied her to her door. Taylor hugged her friend good night, and suggested she be ready at eight the following morning so they could have breakfast together.

Lucas was already late for his meeting. Taylor suggested he go on. She could certainly find her way to their room. The doors were numbered, after all. Lucas wouldn't hear of it. He insisted on making certain she was under lock and key before he went anywhere.

They got into a rather spirited debate concerning the issue of safety in hotels. She felt she was well protected by the vigilant staff. He was certain there were evildoers lurking in every shadow just waiting to pounce on an unescorted woman.

The heated discussion ended when he opened the door to their suite. Taylor rushed through the opening and then came to an abrupt stop. She let out a whispered exclamation. "Oh, Mr. Ross, it's quite lovely, isn't it?"

He smiled over the wonder in her voice. He was a little surprised by her reaction, however, for he assumed she'd been raised in surroundings far more elegant than anything Boston had to offer. She should not only be used to luxury, she should expect it.

He couldn't help but comment on her reaction. "I would think you'd take all this for granted by now."

She shook her head. She was too busy looking over the room to turn to him when she answered. "I have learned, Mr. Ross, never to take anything for granted."

Lucas shut the door, then leaned against it and folded his arms across his chest. He knew he was late for his meeting, yet he didn't want to leave Taylor. It was the first time they'd been alone in a long while, and he found he wanted to spend just a few more minutes with her.

He liked looking at her. Her every expression was so

genuine. Her reactions were damned refreshing, and even when she was disagreeing with him and making him crazed with her illogical, impractical opinions, a part of him was both pleased and amused by her stubbornness and her innocence.

He liked her enthusiasm. Now that he thought about it, he realized he'd never heard one word of complaint from her since the night he'd taken hold of her hand and escorted her out of the ballroom in London. She'd even been polite and agreeable when she thought they were going to drown during that godawful storm. The only worry he remembered her expressing was for her friend, Victoria.

Lucas let out a sigh. Taylor wasn't at all what he supposed she should be.

She wasn't paying any attention to her husband. She was too occupied exploring her surroundings to notice how closely she was being observed.

She thought the room was every bit as elegant as Versailles and made that remark in another whisper of awe. The carpet was the palest of blue in color and so thick and plush she felt as though she were sinking into it. She wanted to kick off her shoes and walk across the room in her bare feet, but she resisted the urge for it wouldn't have been ladylike.

Directly in front of her was a lounging area. A gold-brocaded sofa, decorated with blue pillows, faced the door, though it was still a good fifteen feet away. She immediately went over to test the sofa and found it was every bit as hard as a rock. She still thought it was quite wonderful. There was a low wooden table in front of the sofa. It had been highly polished. She couldn't resist running her fingers across the top.

"I can feel the shine in this cherry wood," she

remarked, though she knew what she'd just said was completely illogical. It made enough sense to her, and she supposed to Lucas as well, for he didn't argue the point with her.

Two pale blue high-backed chairs flanked the ends of the sofa. Taylor felt compelled to test both of them. She then declared they were extremely comfortable.

To her left were two wardrobes, identical in size and design. A door leading to the washroom was at the end of the adjacent wall. To her right was an arched alcove with drapes tied back against the sides. She could see the bed from where she stood. It was a huge thing and without posters. A gold coverlet decorated the bed. There were blue and gold pillows lining the headboard. The sleeping area had obviously been designed for intimacy, and it was, she decided, the most romantic chamber in all the world. With the drapes closed, privacy would be absolute.

Victoria would love it. She deserved such elegance and splendor. Taylor decided that as soon as Lucas left Boston, she would switch rooms with her friend. Taylor knew she would have to remain in Boston at least a week so that she would have sufficient time to purchase the rest of the things she would need in the wilderness. There was also the possibility Victoria would require her assistance in the purchase of a suitable home, and Taylor wasn't about to go anywhere until her friend was settled.

"Do you want me to unlock your luggage or help you unpack?"

Taylor was surprised by the offer. Were American men used to doing women's work?

"Thank you, sir, but no," she answered. "I'm only going to unpack enough for four or five days. How long are you planning to remain in Boston?"

"I'm leaving the day after tomorrow. We're going to have to have a long talk before I go and get some details figured out."

"Yes, of course," she agreed.

He was giving her a curious look. "I thought you were going to stay in the hotel until you found a house to purchase."

She disappeared around the corner without giving him an explanation. Lucas walked over to the arched entrance to the bedroom area and found his wife sitting on the end of the bed.

She was smiling with pleasure. "It's got a wonderful feather mattress," she told him when he asked why she looked so happy.

He nodded. "Why are you only unpacking enough for four or five nights?"

"It's easier," she replied, deliberately giving him only half an answer. Then she changed the topic. "Aren't you late for your meeting?"

"She won't mind waiting a few more minutes."

She? Taylor's back arched. He was meeting a woman? The smile faded from her face. She had to force herself not to become alarmed. There could be any number of innocent reasons why he would be meeting a woman. Perhaps she was a business associate, and though that would be an oddity, it was still possible. She might have inherited money or a company of some sort from a relative. Yes, that was probably it. Lucas had said it was a meeting, after all. She wasn't going to jump to any sorry conclusions until she'd gained all the facts.

"You have a business matter to discuss with this woman?" she inquired.

"No."

Mr. Ross wasn't one to go into detail. She was forced to prod the information out of him.

"What kind of meeting is it?" she asked. "I am simply curious," she added as a hasty explanation.

"It isn't a meeting exactly," he replied. "We just agreed to meet in the lobby at eight. Why?"

She deliberately shrugged. "Just wondered," she replied as casually as possible. "Will there be others joining you?"

"No."

"And?" she prodded, a bit more sharply than she intended.

She suddenly wanted to kick him. In her mind, the conclusions had narrowed considerably. Yet if he was planning a liaison, why was he telling her about it?

She told herself not to overreact. She shouldn't care who he was seeing or why. She did care though. Immensely. She was suddenly bloody furious with the insensitive brute.

She looked thunderstruck to him. He couldn't imagine what had come over her. One minute she was smiling and the next she was glaring.

He was her target, and so he naturally assumed he'd done something to displease her. She'd been perfectly happy when he first mentioned the meeting, and so he concluded going out wasn't what had her pricked now.

"Is something wrong?"

"No."

The hell it wasn't. He waited another minute or two for her to say something more and when she remained silent, he gave up trying to speculate on the cause of her irritation.

"You're going to be late meeting the woman."

"Her name's Belle."

"Belle." She repeated the name in a whisper. She couldn't think of anything else to add. Her heart felt as though it had just been broken. She was feeling crushed and pitiful. She wanted to weep, and it took all her strength to hide her feelings from him.

She told herself she shouldn't have been surprised. Men strayed. She had first-hand knowledge of that hard truth. Her very own fiancé had certainly strayed. While pledging his undying love to her, he was sleeping with her cousin, Jane. Madam had instructed her that it was perfectly all right to love a man as long as she didn't let the love consume her, and as for trust, well, if she really must, then she should spend a considerable number of years weighing all the ramifications before she gave anyone her complete loyalty.

Madam had also warned her about men's peculiar urges. She'd told Taylor they all had uncontrollable cravings. Uncle Andrew happened in on the conversation and took immediate issue with her point of view. He declared it was warped. He insisted that the majority of men didn't have any trouble at all controlling their lust. It was only a base few who let their animal instincts take control of their actions. A heated argument developed. Madam held firm to her belief that men were ruled by their groins and not their minds, and Uncle Andrew took the opposite view. He told his sister she was thinking like a dried-up old prune, and it was all her own fault because she'd never bothered to remarry after her first husband died.

There was only one point both her relatives would agree upon, and that was the fact that all men sowed wild oats. Unfortunately neither her grandmother nor her uncle would go into detail. Taylor was left to guess what in heaven's name oats had to do with sex.

The majority of men and their behavior didn't concern Taylor now. Lucas's behavior was another matter altogether. They were on their honeymoon, after all, and she thought it was damned rude of him to seek out the company of another woman. Taylor didn't particularly care that their marriage was supposed to be in name only. Mr. Ross shouldn't be meeting other women while he was still legally married to her.

Pride kept her from giving him a piece of her mind. "Taylor, you need to get some rest. You look exhausted. I'll see you in the morning."

She let out a gasp. "You're staying out all night?"

"No, but you'll be asleep by the time I get back."

"You're going to be that late?"

He shrugged. No telling with Belle, he thought. His mother's old friend liked to talk. And drink, he remembered. Lord, could she drink. The last time they'd gotten together, she drank him under the table. She was proud of the fact that she could outdrink any man, any time. It wasn't an empty boast. Lucas still vividly recalled the godawful hangover he'd suffered through after their last meeting. History wasn't going to repeat itself tonight, however. Lucas had already decided one drink of brandy was going to be his limit.

"Good night, Taylor," he said before he turned to leave.

"Have a good time," she called out.

"I will," he replied.

She didn't want to kick him any longer. That would have been too kind. She wanted to kill him now.

He had almost reached the door when she jumped off the bed and went chasing after him. She said the first thing that popped into her mind. "Aren't you too tired to go out?"

"No," he replied over his shoulder. "Lock the door after me. I've got a key."

He reached for the doorknob. She rushed ahead and wedged herself between the door and her husband, effectively blocking his exit.

"Exactly how long will you be gone?"

179

"Awhile."

"Oh."

"Oh, what?"

She shrugged. He let her see his exasperation. "What in thunder's wrong with you?" he asked, his bewilderment apparent in both his expression and his tone of voice.

"Nothing," she lied. "Go ahead then. Have a nice evening."

"You'll have to get out of my way first."

She started to do just that, then changed her mind. She'd taken two steps to the side so Lucas could leave, but just as he was reaching for the doorknob again, she rushed back. She threw herself up against the door and splayed her arms wide. She knew she was being dramatic. She couldn't help it.

He was looking at her as though he thought she'd lost her mind. She thought she probably had. She certainly wasn't making any sense. She didn't care. The possibility that her husband might be intimate with another woman made her too ill to think about being sensible.

"Answer one question before you leave."

"What is it?"

"Will you be sowing any oats tonight?"

"What?" He sounded incredulous.

"Wild oats," she explained, being a little more specific. "Will you be sowing any tonight?"

He couldn't believe what she'd just asked him. And then the truth dawned. Taylor was jealous. Lucas was too surprised to say anything. He took a step back and simply stared at her.

She saw the astonishment in his eyes and immediately started blushing like a schoolgirl. His reaction told her he hadn't considered the possibility, and oh,

God, hadn't she just planted the obscene notion in his head?

She let out a loud sigh. She'd gone this far into the murky waters. She might as well go the rest of the distance, or, as Madam was apt to say, finish what she had begun.

"Mr. Ross," she began.

"Are you jealous?" he asked at the very same time.

"No, of course not."

"Could have fooled me," he replied. He did smile then, he couldn't help it.

Her shoulders straightened. Her temper flared. He was, after all, laughing at her.

"Taylor, I'll be happy to explain about Belle."

"I could care less about the woman," she replied. "I don't give a hoot what you do with your time, sir."

It wasn't what she said but how she said it that got him riled up. God, she was stubborn. He decided to let her stew in her own imagination. Come morning, he'd set her straight, but only if she wasn't still sounding like a surly shrew.

"Are you going to get out of my way?"

"Yes."

She didn't move. Lucas decided he was going to have to pick her up, carry her back to the bed, then toss her there with the order to stay put. He reached for her but stopped when she pushed his hands away.

"Marriage is like pregnancy," she announced.

He leaned back. She'd certainly gotten his full attention with that comment. He decided then and there he was never going to be surprised by anything she said to him in the future. Damned if she wasn't the most illogical woman he'd ever encountered. He wanted to laugh but didn't dare. He'd already noticed how sensitive her feelings were. God, she was young.

And inexperienced. And sweet and beautiful and all the things any man in his right mind would want to grab onto and hold close for the rest of his life.

"How is marriage like pregnancy?" he heard himself ask.

"You either are or you aren't," she told him very matter-of-factly.

"Taylor—"

She interrupted him. "There aren't any shades of gray. Until the annulment papers are duly executed, I believe both of us should try to respect our vows. We should be . . ."

"Faithful?" he supplied when she didn't go on.

"Yes, we should be faithful to one another. It would be the polite thing to do."

She bowed her head so he wouldn't see how much it embarrassed her to discuss such an intimate topic. She noticed then she was gripping her hands together and immediately stopped the telling action.

Lucas stared down at the top of her head. Because she couldn't see his expression, he felt it safe to smile.

"Are you telling me I should be celibate?" he asked.

"I'm going to be," she answered.

"It isn't the same thing at all."

"Why isn't it?"

He didn't have a ready answer. In truth, he only just realized how strange his own statement sounded.

"Women have the same urges," he explained. "But they have to be in love first. Men don't."

This reasoning made perfectly good sense to Lucas. Taylor didn't see it that way. She shook her head. "What you're saying, sir, is that the majority of women have virtue and practice restraint, while the majority of men, yourself included, will rut with anything passing by."

"That about sums it up," he agreed, just to irritate her.

She kept her temper under control. It almost killed her. She absolutely refused to get into an argument with him. She'd already said quite enough. Lucas could either accept or reject her opinions. If he proved to be like all the men Madam had warned her about and have the morals of a goat like his half brother, then Taylor decided she was better off finding out sooner than later. She wasn't vulnerable now, because she wasn't in love with him. She had all the symptoms of a woman smitten by an attraction. She became breathless whenever he stood close to her, had difficulty holding onto a thought for more than a second whenever he stared at her, found herself wishing he would kiss her all the time, and wanted him to think she was just a little bit appealing. Lord, wasn't that proof enough she wasn't immune to his charm and his good looks? Warning bells sounded in her head. No doubt about it, she liked him entirely too much. She was going to have to put an immediate stop to it. This one-sided attraction wasn't just dangerous, it was also hopeless.

And all because the obtuse man would rather be hanged than married.

Belle. She hated both the name and the woman. She decided to give Lucas something to think about on his way down to his liaison.

"Ladies don't have urges, sir, as you so indelicately stated. Only common trollops are afflicted with lustful thoughts." *Like Belle,* she silently added.

She tried to walk away from him then. Lucas wouldn't let her go anywhere. He planted his hands on either side of her head, effectively trapping her.

He obviously wasn't finished discussing the issue. "Is that so?" he said.

She looked up at him, thinking to tell him, yes, it was so, and then remind him of the lateness in the hour, but the words got lost in the back of her mind. The look of tenderness in his eyes held her full attention. There simply wasn't room for anything else.

God, he was beautiful.

He was thinking the very same thing about her. Whenever she gave him her full attention, his throat felt like it was closing up on him. Those eyes. They were magical to him and as clear and blue as the sky over Montana Territory.

Yes, she was lovely all right. But she was also as stubborn as an old mule and as opinionated as an out-of-office politician. The innocent was speaking with authority on topics she knew absolutely nothing about. Like urges.

He couldn't seem to quit staring at her. He knew he should leave. Belle had probably already made her way through one bottle of good whiskey. It didn't matter. He couldn't make himself move away from Taylor. The little woman mesmerized him. He wanted to kiss her, then decided he would do just that. He reached over and cupped her chin in his hand. He nudged her head back a little further. Then he slowly leaned down. His mouth brushed over hers in a gentle caress. He knew he'd startled her because she tried to jerk away. He wouldn't let her. He kissed her again, but this time he lingered over the task.

She let out a little sigh of pleasure and grabbed hold of the front of his jacket. It was all the encouragement he needed. His mouth settled on top of hers in an altogether different sort of kiss. The kind that consumed.

His mouth was hard, hot, wet. Her lips were soft, willing. It wasn't enough for him. He forced her mouth open by applying pressure on her chin with his thumb, and once she'd given in to the silent demand, his tongue swept inside to reclaim the taste of her. He stroked the silky interior of her mouth with blatant ownership. God, she tasted good.

Passion ignited with lightning speed. Taylor wasn't the least bit passive. Her arms closed around his waist. Her fingers dug into his back. She could feel his hot skin underneath his shirt. And his strength. She felt that, too. His muscle was as sleek and hard as steel. The heat radiating from his body and his mouth fairly overwhelmed her. God help her, she never wanted him to stop touching her.

He couldn't get enough of her. The taste of her drove him wild. Her tongue dueled with his, and Lord, there wasn't a damned thing timid about her now. He heard himself groan. He thrust his tongue back inside her mouth. She sucked on it. He pulled her up tight against him. His groin rubbed against her. Her hips instinctively cuddled him.

His mouth slanted over hers again and again. They clung together for what seemed an eternity. The way she stroked him told him she didn't want him to stop. Her mouth was every bit as hot and wet as his was. He liked that. There was lots of tongue. He liked that, too.

He ate at her lips, devoured her scent, and damned if it wasn't the most carnal kiss he'd ever experienced.

She whimpered low in the back of her throat. The sound drove him to the limit of his control. He knew it was time to stop. He was already picturing her naked and thinking how good it was going to feel when he was fully imbedded inside her, with her legs wrapped around him and her breasts rubbing against his chest.

The groan gathering in the back of his throat turned into a growl. Lucas tore his mouth away from hers and tried to regain control over his body. His breathing was harsh, ragged. His forehead was pressed against the door now, his eyes tightly closed, and he had to force himself to let go of her.

Taylor wasn't making it easy for him. She was still stroking him, making him burn for more. He could feel her trembling. He was arrogantly pleased over that notice.

The hell she didn't have urges.

She had never felt so overwhelmed by anything in all her life. She was shaking just like she had on the ship when she thought they were going to drown. Fear had been the reason then. Passion was the culprit this time.

Oh, God, she was a trollop. Her hands immediately dropped to her sides. She stood rigid against him and closed her eyes while she concentrated on getting her breathing to slow down.

He noticed the change that came over her. He wondered what absurdity she was thinking about now.

She wanted him to put his arms around her again and give her another make-me-senseless kiss. Lucas wasn't helping her recover her ladylike facade either, for he leaned down and started to nibble on her earlobe. She shouldn't have liked it, but she did. A warm shiver passed down her spine. His breath, so warm and sweet, tickled her skin. Her knees were once again feeling weak. Lord, she could feel her control slipping away again.

"Whatever are you doing?"

"Kissing you."

Yes, yes, that much was obvious, but why, Taylor wanted to say. She couldn't get the words out. Her sigh of pleasure was all she could manage.

"Do you want me to stop?" he asked in a husky whisper.

Of course she wanted him to stop. She'd only just remembered where he was going and who he was meeting. The brute. Kissing her one minute and running off to another woman the next.

"Do you?" he asked again.

She put her arms around his waist. "I don't know," she answered.

The man was driving her to distraction. His mouth was open and hot against the side of her neck. She tilted her head to the side so he'd have better access.

"You smell nice. Like flowers."

Soap, she wanted to say. It was scented. She couldn't get that explanation out of her mouth either.

Mr. Ross was turning her mind into mush.

"Farmers name their cows Belle."

He smiled against her neck. He acted as though he hadn't heard her comment. She felt compelled to repeat it. "I read it in Mrs. Livingston's journal, and since it was published, it has to be true. They definitely name their cows Belle." Think about that while you're wooing your friend.

He kissed her forehead. "You'd like me to keep on kissing you, wouldn't you, Taylor?"

Lord, he was arrogant. And right. She was honest enough to admit the truth. "Yes," she said.

"You know what I think?"

The way he asked the question made her want to sigh again. His voice was deep and husky and how she loved his slow drawl.

"What do you think?" she asked breathlessly.

"You've got a few urges of your own. Do you understand what that means?"

He wanted her to admit that women had the same lustful cravings as men and that he'd been right all along.

"Yes, I understand what it means."

Her shoulders slumped. She pushed away from him and tried to walk away. He grabbed her from behind, wrapped his arms around her waist to hold her still, then leaned down and demanded she explain.

"Tell me what you just learned," he ordered, impatiently waiting for her answer so he could do a fair amount of male gloating.

"I'm a trollop. There, are you happy now? Belle's going to get weary of waiting for you."

"She'll keep on drinking until I get there."

"She sounds delightful."

"She is," he replied. "You aren't a trollop."

She pushed away from him and then turned around to confront him. Her hands settled on her hips. "I'm usually not," she corrected. "But you make me want to do things I normally wouldn't think about doing. When you touch me, I . . . well, I'm only a trollop around you. I therefore suggest we stay away from each other. Please leave now before I disgrace myself again."

She looked like she wanted to cry. He felt guilty because he'd teased her. He was also feeling inordinately pleased with her. The compliment she'd given him, deliberate or not, made him want to smile. She got rattled when he touched her. A man couldn't ask for more than that.

He felt he should say something to calm her. He was her husband, after all, and it was the least he could do. Husbands should try to soothe their wives when they were upset, shouldn't they? What difference did it make that they were only going to be married for a little while?

"You're my wife. It's all right to be a trollop with me."

She caught herself before she snorted. Her expression showed her vexation, however. "But you'd rather be hanged than married, remember?"

Lord, she was a sight when she was riled up. Her eyes blazed with anger and the look on her face would have made a weak man immediately contrite. He wasn't weak, he reminded himself. "You've got that right," he replied.

She threaded her fingers through her hair in obvious agitation. "Do leave, sir."

He thought that was a fine idea. He walked over to the door, reached for the knob, then stopped. His right hand went to his vest pocket to make certain he had his key, then to the other pocket when the first was empty.

He turned around again and walked over to his wardrobe. Taylor watched his every move. She was trying to get her emotions under control. Honest to heaven, she didn't understand her own mind anymore, she decided. Mr. Ross hadn't done anything to cause her to get this upset. Yet she still wanted to weep.

He found the key in the pocket of the jacket he'd worn earlier in the day. Lucas closed the wardrobe, then turned to look at Taylor.

"Belle fed me when I was a boy . . . after my mother died. They were close friends."

He wasn't certain why he offered the explanation. He guessed it was because he didn't want her to worry. He also didn't want her to think he was an ogre.

Taylor was fairly overcome with relief. Belle wasn't a cow. She was a friend of the family.

He'd been honest with her, and so she decided it was now her turn. "I was jealous," she blurted out. "You were right about that."

He was pleased by her confession. From the strain

he heard in her voice, he knew the admission had been difficult for her. Because she looked so solemn, he didn't smile. He gave her an abrupt nod before he turned away.

She didn't want him to leave on a sour note. Perhaps, she considered, if she engaged him in a pleasant conversation, even if it only lasted a minute or two, his mood would improve. She didn't want her husband to greet his mother's friend with a scowl on his face. Belle might jump to the conclusion Lucas wasn't a happily married man.

Oh, God, she really was losing her mind. It didn't seem to matter much to her at the moment. Lucas was going to leave smiling, even if it killed her. Taylor hunted for a topic to talk about, and just as he was pulling the door open, she settled on one she knew he was sure to like.

"I can't make up my mind if I should petition for an annulment or a divorce."

"You already mentioned getting an annulment," he reminded her.

"I did? I don't remember. I believe a divorce is probably easier to obtain."

"Why?"

"There seem to be more reasons acceptable to the court," she explained. She was pleased he was listening. "I considered most of them, too," she boasted. "I've memorized them all, you see, but I couldn't settle on a specific . . ."

He smiled. "You memorized the reasons you could give for a divorce?"

She nodded. She was pleased to see his frown was completely gone. "There's desertion, but of course I couldn't use that as a reason. We haven't lived together long enough," she added. She was warming to her topic now. Her voice echoed with enthusiasm when she continued. "Then I thought about drunkenness, and I immediately discarded the reason. I've never seen you take a drink while we've been together. I even thought about charging you with extreme and repeated cruelty, but that would be a complete lie and it didn't sit well with me at all. You have your reputation to consider, and while mine isn't the least important to me, I do have my pride. I would never be married to a man who beat me and I therefore wouldn't like to lie and say I was."

"Men don't waste time on something as foolish as pride the way women do," he remarked.

"Many do," she argued.

"I don't."

Perhaps if he hadn't sounded so arrogant, she would have told him the true reason she was going to give. But that male ego of his was really getting out of hand. It had become a red flag in front of her eyes.

So he didn't have a problem with pride. *We'll see about that,* she thought to herself.

"You don't like to lie?"

"No, I don't," she replied. "You sound surprised."

"I am. An honest woman," he explained with a grin. "That is a surprise."

She refused to be insulted. "You haven't known many good women, have you, sir?"

He shrugged. "Finish what you started," he ordered. "Don't waste my time with what you might have done. Tell me what reason you'll give for the annulment."

"Yes, of course," she replied. She added what she hoped was a sweet smile and walked over to the door. She gently nudged him on his way, all the while explaining the intricate differences between petitioning the court for an annulment and a divorce. When she was finished, she bid him good night and leaned against the doorway. She watched him walk down the hallway. She wondered how long it would take for his curiosity to get the better of him.

Lucas was halfway down the corridor before he realized she still hadn't told him what reason she was going to use for the annulment. He turned around, walked half the distance back to the door so he wouldn't have to raise his voice, and then said, "If I'm not a drunk or a deserter or a lout who beats his wife, what am I?" he asked her with a good deal of exasperation in his voice.

Taylor sweetened her smile and started to shut the door. In a voice filled with cheerfulness, she told him. "You're impotent."

8

Fortune brings in some boats that are not steer'd.
> —William Shakespeare,
> *Cymbeline*

She ruined his evening.

All Lucas could think about was Taylor's outrageous remark. The hell he was impotent. By God he'd go to his grave laughing before he let her put that foul reason down on a petition for everyone in the court to read.

He must have fumed for over an hour before he settled down and thought the matter through. He replayed the conversation in his mind at least a dozen times, all the while picturing the sparkle that had come into her eyes, and when he was finished with his analysis, he came to the conclusion she'd been bluffing. *Pride.* The word popped into his head all at once. The boast he'd made came next. Men weren't plagued with worries about pride the way women were. Hadn't he said that or something similar? And hadn't the glint come into her eyes then? Oh, yes, she'd been bluffing all right. She'd been teaching him a lesson, too.

Lucas started smiling. Taylor, he decided, was one clever lady.

"It's about time you quit frowning and started to enjoy yourself."

His friend Belle made the comment. Lucas immediately shook himself out of his preoccupation and gave his mother's friend his full attention.

Belle had changed considerably over the past ten years. She looked frail to him now. She used to be a big, strapping woman. She was still just as tall, his size actually, but her skin and posture showed her age. She'd been through difficult years. The frontier was hard on women, made them old before their time. Belle wasn't any different. She'd lived in the wilderness for thirty years before moving back east to Boston. The harsh weather had leathered her skin, and the daily workload every woman was expected to carry had made her shoulders stooped and her back curved.

He remembered she used to have dark brown hair. It was white now. Her eyes hadn't changed, however. They were still warm, inviting, kind. Men were still drawn to her, as evidenced by her companion seated next to her, a Mr. Winston Champhill. The elderly man was half her size, but Lucas noticed the look of adoration in his eyes whenever he looked up at her.

Belle had already buried three husbands. Lucas thought Winston might very well become the fourth.

The couple had already taken seats inside the gentlemen's lounge, an area strictly forbidden to women, but Belle hadn't paid any attention to the rule. The attendants didn't want to make a scene. They sent for the hotel manager. Lucas had only just taken his seat across from the couple when the manager appeared at Belle's side. He leaned down and whispered something to her, she said something back, and the man went hurrying out of the lounge with a blush on his face.

Lucas didn't think he wanted to know what she'd said. After he put the matter of his wife out of his mind, he was able to concentrate on listening to all the news from his hometown. Kerrington was the settlement where he'd been born and eventually abandoned. Once Lucas was old enough and strong enough to leave, he did just that. He hadn't been back since. According to Belle, the town hadn't grown much in the past twenty years. She'd returned to Kerrington several times for weddings and family reunions. With so many husbands, there was of course an extremely large extended family. And with her loving heart, she embraced every one of her relatives.

It was well after one in the morning before she finished with what she called her catch-up news. Mr. Champhill had nodded off a good hour before. Belle was vastly amused by her escort's behavior. She motioned to the gentleman, then grinned at Lucas.

"He's plain tuckered out," she told him in a low whisper so she wouldn't disturb her friend. "He's a good ten years younger than me but he still can't keep up. Don't matter how young I pick them, Lucas. Don't matter at all. I still wear them out." She made the last remark with a boast in her voice.

Lucas smiled. "You going to marry him?"

"I suppose I will," she replied. She let out a sigh. "I get cold at night, and he's big enough to warm me. Maybe this one will last longer than the others. What about you, son? You ever going to find a woman and settle down?"

Lucas leaned back in his chair and reached for his glass. He'd been nursing the brandy all evening. He'd never been much of a drinker. He didn't mind the taste. He minded the aftereffects. He was a man who always wanted to be in control and drink robbed him of that ability.

He wasn't one to tell his business either, but he and Belle went way back. She'd been like a mother to him and had in fact taken over his care when his own mother died. She was the closest thing he had to family and the only tie to his Kentucky background.

"I got married, Belle."

It took him several minutes to convince her he was telling the truth, then he had to wait another couple of minutes for her to recover from the surprise of his announcement. She was clearly astonished, especially when he told her the marriage was in name only, and she did a fair amount of laughing and shaking her head.

"If that don't beat all," she repeated again and again.

She wanted all the particulars. Lucas told her almost everything. He gave her his reason for returning to England, explained all about his youngest brother, Kelsey, and how Merritt had suddenly changed his mind and demanded Lucas pay a ransom for Kelsey's release.

Belle was scowling like a hanging judge about to pass sentence by the time he'd finished that part of his explanation.

"Where's the boy now?" she asked.

"On his way to the ranch with Jordan and Douglas. They're stopping in Denver for a week or so. There's a school there Jordan thinks would be good for Kelsey. If it checks out to his satisfaction, the boy will start next fall."

"These older boys . . . they still working your ranch outside Redemption?" Belle asked.

196

Lucas nodded. "The ranch is a day's ride from Redemption," he said. "I'm going to deed it over to the three of them. They'll probably split it in thirds, eventually get married, and . . ."

"Live happily ever after?"

Lucas smiled. "Perhaps. They're fighting now. Douglas wants to farm the flat land and Jordan wants to add more cattle and use the land for grazing. They've worked hard, Belle. They'll work even harder if the land belongs to them."

"What about you and this new bride?"

"I'm going back to the mountains. She's going to live in Boston. She could never live in the wilderness, Belle. She's too tender."

"She'll toughen up."

Lucas shook his head. "She's very refined, a real lady," he explained. "Taylor comes from an aristocratic family. She certainly has never had to do any common work, and I wouldn't like to see her . . ."

He stopped himself before admitting he didn't want to see her get old and tired before her time. "She deserves to live a good life."

"She have money coming from this aristocratic family of hers?"

"Yes."

"Refined ladies with money do just as well as common women without," Belle said. "Fact of it is, son, with money, she can buy all the help she needs."

"Not in the wilderness," he contradicted. "Women are so scarce in Montana Territory they don't have to work for anyone else."

"There's fourteen women living in Bozeman right this minute," she argued. "And more will be settling in the area real soon."

Lucas didn't ask her where she'd gotten her information. For as long as he'd known her, Belle had always had an abundance of facts stored in her head. Most of them were true.

"I don't live near Bozeman," he reminded her.

"Makes no matter," she argued. "You can hire some men to work . . . Now why are you shaking your head at me?"

"I'll be damned if I'll let another man work close to her."

Belle's smile was wide. "So you aren't wanting any other men buzzing around her," she remarked. "That's mighty curious."

Lucas didn't know what to say in response to her remark. He shrugged to cover his sudden discomfort. He found the topic disturbing and wished now he hadn't told her about his marriage.

"Are you hearing the contradictions I'm hearing?" Belle asked. "You just told me you'd be damned before you'd let another man work close to your bride in Montana Territory, but just five minutes ago you said you're going to let her live in Boston all alone while you go riding back to your mountains."

"I know it sounds . . ."

"Contradictory?"

He let out a sigh. She was right. It did sound contradictory. Belle shook her head at him. "You haven't taken the time to think the matter through, have you?"

He wanted to argue with her. Hell, yes, he'd thought it through. It was supposed to be an easy, simple arrangement and only for a limited time. But Taylor made the arrangement complicated. He certainly hadn't counted on becoming attracted to her or feeling the constant need to protect her or experiencing such raw possessiveness every single time he looked at her.

"Of course I can see why you'd agree to the marriage. You gave your protection for the money to buy the boy's freedom. What was his name again?"

"Kelsey."

She nodded. "You recall the youngun named MacCowan? I seem to recollect the time you killed yourself a pair of vermin to get the boy out of their clutches. Then there was that little Irish girl. Now what was her name?"

"It happened a long time ago, Belle, and it doesn't have anything to do with my marriage."

"I'm just reminding you it's in your nature to protect," she countered.

"It's also in my nature to be free," he said then.

She chuckled. "I heard another contradiction, son. You said you're married, then you said you aren't. How long do you plan to go on like this?"

"I'm going to have to talk to Taylor and find out how long she wants to stay married. We've talked about getting an annulment or a divorce. I don't think it matters to her."

"Which do you prefer?"

"An annulment," he answered. "There would be less of a stigma."

Belle snorted with disbelief. "If she comes from money, she's social. She's going to be shunned either way. Does she realize that?"

"She doesn't seem to care."

"Now that's mighty odd," Belle remarked. "Most ladies would care."

Yes, Lucas thought. The majority of women would care. Why didn't Taylor? He recalled a remark she'd made earlier in the evening when she was going on and on about the list of reasons she'd memorized that were legally acceptable to the court for a divorce petition, and during the long-winded explanation, she mentioned her reputation didn't matter.

Belle downed the contents of her glass, motioned for Lucas to pour her another drink, and then leaned forward.

She grilled him with question after question about Taylor. She wanted to know how she dressed, what she ate, what she drank, how she behaved, how she treated others, and how she expected to be treated.

The contradictions piled up. Taylor came from wealth and luxury, yet on the voyage to Boston, she certainly hadn't behaved like a spoiled young lady in need of pampering.

"She pretty much does for herself," Lucas confessed.

"Nothing about your bride adds up," Belle announced. "Only one thing is certain in my mind, son. She had another reason for marrying you, one more important to her than her reputation."

The greater good. Lucas remembered that after prodding her to tell him the real reason why she'd married him Taylor finally admitted protecting her inheritance from her uncle hadn't been her only motive. She'd also married him for what she called the greater good. What in thunder was that supposed to mean?

Lucas decided it was high time he found out.

It was a fact he hadn't cared enough before the wedding to look into Taylor's background. Hell, he hadn't even bothered to look at his bride beforehand. No, he hadn't cared enough, and what she looked like hadn't been the least bit important to him. The truth of the matter was that he'd been in too much of a panic at the time. Desperation. He'd been desperate all right. He would have done anything to get Kelsey away from Merritt. When he'd seen how sickly and mistreated the boy had been, Lucas had even considered killing the jackal. Then Taylor's grandmother came up with a solution to his problem that wouldn't get him thrown in prison. Lucas immediately took the money and accepted the debt. And now what?

Belle drew his attention when she reached across the table to shake her escort awake. The pair left a few minutes later. Lucas accompanied them to the lobby doors.

"If I weren't leaving for St. Louis tomorrow, I'd insist on meeting your bride, Lucas. I'd get a few questions answered."

Lucas smiled. He could just picture Belle trying to browbeat Taylor into telling her what she wanted to know. His mother's friend was certainly older and more experienced, but Taylor was a bit more clever. She'd hold her own.

He kissed Belle good-bye, then went upstairs. He fully intended to get his questions answered, but he knew he'd have to wait until tomorrow. Taylor was sound asleep, or should be, and he wasn't in the mood for a lengthy conversation tonight. Taylor needed her rest, and so did he. He felt weighed down, worn thin. The city had done that to him. He couldn't be himself here. He had to be polite. He couldn't wear his guns. He felt naked and vulnerable without them. The air wasn't invigorating like the mountain air. Taylor and her friend marveled over how clean the air seemed. They didn't know any better, and he supposed Boston wasn't as stifling as London. It was still godawful to him. Every big city was. He felt as though the soot constantly spewing out of thousands of chimneys was coating his insides. Boston had become as crowded with people and crime as every other big city. Only those people who had never seen the mountains and the plains would be content to live in such a crowded area. They lived in ignorance. It was the only reason Lucas could come up with for why anyone would live in such a loud, hustle-bustle environment.

A man could only take so much, and Lucas had about had his fill. He needed to go home.

He tried to be as quiet as possible when he unlocked the door to their room and walked inside. He spotted Taylor immediately. She was sleeping on the lounge directly across from the door. The moonlight filtering in from the windows gave her hair and shoulders a golden glow. She looked like an angel to him. Her hair was spread out on the pillow and her hands were folded demurely at her waist. She was using her white robe for her blanket.

He stood there for a long while staring at her. He had to force himself to move. He turned and shut the door, locked it, and then crossed over to the alcove. He discarded his jacket on the way to the side of the bed, bent down, and pulled the covers back and then went to get Taylor. His intent was to trade places with her. She would sleep in the bed and he would take the lounge.

Although they'd slept next to each other before, he didn't trust himself to share the bed with her tonight. He wanted her too much. From the moment he'd walked into the room, desire had taken hold. Lucas shook his head. He realized he wasn't being honest with himself. He'd wanted Taylor from the moment he spotted her across the ballroom. The need had grown inside him with each step he took toward his bride. And when recognition finally dawned in her eyes and she gave him that wonderful wide-eyed, Oh-God-what-have-I-done look, he'd had the almost overwhelming urge to pick her up, toss her over his shoulder, and find the nearest bed. Yes, he'd wanted her from the very beginning, and heaven help him, it was becoming impossible to continue to behave like a gentleman.

He gave his word and he was going to keep it, even if it made a eunuch out of him. He'd promised Taylor's grandmother he would protect his bride. Never was the word *ravish* mentioned in the conversation.

Taylor rolled onto her side. The movement pulled him back to the task at hand. He nudged the table out of his way so he could get to her, then knelt down on one knee and started to reach for her. He suddenly stopped when he noticed the paper she was clutching in her hands. He could make out only part of the heading, but it was enough. The paper was a telegraph form. His gaze turned to her face. He was close enough to see the tears on her eyelashes. Her cheeks were still wet. He was suddenly filled with dread. Whatever the message was, it had obviously devastated Taylor, for she'd cried herself to sleep.

Taylor had a death grip on the paper. He had to gently pry her fingers away so that he could read the message. He had already guessed the news, but he wanted to be certain.

The paper was also wet. God, she'd wept all over the form. Lucas slowly unfolded the telegram and read the missive.

Madam was dead.

Taylor's heart had to be breaking. Lucas bowed his head and closed his eyes. He wasn't a praying man, but he found himself reciting a prayer Belle had taught him years ago. He could only remember a few phrases, but he figured God would understand his petition anyway. He asked his Maker to give Madam peace and happiness. The prayer was an instinctive reaction, because he hadn't been unaffected by the news. In truth, he was filled with sadness. He hadn't known Lady Esther long, but she'd still made quite an impact upon him. She was such a strong, opinionated, passionate woman. She gave the word *elegance* definition. She was quite a tough old lady, all right, but what most affected Lucas was her determination and drive to do anything and everything to keep her granddaughter safe.

Lucas opened his eyes and found Taylor staring at him. She didn't say a word, and neither did he. He simply put the telegram down on the table, then reached for her. She didn't resist. Lucas lifted her into his arms, stood up, and carried her to her bed. He settled her in the middle of the sheets, then stood by the side to undress. Taylor wasn't watching him disrobe. She'd closed her eyes, rolled onto her side, away from him, and curled herself up into the blankets.

He wasn't going to let her withdraw from him. She needed to let her pain out, to weep without holding back . . . to begin to mourn.

Lucas got into bed and took her into his arms. She fought him but only for a second or two, and then she put her arms around his waist, buried her face in the crook of his neck, and started shaking almost violently.

He comforted her the only way he knew how. He stroked her back with his hands while he whispered words he hoped would soothe her.

He held her close, and even after he was certain she'd fallen asleep, he continued to keep her in his embrace.

He never wanted to let go.

He woke up on top of her again. It was the dead of the night, almost four in the morning. Awareness slowly eased up on him. He was nuzzling the side of her neck and trying to wedge his knee between her thighs when he realized what he was doing. He had already worked her nightgown up around her hips. She wasn't wearing anything underneath. She wasn't fighting him either. Her legs were entwined with his, her arms were wrapped around his neck, and Lucas, still more asleep than awake, thought she must be having the same kind of erotic dream he was having because she was kissing his neck the very same way he was kissing hers.

He didn't want to stop. His hand moved up, under her gown, stroking, caressing. He cupped the underside of one breast. His thumb brushed across her nipple. She let out a low moan against his ear and tightened her hold on him. He suddenly needed to taste her. He became rough in his quest. He grabbed hold of the back of her neck and forced her to turn toward him. His mouth sealed any protest she might have made. His tongue swept inside to find and mate with hers. He kissed her ravenously while his hands caressed her neck, then moved lower until each covered her breasts. The heat from her skin drove him wild. Her scent, like flowers, faint but irresistible, wooed him, drugged him, and all he could think about was getting a little closer to her clean, feminine fragrance. Her skin felt silky. He wanted to taste every inch of her. His hands moved lower. They spanned her waist, then moved lower still, until he was touching the very heat of her. Her back arched upward and she let out a low gasp.

Then she started trembling. He tore his mouth away from hers and started to unbutton his pants. He was hard, throbbing now with his need to plant himself solidly inside her.

His breath was ragged with his desire. He couldn't

quit kissing her while he was stripping out of his clothes, however, and it wasn't until he tasted the salty tear on her cheek that reality finally set in.

What the hell was he doing? Lucas felt as though he'd just been drenched in iced water. He took several deep, shuddering breaths in an attempt to get his heart to slow down. His first logical thought wasn't a pleasant one. He realized he was taking horrid advantage of Taylor. She couldn't possibly be thinking straight. She'd only just gotten the news her grandmother had died. She needed comfort now, not debauchery.

He tried to get off of her. He pulled her nightgown down and forced himself to roll to his side. It took every ounce of strength he possessed, but he did accomplish the feat. The problem, however, was that Taylor came with him. She couldn't let go of her hold either. Her opened mouth was on his throat, and she was moving erotically against him, urging him without words to come back to her.

He was having none of it. He pulled her arms away from his neck and tried to get her to move back to her side of the bed. She wouldn't leave. She wrapped her arms around his waist and held on for dear life.

She needed him to love her. The second that realization popped into Taylor's mind, she stiffened against Lucas. Oh, God, what was she doing?

She was suddenly overwhelmed with self-pity and desolation. Madam was gone. That fact was all Taylor could focus on. She couldn't imagine life without her. How could she go on, all alone? Madam had become a safety net. If the problems of living in the wilderness became overwhelming, Taylor knew she would have written to her dear grandmother to seek her council . . . and her love. Madam would have told her what to do and even if Taylor hadn't taken the advice, she would have felt that someone else cared. Madam had acted as Taylor's mother in every sense of the word. There was still Uncle Andrew, of course, but he wasn't at all like a father. He was her dear, eccentric, reclusive uncle, her playmate, actually, when she was a little girl and her dear friend now. Who else but Uncle Andrew would have insisted she live in a soddie for a month to find out if she had the gumption and fortitude it would take to live on the frontier if ever she had the chance. Yes, there was still Uncle Andrew she could write to, but it wasn't at all the same.

She missed her mama. The pain was staggering. She thought she'd been prepared to lose Madam. Oh, God, it hurt, so much in fact that she'd deliberately set out to seduce her husband in an attempt to find comfort . . . and love, mock though it would have been, just to ease the horrendous ache in her heart.

"Don't you want me, Lucas?"

He heard the catch in her voice. He couldn't believe she needed to ask the question. He wasn't very gentlemanly in giving his answer. He rolled onto his back, grabbed hold of her hand, and roughly placed it on his groin. Words weren't necessary after that. Taylor's reaction was just as he expected, too. She pulled her hand away as though she'd been burned.

She moved away from him and sat up. "Then why did you stop?"

He stacked his hands behind his head before answering. He counted to ten. He was fully occupied trying to keep himself from tearing his pants off and having his way with her.

"I didn't want you to stop."

He groaned. His jaw was clenched tight and his brow was covered with perspiration. In the darkness, Taylor could barely make out his expression. Tears were streaming down her cheeks. She wiped them away with the backs of her hands. She felt humiliated and miserable. She wanted to hide and weep and, oh, God, she wanted Madam back.

Taylor didn't say another word. She scooted over to the very edge of the bed, trying to get as far away from him as possible, then pulled the covers up. She squeezed herself into a ball, closed her eyes, and fought to keep herself from openly sobbing.

Several minutes passed in silence. She thought he'd fallen asleep. She wanted to leave the bedroom and go back to the parlor. She'd sleep on the lounge again. She knew she was close to losing her composure, for she could feel it disintegrating even now, and she didn't believe there could be anything more humiliating than breaking down in front of him. It had been many years since even Madam had seen her cry. She would have been appalled and ashamed of her granddaughter. Taylor didn't think she could bear it if Mr. Ross witnessed her grief. He would surely find her lack of discipline and control disgusting. She felt ashamed just thinking about the possibility.

She had to get out of there. She tossed the covers back, sat up, and started to swing her legs over the side of the bed. He caught her before she stood up. Taylor didn't even have time to struggle. Lucas moved with lightning speed. He pulled her across the bed, wrapped his arms around her waist, and flattened her against him. Her backside was snug against his groin. His chin rested on the top of her head. He wasn't going to let her go anywhere.

"Taylor?"

She wouldn't answer him. He wasn't deterred. "You wanted me to make love to you for all the wrong reasons."

She tried to move away. He tightened his hold. "You did want me, didn't you?"

She wasn't going to answer his question, but then he started squeezing her and she realized he wasn't going to let up until she gave him what he wanted.

"Yes, I did," she whispered.

"You would have regretted it in the morning."

She thought about his statement a long minute. Then she whispered, "Probably," just to appease him. She didn't believe it though. She wanted Lucas tonight with an intensity she'd never, ever experienced before. The way she was feeling terrified her. Taylor always wanted to be in control. She needed to be disciplined with her emotions and her reactions. Fear had done that to her. And Marian. Taylor had learned from her older sister. Marian hadn't just protected her from Uncle Malcolm's lust, she'd also taught her how to take every precaution imaginable, both mental and physical, to ensure that she would never become a victim to any man.

And then along came Lucas Ross. Taylor didn't know how to protect herself from him. She'd done just fine for quite a number of years, even became engaged to William Merritt and planned a wedding, all the while never giving even a part of her heart away to her fiancé. Although she was devastated by his betrayal, the truth of the matter was that the scandal and the humiliation were more appalling to her than the loss of William. She really hadn't been overly surprised, because Merritt had, after all, lived up to her expectations.

Lucas came from an altogether different kettle of fish. He wasn't at all like the other men she'd known. He was kind and caring and considerate, and oh, God, she really wished he'd stop it. Without even trying, he was tearing away all her shields, and she knew if she wasn't constantly on her guard, he'd sneak right in and steal her heart.

"Taylor?" His voice was a gruff whisper.

"Yes?" she whispered back.

"When I take you, you're only going to be thinking about me."

He rubbed his chin across the top of her head in a gentle caress. "You were thinking about your grandmother tonight. It's all right," he added. "You need to mourn."

She shook her head. "Madam told me I couldn't," she explained. She turned in his arms and rested the side of her face on his chest. "She made me promise I wouldn't wear black. I'm supposed to look to the future, not the past."

The sob caught her by surprise. Lucas rubbed her back and pulled her closer. "What else did she tell you?"

"To remember her," Taylor whispered. The tears were falling rapidly now. Taylor couldn't stop the flow. "She wanted me to tell the babies kind stories about her."

Lucas assumed she was talking about the babies she would have in the years to come. "She'll be remembered," he said then.

He didn't think Taylor had heard him. She was openly sobbing now and apologizing for her conduct every other minute.

"Sweetheart, it's all right to cry."

She didn't agree with his opinion, but she couldn't stop weeping long enough to tell him. She didn't know how long she carried on. It seemed forever to her. Then she got the hiccups, and God, she was a mess, crying all over Lucas and making the most horrendous, unladylike noises.

He didn't seem to mind. He got up, found a handkerchief, got back into bed, and handed it to her. After she'd mopped her face with the thing, he took it away from her, tossed it on the nightstand, and pulled her back into his arms. He was being extremely gentle. The kindness he was showing her only made her weep all the more. After a while, he tried to get her to calm down.

"Hush, love. It's all right."

He must have repeated that promise a good ten times. Nothing was ever going to be all right, she thought. Madam wasn't ever coming back. Taylor was now all alone and fully responsible for two two-year-olds, and Lucas Ross didn't know spit about what was going to be all right and what wasn't.

She was too drained to argue with him. She literally cried herself to sleep while she held onto her husband and let him comfort her. She felt safe and protected. Dear God, she never wanted to let go.

9

Fortune knows we scorn her most when
most she offers blows.
— William Shakespeare,
Antony and Cleopatra

*T*aylor overslept. Victoria came looking for her friend at half past eight o'clock. She was worried about Taylor and explained in a rush to Lucas the minute he opened the door that Taylor was late meeting her for breakfast. Was she ill or had she forgotten they were supposed to dine together in the Ladies Ordinary a half hour ago?

Lucas didn't tell Victoria about Taylor's grandmother. He shook his wife awake, then took over the task of escorting Victoria to breakfast. He wasn't hungry and therefore only ate a single portion of the sausages, fish, biscuits, gravy, baked apples with cinnamon, poached eggs, and potatoes. Victoria ate a single dry biscuit and a glass of freshly mashed and squeezed apple juice.

His wife's friend was nervous this morning. Since

she kept giving worried glances around the crowded dining room, he assumed she was concerned about the other diners. He tried to put her at ease, first by trying to get her to talk about her family. He realized his mistake the minute her eyes started getting misty. Talking about her parents and her friends back in London obviously upset her. Lucas then turned the topic around to her future in Boston. Victoria became even more agitated.

Someone let out a shrill squeak of laughter across the dining room. Victoria jumped a good foot in reaction, then cast a quick look over her shoulder. She had an intense frown on her face.

"Is something the matter?" he asked.

Before Victoria could answer his question, Taylor appeared at the table. Lucas immediately stood up and pulled the chair out for her. She thanked him without looking at him and then sat down.

She kept her gaze downcast but he could still see the faint blush on her cheeks. She was obviously embarrassed about something. He assumed it was because of the way he'd touched her the night before.

She was dressed entirely in black. He didn't care for the color on her and he didn't particularly like the notion that she was deliberately disregarding her grandmother's orders not to wear any colors of mourning.

Taylor's hair was all bound up behind her neck in a knot of some kind. The severe hairstyle made her face all the more flawless. He realized once again how breathtakingly beautiful she was, then found himself glancing around the room to make certain there weren't any male diners staring at her. She belonged to him, damn it all, and he wasn't about to let any other man give her lustful stares.

Lucas realized how ridiculous he was behaving almost immediately. He shook his head over his own contrary behavior and then started barking orders.

"Taylor, eat something. Victoria, tell me what's bothering you."

His wife insisted she wasn't hungry. She drank a full glass of milk, declared she was quite full, and folded her napkin to prove she was finished. She still wouldn't look at him. Lucas was exasperated with both women. He decided to deal with his wife first. He would find out what was bothering her and then take Victoria on. With that decision in mind, he reached over and covered Taylor's hand with one of his own. In a low voice he commanded her to look at him.

She took her time agreeing with the order. He patiently waited. And when she finally looked at him, he said, "You don't have anything to feel embarrassed about. Nothing much happened last night."

He was going to add the reminder that they were married, after all, and that a few kisses and a couple of caresses between a husband and wife was certainly nothing to get all worked up over or cause any embarrassment.

He never got the chance to give his logical argument. She gave him an incredulous look, then said, "I wept in front of you. Of course. I'm embarrassed and ashamed," she added with a nod. The blush intensified. "I promise it won't happen again. I'm usually very disciplined."

He didn't know what to say to that. He started to argue, then changed his mind. Victoria, he noticed, wasn't looking around the dining room any longer. She had become thoroughly engrossed in their conversation. She was glaring, too, and he seemed to be her target.

He wanted to ask her what the hell was wrong with her. Because of her delicate condition, he softened his question. "Is something wrong?"

"Did you make Taylor weep?"

He let out a sigh. She acted as though she believed he'd insulted his wife.

"No," he answered. "She was upset about something else." He decided he'd leave it to Taylor to explain about her grandmother.

"Victoria, have you finished your breakfast?" Taylor asked, trying to change the subject.

Victoria wasn't paying any attention to her friend now. Her attention was fully settled on Lucas. She seemed to be making her mind up about something or other, and just when he was about to get up from the table, she blurted out her request to stay where he was.

"If you knew your wife better, you'd realize she never, ever cries, Mr. Ross."

"Is that so?"

Victoria nodded. Her voice trembled with nervousness when she added, "She never eats anything for breakfast. She always has a glass of milk. You didn't know that either, did you?"

Although he wanted to, Lucas didn't dare smile. Victoria was becoming furious on Taylor's behalf. It was apparent she knew quite a bit about Taylor that he did not.

"She lived in a soddie for—"

Taylor cut her off. She wasn't about to let Victoria tell Lucas anything more about her training for the frontier. He'd start asking questions then, and she wasn't prepared to answer any of them.

"The bankers," she blurted out. "We have to meet Mr. Sherman and Mr. Summers at ten o'clock. Their offices are only a couple of blocks from here. I believe we should walk to the bank, don't you, Lucas?"

He nodded but kept his gaze on Victoria. "She lived in what?" he asked.

Victoria blushed. "Never mind," she replied. "Taylor, I would like to talk about something rather important if you have a minute now."

"Yes, of course," Taylor agreed, relieved the topic was being changed.

"I don't believe I can live in Boston."

After making the statement, Victoria lowered her gaze to the tabletop.

"All right then."

Victoria's head snapped up. "You aren't going to argue?"

Taylor smiled at the surprised look on her friend's face. "Of course I won't argue. You know better than anyone else what you can and cannot do, Victoria."

Her friend felt it necessary to explain. "I've already bumped into old acquaintances," she whispered.

Lucas heard her. He thought her explanation made about as much sense as Taylor's embarrassment over weeping did. "And meeting old friends is a problem?" he asked.

"Yes," Victoria and Taylor answered simultaneously.

He gave up trying to understand. He tossed his napkin on the table and stood up. "If you'll excuse me, I'm going back to our room. Taylor, you're changing your clothes before we go to the bank."

Lucas didn't give her time to argue. He turned around and left the dining hall. Victoria drew Taylor's attention then.

"Why are you wearing black?"

"In memory of my grandmother," Taylor answered. "I received a telegram last night. Madam died four days past. It took my uncle Andrew awhile to locate me," she added.

She'd tried to keep her voice very matter-of-fact, but she wasn't quite able to accomplish the feat. By the time she finished her explanation, she was close to weeping again.

Victoria didn't have any qualms about keeping her emotions under control. Madam would have been appalled by her conduct, Taylor thought, when her friend burst into tears. But she'd like her all the same, because undisciplined as she was, Victoria was extremely loyal to Taylor, and Madam believed loyalty was the second most important quality a person could have. It ranked much higher on her moral ruler than love, and only just an inch or two below the greatest quality of them all. Courage.

Taylor started aching inside. She did her best to hide her feelings, but the effort was fairly overwhelming. The other diners inadvertently helped her regain her composure. Several men and women had noticed Victoria's distress and were giving her curious glances. Taylor found their stares rude and uncivilized. She straightened in her chair, raised one hand, and dramatically waved them back to their own conversations. She added a good frown to ensure their cooperation.

Victoria was mopping the tears away from her face with her napkin. It was a wasted effort, for they just kept on coming.

" 'Honest plain words best pierce the ear of grief,' " Victoria quoted from memory in a whisper.

"William?" Taylor asked, though she knew full well who had written down that bit of advice.

"Yes," Victoria replied. "He was right, too. Plain words are best, and so I'll simply tell you how very sorry I am over your loss. I know Madam was like your mama and your heart must be breaking . . ."

She couldn't go on. She was crying in earnest now.

Taylor wasn't at all embarrassed by the scene her friend was making. She was actually humbled by Victoria's reaction. Taylor wasn't unaffected by her words of comfort either, and she had to take several deep breaths in order to get herself under control.

"You are a dear friend," she whispered once she could trust her voice enough not to break. "I am so fortunate to have found you."

"And I you," Victoria replied. Her voice was muffled by the napkin. " 'Everyone can mask a grief but he that has it,' " she added. "I can tell you're hurting."

Taylor didn't respond for the simple reason that she'd start crying if she did. The possibility was untenable. She wouldn't dare disgrace Madam's memory by breaking such a sacred rule and weeping in public. Taylor thought she'd die first.

" 'To weep is to make less the depth of grief,' " Victoria quoted.

Madam, Taylor thought, wouldn't have agreed with that quote from Shakespeare. She decided to try and lighten the conversation. "And you believe that because your William has written down that dictate, I cannot argue with you?"

Victoria managed a smile. "No, you cannot argue. William is an authority after all."

"Do you know what I'm going to do?"

"What?"

"I'm going to walk to the nearest bookstore and purchase every single one of William Shakespeare's works. I've read him, of course, but I haven't taken the time to memorize every word the way you have. In a month or two, I promise I'll be able to use your William to my advantage whenever I want you to agree with me."

Victoria looked thrilled. She obviously didn't understand that Taylor was teasing her. "I shall be happy to lend you my copies," she said fervently.

Taylor thanked her, then motioned to one of the waiters and ordered a cup of tea for each of them. The dining room had cleared sufficiently for them to have enough privacy to talk.

"Victoria, if you don't wish to live in or near Boston, where would you like to go?"

"With you." She blurted out her answer and then blushed. "If you'll have me," she hastily added. "And if Mr. Ross doesn't care."

"I would love to have your company," Taylor replied. She stopped then to gather her thoughts.

Victoria misunderstood her hesitation. Her shoulders slumped in dejection. "But you don't think it's a good idea. I understand. A pregnant woman would be a burden to you and—"

Taylor interrupted her. "Do let me finish," she insisted. "More than anything in the world I would love to have you come with me. You've become like family."

"But there is a problem all the same?"

Taylor nodded. The waiter appeared with their china setting. He placed the flowered teapot on the table, added two cups and saucers, and then bowed before leaving them alone again.

Taylor poured the tea before continuing. "You cannot make a decision until you know all the facts. You have to understand where I'm going and why. After I've explained—"

"About the babies?" Victoria interrupted with the question.

"Yes," Taylor answered. "Georganna and Alexandra are my older sister's children. The babies are two and a half years old now. Marian . . . my sister, died just a short while after settling in Boston. The children have been under the care of their father, George. He died a little over a month ago. He didn't have any family to speak of, and so the babies have been watched over by their nanny, Mrs. Bartlesmith."

"'When sorrows come, they come not as single spies, but in battalions.'"

Taylor nodded agreement. Shakespeare was right about that. Sorrows did come in battalions.

"Will you take the little ones back to England?"

"No," Taylor answered. "In fact, I want to take them as far away from England as possible. My sister was afraid of our uncle Malcolm. She had good reason to fear him," she added. "She didn't want her daughters near the vile man, and that was her main reason for moving to Boston. Her husband, George, was from America, and he was in full agreement with her determination."

"Are you afraid of your uncle?" Victoria asked.

Taylor felt compelled to be completely honest with her friend. "I would be a fool not to be afraid of him. He's a very evil man."

"Would he harm the babies?"

"Eventually, yes, he would."

"How?"

Taylor shook her head. "I cannot talk about Malcolm without becoming sick to my stomach. However, now that George is dead and Madam, too, the question of guardianship becomes a worry. Uncle Malcolm would petition the court to put the girls in his care, and I would kill him before I let that happen. The little ones would be safer with Lucifer. I'm praying Malcolm has forgotten all about the babies. We didn't inform him of George's death, and because Madam didn't leave any money for the twins, I'm hopeful he won't make trouble. I'm not going to take any chances though. I'm going to have to disappear, Victoria. Don't you see? Until the babies are old enough to fend for themselves, I'm responsible for them. Marian protected me all those years. Now I must protect her daughters."

"I fear disappearing will be most difficult," Victoria said. "The world has grown so small. We have the telegram now and steam vessels that can travel from London to America in less than two weeks. There are trains connecting almost every city, and—"

"I have considered all of this," Taylor told her. "At first I thought I would take the girls to some distant city, but I've changed my mind. There is one place Malcolm won't ever look, and that is the frontier. Mr. Ross told me about a place called Redemption. He said a man could walk for a mile and never meet another person. The babies and I could get lost there."

"In your heart . . . do you believe your uncle will try to find you?"

Taylor nodded. "I don't believe it's an unreasonable fear," she said. "He would like to hurt me. He's a spiteful, vengeful man. He has a scar that crisscrosses his left eye. He almost lost his sight. I gave him that scar, Victoria, when I was just ten years old. I'm only sorry I didn't blind him. Every time he looks in the mirror, he's reminded of what I did to him . . . and why. He'll try to find me all right. I imagine he's been counting the days until he can take over the inheritance and the estates . . . and me."

Victoria shivered. She was beginning to understand what Taylor wasn't telling her. She decided to take a roundabout way of finding out if her guess were accurate.

"If the twins were boys, would Marian have been so obsessed with running away?"

"No."

Victoria let out a sigh. "Is Malcolm a vain man?"

"Yes."

Victoria smiled. "Good," she announced. "And is the scar as unsightly as I hope it is?"

"Yes."

"Very good."

Taylor nodded. She decided she'd said quite enough. Victoria, even though pregnant, was still very innocent in Taylor's estimation. She couldn't possibly understand the twisted appetites of some men. Taylor barely understood herself. Her friend would be appalled and disgusted to know the full truth.

"It's quite ironic," she said then. "My greatest dream was to one day live in the wilderness. Uncle Andrew embraced the notion. Every time I visited him, he would have read something new to teach me. He believed in my dream and wanted me to be prepared. It was a game we played, I suppose."

"Like building a soddie and making you live in it?" Victoria asked.

"Yes," Taylor agreed with a smile. "His servants thought I was as peculiar as he was. It didn't matter. It was just a game."

"Do you know what I think? In your heart you've always known you were going to live in the wilderness of America someday. The twins complicated your plans, and that is why you considered a smaller city somewhere in the West."

"I did think I would eventually end up in the mountains. Ever since I read the first story about Daniel Boone, I was . . ."

"Intrigued?"

"Yes, intrigued."

"I'll do whatever I can to help you," Victoria pledged. "Tell me this, please. What does Lucas say about—"

"He doesn't know anything about Malcolm or the babies, and you must promise not to say a word to him."

"For heaven's sake, Taylor. Think this through. Don't you think he'll notice you're living in Redemption?"

Taylor laughed. "Of course he'll notice, but by then it will be too late. If he finds out my plans now, he'll try to stop me. He doesn't believe I can survive in the wilderness. He thinks I should concentrate on what gowns to wear to the parties in Boston. Can you imagine anything so ludicrous?"

Victoria smiled. Now that she knew Taylor better, it was ludicrous to believe she would fritter her days away on frivolity.

"I want to disappear with you. Hear me out before you caution me. I'm young and strong and somewhat intelligent. I'll do just fine in the wilderness."

"What about the baby? Have you considered what it will be like giving birth in a soddie?"

"Other women have," Victoria argued.

"We're going to have to discuss this at length," Taylor said. "Perhaps it would be better if you join me after the baby's born. It would certainly be safer."

Victoria clasped her hands together. "Then you agree, now or later, I can move to Redemption?"

"Do you have any idea what you're getting into?"

"Yes."

Taylor let out a sigh. Then she nodded. "I believe we should have a toast." She raised her cup of tea, waited until Victoria had done the same, then whispered, "To the wilderness and our new life."

Their cups tapped against each other. "And to freedom," Victoria interjected.

"Taylor, we're going to be late."

Lucas made the announcement. Taylor was so engrossed in the conversation, she hadn't noticed her husband had entered the dining hall.

He didn't look very happy. She forced a smile in an attempt to offset his frown. "We still have plenty of time," she told him.

"I want to get this done," he replied. He took hold of her arm and half dragged her to her feet. "This shouldn't take too long, should it? I'm meeting a friend at noon. I'd hate to cancel out on him. He's got a sound stallion he's interested in selling."

"The meeting shouldn't take more than an hour," Taylor answered. "Victoria, I'll come down to your room as soon as I'm finished with the bankers. Perhaps we should go shopping this afternoon. Will you join us, Mr. Ross?"

Lucas was following the two ladies out into the corridor. The thought of shopping with the two of them made him want to grimace.

"I have an appointment," he reminded Taylor.

"All afternoon?"

"And most of the evening," he said. "The farm is outside Boston. It will take a couple of hours to get there. I won't be back to the hotel before eight."

"Mr. Ross, why are you sounding so cantankerous?"

"I hate being kept waiting."

"So do I," she told him in a gratingly cheerful voice.

"I don't think we should shop, Taylor," Victoria interjected. "You're in mourning."

"She isn't supposed to mourn," Lucas announced. "She promised her grandmother."

"I'm going to find a church and light a candle for her," Taylor said.

"I'm certain she'll like that," Victoria gave her approval.

Taylor wasn't in the mood to shop, but there was a

multitude of items she needed to purchase for the little girls. In truth, all she wanted to do was see the twins. Time was the issue, of course, and she knew she needed to get everything done as soon as possible.

Because Lucas had made plans for the afternoon and early evening, Taylor decided to go and visit the twins. Lucas would never know she'd left the hotel. She wouldn't have to hurry her visit either, she realized, and found herself smiling in anticipation. If luck stayed on her side, she might even be able to talk Mrs. Bartlesmith into going with her and the babies. The notion was highly unlikely, but any hope, no matter how small, was worth a try.

Taylor didn't have any intention of being specific with the nanny until they were well on their way. The less anyone knew about her true destination, the better. She might even hint they were headed for Texas.

Victoria turned in one direction at the landing on their floor, and Taylor and Lucas turned down the opposite corridor. Her husband's long-legged stride was impossible to match without running, and she refused to run in such an elegant hotel.

"Please slow down or let go of me and I'll follow behind you."

Lucas immediately let go of her. He walked ahead, unlocked the door, and then stood there waiting for her.

"Ever heard the expression 'slow as molasses'?" he asked.

Taylor went inside the bedroom before answering. "No."

"It applies to you."

Taylor ignored the barb. She went into the bedroom alcove in search of the papers she wanted to take along to the bankers. She'd made a considerable list of questions to ask and didn't want to forget any of them. Everything had to be settled before she disappeared . . . and before Lucas went back to his mountains.

She collected the papers, folded them, then went in search of her gloves. Lucas blocked her path.

"I meant it, Taylor. I want you to change out of that godawful dress."

"It's appropriate attire."

"You gave your grandmother your word," he argued. He went over to her wardrobe and pulled the doors open. Then he began to sort through her clothes. He wasn't certain why it mattered to him, but she'd given her word, and by God she was going to keep it. A last request had to be honored, and Lucas was going to see that it was.

He grabbed a dress and hanger and turned to Taylor. "Here, wear this. Hurry, we'll be late."

She almost laughed when she saw the gown he'd chosen. "Red? You want me to wear a red dress."

"It will do."

She laughed. "It's an evening gown, sir, and not at all appropriate."

"I like it," he insisted. "And so would your grandmother."

He was walking toward her with the dress in hand. The man was out of his mind if he thought she was going to wear a velvet evening gown to meet the bankers.

"It doesn't fit properly," she lied.

"You're wearing it," he said again.

"Madam would not approve."

She folded her arms across her chest and stood her ground. She wasn't going to give in, and that was that.

From the stubborn set of his jaw, she concluded he wasn't going to give in either. It appeared they had reached a stalemate. Then he went and weighed the argument in his favor.

"Of course Madam would approve. They wear bright colors in heaven, Taylor. I'm sure of it. Now put the thing on. We're going to be late."

She was overwhelmed by what he'd just said to her. He was being completely outrageous. And wonderful. They wear bright colors in heaven. Without a doubt, that was the nicest thing he could have said to her. It wasn't the color or the dress or even what they wore up there, if indeed they wore anything at all, it was the fact that he believed Madam had made it to heaven.

"Lucas Ross, you're a very charming man. Did you know Madam called you my prince when she first told me about you?"

He was exasperated with her. She wasn't making any sense, talking such nonsense. Her voice had turned as soft and soothing as a gentle summer breeze. He couldn't imagine what had caused the sudden transformation. One minute she was shaking her head at him and frowning like an old maid schoolmarm, and the next she was looking like she was going to start crying or kiss him. He didn't know what had come over her, but he was determined to set her straight on this charming business.

"Taylor, I'm neither a prince nor am I charming. I'm only being a gentleman to accommodate you. It's a damn strain," he added. "Honest to God, I don't know how much longer I can keep up the pretense."

She didn't believe him. "Oh?" she challenged. "Pray tell me please, what would you do now, this very minute, if you weren't behaving in a gentlemanly fashion."

"Do you mean tell you what I'd really like to do?"

"Yes."

He grinned. "Get you naked."

She turned as red as the dress. He laughed. "You wanted me to be honest, didn't you?"

"Yes, of course." He had her so rattled, she couldn't think straight. "I'll wear the dress," she stammered out. "With a coat on top." A black coat, she silently added, and one that would cover her from head to ankle. She wasn't going to take the wrap off either, no matter how hot it was inside the banker's building.

She snatched the dress out of his hands and turned to go back into the alcove to change. "It's horribly low cut," she remarked. "I do tend to spill out of the thing."

He reached over her shoulder and grabbed the dress out of her hands.

Taylor ended up wearing a white blouse and navy blue skirt. Lucas was pacing by the time she had added a brightly colored ribbon to her hair.

As it turned out, they were five minutes early. Lucas was quick to point out they would have been late if he hadn't insisted they take a carriage to their destination.

Mr. Harry Sherman met them at the door of the bank. He escorted them into the president's office where Mr. Peter Summers waited for them. Sherman was the elder of the two gentlemen. In England, he'd been a good friend as well as an advisor to Madam for long years. He was almost as old, close to sixty, but five years ago, and just one month after his wife of twenty years had finally succumbed to a long, debilitating illness, he announced he was leaving England. He wanted an adventure, he explained, and had volunteered to help with the opening of the bank's Boston branch. Madam had been astounded, for she believed Harry to be set in his ways. She supported his decision, however, and even helped him get established by depositing a large amount in the American branch. They had stayed friends and wrote to each other at least once every two weeks.

Madam had always said that Sherman had the brains in the business and Summers had the charisma. Her grandmother had certainly been right with her evaluation, Taylor thought with a smile as Peter Summers oozed compliment after compliment. He was as slick as oil and as sincere as a sweet-talking dandy. Taylor didn't remember ever being introduced to Summers, but he assured her they had met. She'd been quite young, he recalled, and had hung onto her grandmother's skirts most of the time he was there. He tried but couldn't coax a smile out of her.

"Your behavior was quite amusing," he told her. "And a bit peculiar. Your uncle Malcolm was there, but each time he left the library, you let go of your grandmother's skirts and became quite the imp. You were into one thing after another. Your grandmother was very indulgent. She let you have free rein. You were busy digging through her desk, looking for treasures I suppose, but the minute your uncle returned to the study, you hightailed it back to your grandmother's skirts again. The pattern was repeated several times, as your uncle was coming and going every other ten minutes or so. I believe he was indulging in a drink or two of whiskey out in the hallway."

"Probably," Taylor replied. "Madam wouldn't allow anyone to drink any spirits in her company."

The banker continued to recollect one humorous incident after another. All involved Taylor's odd behavior around her uncle Malcolm.

She wasn't smiling over the memories. Lucas wondered how long it would take Summers to realize she didn't find anything amusing about her uncle. She'd been afraid of him when she was a little girl. Lucas listened to the stories and came to that easy conclusion. What surprised him was that Taylor was still afraid of the man. The way she clenched her hands together, added to the look in her eyes, indicated her fear bordered on terror.

He was about to change the topic when Summers finished with his recollections and asked Taylor if she'd had a calm voyage from London. Sherman joined in the conversation. Lucas stood behind his wife while the two gentlemen continued to fawn over her. They were harmless enough, he supposed, but he still didn't like the way the younger man stared at Taylor.

Harry Sherman waited until Taylor was once again engaged in conversation with his colleague, then motioned Lucas to the back of the room. In a low voice he asked if Taylor had heard about her grandmother's death.

"Her uncle Andrew sent a telegram," he explained.

Sherman looked relieved. "I hated to be the one to tell her. The two of them were very close, like mother and daughter. I can barely take it in myself. I'll miss her."

Taylor was just taking her seat when Sherman asked Lucas if she were up to going over all the details in the will. "Her grandmother made several changes, and I don't believe Taylor is aware of all the ramifications. The terms are going to cause quite a stir in the family. Mark my words, there's going to be trouble."

An hour later, after all the conditions had been explained, Taylor was feeling sick to her stomach.

Lucas thought she'd become ill. She looked ready to pass out. Her complexion had turned as white as her gloves. Summers had already left his office in search of witnesses to the documents Taylor would have to sign, and Sherman, observing the swift change in his client, went to fetch a glass of water for her. He told Lucas grief was surely the culprit, and talking about dear Lady Esther's last wishes was simply proving to be too much for Taylor to endure.

Lucas sat next to Taylor. He waited until they were alone, then reached over and took hold of her hand.

"Are you going to be all right?"

She didn't answer him. She was staring down at her hands and seemed to be lost in thought.

He squeezed her hand to get her attention, and when that action didn't get any response, he reached over and took hold of her chin. He gently nudged her to look at him.

There were tears in her eyes. She was trembling. Taylor wasn't battling her grief. She was fighting her fear. Her eyes told the truth. She was terrified all right, and he was determined to find out why.

"Oh, Lucas, what has Madam done?" She grabbed hold of his hand and held tight.

He was taken aback by the question. "Are you upset because she left so much of her money to charities, Taylor?" He answered his own question before she could. "No, of course you aren't. You probably suggested she divide her fortune in such a manner. You're still going to receive quite a lot of money. Didn't you expect it?"

"Madam shouldn't have done it. Don't you see? He'll have to come after me now. He won't have any choice. He'll do anything to get the money."

She had a death grip on his hand. She was getting all worked up, and he didn't have a clue as to what to say or do to calm her down. She was going to have to explain the threat before he could confront it.

Taylor turned her gaze back to her lap. She knew she

had to get her emotions under control. Lucas must think she was out of her mind.

"I'm feeling better now," she lied. She managed a weak smile and looked up at him.

He was frowning with concern. "I'm sorry," she blurted out. "I didn't mean to go on and on like that. It was just such a surprise. I'm fine now, really."

He wasn't buying that nonsense for a minute. "You asked the question, What am I going to do? You're married now, Taylor. The question therefore becomes, What are we going to do? Got that?"

He sounded gruff and looked angry. He was acting very like a prince again, she thought.

Her Prince Charming. Lord, whatever had she done to the man? He deserved better. He shouldn't have been saddled with a marriage he didn't want and relatives like Malcolm.

He squeezed her hand then and she realized he was waiting for an answer. She nodded just to placate him. "Yes, I've got it," she said. "The question should be, What are we going to do?"

He grunted. She guessed that meant he was satisfied. "You're a very charming man, Lucas Ross, even when you make those obscene sounds in the back of your throat."

He shook his head at her. He wasn't going to let her change the subject.

"Tell me what it is we have to do something about. I can't help you until I know what the problem is."

"Yes, of course."

He waited a full minute before he realized she wasn't going to say another word.

He decided he would have to prod the worry out of her. "You said, he'll come after you for the money. You were referring to your uncle Malcolm, weren't you?"

She looked up at him and slowly nodded.

"Now that you're married, he can't touch your inheritance."

"I realize that."

She tried to stand up. He stopped her by grabbing hold of her.

"Not so fast," he ordered. "Tell me why you're upset."

She was saved from having to answer him when Summers and Sherman came back into the office. Sherman handed her a glass of water. Lucas had to let go of her hands so she could accept the drink. She took advantage of the opportunity and stood up. She took a sip of the water, handed the glass back to the banker with a thank you for his kindness, and then walked across the office to stand near the window. She folded her arms across her waist, her gaze on the pedestrians rushing back and forth on the street below.

Summers took his seat behind the desk. He turned in his chair to look at his client.

"My dear, you're going to have to sign a few papers in order to gain access to your funds."

She turned around. "What happens if I refuse to sign?"

Summers thought she was jesting with him. The notion that anyone would deliberately turn down any amount of money made him smile.

"It wouldn't matter if you signed or not," he said. "It's really just a formality for the bank's records. The money will stay in trust, earning you a handsome figure in interest if you decide not to spend any of it now."

"Please give me the particulars again. How exactly is the money divided?" she asked.

"Two-thirds of the estate goes to charities, as I explained earlier," Summers said.

She impatiently brushed her hair back. "Yes, yes, the charities. I knew about the charities, but Uncle Malcolm . . . You said he doesn't get the rest. I don't understand. Are you telling me Madam didn't leave her son anything?"

"Let's take this a step at a time," Sherman suggested. He could tell Taylor was extremely anxious and was trying to calm her down by being methodical.

"The third left after donations to her charities still amounts to a sizable sum, my dear. Your great-uncle Andrew will receive a nice allowance and title to the estate in Scotland. The rest is split between you and the children."

Taylor closed her eyes. "Was Madam specific or did she simply say children," she asked.

"She was quite specific. Georganna and Alexandra Henson each receive one-third." Summers turned to Lucas. "The twin girls are Lady Esther's great-granddaughters."

"Has the will been read in London yet?" Taylor asked.

"The reading is scheduled for Tuesday," Summers answered.

"Tomorrow," Sherman said at the same time.

"Didn't Madam leave anything to her son and his family?" Taylor asked.

"Yes," Summers replied. "But it's barely a pittance."

"Not quite so," Sherman argued. "Malcolm will receive a small monthly stipend. It isn't much, but if he adopts a frugal lifestyle, he should get along all right. Lady Esther left Malcolm's wife exactly one hundred pounds. She said it was the amount of weight her daughter-in-law had put on since she married her son. Madam did have a rather twisted sense of humor," he added. He turned to Lucas to once again explain. "Lady Esther didn't much care for Loreen. Said she was a complainer."

"What about Jane?" Taylor asked. "Did Madam leave her anything?"

"She gets the same amount as her mother," Sherman answered. "Exactly one hundred pounds and not a shilling more."

Taylor shook her head. She was filled with dread for the future. "When Malcolm finds out what his mother has done, his roar will cross the ocean. He'll be outraged."

Sherman, who knew Malcolm better than Summers did, nodded agreement. "He'll try to cause trouble, all right. I warned your grandmother, but she wouldn't listen to reason. She told her legal advisers to make certain the will was airtight."

"What about Malcolm's lands?" Taylor asked.

"As you probably know, he had already mortgaged the property. Your grandmother assigned enough money to pay off all of her son's considerable debts. The total is just above fifty thousand pounds."

Lucas seemed to be the only one in the office astonished by the figure. How could any man owe others so much? What had he purchased on credit?

Taylor inadvertently answered his question. "He won't quit gambling," she predicted.

"Your grandmother was well aware of his vice. She decided to give him one last fresh start. If he chooses to run his credit up again, he'll have to find another method to repay. His mother's estate won't bail him out."

"Oh, he'll find another way," Taylor whispered. "Uncle can be very creative."

"Now, now, don't borrow trouble," Summers advised.

Taylor's shoulders slumped. "I know what you're

thinking, my dear," said Sherman. "He won't last a month without trying to beg or borrow from you." He turned to Summers then to give further explanation. "Malcolm's a man of excesses. He won't take this sitting down."

"He'll come after me."

She looked at Lucas when she made the statement. He appeared to be half asleep. His long legs were stretched out in front of him, his hands rested on the side arms, and his eyes were half closed.

"It won't matter," Summers insisted. "Even if you wanted to give him some of the inheritance, you can't. Your grandmother was very specific. What you don't spend will stay in trust for your children."

"And if I die?" Taylor asked.

Lucas took exception to the question. "You aren't going to die."

"But if I did?" She directed her question to Harry Sherman.

"Malcolm still won't get the money. Your husband is the only one who stands to gain." He paused to smile. "From the emphatic way he just spoke to you, I can only surmise he'll do whatever it takes to make certain you live a long, healthy life. Stop this talk about dying, Taylor. Malcolm can't hurt you. You don't have to be afraid of him any longer. I, too, remember what you were like as a little girl. You were certainly frightened of your uncle. But you're all grown up now and married. Put your childhood fears to rest. England, remember, is an ocean away."

"Yes, you're right." She feigned a smile so he'd believe he'd swayed her with his argument to let go of her worry.

They finally got down to the business at hand. Taylor signed the necessary papers, and when the forms had been witnessed and executed, she opened two accounts. One was a joint account in her name and Mr. Ross's, which required both their signatures, and the other account was in Victoria's name.

Mr. Sherman agreed to bring the necessary papers over to the hotel at four o'clock to meet with Victoria and gain her signature. "You've been extremely generous with your friend," he remarked as Taylor was getting ready to leave. She was in the midst of putting her gloves on. Lucas held her coat.

"Madam would approve," she replied.

A few minutes later they were on their way back to their hotel. Taylor wanted to walk. Lucas told her he didn't have time. He wouldn't let her stroll down the street by herself either but insisted she ride with him back to the hotel. He hailed a vehicle, assisted her inside, and then took the seat across from her.

He didn't ease into the topic he wanted to discuss. "Why are you afraid of your uncle?"

She didn't soften her answer. "He's a snake."

"And?"

"I hate snakes."

He smiled in spite of his frustration. The woman had a way with words and an even better way of avoiding direct answers. She would make him crazy if he stayed around long enough to let her.

"When are you leaving Boston?"

He wasn't going anywhere until he was certain she was going to be all right. God only knew when that would be. He was anxious to get going, yet the thought of leaving her made his stomach turn. The truth was staring him in the eyes. He didn't want to go anywhere without her.

He immediately tried to block the notion. He wasn't ready to accept what part of him was insisting was inevitable. He blanched inside and might have even shuddered. No, he wasn't ready to think about anything remotely permanent.

And yet the truth persisted.

Taylor wasn't certain what had come over her husband. He was giving her that mean I'd-rather-be-hanged-than-married-to-you look she was really starting to dislike intensely, and she didn't think she would have been surprised if he'd started growling like a bear.

Her mind took a leap from that thought to another. "Are there any bears in Montana Territory?"

Where had that question come from? "Yes."

"I thought there were, but I wanted to be certain. What kind is most prevalent?"

"The black," he answered. "And the brown, I suppose."

"What about the grizzly?"

"Those too."

"They're terribly clever."

"Is that so?"

Taylor nodded. "They're known to hunt the hunter. They circle back on their stalker. They're mean spirited, too. Daniel Boone killed a good dozen before he was ten years old."

Lord, she was naive. "Is that so?"

"Every time you say, Is that so? you're really saying you don't believe a word I'm telling you. Isn't that right, Mr. Ross?"

He didn't bother to answer her. The vehicle stopped in front of the hotel. Lucas helped her out, paid the fare, then grabbed hold of her hand and dragged her through the lobby.

"I'm perfectly capable of getting to our room on my own, Mr. Ross. Do let go of me."

"You draw a crowd wherever you go," he countered, continuing to pull her along.

She snorted. "You're the popular one, not me."

He was taking the steps two at a time. Taylor was out of breath by the time they reached their floor. "Do people call you by any special name?"

"Lucas," he interrupted. "My friends call me Lucas. And so does my wife. Got that?"

They reached the door to their room. He was digging in his pocket for his key. Taylor collapsed against the wall. If she'd had a fan handy, she would have used it. She hadn't had to run like that for ages.

"It would be greatly disrespectful of me to call you Lucas, but if you insist . . ."

"Why?"

He'd just put the key in the lock but stopped and turned to look at her. He only then realized she was out of breath. He couldn't help but smile. A wisp of hair had fallen out of her prim bun and now curled in front of her ear. She looked utterly feminine. And thoroughly kissable.

They stood just inches away from each other. Taylor couldn't seem to take her gaze off her husband. He had the most adorable smile. His eyes seemed to turn a warm, golden brown. A lesser woman would have melted under his close scrutiny, but she was made of stronger stuff. She let out a long sigh.

"Aren't you going to answer me?" he asked.

She couldn't remember the question. He was forced to repeat it. "Wives in the wilderness call their husbands mister whatever as a way of lifting their status. The hired hands are called by their first names. It's the respectful thing to do."

He didn't look like he believed her. His question confirmed that guess.

"Says who?"

"Mrs. Livingston," she answered. "It was in her journal."

"I should have guessed."

"And while we're on the subject of what is considered proper and what isn't, I would like to point out that the majority of men, married and single, never, ever curse in front of a woman. It's considered bad form, Mr. Ross, and very disrespectful."

"Is that so?"

She was beginning to hate that expression. "Yes, it is so."

He opened the door for her, but just as she started to go inside, he grabbed hold of her shoulders and turned her around.

His head was bent toward her. "Let me get this straight. When you call me Mr. Ross, you're actually being respectful and not trying to infuriate me? Is that right?"

She nodded. He smiled. He didn't let go of her. For a man in a hurry, he was suddenly acting as though he had all the time in the world. Taylor really wished she could stop herself from staring at him. Was it her imagination or had his skin become even more bronzed in the last twenty-four hours? She wondered if he had any idea how handsome he was.

"I'll probably be late."

His right hand moved to the side of her neck. His fingers brushed the strand of hair back behind her ear. A shiver passed down her arms. She had to force herself not to lean into his hand. She couldn't stop staring into his eyes.

He was staring at her mouth. "Don't wait up for me."

"I'll probably spend the evening in Victoria's room," she said. It was a lie, of course, but since she wasn't certain how long it would take to reach Mrs. Bartlesmith's residence or how long she would spend getting acquainted with her nieces, she decided to play it safe. She didn't want Lucas looking for her. "Victoria has quite a few things she wants to discuss," she said. "I could be there until midnight, maybe even later."

He barely paid attention to what she was saying. He wanted to kiss her. He was patiently waiting for her to finish talking so he could.

She took a breath and he leaned down. The thought that he might kiss her had only just registered in her mind when she leaned into him and tilted her head back. His mouth was just an inch away.

A door slammed somewhere down the corridor. A man's laughter sounded in the next instant. Then a woman's. The spell Lucas Ross had cast upon her lifted, and she suddenly realized where she was and what she was doing. She was immediately horrified by her unladylike behavior.

She acted as though she'd just been caught stealing. She literally pushed herself away from him, bumped into the wall behind her, then turned and hurried inside. She called good-bye over her shoulder and swung the door shut.

Lucas couldn't believe what had just happened. Damned if she hadn't just slammed the door in his face. And what in thunder caused her to blush?

"Women," he muttered to himself. Most didn't make a lick of sense. He shook his head and started down the hallway. He stopped when he reached the steps.

Taylor had just collapsed in one of the chairs and let out a loud sigh when a knock sounded at the door. She assumed it was Victoria. She stood up, straightened her skirt, and then hurried across the room. She forced a smile so her friend wouldn't know she was in such an irritable mood and all because she hadn't been kissed and then opened the door.

Lucas filled up the entrance. He was leaning against the door frame, one foot crossed over the other, with his arms folded across his chest, as though he'd been lounging there a long, long time. He was frowning intently.

"Did you forget something, Mr. Ross?"

"Yeah," he drawled. Then he moved. It happened so quickly, she didn't even have time to gasp. He reached out, grabbed hold of the back of her neck with his right hand, and hauled her up against him. His fingers threaded through her hair, the pins holding it up flying every which way. The heavy mass of curls cascaded down her back, covering his arm. His fingers gently pressed against her scalp. He lowered his face until his mouth was directly above hers.

"I forgot to kiss you."

"Oh."

She whispered the word into his opened mouth. It sounded like a groan. His mouth settled on top of hers with blatant ownership, effectively sealing off any other sound she might have made. He kissed her ravenously. Taylor grabbed hold of his jacket so she wouldn't fall down. And when his tongue swept inside her mouth and rubbed so erotically against hers, she felt as though she were dissolving in his arms. Her knees went weak and her heart started pounding a wild beat. She felt hot and yet was shivering at the same time. Her arms found their way around his waist. She held onto Lucas and let him sweep her off her feet. She didn't even try to control her own passionate response. She wouldn't let him stop. She wanted another hot, opened-mouth, tongue-dueling kiss, and Lucas, shaken by her uninhibited reaction to his touch, didn't deny her. They were both just as hungry for each other. She made it impossible for him to hold back. His mouth slanted over hers again and again, and each time the kiss was longer, more sinfully erotic. He was hard and hot. And still he wanted more. His hands moved down her spine, rubbing, caressing. He cupped her sweet backside and lifted her up on her tiptoes until they were intimately rubbing against each other. She instinctively cuddled his arousal between her hips. She moved restlessly against him.

She was making him burn with desire. He knew he had to stop. He'd take her in the corridor if he didn't find a little discipline to pull away from her. God, she was good. He was fast losing all control, and damn but she felt right pressed up against him. She was all soft and feminine, and Lord above, could she kiss.

He was abrupt in his departure. He jerked back, then began to peel her hands off him. He knew he had to put some distance between them with all possible haste, but he made the mistake of looking at her, and when he saw the passion in her eyes, he almost lost the battle. Her lips were rosy and swollen from his none too gentle attack, and all he could think about was tasting her one more time.

Lucas clinched his jaw in frustration. She had the most bemused expression on her face. He found himself arrogantly pleased. She'd obviously been just as affected by their kisses as he'd been. He would have told her to move back so he could pull the door closed when he left, but he didn't think she'd move quick enough to suit him . . . or save her virginity.

She couldn't possibly know how close he was to carrying her to their bed and making love to her.

Taylor was simply too naive and inexperienced to understand her own jeopardy. He understood all right. He was hard and throbbing and aching, and damn it all, if she didn't quit looking at him with those beautiful blue eyes, he knew exactly what was going to happen.

He had to get the hell away from her. With that single thought in mind, he grabbed hold of her shoulders, forced her to move back, then turned around, took hold of the doorknob, and pulled it shut behind him.

She was left staring at the door. "Oh, my," she whispered. She suddenly needed to sit down. She needed a fan, too. It had gotten warm all of a sudden.

Taylor started to cross the room to get to the nearest chair so she could collapse properly when another knock sounded at the door.

Lord, she wasn't up to another round of kissing. Yet she found she was running to the door to answer the summons.

Victoria was standing in the corridor. Taylor could barely hide her disappointment. She invited her friend in, then ushered her over to the seating arrangement in front of the windows.

"Are you feeling ill, Taylor?" she asked. Her voice was filled with concern.

"I'm fine, really. Why do you ask?"

"You look all flushed."

No wonder, Taylor thought. In an effort to keep Victoria from asking embarrassing questions, she changed the subject. "We can't shop this afternoon," she announced. "Mr. Sherman wishes to meet with you in the lobby downstairs at four o'clock. You have to sign some papers, Victoria."

"Why?"

"I told you I was opening an account in your name.

He'll need your signature so you can withdraw funds, of course."

Victoria nodded. "I would thank you again. Your generosity is . . . overwhelming."

Taylor accepted the compliment with a nod, then told her about her plans for the afternoon. "I'm going to write down instructions I wish you to give Mr. Sherman, then I'm going to go see my nieces. I had planned to see them yesterday, but Mr. Ross didn't leave for his appointment until after eight. He would have wanted to know where I was going if I left before he did, and once he'd gone along to meet his friend, it was too late. The little ones were surely already in bed for the night. I can't wait to hold them again. It's better that we go shopping after I've seen them so that I'll have measured their sizes for the amount of cloth I'll need to buy. They're going to need plenty of heavy winter clothes," she added.

"But it isn't even spring yet," Victoria protested.

"We must think ahead," Taylor advised. "We won't be able to get everything we'd like living in the wilderness, and so we must go as prepared as possible. I believe you should start your list as well."

Victoria agreed with a nod. "Your enthusiasm is contagious. Redemption means a brand-new start for me and my baby. I, too, feel I'll be very safe there. What a contradiction that is. There will be wild animals, harsh weather, hostile Indians, and heaven only knows what else, and honestly, Taylor, I cannot wait to get started. I believe I'll go back to my room and start my list immediately after luncheon. Will you go up to the Ladies Ordinary with me? I could use a biscuit to settle my stomach. I seem to have become afflicted with morning sickness in the middle of the day."

Taylor was happy to accompany her friend. They

spent another hour together, and as soon as they finished eating, Taylor told her about the route they would take to reach their destination. Victoria was surprised to learn they would go most of the way by riverboat up the Missouri.

"We must remember to purchase maps when we go shopping," Taylor suggested.

"Will you explain something, please? Does your great-uncle Andrew . . . He is your grandmother's younger brother, isn't he?"

"Yes."

"Does he know you intend to raise the babies as your own?"

Taylor shrugged her shoulders. "I'm not certain if he knows or not. Uncle sometimes forgets things."

"He would forget his great-nieces?"

"Perhaps."

"Did he read all the dime novels you read about the wilderness?"

Taylor smiled. "Oh, yes, he was almost as taken as I was by all the stories about the wild, savage land. We used to argue about living there. I told him I would someday, and he said he didn't know if I had enough gumption."

"And that is why he built the soddie?"

"Yes. We had both read that settlers often lived in mud soddies, and so he had his servants build one for me. They put it right on his front lawn. He directed his staff. I didn't think he would really insist I live in the thing, but he did," she added with a laugh. "And so I moved in and stayed almost a full month. It was horrible at first. Every time it rained, mud would lop down from the—"

Victoria interrupted her. "Do you mean to say the ceiling was made of mud?"

Taylor nodded. "The entire roof was fashioned out of sod. The floor was dirt too, unless it rained. Then it turned to mud. I had a single window without any covering. Anything could fly inside."

"It sounds dreadful," Victoria replied. "Will we have to live in a soddie do you suppose?"

"Not if I can help it," Taylor promised. "But if we have to for a little while, then we will. I learned how to make a soddie into a home. Now that I reflect upon it, I learned quite a lot. After a while, it wasn't completely horrible. By late June, the roof had turned into a garden of lovely pink and purple and red flowers in full bloom. They spilled down over the sides like vines of ivy. From the distance, the soddie was breathtakingly beautiful. Inside, however, was a bit like living in a flowerpot."

"I do hope we'll have wooden floors and a real roof someday. I won't complain if we have to live in a flowerpot though. I promise I won't say a word."

"You won't have to," Taylor replied. "I'll do enough complaining for the both of us."

The two friends continued to formulate their plans for several more minutes. Then they went back to their rooms. Victoria was eager to start her list. Taylor wanted to write a letter to Mr. Sherman, outlining her instructions. Everything had to be settled before she left for the wilderness. She labored over her letter a good long while, and when she was satisfied with the content, she affixed her signature, and then reached for a second sheet of paper. She knew she needed to be as clear and concise as possible. The document would have to stand up in a court of law, she reasoned, and it therefore had to be completely understandable. There couldn't be any nebulous requests or explanations.

Taylor let out a sigh. She didn't relish this task. She

found herself imagining she was attending a fancy ball in London and almost burst into laughter. What a different direction her life had taken. She sighed again, then got down to the business at hand and put her daydream and her past behind her. She picked up her pen, dipped it into the ink well, and began to write her last will and testament.

10

The fear's as bad as falling.
—William Shakespeare,
Cymbeline

*L*ucas fell asleep waiting for Taylor. He thought about walking down to Victoria's room and dragging his wife back to their bed, then changed his mind. She knew what time it was, and if she wanted to stay up half the night talking to her friend, he shouldn't mind.

He did mind though. Taylor needed her rest, and he wanted her to sleep next to him. He liked the way she cuddled up beside him. He liked holding her in his arms and falling asleep inhaling her sweet fragrance. Yet there was more to his need to have her close than the mere physical comfort she offered. When he was sleeping, he was vulnerable. In the past his nights had been as predictable as thunder following lightning. The same nightmare would grab hold of him and squeeze until he felt as though he was being ripped apart. He would wake up with the shout trapped in his throat and his heart feeling as though it were going to explode.

The nightmare never varied. Each night was the same as the night before. Until Taylor, he qualified. Lucas didn't know how it had happened, but she had become his personal shaman. His dreams didn't have any demons sneaking into them when she slept close to him. If he were a foolish, fanciful man, he'd believe her goodness and her purity of soul kept the nightmares at bay.

He shook his head then, trying without much success to push his thoughts aside. Only a fool would let a woman hold such power over him. If he didn't start guarding against her, she'd have him believing he would have it all. He might even start thinking he could be like other men and grow old with a family surrounding him, wanting him, loving him.

Lucas was a realist. He knew better than to embrace such hopeless thoughts. He let out a weary sigh. Maybe Hunter was right after all. Perhaps there had been a reason why he'd been spared. His friend was the only one Lucas had ever confided in after the war. Hunter knew all about the murders of the men in his unit. The other soldiers had all had families waiting for them to come home. Lucas hadn't had anyone waiting for him. Of all the men, he was the most unworthy. He'd been born a bastard and lived like one for most of his life. He shouldn't have survived.

And yet he'd been the only one spared. Hunter insisted there was a reason and that time, and God, would eventually let him know what it was. Time Lucas understood. But God, well, he wasn't so certain about that notion. He believed in His existence, but he couldn't even begin to understand His reasoning. And in a corner of his mind, he still harbored his childhood belief that God had forgotten all about him.

If his own mother couldn't love him, how could God?

Lucas refused to think about the matter any longer. The past was the past. It couldn't be undone. And just where in thunder was Taylor? It was after midnight now. She needed her sleep, he thought again, and he wanted her rested in the morning. And that, he told himself, was the only reason he was worrying about her. The two of them were in dire need of a long discussion about their future. They needed to make plans. He couldn't just leave her alone in Boston, for God's sake, without knowing what was going to happen to her. She told him she had relatives living here. Where the hell were they? Why hadn't they met her at the dock? One question piled up on top of another. Lucas decided he was going to insist upon meeting these relatives. He was going to make certain Taylor would be safe with them before he left her in their company.

He needed to leave Boston soon. The walls of the city felt as though they were pressing down on him. The longer he stayed with Taylor, the more difficult it would be to walk away from her. God, she was making him crazy. She put thoughts into his mind he knew were impossible. Dreams, he thought. Impossible dreams.

Lucas drifted off to sleep thinking about his wife. He'd taken his shoes off, his jacket as well, and had fallen asleep on top of the covers.

He was wide awake the second the key was slipped into the lock of the door, but he kept his eyes closed. A few seconds later, the door was slammed shut. He frowned in reaction. Taylor wasn't being considerate, and that, he realized, wasn't at all like her.

Something was wrong. He sat up in bed and swung his legs over the side just as she came tearing around the corner of the alcove. One look at her face told him something godawful had happened. She looked frantic. Since she'd spent the evening with Victoria, he assumed something had happened to her friend.

Taylor didn't give him time to ask questions. "Do you have your gun with you?"

He couldn't hide his surprise over the bizarre question. "Yes. Why?"

"You have to go back with me. Hurry, Lucas. Put your shoes on and get your guns. I've got one in my valise. Thank God I didn't pack it in one of my trunks."

She turned and ran to her wardrobe. She found the weapon at the bottom of the case. The small box of ammunition was on top of the gun. Taylor stood up, but she was so rattled, she dropped both her valise and her gun. She picked the weapon up first, shoved it into the pocket of her coat, then reached for the box of ammunition. She dropped that, too. Bullets went flying everywhere. Taylor knelt down again, swept a handful up, and put those into her other pocket. She left the rest of the bullets and the overturned valise on the carpet.

Lucas stood next to the alcove watching her. She was muttering something, but he couldn't make out all the words. Something about vermin . . .

"Taylor, what is going on?"

"Put your shoes on," she ordered once again. "You have to hurry."

He wasn't going anywhere until she started explaining. She was obviously beside herself with fear. He needed to calm her down and find out what had caused her panic. If someone had hurt her, he wouldn't need his guns anyway. He'd kill the bastard with his bare hands.

He walked forward, intent on catching her in his arms and demanding some answers. She evaded his grasp, however, and went running across the room. She was determined to get him to do what she'd ordered.

She spotted his jacket on the foot of the bed, swept it up in her hands, and threw it at him. "Don't just stand there. For God's sake, get your guns. You might need two. He'll tell you where he's hidden them. You'll make him tell you. We can't let him get away. I'll never find them."

Her words were tripping over each other. Lucas had never seen her behave like this. She acted as though she'd lost her mind. The look in her eyes showed her terror. She was sobbing now and pulling at his arm, whimpering one word, screaming the next, demanding and begging at the same time.

She knelt down and tried to put his shoes on him. He grabbed hold of her and pulled her up.

"Try to calm down, Taylor," he ordered. "Who won't you be able to find?"

He kept his voice soft, soothing. She shouted her answer. "My babies. He's hidden my babies. Please, Lucas. Help me. I'll do anything if only you'll help me."

He put his arms around her and held her close. "Listen to me. I'm going to help you. All right? Now calm down. You aren't making any sense." He couldn't quite contain his exasperation when he added, "You don't have any children."

"Yes, yes, I do," she cried out. "I have two babies. He's taken them away. My sister . . . she's dead now and I'm, oh, God, please trust me. I'll tell you everything once we're on our way. I know he's going to run away. We can't take the chance."

She was tearing at his shirt while she pleaded with him. He finally caught her urgency. He didn't waste any more time trying to get the straight story out of her. He collected his weapons, checked each to make certain the chambers were fully loaded, then strapped the gunbelt around his waist. He knew his jacket wouldn't cover the guns, and so he went to his wardrobe and put on his black rain duster. The length of the coat, well below his knees, would conceal his weapons from anyone watching as they passed through the lobby of the hotel.

Taylor ran after him carrying his shoes. He put them on at the door, then took hold of her hand and started down the corridor.

"You better start making sense once we're on our way, Taylor."

He sounded as menacing as he looked. The somber black coat echoed his mood. The collar was up around the lower part of his face.

He suddenly looked very much like a gunfighter. Taylor began to have a glimmer of hope. The coldness in his eyes and the mean expression on his face comforted her.

And all because he was on her side. She needed cold and mean now. Lucas, willingly or not, had just become her avenger.

"Please walk faster," she begged.

She was already running to keep up with him. She was still too terrified to realize what she was saying. She was so shaken, she didn't even realize she was crying until he told her to stop it.

He didn't say another word until they were outside the hotel. Taylor gave the address to the cabbie waiting at the entrance.

"Fort Hill? I ain't taking no fare to that part of

town," the driver announced. "Too dangerous," he added with a nervous nod toward Lucas.

The muscle in her husband's jaw flinched when the driver denied the request a second time. Taylor promised to triple the fare, but it was Lucas who finally gained the driver's cooperation. He reached up, grabbed hold of the man's jacket, and almost tore him off his perch.

"You drive or I will. Either way we'll all be leaving in ten seconds flat. Taylor, get inside."

The driver was quick to recognize his tenuous position. "I'll take you," he stammered out. "But once I get you there, I ain't waiting around."

Lucas didn't debate the point. He didn't waste any more time on the man. He got inside and took his seat across from his wife.

Taylor had her gun out. It was a Colt, he noticed, and as shining and unblemished as a new one in a showcase. He concluded she'd only just purchased the weapon.

The bullets were in her lap. While he watched, she deftly flipped the cylinder to the side, loaded the chambers, and then flipped the cylinder closed again. Then she put the gun back in her pocket and folded her hands together.

Lucas was astounded. The fact that she even owned a gun surprised him, but it was the way she handled the weapon that stunned him. She had the gun loaded and ready in less than half a minute . . . and with hands that were almost violently shaking.

"You know how to shoot?" he asked.

"Yes."

"Your uncle Andrew taught you, didn't he? You weren't jesting when you said he taught you how to shoot and how to play the piano. I remember now."

"No, I wasn't jesting. He's a gun collector. He takes them apart and puts them back together. I'm awkward and slow with six shooters, but I—"

He didn't let her finish. She was going to tell him she was extremely accurate, and that certainly made up for speed in her mind. Her uncle told her she had the eye of an eagle, and it really didn't matter how long it took her to get ready. Men, he'd instructed, needed to be quick, for they liked to engage one another in gunfights. Women only needed to be accurate.

"Give me the gun, Taylor. You'll end up killing yourself by accident. You don't have any business carrying a loaded gun around."

"Can't you get the driver to go any faster?"

Lucas leaned out the window, shouted the order, then leaned back in his seat again. He stretched his long legs out, crossed one foot over the other, and folded his arms across his chest.

He looked relaxed, but she wasn't fooled. The anger was there in his voice and his eyes when he spoke to her.

"I take it you were in Fort Hill instead of Victoria's room tonight."

"Yes."

Even though he knew she was going to admit to the atrocity, he was still infuriated by her answer.

"Who went with you?"

"I went alone."

He'd already guessed that answer, too, and now he suddenly wanted to throttle her. He tried to block the image of her strolling around in the city's most threatening area. Picturing her in Sodom and Gomorrah would have been easier to accept.

"Do you have any idea of the danger you were in?"

He hadn't raised his voice. For as long as she'd

known him, Lucas had never shouted. He didn't need to, she realized. The razor edge in his voice was just as effective as a good bellow. She almost flinched in reaction. She caught herself in time.

"Start explaining, Taylor," he ordered. "Don't leave anything out."

She didn't know where to begin or how much to tell him. She was still in such a panic inside she could barely think straight.

She gripped her hands together, implored him to be patient with her, and then told him almost everything.

"I went to visit my sister's children," she began. "Marian died eighteen months ago. She'd been plagued by consumption for several years, and a sudden cold spell that swept through Boston . . ."

"Yes?" he prodded after a moment of waiting for her to continue.

"Marian wasn't very strong. She caught cold, and it settled in her chest. She died after a month of illness. George, her husband, has been raising his daughters."

"And?" he prodded again after another minute of waiting.

"George took ill several weeks ago. Since there was another outbreak of cholera in the area, we believe that is what he died of, but we can't be certain. Mrs. Bartlesmith wrote us with the news."

"And who is Mrs. Bartlesmith?"

"The babies' nanny. She promised to stay with the little ones until I could get to Boston."

"Go on," he told her when she paused again.

"I went to the address I'd been writing to, but Mrs. Bartlesmith wasn't there. The woman who answered the door was very sympathetic and tried to be helpful. She didn't know what had happened to the nanny or the babies. She made me a cup of tea and then spent a good hour digging through her papers until she found the name and address of a couple named Henry and Pearl Westley. They had worked for my brother-in-law. The wife cooked and the husband did odd chores around the house. The Westleys had hoped the new tenants would hire them on, but the woman told me she didn't want them around. She said she could smell the whiskey on both of them. She told them she wasn't in need of their services, but Pearl Westley insisted she keep her name and address in the event she changed her mind."

"And so you went to the Westleys looking for the children," he supplied.

She nodded. "I didn't expect to find them there. I just hoped the Westleys might know where Mrs. Bartlesmith took them."

"So you went to Fort Hill?"

"Yes. It was clear across town, and by the time I got to the address, it was dark. I thank God the driver didn't leave me stranded. He warned me to be quick and promised to wait for me. Henry Westley opened the door. He told me Mrs. Bartlesmith had died. He wouldn't say how or when. His wife was there. She hid in the other room. She kept yelling at her husband to get rid of me. Both of them were drunk. Pearl Westley's voice was terribly slurred. She sounded scared. He wasn't scared though. He was . . . insolent, hateful. He shouted back to his wife that there wasn't anything I could do, that it was too late. He acted extremely defiant."

"Did you go inside?"

"No. I stayed on the porch."

"Thank God you had enough sense not to go inside the house."

"It was a hovel, not a house," she corrected. Her voice shivered with renewed fear. "Henry and Pearl both pretended they'd never heard of the babies. They were lying, of course."

"Did you hear or see anyone else inside?" he asked her again.

She shook her head. "There might have been someone upstairs, but I didn't hear anyone else."

She started crying. She hated herself for showing such weakness in front of her husband, but she couldn't seem to control herself. Lucas started to reach into his pocket in search of the handkerchief he was pretty certain he left back in the hotel room, but she waylaid his intent when she reached across the seat and grabbed his hand.

"I'm not an alarmist, Lucas. I could hear the fear in Pearl's voice. And I could see his insolence. They know where the girls are. You'll make them tell you, won't you? You'll find my nieces for me."

"Yes, I'll find them for you," he promised, his voice a soothing whisper. "Couldn't Mrs. Bartlesmith have taken the children to one of your relatives?"

She shook her head. "Why would the Westleys pretend they'd never heard of the little girls? They both worked for my brother-in-law. Of course they knew. They're hiding something. If any harm comes to the babies, if they've been hurt or . . ."

"Stop it," he ordered. "Don't let your imagination control your thoughts. You have to stay calm."

"Yes, you're right," she agreed. "I have to stay calm. I'll do whatever you tell me to do. Just let me help."

She straightened back against her seat and folded her hands together in her lap again. She was trying to act composed. It was an impossible feat.

"I want you to stay right where you are with the doors locked," he told her.

She didn't argue with him. She didn't have any

intention of hiding inside and leaving him all alone to deal with the Westleys. They were vile and unpredictable people. Lucas might need her assistance, and she needed to be there so she could give it.

She didn't want to lie to him, and so she kept silent. A moment later she turned to look out the window to see if they were near their destination yet, and when she saw the houses they were passing looked disrespectable and dilapidated, she knew they were close to the Westleys' house. The scent in the air had turned sour. They were close all right. Taylor gripped her hands in anticipation. And then she began to pray.

"Did your grandmother know your sister's husband died?"

"Yes," Taylor answered. "I told her as soon as the letter arrived."

"And then what did you do?"

"I wrote to Mrs. Bartlesmith after Madam had formulated her plan."

He waited for further explanation and when Taylor didn't continue, he prodded her again.

"What was the plan?"

"You."

He didn't understand. His frown said as much. She wasn't going to enlighten him. He would understand everything later, after they'd located the babies.

"When I was a little girl, Marian protected me. She was like my guardian angel. I will do whatever is necessary to protect her daughters. They're my responsibility now."

"What did Marian protect you from?"

"A snake."

"Malcolm." He remembered she'd referred to her uncle as a snake when they were leaving the bank.

"Yes," she whispered. "Malcolm." She didn't want

to talk about her vile relative now. She wanted only to concentrate on the little ones.

"What's going to happen to your nieces now that both their parents are dead? Will their father's relatives take them in or were you considering taking them back to England?"

She didn't give him a direct answer. "The little girls are going to need someone who will love and cherish them and raise them to be good and kind and gentle, like their mother. They need a protector. They must be kept safe from all the snakes in the world. It's their right, Lucas." *And my responsibility,* she silently added.

Would she consider taking them back to England, he'd asked. Not bloody likely, she wanted to shout. She was going to go as far away from England as possible. She didn't tell Lucas her plan. Oh, she knew there were dangers lurking in the wilderness, and Lucas would tell her it wasn't a fit place for babies. God only knew she'd already considered every potential problem. Yet no matter how she looked at it, she came to the same conclusion. The twins would be better off living on the frontier than back in England under Malcolm's watchful gaze. He was the far greater threat. She felt sure that age hadn't robbed him of his appetites. Snakes, after all, remained snakes until the day they withered up and died. And Malcolm, ten years junior to Taylor's own father, was just shy of reaching fifty. He had plenty of years of debauchery left in him.

The vehicle was slowing down. Taylor glanced out the window again to see if she recognized the area. The moonlight was bright enough to read some of the signs. The houses, or rather shacks, were so close together they seemed to touch. The streets were deserted, perhaps because of the lateness in the hour, of course, but also because it had started to drizzle, and with the moisture came a blustering March wind.

The Westleys' home came into view. Light radiated through each window on both the lower and the upper floors. The Westleys were still there, for she spotted a figure through the thin window covering on the second floor. Someone was darting back and forth.

She almost wept with relief. They hadn't been able to run away yet. "They're still there," she said. "Look. There's a woman in the upstairs window. She's scurrying back and forth." *Like a rat,* she silently added.

"Looks like she might be packing," he replied. He eased the door open and gently pushed Taylor back against the seat. "No matter what you see or hear, stay inside. Promise me."

"Yes," she agreed. "I'll stay inside," she promised. "Unless you need me," she hastily qualified.

He started to get out. She grabbed hold of his arm. "Be careful," she whispered.

He nodded, got out of the vehicle, and then closed the door behind him. Taylor leaned out the window. "I wouldn't trust our driver if I were you," she whispered. "He's sure to take off while you're inside."

"He isn't going to leave," he promised. He leaned forward, brushed his mouth over hers, then turned and walked up to the side of the perch where the disgruntled looking driver sat.

"My wife's waiting inside until I come back."

The driver shook his head. "Best get her out then. I ain't waiting on anyone in this part of town. It ain't safe."

Lucas acted as though he hadn't heard his protest. He motioned him to lean down so he could hear what he was next going to say.

"When you wake up, you can take us back to the hotel."

The driver wasn't given time to ponder the meaning behind the remark. Lucas struck him hard across his jaw with his fist. The man slumped down in his seat.

Taylor couldn't see what was happening with their driver. She concluded Lucas had been able to convince the man to wait for them. She watched as her husband crossed the dirt road. He went up the front steps of the house, crossed the rickety porch, but when he reached the door, he didn't knock. He tried the doorknob first, then put his shoulder to the task of breaking the barrier down. He disappeared inside.

She started praying. Lucas was gone a long time. It seemed an eternity. Twice she reached for the door handle. And twice she stopped herself. She'd given her word to stay put, and unless she heard a shot fired, she knew she would keep her promise. Unless, of course, Lucas came back empty-handed. If he hadn't found out where her babies were, then she would take a turn trying to find out. Taylor pulled the gun out of her pocket and rested it in her lap. She realized her hands were shaking, but she didn't honestly know if it was fear or anger causing the tremors.

She heard a crash followed by the sound of glass breaking. She pictured a vase slamming down on top of Lucas's head. She couldn't sit still another second. She unlatched the door and jumped down to the pavement. She started forward, then stopped when Lucas appeared in the open doorway.

Taylor hadn't realized how worried she was about his safety until she saw he looked quite all right.

"Thank you, God," she whispered.

She heard the driver let out a loud groan. The man sounded ill to her. "We'll be leaving in just a moment, my good man," she called out. She didn't turn around to look up at the driver when she gave her promise. Her attention was fully directed on her husband. She was trying to discern from his expression if he had good or bad news.

He wasn't giving her any hints. He'd just reached the roadway when a figure suddenly appeared in the doorway of Westley's house. It was a man, and when he shifted his bulk into the light, Taylor could see Henry Westley quite clearly. Lucas had obviously punched the man in his nose, for blood trickled down from the injury and covered his mouth and his chin. She watched as he wiped the blood away with the back of his left hand. His right hand was behind his back. He was staring at Lucas, a look of hatred on his face, and when he raised his right hand, she spotted the gun. What happened next seemed to take place in slow motion, yet only a second or two passed before it was over. Westley brought the gun up and took aim. His target was Lucas, his intent unquestionable. He was going to shoot him in his back.

There wasn't even time to shout a warning. Taylor took aim just as Lucas suddenly whirled around. He fired a scant second before she did. Taylor's bullet struck Westley in his left shoulder. Lucas was more accurate. He shot the gun right out of his hand.

The gunshots shook the driver out of his stupor. He straightened in his seat, grabbed hold of the reins, and was just about to slap the horses into a full gallop when Lucas reached the carriage. He swung the door wide, literally tossed Taylor inside, then followed her. The door closed on its own when the vehicle rounded the corner on two wheels.

Taylor straightened in her seat across from her husband. She was so rattled she didn't even realize she was still holding her gun in her hand. She was pointing the weapon at her husband. He reached over and took the gun away from her before the vehicle hit a bump and she accidentally made a eunuch out of him. Taylor watched him without saying a word. He put the gun in his pocket, then leaned back against the cushion and let out a long, weary sigh.

"How did you know?"

She'd whispered her question. "Know what?" he asked in a much louder tone of voice.

"That Westley was going to shoot you," she explained. "I didn't even have time to call a warning . . . but you knew he was there. Was it instinct? Did you feel him behind you?"

He shook his head. "You warned me."

"How?"

"I was watching you. Your expression told me all I needed to know," he answered. "And when you raised your hand—"

She didn't let him finish. "You shot him before I did."

"Yes."

"I should have killed him."

"You could have, but you didn't. It's simple, Taylor. You chose not to."

"As did you," she replied.

"Yes," he answered. "But for an altogether different reason." He went on to explain before she could question him. "You didn't kill him because of morals I suppose and I let him live because I didn't want to get involved with the authorities. Killing him would have made things complicated. Boston is different from the mountains."

"How?" she asked.

"You don't have to answer to anyone in Montana. It's still . . . uncomplicated."

"You mean lawless."

He shook his head. "No, not lawless. But the law's different out there. Most of the time it's honest. Sometimes it isn't."

Lucas was stalling because he didn't know how to tell her what he'd just learned. It was going to break her heart, and he couldn't think of a way to ease the torment he was going to cause.

"I hate the smell," she blurted.

"What smell?"

"Guns. I hate the smell after you've fired. It stays on your hands and your clothes for hours. Soap doesn't get rid of it. I hate it."

He shrugged. "I never noticed it," he admitted.

Taylor took a deep breath. Her voice was strained when she whispered, "Did you find out anything?"

"Yes," he answered. He leaned forward and took hold of her hands. "The woman taking care of the children . . ."

"Mrs. Bartlesmith?"

He nodded. "She's dead," he told her then. "But it wasn't cholera. According to Westley's wife, the woman keeled over and was dead before she hit the floor. She had a history of heart problems."

"What about the babies?"

"Westley admitted they cleared the house of all valuables and sold off everything. They also took the little girls home with them."

"I see," she whispered. She gripped Lucas's hands.

Lucas couldn't stand to witness her pain. "Listen to me, Taylor. We're going to find them. Do you understand what I'm saying? We will find them."

"Oh, God," she said. She could tell he hadn't told her everything and she was suddenly too frightened to ask.

"They aren't with the Westleys any longer."

"Are they still alive?"

"Yes." His voice was emphatic. She took heart.

"Then where are they? What have they done with my babies?"

Lucas let go of her hands and pulled her into his arms. He settled her on his lap and held her close. He wasn't simply offering her comfort. Honest to God, he didn't want to see her expression when he told her what the bastards had done.

"We're going to find them," he promised once again.

"Tell me, Lucas. Where are the babies? What did they do to them?"

He couldn't soften the truth.

"They sold them."

11

*The world is grown so bad that wrens make prey
where eagles dare not perch.*
—William Shakespeare,
Richard III

She didn't get hysterical. For a long while she didn't say a word. In truth, she was too stunned to show any reaction to the news. Then anger such as she had never felt before took control. It invaded her mind, her heart, her very soul. She became rigid with her fury. She wanted to kill Henry and Pearl Westley, and in those horrible moments of desolation and white-hot rage, she thought she might be capable of cold, premeditated murder. She would rid the world of such vile, contemptible animals and send them to the fires of hell where they belonged.

Reason finally prevailed. The devil would certainly thank her for the gift of two more souls, but then he would also own her soul as well. Murder was a mortal sin. Dear God, she wished she didn't have a conscience. She wanted to make the Westleys suffer the way she was suffering, but in her heart she knew she couldn't become both judge and jury and kill them.

Taylor wanted to lean against her husband's chest, wrap her arms around his neck, and demand his comfort. She suddenly longed to be dependent upon his strength but was so appalled by the notion, she immediately pushed herself off his lap and moved to the opposite seat. She adjusted the pleats in her skirts, all the while praying she would be able to find a few threads of her composure.

"I must be strong now. I can weep later."

She hadn't realized she'd whispered the plea out loud until Lucas agreed with her.

"We'll get them back, Taylor."

He sounded so certain that she took heart. She said a prayer that the little ones weren't being mistreated. *Keep them safe,* she silently chanted to God. *Please keep them safe.*

She suddenly realized Lucas was talking to her and tried to concentrate on what he was saying. Wire his friend? Why? She leaned forward and implored him to start over.

"The little girls were being taken to Cincinnati," he explained a second time. "There's a buyer there." *Waiting,* he silently added.

"How long ago?"

"Two days past."

"Oh, God, they could be anywhere by now."

He shook his head. "It takes forty hours by train to reach Cincinnati, Taylor. If we're lucky, my friend will meet the train."

"But if they didn't go by train?"

"Then it's going to take them longer to get there," he reasoned.

"Yes."

"As soon as we get back to our hotel, I'll wire Hunter."

"Is he in Cincinnati?"

"No, but he's close enough."

"Are you certain you can find him?"

He nodded. "If your nieces aren't on the train, we'll need Hunter more than ever. He's the second-best tracker in the states and the territories combined."

"Who is the first best?" she asked, thinking she wanted Lucas to hire that gentleman as well. The more experts they had looking, the better their chances were of finding the little ones before anything more happened to them.

"I am."

She sighed with relief. "While you wire your friend, I'll get the train schedule and have the concierge purchase the tickets for us. We should leave as soon as possible."

He knew better than to try to talk her into waiting in Boston. Cincinnati could well have been only a stopping-off point and nothing more. There was the real possibility the little girls were already there. Westley said two days ago . . . forty-eight hours. Yes, they could have already reached Cincinnati and be on their way in any number of directions. If they were headed into the hills of Kentucky or the wilderness beyond the Ohio valley, Lucas would insist Taylor stay in Cincinnati and wait there. The city was safer and more civilized. If there was time, he would hire someone to look after her.

"You shouldn't be left on your own."

"Excuse me?"

"Never mind."

"Lucas, I'm going with you. We're going to find them together. I won't slow you down."

"I haven't argued," he countered. "You can go with me."

"Thank you."

She closed her eyes. She was suddenly racked with tremors. "Why is there such evil in the world?"

He stared at her a long while before answering. "Because there's such goodness."

She opened her eyes and looked at him. "I don't understand," she admitted. "Are you saying that if there's one, there must be the other?"

"Seems so," he replied.

She shook her head. "I'm not seeing any goodness now."

"I am," he replied gruffly. "I'm looking at it."

She didn't understand what he meant. Lucas became uncomfortable with the compliment he'd given her the second the words were out of his mouth. They sat in silence for a long moment.

"What are you going to do about Victoria?" Lucas asked finally.

"I'll go to her room tonight and explain everything to her."

Neither spoke again for a long while. Lucas was busy plotting his course of action and listing the items he would need for the journey. Taylor was occupied praying for the babies.

"Lucas?"

"Yes?"

"I know this isn't your battle. The babies are my responsibility, not yours. I want you to know how thankful I am to have your assistance." Before he could respond, she continued. "I'm so sorry this was forced on you. You got more than you bargained for when you married me, didn't you? You should be compensated at the very least, and just as soon as . . ."

He interrupted her. "If you offer to pay me for my services, I'll throttle you."

She was pleased by his anger. She needed a champion now, and Lucas was proving to be just that.

"I'm sorry," she said. "I didn't mean to be insulting. I'm grateful," she said again. She could tell from his expression he didn't want to hear about her gratitude, and so she changed the topic. "Children aren't simply property."

"No, they aren't."

"Most adults believe they are. Most certainly don't believe children have any rights, but they do have rights, don't they?"

He nodded. "They should have the right to loving, protective parents."

"Yes," she whispered.

Her mind jumped to another topic then. "Will the Westleys go to the authorities and bring charges against us?"

"What would they charge?"

"Injury," she answered. "We both shot Henry Westley."

He scoffed at the notion. "They'd have to do some fancy explaining if they talked to anyone," he reasoned. "Do you want to call in the authorities?"

"No," she answered. "It wouldn't do us any good to involve them. Georgie and Allie have already been taken. There would be too much of a delay explaining and filling out forms and . . . unless you think we should, Lucas."

His natural inclination was to distrust anyone with a badge. The symbol gave the man too much power, and power, he'd learned through experience, was like ocean water to a thirsty man. One drink made a man hungry for more and more and more until it became an insatiable craving. Power rarely elevated a man and most often corrupted him.

"It could get complicated and I don't particularly want the law breathing down my neck while I'm looking for your nieces. Answer a question for me."

"What is it?"

"Does Victoria know about your nieces?"

"Yes."

"Why didn't you mention the girls to me?"

She didn't answer him. "Do you trust me?" he asked her then.

She hesitated a full minute before speaking. "I believe I do," she said. "Yes, I do," she added in a more forceful tone of voice. "Madam said I should."

"And if Madam hadn't given you that instruction?"

"You're a man, Lucas."

"What does that mean?"

"Men usually can't be trusted. Victoria and I both have learned that important lesson. Still, you aren't like other men. You're certainly nothing like your half brother. William, I now realize, is a weakling. You're the complete opposite. You'll find them, won't you? Tell me again. I'll believe you."

The jump in topics didn't jar him. He once again gave her his promise.

"Do you think they've been harmed?"

The bleakness in her voice tore at his heart. He was more abrupt than he wanted to be when he answered her. "Don't allow yourself to think about such things. Concentrate only on getting them back. You'll go out of your mind otherwise."

She tried to take his advice. Each time a horrid thought popped into her head, she forced it aside. She made a mental list of all the things she would need to take with her on the trip.

When they finally reached the hotel, Taylor rushed through the lobby in search of the hotel's concierge. She was given a train schedule, and when she read that a train had only just left, she wanted to scream. The next one wouldn't be leaving Boston until ten o'clock in the morning. A messenger was duly dispatched to the station with enough funds to purchase two tickets. The manager suggested he wire their sister hotel in Cincinnati for reservations, and when she agreed, he hurried to do just that. She asked him to be certain to secure a second room for her friend.

Making these plans helped Taylor stay calm. She hurried up to her room, packed her bags, then located the tickets for her trunks and took them with her down to Victoria's room. It was almost two o'clock in the morning when she knocked on her door.

Victoria could barely keep her eyes open until Taylor told her what had happened. The news proved to be as effective as a glass of cold water tossed into her face. She was wide awake and teary eyed in sympathy over Taylor's distress.

"The poor babies," she whispered. "I'm going with you," she added almost immediately. "I'll help any way that I can."

It never entered Taylor's mind that Victoria might decline to help. She had complete faith in her friend. She handed her the tickets for the trunks and instructed her to follow Lucas and her to Cincinnati on the next available train. She explained she had already wired ahead for a room for Victoria, for she hoped her friend would take care of the luggage and then follow her.

"I'm praying they're in Cincinnati," Taylor told her. "I think my nieces are headed west. I want to believe they'll be easy to find. If they've been taken to New

York, where there are hordes of people, finding them would be more difficult."

"What else can I do to help?"

"Go to the bank tomorrow and withdraw as much money as possible. Bring it with you. I'll sign a voucher before I leave in the morning. Please don't tell Sherman or Summers where you're going."

"No, I won't tell," Victoria promised. She embraced her friend, wished her Godspeed, and then remembered the list of items Taylor had wanted to purchase while in Boston.

"Give me your list," she ordered. "Since I will stay in Boston another day to do the banking, I can also do your shopping."

"Yes, of course. I'll give you my list in the morning." She started to leave, then turned back to her friend. "You should also have the staff move your things into our room."

"Why?"

"It's nicer," Taylor explained. She opened the door and started down the hallway. "You deserve luxury, Victoria. I was going to change with you after Lucas left. It would please me to know you're sleeping there tomorrow night."

"And it will please me to know you've found the little ones by then."

Taylor shook her head. "Lucas said it will take forty hours to get to Cincinnati. I can't send a wire to you because you'll be on a train by then. You'll have to wait until you get there. Be careful, dear friend."

"Try to get some sleep tonight," Victoria called out.

The suggestion was given with a kind heart and Taylor pretended to agree to try. She couldn't imagine being able to sleep, but she didn't want Victoria worrying about her.

Lucas returned to their room a short while later. He locked the door, then leaned against the frame while he took her gun out of his pocket and unloaded it. He put the gun and the bullets on the table. Then he packed his things. That chore only took a few minutes.

"Come to bed, Taylor," he ordered. "Tomorrow's going to be a long day."

He was stripping out of his clothes on his way to the washroom when he gave the command. She shook her head. "Not just yet," she told him. She walked over to the window behind the seating area and stood there looking out into the black night.

He didn't argue with her. He thought she probably needed a few minutes of solitude to calm her emotions. He kept his pants on for her sake and slept on top of the covers. He awakened an hour later, knew before he even opened his eyes she wasn't in bed with him, and then spotted her across the room. She hadn't moved from her position by the window. Her head was bowed and her arms were folded in front of her. She was doubled over, and although he couldn't see her face or hear any noise, he knew she was weeping.

Her agony was heartwrenching. Lucas got out of bed and quietly crossed the room. He didn't say a word to her. He simply lifted her into his arms and carried her back to the alcove. He stood her by the side of the bed and undressed her. She neither protested nor offered to help. She simply stood there while he stripped her down to her chemise. He tried not to notice how silky her skin was. His hand brushed across the swell of her breasts, and God help him, he wanted to linger over the task of touching her. He didn't give into the base urge. It didn't seem right or honorable of him to have lustful thoughts about her now. She was too vulnerable. He knew she would let him make love to her, might even welcome his touch, but with the morning light, she would surely have regrets. He wasn't about to take advantage of her.

Hell, he guessed he really was a gentleman.

His gentle little bride had had one hell of a time these past months. The man she believed she loved and was about to marry had betrayed her, the woman who had raised her as a daughter and talked her into marrying a complete stranger died, and Taylor hadn't been given a single hour in which to mourn, and now she surely believed she would never see her sister's children again. Lucas knew she would spend the rest of her life looking for the little girls if that was what was required of her, so strong was her sense of responsibility and family obligation.

Her loyalty staggered him. She acted as though she was going to take on the duty of motherhood. He assumed she meant to help raise her nieces with the assistance of the twins' other relatives.

She called them her babies. Lucas didn't know what her plans for the future were. The present was all that concerned him now.

The babies. He would go into hell if he had to, to get the innocents back.

Evil isn't going to win this time.

Lucas silently repeated the vow over and over again on the train ride to Cincinnati. He didn't know if he was saying a prayer to God or giving Him a challenge. Only one thing was certain in his mind. He would get the children back.

Hunter was waiting for them at the station. Lucas counted his appearance as a sign that luck and maybe even God were on their side. His friend looked trail weary. His tan-colored shirt and pants were covered with a layer of dust. He wore a gunbelt similar to Lucas's, a preference of both men that was considered a bit of an oddity in the West. Most gunfighters and mountain men stuck their guns in their pockets or the belt that held their pants up.

His friend was every bit as tall as Lucas. He was reed thin, with dark blue-black hair and brown eyes. His coloring came from his Crow grandmother. So did his disposition. He was soft-spoken, rarely riled, and had a code of morals most people couldn't begin to live up to. Like Lucas, Hunter had been ostracized growing up. Lucas was treated with contempt because he was a bastard and an orphan; Hunter was despised because of what ignorant people referred to as his mixed blood. They'd become friends out of necessity and loneliness when they were boys. Their friendship had strengthened with the years and their harsh existence. Hunter had returned to the isolation of the mountains before Lucas, but after the war, Lucas had joined him. Each man was loyal to the other, and each had saved the other's hide more than a couple of times. Hunter was the only man Lucas would let stand behind his back. And Lucas was one of the few men Hunter would even talk to, so reclusive had he become over the years.

Taylor took one look at the intimidating man and moved closer to Lucas. Mr. Hunter looked hard and mean. She really couldn't have asked for more.

He tipped his hat to her when Lucas introduced her and said, "Ma'am," and then turned his attention to her husband.

"Couple of possibilities."

Lucas nodded. He latched onto Taylor's elbow and tried to get her moving, but she wasn't going anywhere until she gave his friend her gratitude.

"Lucas told me you rarely leave your mountain home, Mr. Hunter. You'll probably think me foolish indeed, but I believe God sent you on whatever errand it was that brought you so close to Cincinnati. We needed another strong, clever, resourceful man and so He sent us you. I would like to thank you now for whatever assistance you can give us."

Hunter was taken aback by her words and was at a loss for a response. Her acceptance of him, given so quickly and without any apparent reservations, astonished him. He simply stared at her and waited to hear what she would next say. She didn't keep him waiting long.

"Lucas told me you were the second-best tracker in America."

After making that statement she allowed her husband to urge her forward. Hunter fell into step beside them.

"Second best? Who's first?" he asked.

She smiled up at him when she answered. "Lucas is. He told me so."

Hunter couldn't tell if she were jesting with him or being sincere. He felt it his duty to set her straight. "Lucas has it backward, ma'am. He's second best." He nodded.

Lucas spoke up, addressing his comments to his friend. "We'll drop Taylor at the hotel and then . . ."

She interrupted him. "I want to go with you."

He shook his head. "You need to get some sleep," he told her. "You can barely stand up. I slept on the train. You didn't."

"Lucas, I feel fine. Truly."

"You look like hell. If you don't get some rest, you'll get sick."

The argument would have continued on, but Hunter stepped in and put a stop to it with one indisputable fact.

"You'll slow us down."

"Then I'll wait at the hotel," she immediately replied.

It almost killed her to be left behind, but she understood their reasoning. They would be going into places where a lady wouldn't be welcomed. That fact didn't bother her, but she knew Lucas would spend most of his time watching out for her instead of concentrating on the task at hand: finding the little girls.

Taylor didn't have to tell Lucas to take his guns with him this time. He and Hunter helped her check into the hotel room. They stayed less than a minute. After tossing her valise on the bed, Lucas grabbed his gunbelt, loaded his guns, and strapped the belt around his hips on his way out the door. He didn't even waste time saying good-bye.

She paced and fretted for over an hour, then decided to do mundane chores to keep busy. She had a bath, washed her hair, unpacked her clothes, and then stretched out on the bed in her robe. She thought to rest for just a minute or two and then get dressed again.

She slept for a good four or five hours. She awoke feeling disoriented. It took her a full minute to realize where she was. Part of her sleepy confusion was due to the fact that the room she was in was almost identical to the hotel room in Boston. The owners had obviously decided to build an exact duplication of the original. There was the same seating area with a divan and two chairs, the identical alcove housing the bed, and there were even two wardrobes in the room, both set against the same long wall. The colors in the room were somewhat different, however. This one was done in pale shades of gold with white accents. There was also one other difference. There were two doors on the left of the wardrobe instead of one. The first door led to the washroom. The second was an opening to the room reserved for Victoria. The adjoining area was smaller in dimensions and the focal point was a large four-poster bed covered with a royal blue spread. A chair, chest, and wardrobe took up the rest of the space. While the room didn't give the same feeling of intimacy as the alcove did, it had its own charm. It was certainly just as exquisitely appointed and really quite lovely.

Taylor was pleased that the second room she'd reserved was so close to this one. Victoria would be pleased with her accommodations. She'll be exhausted when she arrives, Taylor thought. She wished she had thought to ask Victoria to send a wire ahead telling her of her arrival time, but she'd been in such a state, she hadn't had time to think about such particulars.

Her stomach was suddenly grumbling. Taylor hadn't eaten in a good long while, yet the thought of food made her ill. She was still too churned up with worry and fear to eat anything, and so she went back to her pacing and her praying. A minute seemed as long as an hour. She checked the hour at least a dozen times. It was after eight in the evening. Lucas and Hunter had been gone over seven hours now. She didn't know if they'd come back this evening or not. When she grew too weary to pace, she went over to the window, leaned against the ledge, and stared out into the night. It was pitch black outside, for the moon was covered by rain-swollen clouds.

Where were Lucas and Hunter now? Had they found the babies yet?

There were a couple of possibilities. Hadn't Hunter

said just that to Lucas at the train station? Oh, why hadn't she asked him to explain what he'd meant? She'd behaved like a timid little mouse, that's why. And he'd fairly overwhelmed her, she silently added. She wouldn't dwell on her shortcomings now but would focus on the possibility that they had already found the little ones. Why, they could be on their way back to the hotel with her babies in their arms.

Taylor tried, but she couldn't will the children back. Lucas and Hunter arrived at her door several hours later. They were both empty-handed.

She wanted to push the two of them out and demand they continue their search. Reason prevailed, however. Both Hunter and Lucas looked exhausted.

"Are you going out again soon?" she asked.

"In a while," Lucas answered. "There's a bed in there," he told his friend.

Hunter nodded, then turned and disappeared into the second bedroom. Taylor chased after Lucas. He was on his way to the alcove where their bed was located.

"Did you find out anything? Anything at all?"

Lucas removed his gunbelt, looped it over one of the bed posters, then started to unbutton his shirt. Taylor moved closer to his side. The smell of gunpowder was on his clothes.

"You fired your gun."

He acted as though he hadn't heard the remark. "Hunter and I will start again in the morning. There are a couple of possibilities still to be checked out."

"Do you think they're still in Cincinnati?"

She was wringing her hands together in anxiety and trying without much success to remain calm. He didn't know if they were still in the city or not. Every lead thus far had turned into a dead end. He didn't think he needed to share the dour news with her, however. "We'll find them," he said.

Taylor sat down on the side of the bed. Lucas left the alcove and went to the washroom. He returned a few minutes later, looking clean and refreshed. He smelled of soap now, but there was still a lingering scent of gunpowder. Odd, but she didn't find the smell offensive at all; however, it did remind her he had fired his gun.

"Did you have to kill anyone?"

He was clearly exasperated by the question. "No," he answered, his tone abrupt.

She wasn't intimidated. "But you did fire your gun."

"Yes."

"Why?"

"Just wanted to get a little attention," he told her.

She was beginning to hate his half answers and thought about telling him just that, then changed her mind. She didn't want to get into an argument. Lucas was tired. He needed his rest so he could go back out and look for the babies again.

"You won't give up, will you?" She blurted out her worry and gripped her hands tight while she waited for an answer. Lucas towered over her. The expression on his face told her he didn't like the question. She was quick to guess the reason why.

"Did I just insult you again?"

He nodded.

"I'm sorry," she whispered.

He didn't look placated by her apology. Taylor let out a sigh and got out of his way so he could pull the covers back on the bed.

God, she wanted to believe in him. She should get down on her knees and thank her Maker for giving her

Lucas Ross. Whatever would she have done without him to help her? He really was her Prince Charming and hadn't Madam known that all along?

Heavens, her emotions were getting out of hand. She suddenly felt like weeping. She didn't give into the urge, however, because crying would upset Lucas, and after all the trouble he'd gone to over the past several days, the last thing she wanted to do was make him fret about her. The man needed rest, not more worry.

However, she was too upset to sleep. She decided to go into the other room so Lucas could have some peace and quiet. She turned but had only taken a step or two away from him when he captured her in his arms and pulled her down on the bed with him. He rolled over, keeping her in his arms, until she was flat on her back and he was looming over her.

He shifted his weight so he wouldn't crush her, then braced himself up on his elbows.

"You want to believe I won't ever give up looking, but you're still afraid I might. Isn't that right?"

"If you say you won't give up, I'll believe you."

He gently brushed her hair away from her brow. "Know what I'm going to do?" She shook her head.

"I'm going to tell you a bedtime story."

What had come over him? she thought. He was being so gentle and tender with her. "You need your rest, Lucas. You shouldn't have to try to soothe my fears."

He leaned down and kissed her. Then he rolled to his side, pulled her up against him, and leaned down to whisper in her ear. "Once upon a time . . ."

The story he told her was about a young boy whose only possession had been stolen by an Indian. The treasure was an old, dull-bladed paring knife the boy used for hunting, and while it would have been pretty useless in anyone else's estimation, it was all the boy owned and extremely important to him.

Taylor turned so she could face him. She wanted to ask him where the boy had gotten the knife and why was it all he possessed, but Lucas silenced her by brushing his fingers across her mouth. Then he continued on with his yarn. The boy, he told her, went looking for the knife. He followed the Indians to their wintering home. The lengths the boy went to, to get his knife back were surely exaggerated, for according to the tall tale, he chased the Indian from the back hills of Kentucky all the way to the center of the Ohio valley. Taylor was certain Lucas was making the story up as he went along. No one, especially a young, inexperienced boy, would spend a year and a half chasing after a useless knife.

Lucas certainly knew how to tell a story, however. She was captivated. The tests of courage the boy was given on his journey were fascinating. She laughed out loud when he told her a black bear had run the boy up a tree.

"Bears can climb trees," she reminded him. She wondered how he would get the fictional boy out of that dilemma.

He didn't give her the details. He simply told her the boy was forced to kill the bear before he could go on with his quest.

Taylor didn't scoff. It wouldn't have been polite. And Lucas didn't actually end the story the way she thought he would by telling her he finally found his treasure. He only said the lad eventually found the Indian.

The knife, she supposed, had been lost forever, and the moral of the story was a lesson in courage. She was too practical minded to believe the yarn, of course.

She remembered how tired he probably was when he yawned. Lucas leaned close and kissed her good night. His mouth lingered over the task, and when he at last pulled away from her, she was shivering for more.

He wasn't going to accommodate her. He pulled her up against him again and closed his eyes. He liked to fall asleep inhaling her fragrance. And holding her close. Her back was nestled against his chest, her backside was pressed against his groin, and his arm was wrapped tightly around her waist. She fit him perfectly. It was his last thought before he fell asleep.

Taylor could barely move. Her husband's heat enveloped her. And his strength, she thought with a sleepy yawn. She couldn't stop herself from relaxing against him. She would only rest for a few minutes, she thought to herself . . . just a few minutes.

She awakened an hour later. She eased herself out of the bed so she wouldn't disturb Lucas and went into the other room. She didn't know why, but she felt the need to look in on Hunter, just to make certain he was still there, she supposed.

Taylor didn't make a noticeable sound when she walked into the second bedroom. Hunter was where he was supposed to be. He was sound asleep on top of the covers. Because he was such a tall man, like Lucas he slept diagonally across the bed. He rested on his stomach, one hand down at his side, the other hidden under one of the pillows. He was barefoot and bare chested. Taylor noticed the chill in the room when she started shivering. One of the windows was open, its curtains billowing inward from the stiff breeze. She assumed Hunter had wanted some fresh air, but he surely hadn't realized how cold it would get inside the room. Why, you could almost see your breath. She tried to be as quiet as possible as she walked over to the window and closed it halfway. Then she went to the wardrobe in her room and got one of the blankets stored on the top shelf. She hurried back to Hunter's room and covered Lucas's friend from top to bottom. She noticed the scars on his back and shoulders when she tucked the covers around him, and wondered how he'd come by the marks. His hand moved ever so slightly near the pillow, but she didn't think she woke him. She was shivering by the time she finished her task and went back to her own bed so Lucas could warm her again.

The minute she left the room, Hunter put his hand back on the handle of his gun he'd tucked under the pillow. He was wide awake the second she'd crossed the threshold and had stayed awake all the while she fussed over him. The little act of kindness stunned him. It was thoughtful and caring and sweet.

And damned stupid. He could have blown her head off. He let out a sigh. No, he wouldn't have accidentally shot her. He'd know all the while it was Taylor. He'd heard the rustle of silk first when she walked into the bedroom, then caught the faint scent of flowers in the air when she leaned over him to spread the covers and felt her gentle, feminine touch when she touched his skin as she tucked the blanket around him.

He couldn't frown his reaction away. The pleasure wouldn't leave. He felt . . . comforted, and there wasn't a damned thing he could do about it. He wanted to smile and all because of a simple act of thoughtfulness. It was a new experience for him and it fairly overwhelmed him. She'd fussed over him.

If that didn't beat all. Hunter fell asleep with a smile in his heart.

Taylor fell asleep with her husband on top of her. He had a rather peculiar habit of rolling over until he was completely covering her, then nuzzling the side of her neck while he slept. She could barely breathe, so crushing was his weight. She could have pinched him into moving away from her. She didn't. In truth, she liked having him plastered on top of her. She closed her eyes and pretended he was wide awake and knew exactly what he was doing. Then she wrapped her arms around his waist, held tight, and went back to sleep.

Morning came all too soon. Taylor woke up hugging a pillow. She was all alone in the bed. From the silence surrounding her, she knew both Lucas and Hunter had already left.

She stayed in bed a few more minutes while she formulated her plans for the day. The very first thing she would do was check the train schedule and try to guess when Victoria would arrive. If things had gone according to their plan, she thought her friend would probably be on the four o'clock train.

Her thoughts kept trying to turn to the babies. Were they being cared for? Were they getting enough food? Were they warm? Oh, God, what if they were being hurt now, this very minute, while she . . .

Taylor forced herself to stop the thoughts by saying a prayer that God and his guardian angels would look after the babies until she could find them. She knew she would go out of her mind if she dwelled on all the terrible possibilities, and so she frantically tried to think of something pleasant.

Lucas's story came to mind. It was a blessed diversion. And full of poppycock, she added with a shake of her head. He'd told her a tall tale indeed, and now that she had time to think about it, she decided he was either teasing her or was under the misconception she was a country bumpkin who would believe anything he told her. She wasn't naive, and she'd tell him so when he returned to the hotel. The boy in the story had lived through a bear attack and a windstorm that whistled like a train and lifted full-grown trees out of the ground and hurled them across a valley. Who could even imagine such a thing? Oh, yes, she remembered, the boy had almost drowned, too, and had shared a makeshift barge with a . . . What had he called the animal? She pondered the question a minute or two, then smiled when she remembered. A mountain cat, he'd told her. Necessity and survival had kept the cat too preoccupied to attack the boy.

And if she believed that nonsense, he'd probably try to convince her dirt was as valuable as gold.

The story hadn't simply been a tale of courage. He wasn't just telling her to hold onto her courage, he was also explaining that some people never give up. It was a sweet parable.

God help her, she was feeling teary eyed again. Lucas Ross was an easy man to love. "Enough," she whispered to stop her errant thoughts. If she wasn't careful, she'd start wishing for something she could never have.

Taylor tossed the pillow aside, then swung her legs over the side of the bed and started to get up. She spotted the knife then. It was on the bedside table. She couldn't imagine how the thing had gotten there.

And then came recognition. Taylor was suddenly filled with hope. She stared at the knife a long minute. She didn't need to touch it. She knew it was a useless, dull-bladed paring knife a boy would hunt with.

Lucas was the boy in the story, of course, but he had

surely embellished the tale to make it more interesting. And to have more of an impact, she realized. It
didn't matter. She understood the message. This
morning Lucas had given her his answer to her
question from the night before.

He would never give up.

12

The nature of bad news infects the teller.
— William Shakespeare,
Anthony and Cleopatra

Victoria wasn't on the four o'clock train. Taylor
waited at the station until all the passengers had
departed. She was disappointed but not worried.
Everything would have had to go extremely smoothly
for Victoria to have finished up all their business in
Boston so quickly. Tomorrow, Taylor told herself. Her
friend would arrive tomorrow.

It was unfortunate, but while she waited at the
station, several men did try to accost her. A simple
reminder to behave like a gentleman dissuaded one
man. Two others weren't so easily discouraged. Taylor
ended up having to be downright rude. They didn't
seem to mind. She didn't become alarmed until they
followed her outside. She fell in with the crowd of
people walking down the street but kept glancing back
over her shoulder to see if they were still behind
her.

The two men were there all right and looking quite determined. Their clothes were filthy. So were their faces. The taller of the two kept smacking his lips together. He wore a dark wide-brimmed hat down low over his forehead. The other kept snickering. Taylor could feel herself panicking inside. She frantically looked around her for an avenue of escape.

She had already made one foolish mistake when she'd left the safety of the station. The cabbies were all waiting there for their fares, and why in heaven's name hadn't she jumped into one of the vehicles when she'd had the chance? The safety of the crowd she was hiding herself in was diminishing with each step she took. More than half the number had turned into several buildings, and when they reached the intersection, the group split in half again. Several turned to the left, and more turned to the right. Only an elderly couple continued on straight ahead.

Taylor decided to stay with them. She didn't want to go down any side streets. Not only was she certain she'd get lost, she also knew there was a good possibility one of the streets would turn into a dead end.

She could feel the ruffians gaining on her. She picked up her skirts and hurried on across the road. She kept the elderly couple between her and her stalkers. She spotted several shops ahead. Her panic eased just a little. She decided she would go inside one of the establishments and ask for assistance in handling the men chasing after her.

She was sorry she hadn't thought about bringing her gun with her. Because Cincinnati was such a polished, sophisticated city, she'd never considered the possibility she might need that sort of protection. Why, they were civilized here, for God's sake. Didn't the country ignorants behind her realize that?

She turned to see how far they were behind her and

noticed the couple she'd been using as a shield had turned to walk down the alley she'd just passed. She wasn't about to follow them. God help her, she was suddenly all alone on the street. She heard one of the hooligans giggle. Her stomach lurched in reaction.

She was certainly frightened, but she was also becoming furious. She wasn't going to become a victim, she told herself. By God, she would scream, bite, and kick and make enough racket to draw a good-sized crowd.

Where were all the bobbies when you needed them?

Her panic was growing. What she really needed, she instructed her Maker, was a little miracle. Nothing fancy, she hastily qualified, just a tiny, barely noticeable miracle. Please, God, please . . .

Her prayer was answered. The miracle was just a half a block away. A gun shop. Right smack in the middle of the next block. Taylor had only just finished her prayer when she noticed the boldly painted sign waving like a banner above the shop for anyone and everyone to see.

God bless Mr. Colt, Taylor thought when she reached her destination and saw the display of six-shooters in the window. She let out a sigh of pleasure and rushed inside.

The bell hanging down over the door alerted the shopkeeper she was there. He seemed to be the only other person in the store. She smiled in greeting and hurried down the center of the aisle to the counter at the back of the store.

The owner was actually a little frightful looking at first glance. The poor man had obviously been in a fire, for his face, neck, and hands were covered with thick burn scars. He didn't have any eyebrows at all. Because of his marks, she couldn't judge his age. He had a full head of brown hair though, and because it was tinged with gray, she assumed he was at least forty. He wore thick wire-rimmed glasses. They kept slipping down the narrow bridge of his nose, and he kept pushing them back up.

The owner was obviously uncomfortable about his appearance. He averted his face when she drew close and asked her in a clipped, no-nonsense tone of voice if she required any assistance. He addressed his question to the countertop.

"Yes, thank you," she replied. "I would like to look at the Colt on the shelf behind you. Is it perchance loaded?"

The owner handed the gun to Taylor, then reached behind him to collect a small square box of ammunition. He placed the box on the counter next to the gun.

"We don't keep any of the guns loaded here," he explained.

Taylor opened the box of ammunition, then picked up the gun. Before the owner could stop her, she loaded the weapon.

"Whatever are you doing, miss?" the man asked, his alarm obvious in his tone of voice.

He dared a quick look up at her face. She gave him a wide smile. She was about to explain her reason for loading the weapon when the bell sounded behind her.

"You've got a loaded gun there," he told her in a stammer.

She nodded agreement. "Yes, I do, thank God, and just in the nick of time. Will you excuse me for a moment?"

She didn't give him time to argue with her. She turned around just as the two hooligans started down the center aisle. The wooden floor creaked under the pounding of their boots.

They came to a quick stop when they spotted the gun in her hand.

"It ain't loaded, Elwin," the shorter of the two companions told his friend. He smiled at Taylor then, a nasty, malicious smile, and she noticed he was missing a considerable number of teeth. He was without a doubt the most disgusting individual she'd ever come across.

"She's trying to bluff us all right, Wilburn," his friend said.

The man named Elwin looked around the shop, then nudged his friend. "Lot's of fancy guns in here," he remarked with another loud snicker.

Wilburn nodded. "You the only one working here?" he shouted to the owner.

"I'm betting he is," Elwin speculated.

The owner started to bend down below the counter. "Stay right where you are," Wilburn shouted. He turned to his friend. "Might as well rob the place while we're here. There's got to be a storeroom in back. We could take turns with the little lady in there."

Elwin snickered again. Taylor wanted to shoot him.

"Oh, Lordie," the owner whispered behind her.

She didn't take her attention away from the vile men in front of her when she sought to calm the shopkeeper. "It will be all right, sir."

"It ain't going to be all right for you, little lady," Elwin drawled out. He nudged his friend in his ribs and let out a low giggle. His hat dropped down lower on his brow. She couldn't see his eyes, but she guessed they were as ugly as the rest of him.

They took a step toward her. She cocked her gun in preparation. He stopped, grinned, pushed his hat back on his forehead, and took another step.

Taylor blew his hat clean off his head.

He let out a howl. The sound of gunfire muffled his cry and reverberated throughout the store. The glass in the front window shivered from the noise. The bullet lodged in the door behind the villain.

Elwin looked flabbergasted. Taylor thought that was an appropriate reaction.

"She get you, Elwin?" his friend asked. He squinted at his friend, looking for a mark.

Elwin shook his head. "She didn't even nick me," he boasted.

"She wasn't bluffing," his friend whispered.

Wilburn's face turned red. He took another step toward her. Taylor shot a hole in the tip of his boot.

Wilburn made a try next. Taylor was losing her patience. She shot a hole through his boot, too. He jumped back and stared down at his feet. He wiggled his toes to make sure they were all still there, then glared at the woman who'd just ruined his boot.

"Nope, she ain't bluffing us," he told his companion. "We're going to have to rush her."

Taylor let out a dramatic sigh. "They're really very stupid, aren't they?" she called out to the owner.

She heard his chuckle behind her. "Yes, they are," he agreed.

Elwin didn't like hearing the insult. His face turned as red as a ripe tomato. He started to reach into his pocket. Taylor cocked her gun again.

"We've got to wrestle that gun out of her hand," Wilburn decided.

Elwin shook his head. "You wrestle with her," he suggested in a mutter. "Can't you see where she's got her fancy gun pointed? My personals are in her sights. She's crazy, Wilburn. No telling what she'll do. She might not miss us with her next shot."

Both men mulled the matter over for a few seconds before they started backing away.

"We ain't going to forget you," Elwin promised.

"We'll get you all right," Wilburn added.

The shopkeeper took control then. He snatched up the loaded rifle he kept hidden on the bottom shelf and shouted a warning.

"I'll shoot you both if I have to, and I'll get you in your middles. Now get over there by the wall and keep your hands up high where I can see them."

Taylor turned to the owner. "How much do you want for this gun? I've taken a liking to it. I would like to purchase it, sir."

He shook his head at her. "You can have it without charge. You saved me from getting robbed and most likely killed. I'm in your debt, miss. If you'll only just tell me your name and address, I'll put it in my log. Each Colt is registered, you see, with its own number. It's a way to match the gun up with the owner."

"My name's Taylor Ross," she answered. "I'm staying at the Cincinnati Hamilton House, and I do thank you for this gift."

The shopkeeper kept his rifle trained on the two culprits now cowering together against the wall. Taylor tucked her gun in the pocket of her coat. She took the long way around the men on her way to the front door.

"Will you make certain they stay here for a little while? I don't want them following me."

"Don't you worry none, miss. As soon as my partner gets here, I'll send him to get the authorities."

"Good day to you then," she called out as she opened the door.

"Miss?" the owner shouted.

She paused at the threshold. "Yes?"

"Where'd you learn to shoot like that?"

"Scotland."

She was pulling the door closed behind her when she heard his response to her answer.

"If that don't beat all."

Taylor walked all the way back to the hotel. She stopped at the first Catholic church she came upon and went inside to light a candle for Madam. She sat in the pew for close to an hour. First she prayed, and then she talked things over with her grandmother. She felt better and certainly more in control after her visit to the church. In truth she wasn't certain if it was because she'd prayed or because she had the protection of a gun in her pocket.

It was dinnertime when she reached Hamilton House. As much as the thought of food repelled her, she knew she should eat something. She was already feeling nauseated.

She hurried to the Ladies Ordinary, took a table in the corner, and ordered soup, two biscuits, and a pot of tea. The waiter tried to talk her into eating a more substantial meal. She graciously declined his suggestion. She nibbled on one biscuit and decided to take the other one back to her room in case she started feeling queasy again. She barely touched the vegetable soup, but the tea tasted wonderful to her. When she was finished with her sparse meal, she felt refreshed. The feeling didn't last long. After she'd had her bath and changed into her nightgown, she was worn out. She fell asleep on the settee while she waited for Lucas to come back.

She didn't wake up until the following morning. She found herself in her bed. Lucas must have carried her there. He'd changed his clothes, too, for the shirt he'd worn yesterday was looped over a chair.

They were still looking for the babies. Why was it taking so long? Taylor tried not to become discouraged. She got dressed, then went over to the writing table to make a list of things she could do to help in the search.

The more people they had looking for the children, the quicker they'd be found, she reasoned, and so she wrote out an advertisement to place in the local newspapers. Then she considered hiring several private investigators. If they'd been raised in Cincinnati and kept their ears opened to the goings on around the city, one might have already heard about the twins. Perhaps the hotel's management could recommend a few good investigators.

Taylor also considered making up flyers and pinning them all around the city offering a substantial reward for information about the twins.

If they were still in the city . . .

The day dragged. She decided to show Lucas her list that evening. If he didn't have any valid objections to her plan, she would place the advertisement with the papers in the morning. Perhaps he or Hunter would have a few suggestions to make as well.

Being idle was driving her crazy. She paced and she prayed, but the time still dragged by. Oh, how she wished Victoria were here. She needed someone to talk to and her friend was such a compassionate, caring woman, she would know the torment Taylor was going through.

She prayed her friend would be on the four o'clock train today. It was almost half past three now. Taylor went to the wardrobe to get her coat. She was going to go back to the station, of course, but this time she was taking her gun with her.

She filled the chambers with more of her bullets, tucked the gun in her pocket, and was just putting her coat on when the door opened and Hunter and Lucas walked inside. She was thrilled to see them until she got a good look at their faces. They both looked disheartened.

"You didn't find them, did you?"

Lucas shook his head. He closed the door behind him and leaned against it. "Not yet," he qualified when he saw her crushed expression.

He looked exhausted. The weariness was evident around his eyes. And in his voice.

She wanted to tell him he mustn't lose heart or give up but caught herself before she voiced what he would surely take as an insult.

"You need to get some sleep, Mr. Ross," she said. "Rest will clear your head. Are you hungry? There's a biscuit on the table over there."

She realized how inadequate the offer was as soon as she made the suggestion. "I'll be happy to go and get both of you some proper food."

She turned to Hunter. He was leaning against one of the wardrobes watching her.

"What about you, Hunter?"

"I'll get something later," he replied.

Taylor nodded. Her expression was filled with anxiety. She was gripping her hands together and looking close to breaking down. Hunter looked at Lucas to see what he was going to do about comforting his wife.

No help there, he realized. Lucas looked bone tired. Hunter shook his head at his friend. "You never could keep up with me, could you?"

"The hell I couldn't," Lucas replied.

Hunter snorted. He turned back to Taylor. "We have one lead that could prove helpful. We're waiting to hear."

"Might prove helpful," Lucas stressed before Taylor

could get her hopes up. He didn't want to see her disappointed again.

"We should know in a little while," Hunter interjected.

"Where were you going?" Lucas asked. He seemed to have only just noticed she had her coat half on.

His question reminded her of her errand. "To the station to see if Victoria is on the four o'clock train," she explained while she struggled to get her arm in the sleeve of her coat.

Hunter started across the room. He stopped suddenly and turned back to Lucas. "She's got a gun in her pocket," he told his friend. "She always carry one?"

Because she was standing directly in front of him, she decided to answer his question. "Cincinnati is far more dangerous than I thought it would be," she explained. "I had a near miss yesterday. How did you know I had a gun in my pocket?"

"The bulge," he answered.

She told him how astute she thought he was because he'd noticed, then pulled the gun out of her pocket to show him. "It was a gift," she explained.

Lucas was still leaning against the door. He was so tired he barely paid any attention to the conversation. He wanted a hot bath and hotter food. He needed a good eight hours sleep, but he knew he couldn't waste the time on such a luxury. Time was critical now. The leads were still warm, and if they were ever going to find Taylor's nieces, they would have to move fast.

His instinct told him the little girls were still in the city. Hunter felt the same way. He'd questioned a man, more drunk than sober, but still reasonably coherent, who swore he'd seen the little ones with the Border brothers just two days before.

The Border brothers. Lucas's skin tightened at the mere mention of the name. The two men were as evil as Satan, as sneaky as a jackal, and as mean dispositioned as a rattler. Lucas couldn't wait to get his hands on the bastards. They used to be in the business of selling for a couple of prostitutes. The younger of the brothers took a fancy to cutting up the women, and it wasn't long before his butchering put an end to the enterprise. They moved on to another profitable business. They still bartered anything and everything, but their specialty was children now. Orphans, the man told Hunter, were their preference. No complications, he'd explained. The more fortunate ones were sold to couples out in the wilderness who needed help running their farms. The prettier children weren't as fortunate, for there were men with . . . What had the man said? Unusual cravings.

Oh, yes, the Border brothers. They deserved to die a slow, agonizing death, and Lucas felt he was just the man to deal out the punishment. Hunter would probably get in his way though. He'd already made the claim that he was going to skin the pair alive.

No doubt about it. One way or another, by Hunter's knife or his own hand, the brothers were going to die. Justice would be served.

Lucas pushed himself away from the door, rolled his shoulders to take the stiffness out, then turned his attention to his wife. For the last few days and nights, he'd been forced to move in the shadows of the dark, foul sewer of the city, and he desperately needed to cleanse his mind now. He needed Taylor. She represented warmth and brightness and beauty. He would confront the beast later. For now he wanted only to surround himself in her scent and her magical touch. She was as welcoming as the sun to a man who'd been hiding in the darkness for too damned long.

Hunter was drawn to her as well. Lucas had never seen him spend this much time talking to any woman. He was sure talking up a storm now. Lucas wasn't jealous or even irritated by his friend's behavior. His trust in Hunter was absolute. He understood his need as well, for the two of them were very alike.

Taylor didn't realize how she'd affected his friend. She accepted his smile as an ordinary occurrence. She didn't have a clue how amazing it was for Hunter to ever smile at all.

Hunter looked like he wanted to laugh. Taylor was leaning against his side while she pointed out all the clever little changes in the gun Hunter held.

His friend kept giving him glances. Lucas walked forward. He decided to find out what his friend found so amusing.

"The gun is registered with its own special number," Taylor was explaining. "But did you know that each piece, before it's fitted, is also etched with the same number? If only a part of the gun is found, the number could still be read."

Hunter nodded. "How many times did you say you fired?"

"Three times," she answered. "There wasn't a kick, Hunter. I didn't have to adjust my aim at all. It's a vast improvement over the older models. You must try it sometime."

Hunter handed the weapon to Lucas. "It's lighter," he remarked.

"Is it loaded?" Lucas asked.

Hunter grinned. "After yesterday's adventure, I would imagine it is."

"I cleaned it last night and reloaded this morning," she told her husband. She wanted him to know she took good care of her possessions.

Then she tried to take her gun back. Lucas wouldn't give it to her. "You don't need this," he remarked.

Hunter was smiling again. Something was up all right, but Lucas was too weary to figure it out. Only one fact was registering in his mind. His friend hadn't smiled this much in all the time he'd known him.

"Weren't you listening?" Hunter asked.

"Guess not," Lucas replied.

"She needs the gun."

"This isn't the gun you had in Boston," Lucas remarked, for he'd only just realized the subtle differences in the weapons. "This is brand-new. Where'd you get it?"

"Weren't you paying attention to what I was telling Hunter?"

"No."

She let out a sigh. Her poor husband was so tired, he was having trouble concentrating. "You need to get some sleep, Mr. Ross. Give me my gun back. I got it at a gun shop, of course. Heavens, I'm going to be late for the train's arrival if I don't hurry."

"You still have plenty of time," Lucas told her. It suddenly occurred to him that she was back to calling him Mr. Ross again. He scowled and turned his attention back to the shiny Colt he held in his hand.

"It's nice," he remarked. "Why'd you buy it?"

"It was a gift."

"Why?" Lucas asked.

"Why what?" Taylor replied.

He held onto his patience. "Why was it a gift?"

She didn't care for his tone of voice. It was snappish. She didn't care for the way he was scrutinizing her either. He reminded her of a barrister trying to prove a hidden motive. Taylor's spine stiffened in reaction. She was his wife, not a defendant. The flash of irritation was short-lived however. Then she felt guilty because she was certain she was overreacting. Lucas looked dead on his feet. She should be giving him her sympathy.

Because he didn't appear to be in a very amiable mood, she decided not to go into detail about the near robbery. It might upset him. What he didn't know wouldn't hurt him. "It isn't important," she announced. "My, you look tuckered out. Why don't I go and turn the bed down for you?"

He might have been exhausted, but he was still as quick as ever. He grabbed hold of her arm before she could take a single step away from him.

"Why was it a gift?" he asked again.

She let out a sigh. "The owner was . . . appreciative."

"Why?"

The set of his jaw told her he wasn't going to give up until he had all his answers.

"There was a small, inconsequential altercation in the store and just a hint of a possibility of a robbery," she said with a shrug. "That's all."

"Elwin and Wilburn."

Hunter interjected the names. He was grinning like a naked bandit bathing in gold coins.

"Couldn't you tell I wasn't going to go into detail with Mr. Ross?" she asked Hunter. She added a frown so he'd know she was displeased with him.

He didn't seem to mind. He winked at her. "Are you going to make me sorry I told you what happened?" she asked. She didn't give him time to answer. She shook her head at him and said, "You're supposed to be loyal to me, sir."

"I am?" Hunter asked.

She nodded. She waved her hand in Lucas's direction. "I'm his wife, after all."

"Who in thunder are Wellen and Elburn?" Lucas

asked the question in a surly, someone-better-answer-me voice.

"They're Elwin and Wilburn." Hunter took great delight in correcting his friend's pronunciation.

"Start explaining, Taylor."

"You might become irritated."

She was a little late with that concern. Lucas was already looking angry.

"They're the men who followed Taylor from the train station yesterday. She told me she prayed for a miracle. God gave her one."

"Oh?" Lucas asked, his voice suspiciously soft.

Hunter couldn't wait to explain. "A gun shop."

Lucas nodded. "I see."

"Your eyelid's twitching," Hunter said.

Lucas ignored his friend. He turned his attention to his wife. She was giving him a sweet smile and trying to act as though nothing out of the ordinary had happened.

"And?" he prodded.

"There really isn't anything more to tell," she replied.

Hunter didn't agree. He ended up telling Lucas the entire story.

Just as Taylor suspected, Lucas didn't take it all in stride. His grip on her arm started stinging. She pinched him to make him let up on his hold. By the time his had-to-tell-it-all friend finished giving him every last detail, Lucas's jaw was clenched tight, and there was a noticeable tick in his left eyelid.

It mesmerized her.

"Do you have any idea what could have happened to you?"

She knew that question was coming. "If you weren't so tired, you would realize I used my wits to get out of a worrisome situation. You would be praising me, sir."

The tick intensified. Yes, he should have complimented her. He didn't though. He dragged her over to the settee, forced her to sit down, and then towered over her while he tried to scare the hell out of her.

He didn't raise his voice, and that made his lecture all the worse in her opinion. In great, vivid detail he told her what could have happened to her. He painted a godawful picture. Her face turned as white as snow by the time he was finished listing all the horrors she might have had to endure . . . before they killed her.

Lucas had her dead and buried on a remote country road, and when he at last finished with his ungentlemanly terror tactics, he made her admit she'd done several foolish things. "You never should have gone alone."

"No, I shouldn't have," she readily agreed. Her head was bowed low.

He thought she was being contrite and maybe even a little submissive. He was immediately suspicious. In all their time together, he'd noticed how headstrong she was and how stubborn. But submissive? Never.

Fatigue made his anger over her foolishness more intense. He knew he was overreacting. He didn't care. The thought of Taylor in such danger made him furious and all because it scared the hell out of him. If anything ever happened to her, he didn't know what he would do.

"I made a promise to your grandmother to keep you safe until you got settled . . . where in thunder are you going to get settled? Are you going to take your nieces to their father's relatives? You weren't thinking of taking them back to England, were you? No, of course you weren't. What about Boston?"

She lifted her shoulders in a shrug. The action made him want to throttle her. And then kiss her. He shook his head.

"I'm not a saint," he muttered.

Taylor didn't look at him when she agreed. "No, you certainly aren't a saint, sir."

"How long am I . . ."

He didn't finish his question.

"Stuck with me?" she asked, her voice as whisper soft as his had been when he started the question.

No, that wasn't what he was going to ask her, but thankfully he'd stopped himself before he blurted out the rest. He'd wanted to know exactly how long he was supposed to keep his hands off her. Pretending to be a eunuch around her was taking its toll. He wasn't made of stone. Didn't she understand that?

Lucas let out a sigh. Of course she didn't understand. She was quite astute about most things, but when it came to the marriage bed, she was as innocent as a . . . virgin, just like she was supposed to be.

What was the matter with him? He was trying to make her understand she couldn't just run here and there without protection, and right smack in the middle of his speech on the merits of using caution, his mind turned to thoughts of what it would be like to bed her. Lucas was thoroughly disgusted with himself.

The tension inside the room grew until it was almost unbearable. Hunter had already gone into the second bedroom so Taylor and Lucas could have the privacy they needed. Lucas suddenly wished there was a crowd of people in the suite with them. The questions rambling around in his head, one on top of another and another and another, kept demanding answers. He suddenly felt like a barracuda he'd watched once, fighting against the hook. He'd stood next to a fisherman on the pier and seen how the weathered old man had patiently worked the fish. He'd given him plenty of line, let the barracuda fight until exhaustion finally overtook him, and then the old man had calmly reeled him in.

Lucas pushed the memory away. He kept his gaze firmly directed on his wife. He couldn't see her face, for her head was bowed so low he thought her chin must be touching her chest. God, she looked dejected. He assumed he'd injured her feelings, and hell, what was he going to do about that?

She suddenly straightened her spine and looked up at him. One glance told him he'd been wrong in concluding he'd hurt her feelings. There weren't any tears in her eyes. There was fire. She didn't look like she wanted to weep. Quite the opposite. She looked like she wanted to kill him.

He was at first startled by the notice, then incredibly relieved. Oh, how she pleased him. He felt like laughing and couldn't give a reason why. The woman was making him crazy. Those wonderful, beguiling blue eyes of hers captured his full attention. And his heart.

They stared at each other a long, silent moment. She was trying to collect her thoughts so that she would sound reasonable when she spoke to him.

He was using the time to come to grips with the truth. He expected to be hit by lightning. He wasn't. He didn't blanch or stagger to his knees, and all because the realization wasn't gruesome or horrifying after all. It was in fact quite liberating.

He could feel himself being reeled in. The questions were gone, the answer had been there all along. He realized that now. He'd just been too stubborn and mule headed to recognize all the signs.

He was a man in love with his wife.

Taylor had succeeded in getting her anger under control until her insensitive clod of a husband smiled at her. He'd just asked her the most appalling question and then had the gall to grin over it.

"I'll be happy to answer your question," she announced in a voice that shook with anger. "You're stuck with me until you find my babies. It's that simple. Find them, and then you can leave."

She suddenly bounded to her feet. She put her hands on her hips and glared at him. "Go where the wind blows you, Mr. Ross, if that is your inclination."

Hunter stood in the doorway watching Taylor. Since she wasn't paying any attention to him, he thought it safe to smile. He wanted to laugh. Lord, she was in a lather and she was about the prettiest thing he'd ever seen. He wondered if Lucas knew how fortunate he was to have married her. She wasn't just beautiful, she was also spirited. Hunter found it an appealing combination.

He didn't want to interrupt, but he'd noticed the lateness in the hour and thought he'd offer to go to the train station to collect her friend. He guessed he'd have to wait until Mrs. Ross was finished giving Mr. Ross hell before he could find out if she wanted him to go on the errand or not.

Taylor kept her attention on her husband. She was determined to make him understand how she felt and why. Her mind raced from one argument to another.

"What either one of us wants isn't the least important," she began. "Both of us must put the children first. Every adult should," she added in a whisper.

Then she remembered an incident from her past she thought would best explain her position.

"I saw a woman strike a boy across his face. It was at the annual fair held on my grandmother's estates. The woman used her fist and the blow lifted the lad off the ground. He landed in the mud. It was a miracle his neck wasn't broken."

Lucas didn't show any reaction to the remembrance. He waited to hear the rest of the story.

"Quite a few people witnessed the act of cruelty, but none of them did anything about it. He was just twelve years old. Someone should have come to his rescue. She was cruel and malicious."

"You did something though, didn't you?"

"I certainly did. The woman was employed by my grandmother. I made her promise not to strike the boy again. I threatened to ask Madam to fire her if she ever raised her hand against him again."

"How old were you?"

"Ten."

"You were awfully young to . . ."

"My age isn't important to this story," she interrupted. "The woman told me the boy was a distant relation she'd been forced to take in and feed. She didn't want him and she certainly didn't love him. I made certain the boy was taken out of harm's way. That was all that mattered to me."

"How did you accomplish that?"

"I took him home with me."

He smiled. Of course she took him home with her. He couldn't imagine Taylor doing anything less, even at the tender age of ten.

"I would like to meet him someday," Lucas remarked.

"You already have, Mr. Ross. Thomas took over the arrangements for our wedding. He made certain there weren't any problems. He did a fine job."

Lucas remembered the young man. "He was your grandmother's butler."

"Yes. Mr. Ross, the only reason I shared the incident with you was to help you understand that it doesn't matter if you're inconvenienced or taxed or even stuck with me as you so eloquently stated. You and I, and Hunter, too, all have the same responsibility. It is our obligation, indeed our sacred duty, to protect the innocent from harm. I can't take the babies home and keep them safe until you find them.

"I've already given you my word I'll find them. Are you now suggesting I might abandon you?"

She could tell he was getting angry. She didn't care. "You did ask me how long you were going to be stuck with me," she reminded him.

"No," he corrected. "You assumed that was what I was going to ask. Don't jump to conclusions. They're usually wrong."

He moved forward until he was standing just on the other side of the table facing her. "And don't ever tell me what I may or may not do. We aren't at odds over the issue of the children. I recognize my responsibility and so does Hunter. Do we look like we're going to bolt?"

She shook her head. "You really weren't going to ask me how long you were stuck with me?"

"No."

She felt like a fool. She was mortified by her own conduct. She could feel herself blushing. Lord help her, she'd lectured him, insulted him as well, and simply telling him she was sorry wouldn't be adequate.

"I'll pay you," she blurted out.

"What did you say?" He was certain he hadn't heard correctly. She wouldn't deliberately insult him again by suggesting he would take money for doing what she had just pointed out was his sacred duty.

"I'll give you anything you want," she explained in a rush.

She added a nod to let him know she was sincere.

The tick was back in his eyelid. Her offer obviously hadn't pleased him. She was bewildered. "I meant no offense, sir. I was simply being practical. I know you'll find the babies with or without compensation. Honestly, there isn't any reason to get huffy."

"Huffy?" He choked on the word.

"Oh, how like a man to get riled up over a practical matter." She waved her hand in the air. "Forget I made the offer."

"Too late," he told her.

She let out a sigh. She'd hurt his pride, she realized, and it was up to her to repair the damage. The problem was simple; the answer eluded her, however. She didn't know how to soothe him.

Mr. Ross seemed to take exception to everything she said. She was going to tell him she believed he was a bit high-strung when he turned her attention.

"I'll take you up on your offer."

Taylor wasn't the only one surprised by his turn-about. Hunter raised an eyebrow in reaction. He was astonished.

"You will?" she asked.

"Yes, I will," he agreed. "You did say I could have anything I wanted, isn't that right?"

"Yes." She hurried to add, "After we've found the babies."

"Of course."

He gave her a wide smile and then turned to look at Hunter. "Do you want to go with me to the train station? We could get something to eat on our way back."

Hunter checked the time before answering. "The meeting's set for six," he reminded his friend.

"We'll be back by then."

Lucas started for the door. Taylor skirted her way around the table and chased after him. She grabbed hold of his arm and asked him to stop.

"Do you know what you want?" she asked.

"Yes. I know exactly what I want."

Hunter opened the door and walked out into the corridor. Lucas tried to follow him. Taylor grabbed hold of him again.

"For heaven's sake," she began. "If you know what you want, kindly tell me."

He turned around to look at her. He wanted to see her expression when he enlightened her.

"I want"—he leaned down and kissed her hard—"a wedding night."

13

Love sought is good, but giv'n unsought is better.
—William Shakespeare,
Twelfth Night

*H*e rendered her speechless. He was out the door and halfway down the corridor by the time she recovered her wits. Then she went running across the room, almost ripped the door off its hinges when she opened it, and called after him.

"Are you out of your mind?"

He didn't turn around when he answered her. "Must be," he called out in a gratingly cheerful tone of voice.

Taylor sagged against the door frame. Her shouted question caused a bit of curiosity with some of the other hotel guests. Three doors opened along the hallway. Two men and one woman peeked out to see what all the commotion was about. Lucas and Hunter disappeared down the stairwell. She was left to deal with the neighbors. She considered calling out an

315

apology, then changed her mind. She hurried back inside her room and shut the door.

She collapsed in the nearest chair and tried to reason through Mr. Ross's outrageous request. Or was it a demand? She sighed then. It had certainly sounded like a demand.

Didn't he realize how complicated things would become if they became intimate? She didn't want to think about it. That man. What in thunder was wrong with him? Didn't he remember he didn't want to be married?

"He's bluffing." She whispered her conclusion. The possibility filled her with relief, for sharing a wedding night with Lucas Ross would complicate everything.

Wouldn't it?

Lord, she could barely catch her breath. The image of Mr. Ross in bed with her without his pants on made her heart skip a beat. He had to be bluffing. She repeated the thought. He didn't want any complications either. Or commitment, she added with a nod.

The man was downright rude to gct her all riled up with his games. Taylor forced herself to put her husband out of her thoughts. She had more important things to think about.

Like Victoria. Since Hunter had taken over the adjacent bedroom, Taylor decided to secure yet another room for her friend. She didn't have to go down to the lobby. She rang the bellpull in her room. By an intricate set of levers built into the hotel, a peg with her room number was lifted down below. Less than ten minutes later, one of the hotel's courteous staff was at her door to offer assistance.

Lucas and Hunter returned to the hotel an hour later. The train, Hunter explained, was going to be four hours late. They grabbed something to eat and were now going to meet with a man they hoped would lead them to the twins. Lucas assured Taylor that either he or Hunter would meet Victoria. Taylor, he added with a meaningful scowl, was to stay in the room.

Her husband went into the bedroom. She followed him to ask him if she could go along to the meeting. He told her she was out of her mind. She guessed then he wasn't going to be reasonable.

Lucas had gone in search of his money belt. He knew the man they were going to meet would demand compensation for selling out his friends. Lucas was going to give him whatever he wanted. He found the money, put half the amount in his pocket, and then turned his attention to his wife. He almost smiled when he saw her expression. Lord, she looked disgruntled. He told her no again but in a kinder tone of voice and even added the explanation that the man they were going to meet might not talk as freely if a woman was along.

It was a lame excuse. He didn't care. Like it or not, she was going to have to wait for them to return. He needed to know she was safe, but he didn't tell her that.

Lucas left a few minutes later. Hunter was getting as bossy as her husband. He followed Lucas out the door, then turned around and ordered her to keep the door bolted until they returned. "Don't let anyone in, no matter what the reason. Got that?"

"Yes, of course."

He started to leave, then paused again. "He's got enough on his mind. He shouldn't have to worry about you."

"And you have enough to worry about as well, Mr. Hunter. I won't let anyone in. I promise."

Hunter pulled the door closed, waited until he heard the bolt slip into place, and then left.

Lucas was waiting for him at the steps. They planned to meet their man in the lobby. They hoped he'd have information for them.

His name was Morris Peterson. He wasn't a bad sort, for he hated the Border brothers as much as Lucas and Hunter did. He didn't hold with the practice of buying and selling of people, but he didn't have any problem taking money for the information he supplied. He was taking a risk, after all, and if the Borders found out he squealed, they'd cut his throat for sure.

Lucas paid him the cash he wanted. They stood together in the corner of the lobby. It was crowded with businessmen, and no one paid them any attention. Morris still insisted on keeping hidden behind Lucas's sizable bulk.

"I can give you a name," he whispered. "Boyd," he added with a nod. "He drinks every night at the saloon on the corner of Hickery. You know the place I'm thinking of?"

"We'll find it," Hunter said. "What can Boyd tell us?" he asked.

"He was talking last night," Peterson whispered. "Bragging, he was, about the money he was going to make. I heard him say he was going to get double the money. Then he laughed real hard . . . like he knew a secret. I'm thinking he was referring to the twins you've been asking about."

"When does he usually start in drinking?"

"After dark," Peterson replied.

"Anything else?"

Peterson shook his head. He pocketed the money Lucas had given him and left a few minutes later.

"Could be another false lead," Hunter cautioned.

"Could be," Lucas agreed. "But you know . . . I got this feeling . . ."

Hunter smiled. "I got the same feeling," he admitted. "My instincts are telling me Boyd's going to lead us to the Borders."

Things were looking up. "It's only a little after six. I'm going back upstairs and sleep for an hour. After I meet the train and bring Victoria back to the hotel, you and I will go find Boyd."

"I'll go get Victoria. You can sleep until I get back."

"What about you? Aren't you tired?"

"I didn't lose forty hours on a train. You did. What does Taylor's friend look like?"

"Red hair, green eyes."

Hunter filed the information. "I think I'll go find this saloon. It will save us time later."

The two took off in opposite directions. Lucas told Taylor what had happened while he stripped out of his shirt and shoes. He was sound asleep on top of the covers five minutes later.

Hunter found the saloon, then backtracked to the train station. By the time he got there, the passengers had all disembarked. He told the driver to wait, tossed him a coin to keep him patient, and then went looking for Victoria.

Red hair and green eyes. Easy enough to spot, he thought. And yet he almost missed her. She was hidden behind three gigantic trunks the size of an ordinary carriage. The trunks were stacked one on top of the other, and if he hadn't noticed a bit of skirt when he turned to leave, he would have thought she hadn't been on the train.

The station was almost deserted. One of the porters had gone in search of a wagon sturdy enough to haul her trunks. Victoria was certain the man had forgotten about her. She prayed she was wrong, for she was too weary and too ill to do more than slump against the trunks and wait.

She was feeling horribly nauseated. She shouldn't have eaten the apples. They were green and not at all ripe, but she'd been hungry and feeling queasy, and she foolishly thought the apples would calm her stomach.

Quite the opposite was the case. The apples were giving her fits. She felt like she was going to throw up any minute. She stood as still as possible, afraid any movement at all would make the illness worse, and prayed she wouldn't disgrace herself.

Ladies did not lose their suppers in public places.

"Victoria Helmit?"

She turned at the sound of her name. Then she backed up a space. The man who'd addressed her took her breath away. He gave her quite a fright as well. He was extremely dangerous looking, until he smiled. Then he turned handsome. He had dark, rugged good looks. His hair was as black as midnight. So were his eyes. His gaze was piercing, his clothes were rumpled, and he was in dire need of a shave.

Who, in heaven's name, was he?

He repeated her name again. She might have nodded, she couldn't be certain. She could feel the bile in the back of her throat. She took a long breath and tried to stay upright.

He thought she was afraid of him. She was a pretty thing, with those wide green eyes and fiery colored hair. It was a mass of curls now. Pins hung from the copper locks about her face. The ribbon holding her hair behind her neck had come untied. The blue and white checkered strip was dangling down her back.

"My name's Hunter," he told her. "I'm a friend of

Lucas Ross. I'll take you back to the hotel. Are these trunks all yours?"

She couldn't answer him. Her throat felt as dry as parchment paper. She swallowed and tried to find her voice. She could taste the bile now. Oh, God, she knew she was going to be ill any moment. Victoria took several deep breaths in rapid succession in a bid to stall the inevitable.

Hunter couldn't imagine what had come over her. He knew most women were a little nervous around him. He thought it was because of his size and his customary frown. Her reaction went way beyond nervousness, however. She was staring up at him with a look that suggested he'd turned into a gargoyle.

Hell, he wasn't that godawful looking, was he?

With an effort, he held onto his patience. Then he introduced himself again. He kept his voice as mild as a summer breeze. He was trying to calm her. Her eyes were wide with panic. He wasn't going to do her any harm, but he guessed she didn't know that. His ego was taking one hell of a beating.

"My name is Hunter," he repeated.

"I'm . . ."

She was choking on the word. He wanted to whack her between her shoulders to help. He stopped himself in time. If he touched her, she'd probably faint or start screaming.

"Yes?" he asked, trying his damnedest to sound reasonable. He clasped his hands behind his back in what he hoped was a casual stance.

She glanced to her left and then her right. She was obviously looking for a means of escape.

"How about if I put you in one of the carriages and I take another to the hotel? Will you feel comfortable with that arrangement?"

She frantically shook her head at him. When she

started taking great gulping breaths again, he lost his patience.

"Look, lady, I'm only doing Lucas a favor. If you don't . . ."

She grabbed hold of his arm. He was so surprised by her touch, he forgot what he was going to say.

Her bizarre behavior made sense to him a minute later, but by then it was too late.

"I'm going to be sick."

And she was. All over his favorite pair of boots.

Hunter pounded on the door to Lucas's room, then bent over to take his boots off. He left them outside the door.

Taylor opened the door for them. The second Victoria spotted her friend, she burst into tears.

Lucas was in the process of buttoning up his shirt. He walked into the room just in time to see Victoria hurl herself into Taylor's arms.

"Whatever happened? Why are you so upset, Victoria?" Taylor asked. She hugged her friend while she glared over Victoria's shoulder at the man she thought was responsible for her pitiful condition.

Hunter glared back. Taylor noticed he wasn't wearing any shoes.

"I'm not feeling at all well," Victoria confessed.

"What happened to your boots?" Lucas asked Hunter. He stood behind the women.

Hunter stalked into the room. "Never mind," he muttered.

"You're just tuckered out," Taylor told Victoria. "You'll feel better after you've had a bath and a nap. Come into your bedroom and I'll help you get settled."

Hunter stood in the middle of the room glaring at

Victoria. He waited until Taylor had taken her into the adjoining room, then turned his glare on Lucas.

"What happened?" Lucas asked.

"I introduced myself."

"And?"

"She threw up all over me."

Lucas smiled. He wanted to laugh but he didn't dare. Hunter would have killed him. He turned away, coughed to cover his amusement, and then finished getting dressed by tucking his shirt into the waist of his pants.

"Don't ask me to do you any more favors," Hunter snapped.

Taylor's laughter suddenly filled the room. Her friend had obviously confessed what she'd done. A moment later Lucas and Hunter could hear Victoria laughing.

"It wasn't funny," Hunter muttered.

"You sure have a way with women," Lucas told him. He was thoroughly enjoying his friend's irritation.

"The cabbie charged four times his usual fare."

"Why?"

"She threw up inside his carriage. I couldn't get her to calm down."

Lucas did laugh then. He pictured Hunter trying to soothe Victoria and being completely inept. God knew he would have been inept. Neither one of them had any experience dealing with persnickety ladies, and Lucas was suddenly damned thankful he hadn't been the one to go after Taylor's friend.

"I wasn't responsible for her condition," Hunter said. "She told me it was the rocking motion of the train that made her sick. God, I need a bath. Will she get hysterical if I go in there and get my clothes?"

"Taylor already had your things moved to your room. It's on this floor, just three doors down the hall. The key's on the table."

Hunter couldn't hide his surprise. "They gave me a room in this fancy hotel?"

The question was telling. Hunter was used to the prejudice against him. Lucas wasn't. Hunter pretended to take it all in stride. He never made a scene when he was discriminated against. He told Lucas once he didn't have to stand up for himself and his rights. Lucas took over the task for him.

"You weren't here to sign the register," Lucas pointed out. "Taylor put the room under her name."

They both knew Lucas wasn't being completely honest. The hotel management would never have given Hunter a room on his own. Arms would have had to be twisted. Lucas would have seen to that, but Taylor, unwittingly, had averted a scene.

Hunter was ready to move on to a more important topic in his estimation.

"When do you want to leave?"

"As soon as you're ready."

Hunter picked up the key and left. He returned to Lucas's room a half hour later. Taylor had spent her time helping Victoria get settled and seeing to the chore of cleaning Hunter's boots.

He found them waiting for him inside the door. His boots looked brand-new.

Taylor walked into the room just as Hunter was putting them on.

"It was thoughtful of you to have them cleaned, Taylor. I didn't think there would be enough time."

"Taylor cleaned them," Lucas told his friend. He leaned against the arch to the alcove. His gaze was centered on his wife. She looked flushed to him.

"You feeling all right, Taylor?" he asked.

She looked at the floor when she answered. "Yes."
It wasn't like her to act timid. Something was wrong, he decided. He put his gunbelt on, checked to make certain each of his two guns was fully loaded, a ritual that gave him a considerable amount of peace of mind, and then told Taylor to come to him.

She took her time walking across the room. When she reached his side, he took hold of her hand and pulled her into the privacy of the bedroom area.

"Look at me," he commanded.

She took her sweet time obeying that order as well. "Why haven't you asked me if you could come along with us?"

Her eyes widened in surprise. "Would you let me?"

He shook his head. "No, but you didn't ask. What's the matter with you?"

She ignored his question. "I should go with you, you know. When you find them, I should be there. They'll be afraid, Lucas. They'll need me."

She gave a valid argument. He nodded. "All right then. When we find them, I'll come back and get you."

"Thank you."

"You still haven't told me what's bothering you."

She let out a sigh. "Were you bluffing?" she asked. "I was certain you were, but now I find I need to hear you admit it."

"I never bluff."

"Oh, all right then."

"Taylor?"

She started to turn away. He put his hands on her shoulders to keep her there.

"Yes?"

"What are we talking about?"

"Your wedding night."

He smiled. Then he leaned down and gave her a quick kiss. "Our wedding night," he corrected.

She looked thoroughly disgruntled with him. "Don't you realize how complicated you're going to make . . ."

His mouth silenced her argument. It wasn't a gentle kiss. He wanted to overpower her. His mouth took absolute possession. His tongue thrust inside. She melted against him, wanting to be swept away, to pretend, if only for a moment or two, that everything was as right and as clean and as beautiful as sunshine after the rain.

She knew he wanted her. She wanted him to love her. But he'd rather be hanged.

She pushed herself away from him. "You forget yourself, Mr. Ross," she stammered out. She was panting and blushing and diligently trying to act prim and proper.

He was having none of it. He pulled her back into his arms, kissed her again, long and hard, and when at last he pulled away, she could barely form a coherent thought.

He left her sitting on the side of their bed. Taylor came to her senses a minute later. The whistle did it. Lucas made the arrogant noise as he sauntered out the door.

Taylor patted her hair back in place, let out a loud sigh, and then went to check on Victoria. Her friend was sound asleep. Taylor tucked the covers around her, closed the window so she wouldn't catch a chill, and then tiptoed out of the room. She suddenly remembered the notes she made and wanted to discuss with Lucas. She caught herself before she let out an unladylike expletive. She would just have to wait until tomorrow to find out what her husband thought about placing an advertisement in the papers and hiring a private investigator. She couldn't imagine he would have any objections, for they needed all the

help they could get, but she still felt that because he
had taken charge of the search, the suggestions should
first be discussed with him. Taylor got the paper out
and put it on the table so she wouldn't forget again.

Then she sat down. She'd started a ritual of her own
the night she found out the babies had disappeared.
Every time Lucas left to search for the little girls, she
prayed for him. Her plea to God was twofold. She
asked Him to keep Lucas safe from harm and to help
him find the babies. When Hunter had joined in the
search, she of course added his name to her petition.

She couldn't sit still long. Pacing, it seemed, had
also become a ritual. She would worry and pray and
pace until Lucas and Hunter were safely home.

Perhaps tonight they wouldn't come back empty-
handed.

"Please, God," she whispered over and over again,
"let them find my babies."

Hunter and Lucas both felt they had a solid lead
this time. They found the man named Boyd. They
were in the process of becoming his best friends, and
all because Hunter was paying for his whiskey. They
sat with him at a round table in the corner of the
saloon. Their goal was to get him liquored up enough
to betray his own mother.

An hour later, they had accomplished their goal.
Boyd took one look at the money Lucas was offering
and started talking. He thought he was doing the
Borders a good deed, because Hunter had hinted at
the possibility of buying the twins. Money, Hunter
boasted, wasn't a concern since he'd made his fortune.

Boyd was an extremely unpleasant individual. Demons, after all, usually were. He was completely
devoid of morals. He was also as ugly as sin. He had
thick, pockmarked skin and eyelids so heavy, the folds
hung down over his eyes. He squinted in order to see.

He had the disgusting habit of puckering his lips together every time Hunter mentioned money. It was as though he was tasting his own greed.

Lucas barely spoke a word. He was afraid his voice would betray him. His loathing for the creature sitting across from him made his insides burn. The animal pretending to be a man was calmly discussing the pleasures to be had from young flesh.

Lucas wanted to kill him.

He had to give Hunter his due, however. He knew his friend was just as repulsed by the obscene man. Yet he didn't let his hatred show in his expression or his voice.

"How'd you come by so much money?" Boyd asked Hunter. "You're a half-breed, ain't you?"

Hunter ignored the second question and answered the first. "Gold," he lied.

"You hit a strike?"

Hunter nodded. Boyd grinned. "Must have been a mighty big one," he remarked.

"What about the Borders?" Hunter asked, trying to bring the man around to the main discussion.

"They already got themselves a buyer," Boyd said. "They could be convinced to go back on their word. It was a woman buyer, after all."

"A woman?" Hunter asked. He couldn't quite hide his surprise.

Boyd gave Lucas a worried glance. "Your friend doesn't talk much, does he?"

Hunter didn't answer him. "You said the woman was a buyer?"

Boyd nodded. "She wants twins for her brothel. Least that's what she told the Borders. You really willing to pay triple the asking price?"

"I got the money," Hunter replied. "Might as well

use some of it. If the twins are worth it," he added. "I'd have to see them first."

"And you'll give me a split because I told you about them?"

"I already said I would."

"What if they ain't twins?" Boyd asked then. "I can't be certain they are," he admitted. He took a long swallow of whiskey, let out a loud belch, then wiped his mouth on the back of his sleeve. "I haven't seen them. I heard the brothers had a pair of twins and their older brother. The boy's a half-breed. Could be his sisters are, too. If that be the case, none of them will be worth a plug nickel."

Hunter turned to Lucas. The message was clear in his eyes. He wanted to kill the bastard. He couldn't stand to look at him another minute, and he'd heard quite enough. He reached for his knife.

Lucas shook his head. "Not yet," he told his friend.

"Not yet what?" Boyd demanded to know.

"Tell me where they're keeping the children," Lucas ordered. He couldn't keep his anger out of his voice and didn't even try. Boyd didn't seem to notice. His full attention was directed on the stack of bills Lucas had just placed on the table.

Boyd's gaze was riveted on the sight. He puckered his lips together and reached for the money. Hunter's knife stopped him. The blade sliced through the crack between Boyd's fingers.

"Not so fast," Hunter announced after Boyd had finished screeching at him.

"Give us the address first," Lucas insisted. He poured Boyd another drink under the guise of friendship.

Boyd gave Hunter a glare and then drained his glass. He stared at the money another long minute, obviously trying to make up his mind. Then he blurted out the address.

"You won't be telling how you found them, will you?"

Hunter wasn't paying any attention to Boyd. He stared at Lucas, waiting for permission, no doubt, to kill the bastard.

Lucas denied him once again. "Boyd's going with us," he explained. "If he's lying, you can kill him."

"And if he isn't lying?"

Since Boyd was following the conversation, Lucas lied. "We'll give him the other half of the money."

"I got me enough money here," Boyd argued. He was so drunk now, his words were slurred together. "I ain't going anywhere with you."

It took all Lucas's discipline not to reach across the table and grab the bastard by his neck. He forced a mild tone of voice when he spoke. "My friend likes to use his knife," he said with a nod toward Hunter. "He does some pretty fancy work with his blade."

Hunter raised an eyebrow, then smiled. "Thank you," he replied, pretending to be pleased by the outrageous lie.

Boyd's face was turning pale. It wasn't good enough for Lucas. He acted as though he was discussing the weather when he continued. "He's partial to skinning a man. He keeps him alive while he works on him. Isn't that right?" he asked his friend.

Hunter nodded. "Wouldn't be any fun if he were already dead. What's the point then?"

"Exactly," Lucas agreed. "What's the point?"

Boyd was shaking now and giving worried glances around the saloon. He was apparently looking for someone to help him.

No one was giving him the time of day. "I'm a white man," he protested.

Hunter smiled. "It's all the same to me," he drawled out.

Lucas nodded. "You called it, Boyd. My friend's a half-breed and therefore a savage, right?"

Boyd nodded, then shook his head. He couldn't seem to make up his mind to agree or disagree. He snorted. "You aren't going to take me anywhere. I'm staying right where I am. There are too many people in this here saloon. Witnesses," he added with a smug smile.

Five minutes later, Boyd had tears in his eyes. He was being dragged down the street between Lucas and Hunter.

They were looking for an alley. They found one two blocks later. They left Boyd there, bound and gagged and unconscious, behind a stack of wooden crates. They didn't want Boyd having second thoughts and possibly alerting the Border brothers of trouble, and as Lucas patiently pointed out to Hunter when he demanded the right to kill the son of a bitch, they might need to ask Boyd more questions if the Borders had moved the children to another location. There was also the telling fact that neither one of them was a cold-blooded murderer.

"We might want to kill him, but we won't," Lucas said.

Hunter didn't like being reminded of the truth. He growled low in his throat. "If we were in Montana Territory . . ."

"It would still be murder," Lucas countered. "When this is finished, we'll make certain everyone in town knows Boyd sold out his friends. That should make his life miserable."

Hunter cheered up. He fell into step beside Lucas and walked down the main street. Neither said a word for several minutes. Then Hunter broke the silence.

"So I like to skin a man alive, do I?"

Lucas grinned. "I thought it was a nice touch."

Hunter laughed. "Expectations," he said with a nod. "He expected me to behave like a savage."

"And I merely reinforced his own ignorant beliefs."

The two men put Boyd out of their minds. They found the address they were looking for twenty minutes later. They had to backtrack twice. They were in the heart of the slum of the city, surrounded by tenement buildings. Clothing hung down from broken rails, windows were broken or altogether missing, and the sound of human misery echoed all around them. Babies cried while adults shouted. The dilapidated buildings were gray. The ground surrounding the housing was covered with garbage and worse. The stench was almost unbearable.

"They're inside. I feel it in my gut, Lucas."

"I got the same feeling," Lucas said. "I'm going to have to go and get Taylor."

"Why?"

"She's the only one who will know for certain if the twins are her nieces," he said. It was a lame excuse and they both knew it.

Hunter rolled his eyes heavenward. "How many twins do you think the Borders have up there? For God's sake, Lucas, either way we're going to get those children out of there."

Lucas nodded. "I know," he agreed. "But Taylor deserves to go with us. I promised her."

Hunter quit arguing. "I'll wait here," he said. He was already moving into the shadows between the two buildings, looking for a spot where he could keep his gaze on both the front and the back doors. If the Borders decided to move the children, he wanted to know about it.

Lucas hailed a cabbie three blocks away. He had the

driver wait for him in front of the hotel while he went upstairs to get Taylor.

She opened the door for him. She took one look at his dark expression and tried to brace herself for bad news.

He stopped her questions with an abrupt order. "Get your coat."

She didn't take the time to ask him where he was taking her. She ran to the wardrobe, grabbed her coat, and went running back to her husband. She patted the pocket to make certain her gun was still there.

Lucas gave her only a partial explanation of what had happened. He didn't go into any detail about Boyd. He didn't want to waste the time.

Taylor was gripping her hands together. She was tense and frightened.

"You say the little girls have an older brother with them?"

"That's what we were told."

They reached the vehicle. Lucas assisted Taylor inside. She waited until they were on their way before speaking again.

"If they have an older brother, they can't be my sister's twins."

"Do you want to go back?"

"Of course not," she cried out. "You insult me by asking such a question. We're going to get these children away from the vile animals first. Then we keep looking for my babies."

He was pleased with her answer. "I want you to stay between Hunter and me the entire time we're inside."

"Yes."

"You'll do exactly what I tell you to do. No arguments."

"No arguments," she promised.

The list of his orders continued. Taylor understood

why he was being so harsh and sounding so angry. He wanted to keep her safe. Worry made his voice take on a hard edge. She found it comforting.

They were nearing the tenements when Lucas finished with his instructions. Because she looked so frightened, he decided to give her something positive to think about.

"By next week, you could be on your way to George's relatives with the twins. Think about that happy reunion, Taylor." He was offering her a glimmer of hope. He was surprised when she shook her head. She was staring out the window, taking in the godawful view, and barely paying any attention to what Lucas was saying.

The smell of boiling cabbage and human stench made her want to gag.

"Did you ever meet any of George's relatives?" he asked.

He had to repeat his question because of her inattention. "The twins' father," he said. "Did you meet any of his relatives?"

She couldn't imagine why he was asking such a strange question now.

"No, George was an orphan. He didn't have any relatives. Look, there's Hunter. He's walking toward us."

Taylor had the door opened before the vehicle came to a complete stop. Lucas paid the driver and offered the man a handsome bonus if he would wait for them. The lure of the money outweighed the cabbie's concern about the safety of the neighborhood. He pulled out a rifle from under his perch, put it across his lap, and then promised to wait as long as thirty minutes.

Taylor waited next to Hunter until Lucas crossed the street. Then she moved to his side and took hold of his hand. She put her other hand in the pocket of her coat and held onto her Colt.

They walked in silence up the rickety steps of the tenement. Lucas went inside first. Taylor followed. Hunter was right behind her.

The apartment they were looking for was on the third floor and in the very back of the building. The floorboards creaked, but there was so much noise inside, they could have pounded their way down the hallway and not been overheard.

The walls were paper thin, as were the doors. When they reached the number they wanted, Lucas motioned for Taylor to stand against the wall several feet away. If there was gunfire, he didn't want a stray bullet hitting her.

Hunter already had one of his guns out. Lucas readied his own, nodded to his friend, and then slammed his shoulder against the door and rushed inside. Hunter followed him.

A young man, around the age of twenty, had been asleep on the divan. He awakened to find Hunter's six-shooter pressed against his temple.

A woman twice his age came running into the living room from the kitchen. She wore only a sheer nightgown. She had orange-colored hair and a heavily painted face. She didn't try to cover herself. She sneered at Hunter and went running toward him with her hands out and her jagged nails ready to do injury, but she came to a quick stop when he pulled out his second gun and leveled it at her.

She apparently decided to take a different approach. She put her hands on her hips and pulled the material of her nightgown tight against her so he'd be sure to see what she was offering and thrust her breasts out. "My name's Shirleen. I do my business out of the bedroom back yonder. Why don't you put your guns away, sugar? I can show you a real good time. It will only cost you a dollar, two if you want to use my mouth. I'm worth the money, aren't I, Charlie?"

The man on the divan was too frightened to answer her. He didn't even nod.

"You wouldn't shoot a lady, would you, sugar?" she crooned at Hunter.

His voice was devoid of emotion when he answered her. "I'm not looking at a lady."

She didn't care for the insult. Her eyes became bare slits again. Hatred glowed from her expression. "You're in the wrong place," she told him. "This here belongs to the Borders." The sneer was back in her voice. "They don't take kindly to being robbed. They'll cut you good if they catch you. You'd best get out of here while you still can."

Hunter didn't show any reaction to her threat. He simply stared at her and waited for her next move. Lucas had already made his way around the cramped apartment. There were two bedrooms. The first was empty, and from the rumpled and soiled bedding, he assumed that was the room the woman used to conduct her business. The second bedroom door was locked. He started to use his shoulder to break the barrier down, but then he heard the sound of a child crying. The noise was faint, yet still recognizable. Lucas stepped back. He was afraid to crash through the door for fear he would injure the child if he or she were standing close to the opening.

He needed the key.

"Surely you've heard of the Borders," Shirleen muttered. "Everyone has heard of Billy and Cyrus." She snorted with laughter. "You got to be new in town, sugar, or you'd know how dangerous and fool-hardy it is to dare to rob . . ."

"Give me the key to the bedroom door."

Lucas issued the order from behind the woman's back. She jumped a foot and whirled around. Until he spoke to her, she hadn't realized there was more than one man inside the apartment with her.

This one was far more threatening to her than the other one holding Charlie captive. He didn't make a sound when he moved. Only a man used to breaking the law knew how to walk like a shadow. Shirleen took a step away and tried to hide her fear.

Taylor walked inside then. Hunter told her to shut the door. She did as she was ordered, then turned around again.

She gave the scantily clad woman only a passing glance. It was enough, however, to convey her disgust. Her gaze moved on to the man stretched out on the divan. She noticed what he was doing, and since both Hunter and Lucas were watching her, she gave the warning.

Her gaze was on her husband when she spoke to Hunter. "He's reaching for his gun. It's probably under one of the cushions."

Hunter smiled. "I know."

She didn't understand. If he knew what the man was doing, why didn't he stop him?

Lucas understood. Hunter was waiting for an excuse to kill the vermin.

"No gunfire," he called out to his friend.

Hunter frowned with disappointment. Then he let out a sigh. He flipped the gun around in his hand, and before his prisoner understood his intent, Hunter slammed the butt of his gun against the side of his head. He didn't kill the man, but when he woke up, he was going to wish he were dead. His head was going to feel as though it had been split in two.

Hunter shoved the unconscious man onto the floor,

then reached down between the cushions. He found the pistol hidden there and tucked the weapon in his belt.

It suddenly dawned on Shirleen that the strangers weren't there simply to rob the place. Her gaze was locked on Taylor. She watched Taylor cross the room to the bedroom door, thinking that she looked like an angel. And for that reason alone, the threat she issued carried all the more substance.

"He might not kill a woman, but I would. You have five seconds to give me the key," Taylor said, a chilling look in her eyes. Shirleen didn't think twice about arguing with her. She believed with all her heart the angel with eyes as cold as blue ice was about to kill her.

"One . . ."

Shirleen ran to the stack of boxes near the window, reached into the top one, and pulled out the key.

"I didn't have anything to do with taking those brats. I only work here, that's all. What Billy and Cyrus do doesn't concern me."

Lucas snatched the key out of her hand, motioned for Hunter to keep his eye on her, and then unlocked the door. He wouldn't let Taylor go inside first. He wanted to make certain there wasn't someone else in the bedroom with the children.

It was dark inside, too dark to see his way around the room. Lucas lit one of the lamps after first scanning the area for signs of shadows moving about.

He spotted the little girls across the room. His heart suddenly felt as though it was going to explode with relief. And with rage.

The two little ones were sound asleep on the floor in front of the closet door. They clung to each other. One was softly weeping with her dream. Lucas couldn't see the other one's face. She had her head tucked under her sister's chin.

They were beautiful children. Babies, he silently corrected. They were so tiny, they couldn't be three years old yet. The one he could see clearly had coloring identical to Taylor's. Both twins had white blond hair. The resemblance was close enough to make anyone believe the twins were her daughters. No doubt about it, they belonged to her.

He motioned for Taylor to come inside, then put his gun away. He moved back to the doorway to watch from a distance. He knew he would frighten the little girls if he got too close to them. He wanted them to see Taylor first.

"They're hers, aren't they?" Lucas heard the woman ask Hunter.

Taylor wasn't paying any attention to Shirleen. She hurried into the bedroom. She stopped just as suddenly when she spotted the babies. Her hand went to her mouth and she let out a low, pitiful moaning sound that tore at Lucas's heart. She stared at the babies and slowly walked over to them.

She felt faint with relief and jubilation. She was crying by the time she reached the children. She knelt down on the floor in front of them but didn't touch either one of them for a long minute. Her head was bowed and her hands were tightly folded together in front of her. Lucas thought she might be praying.

She then reached out and gently shook her babies awake. "It's time to go home now," she whispered.

One of the little girls opened her eyes. She sat up, rubbed the sleep from her eyes, and stared up at Taylor. She looked curious and only mildly afraid. When Taylor stroked the side of her face and smiled at her, she put her thumb in her mouth and leaned forward. Taylor gently lifted her onto her lap. She held her close and crooned to her, and when the baby at last relaxed against her, she reached for her sister.

The other twin woke up crying. She was quick to stop her tears when she saw Taylor. She seemed to recognize her. Taylor knew that wasn't possible, of course, for the twins hadn't even been crawling when she'd seen them last. The little girl put her arms out to be held. Taylor lifted her onto her lap next to her sister and hugged her tight.

Taylor couldn't quit crying. She rocked her babies in her arms and told them over and over again that everything was going to be all right. She was taking them home.

One fell asleep in her arms and the other let herself be cuddled for several minutes, then began to squirm. She wanted to look up at Taylor, and after she'd wiggled her way around and could see Taylor's face, she pulled her thumb out of her mouth and reached up to touch Taylor's hair.

"Are you my mama?"

"Yes."

"Are you Allie's mama, too?"

"Yes."

It was all Georganna wanted to know. She leaned back against Taylor, put her thumb in her mouth again, and closed her eyes.

Lucas walked over and hunkered down next to his wife. "Are they all right?" he asked in a whisper.

"I think so," she answered. The babies were wearing wrinkled blue-colored day dresses. Their legs and arms and gowns were covered with dirt. They hadn't been taken care of properly, but Taylor was relieved that she couldn't see any bruises so far.

"Let's get them out of here, Lucas."

He was in full agreement. And yet he hesitated. He turned, bent lower, and looked under the bed. Then he stood up. Where was the boy they'd heard about?

He lifted one of the twins into his arms. She didn't wake up. Her head dropped to rest on his shoulder. Taylor handed him the other baby, and then she also stood up.

Lucas wanted to question the woman about where the boy had been taken. He wouldn't rest until he had all three of them. He led the way into the living room. Hunter held up three fingers. Lucas shook his head. Then Taylor drew his attention. She reached out and touched his arm.

"Wait," she whispered. She turned around and went back into the bedroom. Something wasn't quite right, but she was so exhausted with worry and relief over finally finding her babies, she couldn't figure out what was wrong.

Lucas followed her. "What is it?" he asked in a whisper so he wouldn't disturb the babies.

Taylor shook her head. She started to turn around again, then stopped. "Why were they sleeping on the floor in front of the closet?"

She didn't give him time to speculate on the oddity. She hurried over to the closet door and tried to open it. The door was locked.

"Get the woman in here," Lucas called out to Hunter.

A few seconds later, Shirleen appeared in the doorway. Hunter stood behind her.

"Why is this door locked?" Taylor asked. She could barely stand to look at the woman, so repulsed was she by the sight of such evil.

"No reason," Shirleen blurted out. "Just is." Her words were hurried when she added, "There aren't any clothes in there for your girls. They're all in a box by the front door. I'll show you where they are," she added. Hunter stopped her from moving.

"Open the closet door," Taylor demanded.

"Whatever for? I told you already," Shirleen muttered. "There's nothing inside for you to want."

She sounded agitated now and started rambling again to cover her nervousness. "The Borders thought your girls were orphans. With their curly white hair and their big blue eyes, why, they got to be yours. They're your mirror image. Billy and Cyrus will still try to keep them. They already got themselves a buyer. I'd hightail it out of here if I were you."

"Unlock this door," Taylor ordered.

Shirleen forced a shrug of indifference. "I don't know where the key is," she said. She folded her arms across her middle and glared at Taylor.

"Want me to kill her?"

Hunter asked the question. His voice was devoid of all emotion, which made the inquiry all the more chilling. Shirleen let out a gasp, glanced up at Hunter, and then turned her full attention to Taylor. She held her breath while she waited for her answer.

She missed Hunter's wink. Taylor didn't. She understood he was bluffing. He wanted to rattle the woman. Taylor wanted to worry her. She waited several seconds so Shirleen could think about the possibility, then looked at Hunter.

"Yes, please," she called out in an oh-so-polite tone of voice that sounded very like she was ordering a second cup of tea from a solicitous waiter.

Even though Shirleen's face was covered with makeup, she still paled considerably. When she felt Hunter's hand on the back of her neck, she cried out, "It's the same key that opened the bedroom door. I'll get it."

Hunter ordered her to stay where she was. He removed the key from the lock. He didn't want to leave the doorway. From where he stood, he could watch the front door. If one of the Border brothers came strolling in, he wanted to be prepared. For that reason, he didn't hand the key to Taylor, he tossed it to her.

She caught the key in midair, turned around, and unlocked the door. She opened it only a fraction and started to move back so she could pull the door wide, when it suddenly seemed to explode in her hand.

Taylor was knocked backward by the force of the door being slammed against her. The doorknob caught her in her side. She was thrown against the wall behind her, righted herself as quickly as possible, and then grabbed hold of the door before it could hit her again.

Lucas shouted the warning for her to stay back. Hunter leveled his gun on the opening of the closet. It was so dark inside, he couldn't see the threat. He wasn't taking any chances. There could be a man inside, hiding there with his gun ready, waiting to get a few of them in his sights.

Lucas was having the same thought. He moved out of the way, then half turned so the twins would be better protected. If a gun were fired, the bullet would have to pass through his back before getting to one of the babies.

Taylor started to walk forward. Lucas told her to stop. His voice was hard, abrupt. He turned to Hunter, gave him a quick nod, letting him know it was up to him to take care of the matter.

Hunter was going to do just that. He took a step to the side, thinking to approach the doorway from a safer angle, but he'd only moved a foot or two when he came to a sudden stop.

He couldn't believe what he was seeing. A little boy, surely no older than six or seven, came flying out of his prison. He was so quick, he was almost a blur. It wasn't until he stopped in the center of the room and frantically looked around him that Hunter and Lucas both got a good look at him. Taylor stood behind the boy and therefore couldn't see his face.

He had dark black-brown hair that nearly reached his narrow shoulders in length. His eyes were the same color. They were wide with panic. His stance was rigid. He looked ready to spring into action.

No one said a word for several seconds. Lucas was so filled with rage on the boy's behalf, he was shaking with it. God only knew how long the child had been locked inside the closet. Animals weren't treated with such cruelty.

Hunter was just as outraged as Lucas was. He stared at the boy and saw himself as a child. The ache he felt inside made bile rush up into his throat. He burned with the fever of revenge.

Taylor was so astonished by the sight of the boy, she leaned back against the wall and tried to recover her breath. And then the enormity of the atrocity committed against the innocent child struck her full force. Her eyes filled with tears. Dear God in heaven, someone should pay for this sin.

Thoughts of revenge were fleeting. The little boy was obviously terrified. He needed to be comforted now. Taylor started toward the child with that single thought in mind.

He wasn't paying any attention to her. He spotted the twins in Lucas's arms, let out a howl of fury, and then lowered his head and went running at the man who dared to touch his charges.

Hunter put his gun away and intercepted the boy just as he was about to butt his head into Lucas's hip.

The child was screaming and kicking and biting. Hunter held him around his waist and lifted him up off the ground. He quickly caught hold of his hand when he realized the boy was going after his gun.

He ordered the child to quit his struggle. The command was ignored. He didn't know what he was supposed to do next. He wasn't going to hurt the child, but he doubted the little one realized that. And so Hunter looked at Taylor for help.

She came running. "Put him down," she told Hunter.

"He's a little savage," Shirleen called out. "You can see he's a half-breed. He thinks he's the girls' protector. They had to lock him in the closet," she added. "He wouldn't let anyone near . . ."

She quit her explanation when Taylor looked at her. The fury in the angel's eyes terrified her. Her hand went to the base of her neck and she caught a quick breath.

"He calls himself their brother," she whispered. "He's lying, of course. Just look at him and you can see they aren't related," she added with a snort.

"He is their brother." Taylor made the statement in an emphatic tone of voice.

The boy stilled in Hunter's arms and looked up at her.

She nodded. He didn't understand what she was telling him. As soon as he was freed from Hunter's hold, he tried to run past her to get to the little girls again.

Taylor grabbed hold of his hand and pulled him into her side. Dark hair hung down over his forehead. She gently brushed the hair away from his brow. He wouldn't look up at her now but kept his attention fully directed on Lucas.

"We're going home now," she told the child.

He dared a quick look up at her. "You can't take them away from me. I won't let you."

She could feel him trembling. She wrapped her arms around him and leaned down to whisper in his ear. Lucas couldn't hear what she was saying to the child, but when she at last straightened away from him, he was looking up at her with tears in his eyes.

She put her hand out. He clasped hold of it. He was still afraid to trust her. She could see it in his eyes. She slowly nodded, telling him without words she meant what she had just promised him.

He tightened his hold on her hand. She wanted to weep.

"Where are your shoes?" she asked. Her voice shivered with emotion.

"I don't have any. They threw them away."

Taylor didn't show any outward reaction to his remark. "We'll get you a pair tomorrow."

His eyes widened in surprise over her promise.

She smiled at him and then turned to Hunter. She wasn't about to let the child walk barefoot outside. "We're ready to leave now," she told him. "Will you carry him?"

Hunter nodded. The boy pulled back when Taylor tried to lead him across the room. He was obviously afraid of Hunter, and Lucas as well, she surmised, because he kept giving both giants fearful glances.

She wasn't about to introduce the men. She didn't want the horrible woman to hear their names. They had enough to contend with, and Shirleen would certainly give the Border brothers as many particulars as she could remember. If she had their names, trouble would follow.

Taylor drew the child into her arms again and leaned down to whisper to him. Both her husband and his friend patiently waited. It didn't take long, and when Taylor was finished, the little boy was smiling.

Lucas and Hunter were both curious. The change that came over the child was startling. Whatever had Taylor said to him?

The boy let go of Taylor's hand and walked across the room. He had a cocky bounce to his stride. He smiled up at Lucas as he passed him. He certainly wasn't afraid of Hunter either, for when he reached his side, he reached out to clasp hold of his hand and stared up at him with wide eyes and a look of awe on his face.

Taylor looked at Lucas. He raised an eyebrow and motioned toward the child. She simply smiled at him, then suggested once again that they leave.

Shirleen followed them to the front door. Lucas was the last in the procession. Just as he was passing by the divan, the man resting there let out a low groan. Lucas shifted the babies so that he could hold them with one arm, then reached down with his right hand and slammed his fist into the man's jaw. He knocked him out cold and never broke his stride.

Taylor requested a moment alone with Shirleen. Her husband denied her by shaking his head. Taylor turned to the obscene woman. "I'm going to make certain you spend the rest of your life in prison."

"I didn't have anything to do—"

Taylor didn't let her finish her protest. "You knew what was happening. You could have helped the children. You didn't."

She started out the doorway when Shirleen turned and ran toward her bedroom.

"We'll be back."

Lucas made the comment. It wasn't a threat. It was a promise.

They took the back steps. Taylor led the way. She kept her hand in her coat pocket, her fingers curled around her gun.

They didn't run into trouble. When they reached the street and started across, Taylor offered to take one of the babies. The cold air had awakened both the twins. Georganna had leaned away from Lucas and was staring at him. Alexandra also stared but not quite so blatantly. Both babies had their thumbs in their mouths. Georganna made a smacking sound when she sucked. Alexandra didn't make any noise at all.

"They're fine where they are," Lucas told Taylor. "Take hold of my arm," he ordered then.

Hunter moved up to Taylor's other side. She reached up to pat the little boy's arm, then turned to stroke one of the twins.

She wanted to hurry to the vehicle for it was chilly out and she didn't want the children to catch cold. She worried about the possibility as she walked along.

Hunter wanted to get the hell out of the neighborhood before the Borders came home. He didn't like the notion of killing the brothers with the boy in his arms. He thought about that possibility on their walk to the carriage.

Lucas's mind was on another matter altogether— the twins' father. George, she'd said, had been an orphan. He hadn't had any relatives. Of course he hadn't. Orphans never did.

And she'd known all along. The greater good. She'd told him that was why she'd married him. For the greater good. The cryptic remark finally made sense.

Madam's master plan. Do you like children? Taylor had asked him the question. Oh, yes, the greater good.

"I'll be damned."

He whispered the remark so low only the twins heard him. Georganna pulled her thumb out of her mouth and smiled at him. Alexandra shyly smiled up at him as well, but she kept her thumb in her mouth.

They reached the vehicle a few minutes later. Taylor got inside first. Hunter put the little boy inside next. He sat next to Taylor.

Lucas handed Georganna to her. She put the baby on her lap and reached for the second twin. Alexandra was duly settled on her lap next to her sister.

Taylor put her arm around the little boy so he would be included in her embrace, leaned back against the cushion, and closed her eyes. She let out a sigh of contentment.

Hunter and Lucas were having a difference of opinion outside the carriage. Hunter insisted on returning to the tenement to wait for the Borders. Lucas didn't have any problem with the plan. He just didn't want to be left out. Since he couldn't leave Taylor with the children, he demanded that Hunter return to the hotel with them. Once everyone was settled in for the night, he would go with his friend to confront the bastards.

Taylor ended the argument. "These children are going to freeze to death if we don't get them out of the cold air. Do get inside, both of you."

A moment later, they were on their way. The moonlight was bright enough to see each other inside the carriage. Lucas's gaze was on his wife.

"Taylor?"

There was a hard edge to his voice. She ignored it and gave him a smile. Lord, she was content. "Yes?" she asked.

His gaze turned to one little girl and then the other.

It was almost impossible to tell them apart. Then his frown settled on his wife again.

"Tell me something," he ordered.

"Yes?" she asked again.

He nodded to the twins. "Which one's greater and which one's good."

14

O' while you live, tell truth, and shame the devil.
—William Shakespeare,
Henry IV

The twins conquered their shyness in no time at all. The night air had revived them as well. They talked nonstop all the way back to the hotel while they climbed all over Lucas and Hunter.

The two men had never considered themselves family men. They hadn't ever been around such little children, and they both felt awkward and inept holding such fragile little things.

The babies didn't feel awkward around the giants, however. They took to the two men the way ducks take to water.

Taylor had her full attention on the little boy. She asked him his name. He told her he didn't have a real one or at least he couldn't remember one, and then, while he wrung his hands together with worry, he whispered all the names he'd been called. He ended his explanation with a shrug.

"I guess you could call me Sneak. That's what everyone calls me the most."

Taylor was appalled and horrified, but she hid her reaction from the child. She didn't want to embarrass him. Most of the nicknames he rattled off were grossly obscene. He was too young to understand their meaning, of course, and she counted that fact a blessing.

Both Lucas and Hunter were listening to the conversation. When Lucas heard the nicknames, he became infuriated. Hunter wanted to kill someone.

"We will never say those words again," she instructed the child. She kept her voice a gentle whisper. "I want you to forget you ever heard them."

"Then what will you call me?" he asked. He sounded as worried as he looked.

Lucas and Hunter weren't helping matters. They were both scowling like bandits. She didn't want the child to believe he was the reason for their foul moods. She gave both men a quick glare she hoped they would interpret to mean she wanted them to quit looking so dour, then turned back to the little boy.

"You don't remember a name your mother or father used to call you?"

"Mama died. I try, but I can't remember her face anymore. I didn't have a father."

Hunter leaned forward to question the boy then. He began by telling him not to be afraid of him, then asked him what happened after his mother passed away.

The child lifted his shoulders in a shrug. "I slept in a crate behind Stoley's store."

"You didn't have family to go to?" Hunter asked then.

The child shook his head. He straightened up in his seat and smiled. "I'm not afraid of you, not since she told me . . ."

Hunter glanced over at Lucas. "Told you what, son?" Lucas asked.

"You know," he whispered.

"Tell us anyway," Lucas encouraged. His curiosity was pricked, of course. The boy was staring at him with a look of adoration on his face. He wanted to know why.

"She said you two look scary, but it's all right. You're supposed to," he explained.

He turned to smile up at Taylor. She nodded.

"We're supposed to look scary?" Hunter repeated.

"Why?" Lucas asked.

The boy answered him. "Cause you come in all shapes and sizes."

He acted as though Lucas should already know that important fact.

Both men turned their gazes to Taylor. They obviously wanted her to explain. She didn't say a word. She simply looked back at them and gave them a sweet smile.

The riddle intrigued Lucas. "What comes in all shapes and sizes?" he asked.

Hunter shrugged. "I'm still trying to figure out why we look scary."

The child answered their questions, his voice whisper soft. "You're my guardian angels."

"Helpers," Taylor reminded the little boy in a whisper only he could hear.

She was too embarrassed to look at her husband or his friend. She patted the child and turned her attention back to the matter of a suitable name to call him.

Lucas coughed to cover the laughter he was suppressing. Hunter shook his head. "We are not angels," he muttered.

The boy brightened up. "She told me you would say you weren't."

"Now listen here, son . . ." Lucas began.

Taylor interrupted him. "I happen to have two fine names in mind to call you," she announced. "Daniel and Davy, though I would imagine we would use the formal David in this instance. Yes, Daniel or David."

Lucas leaned back. "Here we go again," he whispered to Hunter.

Taylor immediately defended her choices. "They are both proud, honorable names, aren't they?"

Lucas nodded. Hunter looked confused. He didn't know about Taylor's obsession with the mountain men and their legends.

"Daniel and David," said the little boy, trying out the names.

"Yes," Taylor said. "You must take your time to decide which name you want. It's an important decision, you see, because you'll carry the name for the rest of your life. I shall be happy to help you decide."

"How?" the boy asked.

"I'll tell you a story about each courageous man before you go to bed at night. One story will be all about Davy Crockett and the other will be about Daniel Boone."

"Will I be David or Davy Crockett then or Daniel Boone?"

"David," she corrected. "It's a bit more proper. Your last name is going to be Ross."

"It is?"

She smiled. "Yes, it is."

"Will the men be mad if I borrow their first names?"

"No, no, of course not," Taylor replied. "They're dead. They won't mind at all."

Taylor told him who the famous men were and that they were so admired that books had been written about them. The child became enthralled. She couldn't have hoped for a better reaction. She wanted him to love the mountain men as much as she did. More important right this minute was the fact that the little one wasn't wringing his hands together any longer.

"Family isn't about blood," she explained. "It's about making a commitment to one another."

He didn't understand what she was telling him. Taylor didn't try to explain further. She understood, and in her mind, that was all that mattered.

Two hours later, everyone was bedded down for the night. Lucas and Hunter were forced to take over the duty of bathing the little girls. David Daniel had already had his bath and his hair trimmed. While he played in the tub, his clothes were washed and dried by the hotel's laundry service. The twins' clothes were also cleaned. Taylor was kneeling on the floor washing the babies when Victoria demanded her attention. She had started to violently throw up again.

Since neither Hunter nor Lucas wanted to get near her, Taylor made them take over the chore of scrubbing the babies. She ordered them not to let them drown, then went running with a wet cloth to Victoria's side in the other washroom.

The two-year-olds were wide awake and talking up a storm. Lucas lathered up one of the twins, then realized his mistake. He lost her under the water. She came up sputtering and giggling. The soap made the babies as slick as greased piglets, and both Hunter and Lucas were drenched through by the time they got the pair out of the tub.

They dried them with towels, put their clean drawers back on them, and then sat them on Victoria's bed.

They stayed there less than a second. They weren't

at all tuckered out. Lucas and Hunter were exhausted. They sat side by side on the settee, feeling helpless and weary, while the babies climbed all over them.

Georganna was the more talkative of the two, though Alexandra certainly held her own. Both girls asked question after question, and if they didn't get an answer, they just kept repeating it over and over and over again.

They called each other Georgie and Allie. Hunter still couldn't tell them apart, but Lucas could.

While the men kept watch over the babies, Taylor ordered a day bed for the adjoining bedroom and secured yet another room on the same floor for Victoria. She was finally feeling fit again. Her things were moved down the hall into the room next to Hunter's. David Daniel, wearing one of Lucas's undershirts, was tucked into the day bed and told a story about Davy Crockett and another about Daniel Boone. By the time Taylor leaned down to kiss him good night, he was sound asleep.

The twins were winding down as well. They had both squeezed themselves between Lucas and Hunter. Their eyes were droopy and their thumbs were in their mouths. They were being lulled to sleep by the men's conversation.

"Did you hear her tell the boy his name was Ross?" Hunter asked in a low whisper.

"I heard," Lucas replied. He grabbed hold of Georgie's foot before it slammed into his groin.

"She know what she's taking on?" Hunter asked then.

Lucas yawned. "Seems she does," he drawled out.

"The boy won't have anyone looking for him," Hunter remarked. "But what about these two? Are there any relatives waiting or wanting to take them in?"

Lucas was about to answer his question when Taylor walked into the room.

She wanted to discuss their sleeping arrangements. Lucas straightened up. Her remark gained his full attention.

She thought it would be a fine idea for her to sleep with the twins in the large bed next to David Daniel.

He had to put his foot down. She was sleeping with him, and that was that.

"We'll leave the door between the rooms open."

"What if one wakes up crying?" she asked.

"I'll hear them," Lucas promised.

Hunter grinned. "I'll probably hear them, too," he jested. "They're little, Taylor, but they both have a mighty roar. Didn't you hear them when they were in the tub? They were making enough noise to reach the lobby."

Taylor didn't look convinced. Hunter gave up. He turned to his friend and reminded him of their errand. Lucas assured him he hadn't forgotten. He stood up, handed one of the babies to Taylor, then leaned down and kissed her good-bye.

"Where are you going? It's after ten," she told him.

He didn't answer her. Hunter drew her attention then by giving her the second twin. He tweaked the baby's nose, winked at the other one, and then followed Lucas to the door.

"Mr. Ross, tell me where you're going?" she demanded.

"Lock the door, Taylor. Don't let anyone in."

She couldn't go after him to stop him and demand an explanation. She had her hands full of squirming babies.

She put them to bed, covered them up, then tiptoed out of the room. When she reached the alcove of her own bedroom, she turned around and found them right behind her.

It took her three tries before she finally got them to stay in their own bed. Allie fell asleep first, but Georgie quickly followed.

Victoria came down to her room a few minutes later. She took over the duty of watching the children while Taylor took her bath.

Once she was dressed in her nightgown and robe, she sat down in one of the chairs adjacent to the divan and brushed her hair while she and Victoria caught up on everything that had happened. Taylor didn't leave any of the details out. She lingered over her description of the foul woman named Shirleen and the disgusting man lounging on the divan while David Daniel had been locked in the closet. Victoria was properly outraged.

"Why didn't you alert the authorities?" her friend asked.

"My first concern was to get the children away from there," Taylor explained. "I'm not about to give up David Daniel," she added. "But since I'm not his mother according to the law, I was worried he might be taken away from me. I couldn't risk it."

"Those vile people should be punished for their sins," Victoria said. "And what about these brothers? Will they go right on their merry way?"

Taylor shook her head. "If I have them arrested, there will be a trial. In America, everyone is considered innocent until proven guilty. There would probably be articles written in the papers. The twins would be mentioned, of course, and my name would appear."

"Malcolm," Victoria whispered. "You're concerned about your uncle, aren't you?"

She nodded.

"Cincinnati is quite a distance away from London, Taylor."

"Yes, of course it is. Victoria, what would you do?"

Her friend didn't have a ready answer. "What does Lucas suggest?"

"I haven't told him about Malcolm."

"I realize that," she countered. "But what about the Borders? Doesn't he think they should be punished?"

Taylor straightened in her chair and dropped her brush into her lap. "Lucas and Hunter went back to the tenement," she whispered.

"Why?"

"To wait for the Border brothers," Taylor said. "Dear God, there's bound to be trouble."

"Lucas can take care of himself. And so can Hunter. It's out of your hands now. Those two will surely drag the brothers off to the authorities."

Taylor wasn't so certain either her husband or his friend would involve the police. They might want to deal with the brothers themselves. She had seen the looks on their faces.

"There's always a chance the brothers won't go home tonight," Victoria remarked. "You could be worrying for no purpose."

"We should leave Cincinnati the day after tomorrow. We'll only allow one day to purchase the things we'll need."

The switch in topics took Victoria by surprise. "Yes," she agreed after a moment's pause. "I purchased all the items you'd written down."

"The children need shoes."

"We'll get them tomorrow. Taylor, what in heaven's name are you going to tell Lucas?"

"His duty is done," she replied. "He'll probably leave tomorrow. I shall suggest that very thing."

Victoria rolled her eyes heavenward. "Do you honestly believe he would leave you with three children stranded in this city? I think not. You're fooling yourself if you believe that nonsense."

Taylor's shoulders slumped. "Poor Mr. Ross," she whispered. "He didn't ask for any of this. He doesn't even want to be married."

"He may not like being married, but he's certainly beginning to like you. Don't look so surprised, Taylor. Haven't you noticed the way he stares at you?"

"Do you mean the if-it-wasn't-against-the-law-I'd-throttle-you look he gives me all the time?"

Victoria smiled. "I must admit I have seen that look several times. What about hired help? You mentioned you wanted to employ a cook and a nanny and a maid. Is there time to interview?"

Taylor shook her head. "I would have to run an advertisement first. No, there isn't time. I'm afraid we'll be on our own for a time. Perhaps we'll find suitable help in Redemption."

It was a false hope. How many cooks could there be in a two-block town?

Victoria was thinking along the same lines. "I have taken the liberty of purchasing a book full of recipes," she told Taylor. "They don't look too difficult."

They continued to talk about the problems they might encounter and worked on their list of things to be purchased in Cincinnati. It was almost midnight when Victoria went back to her room. Her friend offered to help take the children to breakfast the following morning.

Taylor was too keyed up to sleep. Her mind kept turning back to the Border brothers. She wasn't the vengeful sort, but she felt it was her duty to see that their business was stopped. There would be other children at risk unless something was done.

She finally came up with what she believed was a suitable plan.

Lucas came back to their room a few minutes later. He spotted Taylor sitting at the desk, diligently writing something down on paper. She was so engrossed in what she was doing, she barely spared him a glance.

It was safe to stare at her because she wasn't paying him any attention, and Lucas did just that. She made him feel clean. The realization made him smile. He knew he wasn't being reasonable. He didn't care. He'd just come back from the filth in the city. Hell. The area he'd been in was surely what hell would be like. And looking at the Border brothers in their seedy quarters was very like staring at a couple of demons.

Now Lucas felt as though he'd made it all the way to heaven. Taylor. With her golden curls and wonderful blue eyes. God, he even liked her frowns.

He wanted her so much he was shaking with his need. He took a bath instead. When he returned to the main room, she was still laboring over her task.

And he still wanted her. He listed at least ten sound reasons why he should leave her alone tonight. The last was the least substantial. It was after midnight. She was exhausted. She needed her sleep.

It didn't matter. By the time he'd crossed the room, he knew what was going to happen. Gaining his wife's cooperation was all that mattered to him now.

"What are you doing?" he asked.

She put her pen down and looked up at him. "I've just finished writing out an advertisement. I'm offering five thousand dollars for information leading to the arrest and conviction of Billy and Cyrus Border. Do you think I should offer more?"

He shook his head. "Their friends would sell them out for a whole lot less."

"That's what I thought," she told him. "I'm going to deposit the money in one of the banks here and put an officer in charge of the disbursement. My hope is that the reward will force the brothers to run for the rest of their lives."

"They aren't going to bother anyone ever again."

She jumped to her feet. "What happened?"

He shrugged. Billy and Cyrus were both dead, but he didn't tell her that. The truth might upset her. She was such a gentle woman, she wouldn't understand. It had been a fair fight. Lucas made certain of that. In the end, Cyrus tried to shoot Hunter in the back. Lucas had taken him out, and Hunter had taken care of Billy. He could have killed him in cold blood. He didn't though. He waited until Billy drew on him. Then he shot the son of a bitch through the center of his black heart.

He didn't want to talk about or think about the vermin any longer.

"They're gone," he told her.

"Do you mean to say they left the city?"

He had to think about the question a long minute. He guessed they had left. Their souls were probably already in hell, and their bodies were already starting to decay wherever Hunter had buried them.

"I guess you could say they have."

She put her hands on her hips. "Tell me exactly what happened tonight," she demanded.

"Hunter and I took care of the matter. That's all you need to know, Taylor. Are you tired?"

"No, but—"

"Good. Come to bed now."

He caught hold of her hand and dragged her into the alcove. He was barefoot and shirtless.

His back was broad, unblemished, deeply tanned.

She knew his skin would be warm to her touch. She tried to block the thought. She started feeling breathless. He stopped and turned around to look at her when they reached the side of the bed. His pants were unbuttoned. She could see the dark, curly hair in the opening.

She started blushing. She said the first thing that came into her mind. "You shouldn't walk around like that. You'll catch a chill. Aren't you cold?"

He reached for the tie to her robe. "No. Fact is, I'm hot."

She let him take her robe off. The way he was looking at her made her feel warm inside.

"You must be exhausted," she blurted out.

He shook his head. "I'm not at all tired."

She frowned up at him. "If I'm not tired, and you aren't either, why are we going to bed?"

He let her figure out the answer to that question. He walked over to close the drapes. When he was finished, the room had turned into a cozy cocoon.

Taylor sat down on the side of the bed. She removed her slippers and then stood up again.

She wanted to check on the children. He caught her when she tried to walk past him. "I already looked in on them," he assured her. "The babies got in bed with the boy. They're sound asleep."

She nodded, turned around, and got into bed. She fluffed her pillow behind her head, pulled the covers up, and then smiled at him.

He got into bed beside her. "You forgot to douse the light," she told him in a whisper.

He rolled to his side, propped himself up on his elbow, and stared down at her.

"I didn't forget."

He wanted to see her passion. He wanted to look

into her eyes when she found fulfillment. He didn't think it would be a good idea to tell her the truth, however. She was skittish enough. The way she was gripping her hands together told him how nervous she was.

He leaned down to kiss her. She turned her head away. "Do you remember that first night in London at the ball?"

The question caught him off guard. He leaned back. "Yes, I remember. We were married that day."

"At the party your half brother told you he had been intimate with me. Do you recall his boast?"

Lucas frowned. He couldn't imagine why she would bring up that topic now. He guessed he'd have to wait to find out where she was leading him. "Yes, I remember," he told her.

She turned to look up at him. "It wasn't true," she whispered. "He never touched me. No man has. I just thought you should know."

His smile was filled with tenderness. She was trying to tell him she was a virgin and blushing enough to make him think she considered the topic horribly embarrassing. "I already knew," he whispered back.

"Oh." She said the word with a long-drawn-out sigh.

Lucas draped his arm around her waist and leaned down to nibble on her earlobe.

"What are you doing, Mr. Ross?"

"Complicating things."

He started to laugh. He moved lower to place wet kisses along the column of her throat. She could barely catch her breath. She moved her head to the side so he'd have better access even as she embraced the thought that he should stop this nonsense immediately. He shouldn't be amused either. If he made love to her, it really would complicate things. She certainly couldn't get an annulment, could she? Did she even want one? What about a divorce? Did she want one of those? Oh, God, it was already complicated.

The truth all but smacked her in the face. She was the one complicating things, not Lucas, and all because she was falling in love with him.

She was thoroughly disgusted with herself. Hadn't she learned her lesson yet? Was it going to take another heartbreak before she finally figured it all out? Men weren't to be trusted. *Except Lucas,* a voice whispered deep inside her. She could trust him. But what did it matter? And how in God's name could she love a man who looked ready to gag every time she reminded him he was married to her?

Taylor rolled over to face Lucas. She was going to tell him to keep his hands at his sides and leave her alone. She neither wanted nor needed him. If she said the words with enough authority and feeling, she might even believe they were true.

"Mr. Ross?"

He cupped her chin with one hand and nudged her face up. His mouth hovered directly over hers. "Yes?" he asked in a voice as rough as sandpaper.

She suddenly wanted him to kiss her. *Just one kiss,* she told herself. Then she'd tell him to leave her alone.

"Just one," she whispered.

His mouth brushed over hers. "One what?"

She forgot. It was his fault because he had such beautiful eyes. He robbed her every thought when he stared at her with such intensity, such passion. She was powerless to do anything more than stare back.

She wished he'd kiss her. That realization made her remember. "Just one kiss," she blurted out before she forgot.

He nudged her onto her back. Then he covered her with his body. He braced himself on his elbows so he wouldn't crush her and stared down into her eyes.

"And then?" he asked.

"And then what?"

She was having trouble concentrating. He thought that was a nice reaction. He knew he was rattling her. She was blushing enough to make him think she could feel his hardness pressed against her. He rested between her thighs. Her nightgown had gotten bunched up around her hips. Taylor was trying to push the gown down and stay perfectly still at the same time. Oh, yes, she felt him all right. God knew he could feel her heat. It made him harder, until desire mixed with pain and he was throbbing with his need to plant himself solidly inside her.

"Just one kiss," she whispered. "And then you . . ."

His mouth silenced her explanation. He took complete possession. His mouth was hard and hot, as hard and hot as the rest of his body. His tongue swept inside. She groaned low in her throat and wrapped her arms around his waist. Her nails dug into his waistband. He grunted in response. She thought it was the most arousing sound she'd ever heard.

She loved everything about him, his scent, his taste, the feel of his hot skin under her fingertips. He was so strong he could easily crush her, and yet he was incredibly gentle whenever he touched her. He kept his strength contained. His power surrounded her, comforted her.

He wooed her with his mouth, his tongue, and his hands. He stroked her wild and made her feel as though she was the most precious thing in the world. He made her feel wanton and desirable. And powerful. He reacted to her every touch. She could make him groan by simply brushing her fingertips across his shoulders. When she moved against him, he deepened his kiss and pulled her tight against him.

She couldn't seem to get enough of him. He pulled her hands away from his back but only for a second or two. He tugged on the sleeves of her gown, and then demanded in a rough whisper that she hold onto him again. His mouth left hers. Before she could protest, he was kissing her again. She wished he wouldn't tease her. She never wanted the kiss to end, and when at last he did pull away from her, she was panting for breath and clinging to him.

He was in much the same condition. He thought he sounded as though he'd just run up the side of a mountain.

She felt as though she was floating in a pool of sunshine. She couldn't catch hold of a single worry. Desire made her blissfully carefree. Lucas had done that to her. One kiss and he'd filled her mind with butterflies.

He wasn't finished wooing her. He kissed a path down her neck, lingered over the pulse beating frantically at the base of her throat, and then moved lower still. She let out a sigh of contentment and closed her eyes.

He was determined to go slowly. He wanted to savor their coming together, but more important, he didn't want to frighten her. He'd taken her nightgown off but kept his britches on, and he wondered how long it would take her to realize she was naked. He prayed it would be later instead of sooner. He wanted her to be as caught up in desire as he was. He would stop if she asked him to, but damn, he didn't even want to think about the possibility. He was already burning, and all he wanted to do was feel her squeezing him while he poured his seed into her. She was going to be hot and tight and wet, just like he'd fantasized all these past weeks.

He let out a low groan in anticipation.

She had the softest, the smoothest skin he'd ever felt. He wanted to taste every inch of her. God, she smelled as wonderful as heaven. He buried his face in the crook of her neck and inhaled her sweet fragrance while he slowly eased himself down on top of her.

His chest covered her breasts. She let out a gasp of raw pleasure and wrapped her arms around his neck to bring him closer. The thick mat of dark hair covering his chest tickled and tantalized her breasts. The heat from his skin made her nipples hard. She was overwhelmed by the erotic feelings flooding her body. She moved restlessly against her husband, wanting something more from him to ease the heaviness in her breasts.

He seemed to know what she wanted. His hands moved down from her shoulders to stroke her breasts. He took each into the palms of his hands, then slowly rubbed the pad of his thumbs across her sensitive nipples.

She let out a little cry. Her nails dug into his shoulder blades. He grunted in response to the pain-pleasure she gave him, then moved again down her sweet body so that he could caress her with his mouth. He kissed the valley between her breasts with loving attention. Her skin was so sensitive to his touch, the day's growth on his face felt rough and scratchy, and dear God, it was the most incredible feeling. She felt as though she were coming off the bed. She arched up against her husband, begging him without words not to stop his torment.

She didn't think it was possible to feel more pleasure. And yet, when his mouth covered one of her nipples and he began to suckle, she couldn't remember to breathe. The pleasure was so intense, it consumed her. And just when she was certain she was going to die from the ecstasy he was giving her, he rolled away from her.

He stood up by the side of the bed. They stared at one another for a long silent minute. He was savoring the look of passion in her eyes. They were a misty blue now. Her lips were swollen, her skin flushed, and God but she was the most sensual woman in all the world.

Their mating would be good no matter what, but he wanted perfection. For her. Only for her. She had to want him as much as he wanted her. Since he had never taken a virgin to his bed before, he wasn't certain how long it would take to make her feel the way he did. He was determined to make her burn for fulfillment, to feel the intensity. He craved her.

He only hoped he had the stamina and the strength to hold back until she was ready. His hands shook and his actions were jerky as he tore the buttons open and peeled off his pants.

Taylor couldn't take her gaze away from his face. The smoldering look in his eyes made her heart flutter a wild beat. Every fiber in her body responded to him. The night air chilled her skin but the warm knot inside her was spreading down her middle, reaching the very core of her femininity. She wasn't covered with a nightgown or a blanket. She should have felt embarrassment. She didn't. She rested on her back on top of the rumpled sheets, staring up at her husband without any shyness at all.

The unknown did frighten her, and for that reason she didn't look below his chin. She'd seen Lucas naked before, but only his backside. She'd never seen the front of him.

Curiosity won out. She slowly lowered her gaze to

his waist. She saw the dark hair springing free from the V in the opening of his pants, but then Lucas bent over to take his pants off and he blocked her view.

And then he was covering her once again. She tried to keep her legs together. He wouldn't let her. He used his knee to wedge his way between her thighs, and before she could move out of his way, he came down on top of her. He gathered her in his arms and held her tight. His hardness was pressed intimately against her pelvis. Pleasure warred with fear. He felt huge against her. Her mouth went dry. She tensed against him in trepidation. Her hands were fisted at her sides. She squeezed her eyes shut and waited for the inevitable pain.

A full minute passed and still he didn't move. The heat from his body began to help her relax. She started breathing again and opened her eyes.

Lucas braced himself up on his elbows and stared down at her. He gritted his teeth against the incredible surge of pleasure he felt pressed against her.

Taylor noticed only the tenderness in his eyes. She was suddenly overwhelmed by his gentleness. She reached up and stroked the side of his face. He leaned into her hand, then kissed her palm. A shudder of desire caught her by surprise. She wanted him to kiss her again, hard, on the mouth. She wanted him to use his tongue. She wanted . . .

"You may . . ."

She whispered the request and stared into his eyes while she waited for him to understand.

He leaned down and kissed her brow. "I may what?" he asked. His voice was as gritty as the sound of crushed leaves. It was incredibly arousing.

"You may kiss me again," she explained. She sounded breathless.

He slanted his mouth over hers and her lips parted.

His tongue swept inside, plundering, tasting, giving. Her hands went to the back of his neck and her fingers splayed upward into his silky hair. She never wanted him to leave her. Her tongue rubbed against his with a boldness that surprised both of them. And then the kiss took on an urgency that left them both desperate for more.

His hands moved down between their bodies. He stroked her breasts and then moved lower. His fingers circled her navel. She instinctively moved against him.

He shifted his position, his mouth sealed with hers all the while, and then his hand moved lower still until he found what he most wanted to touch. His fingers surged through the soft, curly hair between the junction of her thighs. He stroked the smooth petals shielding her virginity and then began to caress the kernel of desire he knew would drive her wild.

She would have screamed with the pleasure he gave her if she'd had the strength. She let out a low whimper instead. She couldn't stop herself from moving erotically against his hand. His fingers were magical.

The rhythmic motion of his fingers against her made her wild, wanton. She arched against him, demanding more. Her nails scraped his shoulders, and she softly moaned his name.

Her uninhibited response to him made him lose his own control. His actions were rough now, determined. He grabbed hold of a fistful of her hair, pulled her head back, and sealed her mouth with his. His tongue thrust into her mouth just as his finger penetrated her tight sheath. He could feel her wetness, and it drove him wild. She cried out against his mouth. He knew he was hurting her.

He eased his finger out and tried to soothe her with

another drugging kiss. And then, before she realized his intent, his mouth replaced his fingers and he was kissing her there, stroking her with his tongue and his lips. The taste of her was intoxicating. She writhed against him even as she begged him to stop the blissful torture.

He wouldn't be deterred. He used his tongue to stroke the passion in her, and only when she was trembling and burning and pleading with him to come to her, did he at last make her completely his.

He knelt between her thighs but didn't immediately enter her. He took hold of her hands and placed them on his hard shaft. She let out a low moan. The deep guttural sound he made in the back of his throat, filled with raw pleasure, made her feel heady with power. She stroked him, squeezed him. Her finger brushed across the very tip. She felt the moisture there and leaned up to taste it with her mouth.

He almost came then and there. Her tongue flicked across the tip of his arousal and her sweet, soft lips closed around him. She started to suckle. Lucas's composure vanished. He didn't want to come in her mouth, not this time. He wanted to give her fulfillment first. Even if it killed him.

His movements became rougher now, more uncontrolled. He pushed her back against the sheets, lifted her hips up high on the front of his thighs, and when he was about to enter her, he demanded she look at him.

"We're a family now, Taylor. You're my family. Do you understand?"

She put her arms around him and drew him down to her. "Love me, Lucas. Please," she whispered.

And still he hesitated. "I understand," she said then.

"I'm going to hurt you. I'm sorry, baby. God, I'm sorry."

He kissed her then, long and hard. His tongue moved inside to mate with hers, and then he tried to slowly ease inside her tight sheath. It was agony. He wanted to be gentle. He couldn't. His body demanded completion, and he was powerless against the primitive instinct. Her permission had pushed him beyond control. He thrust deep, breaking her virginal barrier with one hard push, and he was finally planted solidly inside her. He captured her cry with his mouth, and though it didn't seem possible to him, he sank deeper inside her.

He was surrounded by her, caressed by her incredible tightness, flooded with such intense pleasure he thought he would die from it.

Taylor felt a searing pain and believed with all her heart that Lucas had just torn her apart. It hurt so much she started to cry. Yet within the space of a heartbeat, the pain began to lessen. A dull ache lingered, and when Lucas leaned down to kiss her tears away and whisper sweet lies about how beautiful she was, the pain was all but forgotten.

He wanted to give her time to adjust to him. The determination to hold back lasted less than a few seconds. She restlessly moved against him and began to stroke his shoulders. He rocked against her. Sensation after sensation flooded him. He slowly withdrew, then thrust back inside her. The rhythmic mating motions became more forceful, much quicker. Each time he sank back into her was better than the time before. He became mindless to everything but giving her fulfillment and finding his own. Her arms were wrapped tightly around his neck. He pulled her legs up to hold him around his hips. And then she began to move with him. She arched up when he pulled back, until the ritual became wild and wonderful and exhilarating. They moved in perfect harmony. With each thrust, he became harder, fuller. He knew he was about to climax. He wanted her to be there with him. He reached between their joined bodies and stroked the nub hidden between her velvety folds until she coiled all around him and cried out his name. Tremors racked her body. She chanted his name in the throes of her orgasm, and only then did he allow himself the freedom to gain his own. He surged forward again and poured his hot seed into her.

His ecstasy was so shattering and gratifying he thought he'd died and gone to heaven. His head fell down to the crook of her neck. He groaned low in his throat. His heart was slamming inside his chest, and he took several deep, gulping breaths. He felt weak and powerful at the same time. The contradiction didn't make any sense. It didn't need to, for reality had turned out to be much better than all the fantasies he'd had.

She'd given him perfection.

Taylor felt as though she'd just reached the stars and was now gently floating down to earth again. She had never known such passion was possible. It overwhelmed her, consumed her. She clung to her husband, feeling safe and protected in his strong arms, until her heart quit beating so erratically and she could draw a deep breath.

They lay complete and exhausted in each other's arms, each listening to the other's heartbeat for a long while. Lucas was the first to gather enough strength to move. He let out a loud groan and rolled to his side. He couldn't quite bring himself to let go of her though and so he took her with him. Her eyes were closed. He couldn't stop staring at her. She was so beautiful to him. She had incredibly long eyelashes. He'd never noticed before, but only because he'd been too occupied staring into her enchanting blue eyes. Her complexion was flawless and with a lovely golden hue. She was flawless, he decided then. His gaze turned to her mouth. She had full, pouting lips that could drive him to distraction. He couldn't leave them alone. He rubbed his thumb across the silky texture, then tilted her head back and kissed her, savoring once again the taste and the feel of her softness against him.

When he pulled back, she opened her eyes and looked at him. She was shaken by his gentleness. Tears threatened to spill down her cheeks. Did he think the marriage act they had just shared had been as wonderful as she did? Had he been just as overwhelmed?

Madam had called it rutting. Taylor had believed her. She understood the truth now. It was anything but rutting. Loving Lucas had been pure and joyful and fulfilling, and it was surely the most wonderful experience of her life. She would always cherish the memory.

Lucas spotted the tears in her eyes and immediately became alarmed. "I couldn't help hurting you, sweetheart. Are you in pain now?"

She shook her head. She scooted closer to him and closed her eyes. "It was beautiful," she whispered.

He hugged her tight. He was arrogantly pleased with her admission. "It was, wasn't it?" He let out a loud yawn and then added, "It was perfect."

He fell asleep a few minutes later. He had a smile on his face.

It took Taylor much longer to relax. The afterglow was slow to leave but eventually reality returned. And with it came new worries, one on top of another. At the root of all her fears was the simple realization that she was in love with her husband. She was vulnerable now, and God, how that terrified her. She had three precious children dependent upon her. She couldn't afford to let her actions be ruled by her heart.

She needed to be strong. She repeated her determination over and over again while she got out of bed and went to wash. When she got back into bed, she stayed near the edge of the side of the bed so she wouldn't touch Lucas. She wanted to take hold of him and never let go. She fought the urge. God, how she wished she could lean on him and let him share a little of her burden. She didn't have any idea how she would ever be a good mother. She lacked all the necessary skills, or so she believed, and while she was growing up, she never even held a baby in her arms. Her experience was limited to speculation, and her terror was that she would do something so terribly wrong, the babies would be marred for life. And so would Davy Daniel, she realized. He needed more than simple comfort. He needed someone to help him understand his own value. Could she build up his self-esteem? Dear God, she didn't know how.

Oh, yes, she wanted to lean on Lucas and borrow some of his strength. She didn't dare. How easy it would be to let him take care of all of them. He was too noble to turn his back on her and the children. Still, it wouldn't be right or fair of her to ask. He didn't want to be married, and he certainly hadn't wanted a family. He was a loner who liked living that way. Besides, he'd done enough for her. More than enough, she thought. He could have walked away once they'd reached Boston, but he'd stayed on and searched for her nieces. He hadn't given up. Other men would have or gotten rid of the problem by handing it over to the authorities. Lucas had been as noble as a prince, and it wouldn't be honorable of her to become dependent on him. She had to stand on her own two feet. The children were her responsibility. Hers alone.

Was it wrong for her to want to live close to him? Redemption. Even the name signified a safe haven to her now. And Lucas Ross had become her safety net. She didn't want to trap him. No, of course she didn't. But the children came first and if they needed something, or if there were trouble she was having difficulty handling, she wanted to be able to turn to him for help. He could still go riding off into his mountains. It wasn't so uncommon to leave a wife behind. Daniel Boone left his wife all the time, sometimes for several years. According to the stories, Mrs. Boone never complained, and from the number of children she had, Taylor assumed Daniel came home every now and again.

Divorce. The word left a sour taste in her mouth. Yes, Daniel Boone had left his wife behind, but he always came back. He wanted a wife.

Lucas didn't. Taylor closed her eyes and tried not to cry. She owed her Prince Charming his freedom.

Lucas woke up on top of her again. It was a little before dawn, his usual time to wake up, but he was having trouble clearing his mind this morning. He thought he was having an erotic dream. He was nuzzling the side of her neck and rubbing against her, and what made the dream so real to him was the feel of her warm skin against him. She wasn't wearing any clothes. Neither was he. His hands cupped her breasts. Her nipples were hard pearls. He moved down and took one into his mouth. She let out a little moan and began to move restlessly against him. Her legs were entwined with his. He shifted so that he could kiss the other breast and as he began to suckle, his hands stroked a path down to span her narrow waist. Her stomach was flat, smooth, her skin silky against his fingertips. His hand moved lower. He caressed the tilt of her hip, then trailed his fingers down the smooth skin on the outside of her thigh. And then he stroked a hot path up the inside until he brushed against the dewy curls at the junction of her thighs. He caressed her with his fingertips, making circles around and around the nub of her desire, until she was moaning and writhing against him, and when at last he began to caress the very spot he knew would drive her wild, she arched upward and let out a cry of raw pleasure. He didn't stop his sweet torment until she was damp with desire and begging him with soft whimpers to come to her.

He wasn't certain if she was completely awake or not. It didn't matter. She touched his arousal when he moved between her legs, and he knew he would die if he didn't mate with her. He burned with the need to feel her tight walls surround him, squeeze him, milk him.

He wrapped her in his arms, covered her mouth with his, and then thrust deep inside her. He wasn't gentle, and only when he was planted solidly inside her and was flooded with intense, throbbing pleasure did he realize he was hurting her. He was too caught up in his own passion to translate any subtle messages.

She wasn't subtle. She pinched his shoulder and told him she was in pain.

He stilled his movements immediately. She tried to move away from him. He clenched his jaw against the incredible pleasure she inadvertently gave him. He couldn't bring himself to leave her, yet he knew he was going to. What in God's name was the matter with him? Of course she was sore. She'd been a virgin, and it hadn't even been a full day since he'd bedded her.

He took a deep breath, willing some strength back

into his mind and his body and then started to pull back. She stopped his retreat by putting her legs around his hips and bringing him back.

His head dropped to her shoulder. "If you want me to leave you alone, you're going to have to let go of me."

Under the circumstances, he thought his explanation was damned reasonable and noble. Her response was to put her arms around his neck and kiss his earlobe.

"Lucas." She whispered his name like an enchantress.

She brushed her hand across his shoulder. She knew she was giving him mixed signals, and it was the fact that he would do whatever she asked him to do that made all the difference to her. She ached from the pain of his invasion; but there was pleasure as well, and she knew that soon, with his kisses and caresses, the pain would be forgotten.

"I don't want you to leave me," she whispered. "I just want . . . I want . . ."

He moved inside her. One slow, long stroke. She let out a low sigh. "This?" he asked.

"Yes."

His mouth covered hers then in a long, drugging kiss. He was determined to go slow. He was going to be gentle with her, even if it killed him.

His promise only lasted a minute or two. Once he started moving inside her again, she quickened the pace. The pain was forgotten, replaced with such incredible pleasure, she thought her heart would surely stop and she would die the sweetest of deaths.

She wasn't a passive lover. Lucas was shaken by her uninhibited responses. Her mouth was every bit as wild and wet as his was, and she stroked him with just as much loving curiosity. She found fulfillment before he did, and when she tightened all around him and cried out his name, he allowed his own release. They held each other close while tremor after tremor of passion consumed them. He collapsed on top of her. The scent of their lovemaking filled the air around them. It made him drowsy with satisfaction. He was still fully imbedded inside her. He couldn't bring himself to leave her just yet. He knew he should get up and act the part of a gentleman by fetching her a cool, wet cloth. He would play her lady's maid like any good husband would.

Just one more minute, he thought. Then he'd get up. Just one more minute . . .

He was snoring with contentment a second later.

Taylor was too content to move. She knew she should get up. She would go and get a washcloth to freshen herself and then put on a clean nightgown. She didn't know what time the babies or Davy Daniel would wake up, and she wasn't about to be caught in bed with Lucas without a stitch of clothing on. The possibility was too mortifying to even think about. Yes, she would get up. In one minute, she thought. She snuggled closer to her husband and let out a loud yawn. In just a minute . . .

15

Passion, I see, is catching.
—William Shakespeare,
Julius Caesar

"Mama's naked."

Taylor bolted up in the bed when she heard one of the twins make the announcement. She thought it might be Georgie. She was the more outspoken of the babies.

Then she heard Hunter's deep voice. "Is that so?"

She wanted to die. She let out a low groan and pulled the sheet up to cover her breasts. Lucas had been sleeping on his stomach. When he heard the conversation going on in the other room, he rolled onto his side and glanced toward the alcove entrance. Thankfully the drapes were still closed.

"The man's naked, too."

Allie made that important announcement. She obviously didn't want to be left out.

Hunter laughed. "About time," he called out in a voice deliberately loud enough to reach his friend.

Taylor's face was burning with embarrassment. Lucas didn't dare smile. She gave him a glare he translated to mean she blamed him for the awkward situation. He didn't think laughing would be an appropriate response. She'd only get more riled up. He yawned so she'd know he was taking it all in stride and then reached over to trail his fingers down her spine.

She tried to scramble off the bed. He caught her around her waist and dragged her down next to him.

"Put your pants on," she implored him. "Oh, God, how am I ever going to face Hunter again?"

"First things first," he insisted. He rolled on top of her, smiled because she felt so damned good against him, and then kissed her. She struggled against him, but only for a few seconds, and then she wound her arms around his neck and kissed him back. She was reluctant to let go of him. He was so pleased with her reaction, he kissed her again. Then he got out of bed and put his pants on.

He walked into the other room to see what Hunter wanted. From the brightness of the sunshine streaming in through the windows, he guessed it was almost eight o'clock.

"The boy let me in," Hunter explained before Lucas could ask. His friend was sitting on the divan, patiently letting the little girls climb all over him. "He made certain he knew who it was knocking on his door first," Hunter added with a good deal of praise in his voice. "He's a smart one."

"Where is he?" Lucas asked.

"Getting dressed. These two need a little help," he said with a nod toward the twins. "Is Taylor up yet?"

Lucas nodded. Hunter grinned. "You look like a married man."

"Did you look in on Victoria?" Lucas asked, deliberately changing the subject.

Hunter's mood immediately soured at the mention of the woman. His expression showed his irritation. "I tried to check on her. Honest to God, I did. I'm telling you straight, Lucas. I won't be getting near her again. Enough's enough."

Lucas hid his smile. "What happened this time?"

"She opened the door, started in gagging, and then slammed the door in my face. What the hell's wrong with her?"

Allie had started bouncing up and down on the settee and was now leaping high enough for Lucas to be concerned she might throw herself into one of the windows and crack her head. He caught her in his arms, told her to behave herself, and then tried to put her down. She had other notions. She wiggled around in his arms and held onto him. He settled her against his chest and turned his attention to Hunter again. Georgie wasn't about to be ignored, however. She scooted off Hunter's lap and went running to Lucas. Then she put her arms up and gave a rather imperious command.

"Up."

Lucas bent down, lifted her into his other arm, and then straightened up again. Allie started pulling the hairs on his chest. He told her to stop it. Georgie had become fascinated by the stubble on his jaw. She rubbed her fingers down his cheek and squealed with delight.

"You've got that look," Lucas told his friend.

"What look's that?" Hunter asked.

"Like you've got something to say."

Hunter nodded. "I ran into a couple of bounty hunters this morning. They had some interesting news. Caulder was seen outside Kansas City. They got a posse together and chased after him but he got away."

"What are you talking about? A posse? When I left for England, Caulder had just gotten another promotion. Now you're telling me he's a wanted man? What the hell happened while I was away?"

Lucas had made it his business to know everything about the bastard he was going to kill. The only reason he'd let him live this long was because of the gold he'd stolen. Lucas hoped Caulder would lead him to the fortune. The gold was the evidence he needed to convince the authorities. He wanted the world to know what Caulder had done to eight honorable men.

He'd spent almost all the money he had accumulated paying men to watch Caulder when he couldn't. His patience had finally been used up, however, and he'd made the decision before leaving for England that when he returned he would hunt the man down like the animal he was and kill him. To hell with the evidence.

"The way I figure it, that fancy government man you talked to must have believed you."

"Travis?"

"You told him about the gold, didn't you?"

"Yes."

"You told me he wasn't a bad sort," Hunter reminded his friend.

Lucas nodded. Travis was a good man. He'd listened to Lucas, and although it had only been his word against the army officer, Travis still used his authority to change the records. The eight missing men had been listed as deserters. Travis cleared the charge. Lucas remembered where the bodies were buried. He thought they should be shipped home to their families. Travis wanted to leave them where they were resting. The issue had still not been resolved.

"Caulder finally went for his gold, didn't he?"

"And Travis followed him," Hunter said.

"Damn."

Lucas whispered the blasphemy. He was so lost in his own thoughts, he didn't hear the twins repeat the expletive.

"I take it he got away from Travis?" Lucas muttered.

"Yes," Hunter replied. "He had some help from his friends. Travis took a bullet, but it wasn't anything serious."

"What about the gold?" Lucas asked.

"Caulder has it."

Lucas let out a sigh. First Allie and then Georgie imitated the sound.

"The bounty hunters wanted me to help them track Caulder," Hunter remarked. "There's a sizable reward. They're sure he's headed west."

"You tell them any different?" Lucas asked.

"No."

Lucas nodded. "Caulder's headed north. His brother will hide him."

"Chicago," Hunter agreed. They both knew that was where the brother lived.

"Yes," Lucas said. "Caulder's definitely in Chicago."

Taylor walked into the room in time to hear Lucas's last remark. She was glad for the diversion. She kept her head bowed while she pretended to fuss over tightening the belt to her robe and walked over to her husband.

She kissed each baby good morning, smiled when they giggled, and then asked Lucas who Caulder was.

"No one important," he lied. "Victoria isn't feeling well this morning. You might want to look in on her."

"She's sick again," Hunter quickly added.

They were both trying to change the subject. Taylor went along with their scheme. She would wait until later to find out who Caulder was. She didn't believe for one minute he wasn't important to Lucas because of the hard look that came into his eyes at the mere mention of the man's name.

She left Lucas with the twins and went into the connecting room to see what David Daniel was doing.

The dear child was trying to make his bed. She gave him a good morning kiss and then helped him finish his chore.

He was shy with her this morning and very solemn looking. She sat down on the side of the bed and drew him close to her.

"Is something worrying you, David?"

"I'm Daniel today," he told her.

She smiled. "All right, Daniel. Now tell me what's worrying you."

The little boy had quite a few fears stored up inside, all of them concerning the babies, and the most important one was about food. Babies needed to eat often, he told Taylor, and since none of them had any shoes to wear, how could they go outside to get something to eat barefoot? He didn't want anyone laughing at his sisters.

She told him they would eat their breakfast in the hotel room. Then she needed to go to the bank. The errand would only take her a little while, and Victoria would stay with them until she got back. Then they were all going shopping. They would buy shoes first.

He still looked worried to her. "Was there something else you wanted to talk about?" she asked.

He grabbed hold of her hand and stared down at the floor. "What am I supposed to call you?"

"What would you like to call me?"

"Georgie calls you Mama. She calls every lady she sees Mama," he added. "She gets confused. Allie called you Mama this morning. I heard her. She must be confused, too."

"I want them to call me Mama," Taylor said.

"Then maybe I should, too," he blurted out. "That way they wouldn't get confused, would they? If I call you one thing and they call you another . . ."

The yearning in his voice made her heart ache. "I was hoping you wouldn't mind calling me Mama."

"Are you old enough? You don't look old enough."

His worries were endless. Taylor smiled. "I'm old enough," she assured him. "Have we settled this?"

He shook his head. "I still shouldn't call you Mama. I'm too big. I'm seven now. Babies say Mama. I should call you Mother."

She thought that was a fine idea. She put her arm around his shoulders and hugged him. "Mother it is," she whispered.

The quiet interlude was the last peaceful minute she had for the rest of the day. Lucas wouldn't let her go to the bank alone. He insisted upon accompanying her.

She hurriedly dressed in a white blouse with lace around the stand-up collar and a plain pleated black skirt. She brushed her hair and then tied it with a ribbon behind her neck.

The outfit was something a prim schoolmarm might wear, but on Taylor, the effect was devastating to Lucas. He fought the sudden urge to tear her clothes off her and make love to her. She looked proper, but he alone knew all about the passion hidden inside her, and oh, how he remembered her silky, golden skin beneath all the layers of clothing.

Victoria arrived at the door just as the waiter delivered their breakfast. Taylor's friend looked radiant. There was a pretty blush in her cheeks and a smile on her face. Her bout of morning sickness had obviously passed.

Georgie put her arms out to Victoria, called her Mama, and demanded to be held. She lifted the baby up, told her her name was Victoria, and then pointed to Taylor. In a whisper she said, "She's your mama now."

Victoria put the baby down on the settee. Hunter was standing by the window. She smiled at him. He frowned back. She thought his behavior was rather rude. She was going to offer to pour him a cup of tea, then decided against it.

Victoria was happy to watch the children while Taylor went on her errand. Hunter tried to leave then. Lucas asked him to stay. He ignored the hot glare his request evoked, opened the door for Taylor, and left his friend fuming behind him.

Lucas didn't go inside the bank with her. He waited outside the door. It was too fine a day not to stand outside in the sunshine. She was thankful for the privacy. She wanted to withdraw a large sum of money, and she didn't want Lucas asking her any questions. The cash was for the journey into the wilderness. The transaction took almost thirty minutes. The banker had to wait for confirmation by wire from the Boston bank. He wrote down her temporary address for his bank's records and finally handed her a thick envelope filled with crisp bills.

She tucked the envelope into the pocket of her coat, assured the worried-looking bank officer she didn't need an armed guard escorting her back to the hotel, and went outside where Lucas waited for her.

He was preoccupied on their walk back to the hotel and said hardly two words to her. They had just reached the lobby doors when he turned to her.

"You and I have to have a long talk."

"We do?"

"Damned right we do."

Her eyes widened over the vehemence in his tone. "All right," she agreed. "Will tonight be soon enough to suit you, Mr. Ross?"

"It will have to do, Mrs. Ross."

He added a brisk nod, then took hold of her hand and pulled her through the entrance.

"What are we going to talk about?" she asked him on their way up the stairs.

He couldn't believe she'd asked the question. "The children, Cincinnati, our marriage. Taylor, do you have the slightest idea what you've taken on?" He realized the question was a little late in coming. "We're going to have to figure out . . ."

She interrupted him. "You really shouldn't worry so, Mr. Ross. Worry ages a person."

There was such a crowd of people on the gallery level, they had to thread their way around clusters of people to get to the next staircase. She kept her hand in her pocket covering the envelope. She wasn't about to let a pickpocket near her. The guests all looked respectable enough, but one could still be a clever thief.

Lucas wasn't able to talk to her again until they were on the way up the second flight of steps. "I've been accommodating, haven't I?" he asked her.

"Yes, of course," she replied. She was out of breath from running to keep up with him. Mr. Ross was taking the steps two at a time. He acted as though he was running from an angry mob.

389

"Do slow down," she ordered. "You've been a perfect gentleman . . . most of the time. I cannot keep up with you, sir."

"I can't keep it up, Taylor."

"Then slow down, for heaven's sake."

It dawned on him they weren't talking about the same thing. "I meant I can't keep on being a gentleman. It isn't in my nature."

He didn't look like he was jesting. "Are you apologizing for being nice?"

"I'm not apologizing for anything," he muttered. "I'm simply telling you I can't keep it up."

"It's all been a . . ."

"Yes."

She bowed her head so he wouldn't see her smile. She didn't want him to think she wasn't taking his remarks seriously. She wasn't, of course, but she didn't want him to know it. He sounded so sincere and earnest.

"If you don't like being nice, why are you?"

He was ready for the question. "Your grandmother gave me money and in return I promised to look out for you. There were other conditions attached, and I kept every one of them."

"Name one of the conditions, please."

They reached the door to their room. Neither one of them reached for the doorknob.

"I shared the same cabin with you on the ship," he said. "That was one of your grandmother's stipulations."

She shook her head. "You told me she only wanted you to secure one room. I'm certain Madam didn't want you in my bed."

He snorted. She folded her arms in front of her in response to the rude noise. Lucas seemed to be spoiling for a fight, and she was suddenly quite happy to accommodate him.

"Are you telling me being a gentleman was one of Madam's conditions?"

"Yes."

"Was it also a condition for you to share the hotel room in Boston with me?" she asked. "And this hotel room as well?"

"No."

"Then why did you?"

He couldn't come up with a single answer that sounded remotely logical.

"Where I slept isn't important," he argued. "I'm concerned about the future, not the past."

He wanted her to understand there would have to be changes. They were man and wife now, and she was going to have to make a few allowances. When she realized he was willing and determined to live in the city so the children could have every advantage, she would surely be willing to put up with his surly moods.

She should also try to love him a little.

He'd explain everything tonight. He'd start by telling her he wasn't going to leave her to raise the children on her own. "You and I are going to have to work out the details. We'll sit down after the children are in bed."

She wasn't listening to a word he'd just said. She was still thinking about an earlier remark. "Why did you stay on in Boston?" she asked. "Now that I think about it, you really could have left as soon as the boat docked."

"Ship," he corrected.

"Excuse me?"

"It was a ship, not a boat. And I stayed on in Boston

because you wanted me to, remember? There were papers to sign. After that, there were a couple of babies to find. Remember them?"

"There isn't any reason to become sarcastic, Mr. Ross. Your anxiety over the situation is clearly apparent to me. I believe I understand the reason behind it."

"You do, do you?"

His left eyelid flickered once. Then again. She knew he was getting upset. She didn't care. "Yes, I do know what's bothering you. You slept with me and we . . . were intimate."

"And that has made me anxious?"

She nodded. He shook his head. Anxious? Hell, no, he thought. Relief was a far better description for what he was feeling. She belonged to him now, and it didn't matter if she wanted to be his wife or not. What was done was done. There wasn't going to be any damned annulment, and if she so much as mentioned the word *divorce,* he'd probably break a tooth clenching his teeth together to keep from shouting at her.

The flicker had moved into the side of his cheek. She knew she was getting him riled up. She couldn't understand why. She was only telling him what he already knew. "I told you it would complicate matters if we became intimate, but you wouldn't listen, would you? Now you're sorry. You're feeling hemmed in, trapped. You want to go back to your mountains."

Lucas didn't know how the conversation had gotten so far out of hand. Her conclusions were all wrong, and it suddenly dawned on him that she might be telling him her own fears. Was she afraid he wanted to abandon her? He decided to find out. He would use reason to get her to realize how incorrect her conclusions were and then coax her into admitting she was afraid.

"If you're so certain I want to go back to the mountains, why haven't I?"

"Because of the children," she immediately answered. "You only just found them, remember? You also feel responsible and even a little guilty because you think I might think you're running out on me."

Hunter opened the door. Taylor was thankful for the interruption. She hurried inside.

"We'll continue this discussion tonight," Lucas promised.

"If you insist."

Lucas caught up with her and leaned down close to her ear. "By the way, Mrs. Ross, I have never felt guilty about anything in my entire life."

The look she gave him told him she didn't believe him.

She turned her attention to getting the children ready to go shopping. She accidentally called Georgie Allie and five minutes later repeated the error. She was having a terrible time telling them apart, and it was a strain keeping her confusion a secret. David Daniel didn't have any difficulty, nor did Lucas, she remembered, and she found her problem not only embarrassing, but also humiliating. A mother should be able to tell her babies apart. She even sat them down side by side on the settee, knelt down in front of them, and stared at the two of them long and hard, searching for subtle differences. She couldn't find any. Their every feature seemed identical. Their violet-colored eyes appeared to be the same shade, their blond curls parted at the same spot, and even their chubby cheeks looked identical to her.

The differences were in their personalities. Georgie was the more outgoing of the two. She didn't seem to be afraid of anything. She had all the qualities of a leader, a bossy one at that, Taylor thought with a smile, while her sister, Allie, was already showing signs of being a peacemaker and a lady. She held her own with her sister, however, and when she wanted attention, she could scream just as ferociously.

Neither twin seemed to be suffering any ill effects from their ordeal with the Border brothers. Taylor was both surprised and relieved.

While she helped Daniel tuck in his shirt, she told him how thankful she was that none of them had been hurt.

"I wouldn't let anyone hurt my sisters," he told her with a good deal of arrogance in his voice.

"They were fortunate to have you to look after them," she praised.

"I made sure they fed them good, too," he told her. "They were scared a lot. Mostly at night. They still get scared," he added in a whisper so Allie wouldn't hear him. She was trying to climb up on his bed. "After everybody goes to sleep, they get in bed with me. Georgie has to hold my hand."

"You've been their guardian angel," she told him.

Daniel shook his head. "Maybe a helper," he whispered. "Like Hunter and Lucas."

Daniel was only seven years old and yet he had been forced to behave like an adult. She made a promise that when they reached Redemption and had a home of their own, she would help Daniel learn how to be a little boy again. He'd shouldered responsibilities most grown men would have trouble carrying. On the surface, Daniel was everything a mother could want in a son. He was polite, thoughtful, courteous, appreciative of every little thing she did for her, and oh, how he wanted to please her. Those were all wonderful qualities, but in her estimation, not at all normal in a seven-year-old. She would love to hear him shout or show anger or even become a little stubborn upon occasion.

Time was on her side. Daniel wasn't going to relax his guard until he learned to trust her. Once he understood her love wasn't conditional, she felt certain he would start smiling.

She put the worry aside for the moment and went back to getting the twins ready. It took her a full hour to get everyone organized. Lucas hired a cabbie for their use for the day. She thought he was being extravagant and thoughtful.

Just as she'd promised Daniel, they purchased shoes first. Each child got three pairs. Two were larger sizes for the children to grow into. Daniel was easy to purchase clothing for as the general men's store carried ready-made clothing for both boys and men. When they left the store, the child had a complete wardrobe.

The twins were another matter. There weren't any ready-made dresses available. The clerk had recommended Madame Mason's fine establishment. The shop not only carried a full selection of fabrics, but also had a full staff of dressmakers available for fittings.

Madame Mason personally measured the twins, and Taylor ordered a large assortment of clothing to be shipped to General Delivery, Redemption, Montana Territory. She then took the owner aside and explained that the children were in dire need of clothing now. Was it possible to finish a few of the outfits right away?

Madame Mason was led to believe everything had been lost in a fire. She was extremely sympathetic and came up with an alternative suggestion she was sure Taylor would appreciate. She took her into the back room to show her the second-hand garments available to families whose finances were strapped. Madame Mason hoped Taylor wouldn't be offended. The opposite was the case. Taylor didn't have any qualms about buying hand-me-downs. Clothes were clothes, and the owner assured her she had only purchased barely worn, high-quality items.

They spent two hours in the back of the shop, and when they were ready to leave, they had complete wardrobes for the little girls. Victoria had already purchased fabric to make clothing for her baby, but there were such adorable little sleeping gowns available and soft receiving blankets, she couldn't resist buying a full selection. Daniel certainly didn't need anything more, but Taylor couldn't resist three shirts, two pairs of pants, and two belts she declared were too handsome to pass up.

They had lunch in a restaurant that catered to families, then went to purchase books and maps. Because the children had been so agreeable, Taylor let each of them pick out a toy. Daniel chose a small wooden horse, and Georgie and Allie both wanted rag dolls.

All in all, the day was both delightful and productive. There was only one minor inconvenience. When Taylor told Georgie she couldn't climb up on the counter in Hansen's Linen Shop, the little girl threw herself down on the floor and went into a full-blown temper tantrum. Taylor had never seen anything like it. The little imp was kicking and screaming loud enough to draw a good-sized crowd. She sounded as though she was being tortured. Allie was the only one not horrified by her sister's conduct. She fell asleep on Victoria's lap while she watched Georgie's theatrics. Taylor was at a loss as to what to do to calm her angel-turned-hellion. She knew exhaustion was the culprit. Georgie was in dire need of a nap.

One well-meaning woman suggested Taylor give the little girl a good smack on her backside, but Taylor couldn't imagine what hitting would accomplish, and she didn't believe in corporal punishment anyway. She simply stepped over her writhing daughter, paid for her purchases with all possible haste, and then scooped up the screaming child in her arms and carried her outside to the waiting vehicle. Georgie wore herself out in no time at all. She fell asleep the minute the carriage was in motion.

Taylor learned a valuable lesson about two-year-olds. One couldn't always reason with them.

Early that evening, she and Victoria took the children downstairs for supper. Daniel kept nodding off during the meal. Taylor all but hand-fed him. The twins were blessedly subdued. They were hungry, yet still managed to get more food on their dresses than in their mouths. Their table manners were deplorable. Taylor made a note to herself to start training them tomorrow in the proper use of utensils. They were too sleepy to listen to her instructions tonight.

The twins demanded to be carried back to their room. Victoria carried Georgie and Taylor carried Allie. Daniel held onto her hand. They were all so weary, their feet dragged.

Victoria offered to help get the children ready for bed. Because she looked dead on her feet, Taylor told her to go on to her own room.

"Sleep well, Victoria. Tomorrow's going to be another long day."

"Then we're leaving tomorrow?"

"If we can get everything ready in time."

"Should I pack tonight?"

"We're all too sleepy. We'll pack tomorrow."

Taylor happened to look down and catch Daniel's expression. The child looked terrified. She guessed the reason immediately. "Daniel, wherever I go, you go. I would never leave you or your sisters behind. We're always going to be together."

"Do you promise?"

Lord, he looked solemn. "Yes, I promise."

His nod told her he was convinced. "Where are we going?" he asked her in a whisper.

Taylor gave him only a partial answer. She told him they were going on a train.

Daniel was thrilled. She handed him the key to their room and let him undo the lock. Victoria handed Georgie to her but didn't immediately leave.

"Where did Hunter and Mr. Ross go today?" she asked.

"They didn't tell me," Taylor replied. "I imagine they had errands of their own."

"Will we ever see Hunter again?"

"I imagine we will," Taylor answered. "He and Lucas have been friends for a long time. I believe Hunter lives near Redemption. Why? Do you want to see him again?"

Victoria shrugged. "He hasn't said more than ten words to me. Have you noticed how he frowns whenever he looks at me?"

Taylor smiled. "You threw up all over the man," she reminded her friend. "I think he's just being cautious around you. Besides, men of few words are the best men."

Victoria laughed. "I don't believe Shakespeare was right about that."

She started to go to her room, then stopped. "I told him I was married and that my husband only just passed away. I didn't mention the baby."

Daniel had the key turned upside down. Taylor helped him get the key into the lock, then turned back to her friend. Georgie had put her head down on Taylor's shoulder, and Allie was playing with her hair.

"Why didn't you mention the baby?"

"He didn't seem at all interested in anything I had to say. He's quite rude."

Taylor wasn't given time to argue in Hunter's defense. Victoria went hurrying down the hallway. Daniel finally got the door unlocked and ran inside. Taylor followed.

The twins were more than ready to sleep. They were both sucking on their thumbs and rubbing their eyes. She got them ready for bed, gave them their new baby dolls to sleep with, and then tucked them under the covers.

Daniel had placed his wooden horse on the window seat near the head of his bed. He was already under the covers, waiting for a story. She told him two. Daniel Boone and Davy Crockett were going to get equal attention.

She realized he was still wearing his boots when she went to tuck the covers around him. She made him take them off and put them on the floor next to his bed. When she returned to the room an hour later to check on the children, she found Daniel sound asleep with his boots wrapped in his arms. He appeared to be hugging them.

She stood there a long while staring down at the child. She tried to imagine what his life had been like before he'd been taken from the streets by the Border monsters.

Lucas whispered her name. She turned around and found him leaning against the door, watching her. She didn't know how long he'd been standing there. She walked over to him. The rustle of silk was the only sound in the room.

"Is something wrong with the boy?" Lucas asked.

"No, he's fine. Could there be someone looking for him?"

"It's doubtful," he answered. "He doesn't remember any family, and he lived on the streets a long time. If a relative had been searching, probably he or she would have found the boy by now. It might be a good idea to let the authorities know he's with you, though," he added.

"I won't let any official take Daniel away from me."

"You're afraid that might happen if you make out a report?"

She nodded. He let out a sigh. He didn't know what advice to offer her. "Let's think about this," he suggested. "With the number of children left on their own out in the cold . . ."

"Are there many?"

"Too many." He sounded disheartened.

They had been talking in whispers. One of the twins muttered in her sleep and rolled over. Lucas didn't want to wake her. He took hold of Taylor's hand and turned around. He pulled her along behind him across the main room and into the alcove housing their bed.

She was ready for sleep. She'd washed and put on a pale blue nightgown and robe. The back of Lucas's hair was wet, she noticed. He'd obviously bathed as well. He was dressed in day clothes, though, a pair of black pants and a white shirt. The collar was crooked in the back. It was half turned up. She resisted the urge to straighten it.

When they reached the side of the bed, he turned to face her. His eyes, their color so wonderfully intense, mesmerized her. The way he was looking at her made her breath catch in the back of her throat.

He stared down at her a long minute, then shook his head. "This was a bad idea. We should go back in the other room to have our talk. I didn't want to wake up the children, but I can't discuss anything important here."

"Why not?"

"The bed's too close."

"Oh."

Neither one moved. Lucas still held onto her hand. He couldn't seem to make himself let go.

"I have to leave tomorrow," he said.

The jolt of pain she felt took her by surprise. She had expected him to leave. Her own plans depended upon his going away. Why then did she feel as though her heart were breaking?

He waited for her questions. After a minute standing there staring down at her, he realized she wasn't going to ask him any. He'd already decided he wouldn't tell her much. He'd give her only a few details. She'd worry about him otherwise. She had enough to think about. He didn't want to add another problem.

In his entire life no one had ever worried about him. Until Taylor. Every time he'd left the hotel to search for the twins, she'd whispered her order for him to be careful. She didn't want anything to happen to him because she was relying on him to find her nieces. But there was another motive for her concern. She was softening toward him, and in time she might begin to love him. Family. Worrying was all part of this family business, he decided. He was now accountable to her for his actions, just as she was accountable to him.

She cared about him all right. She was appreciative and thankful and even beholden to him. He wanted more.

"Hunter's going to stay here with you and Victoria and the children."

"He doesn't need to stay. We'll all be fine."

"He's staying."

He waited for her agreement. She reluctantly nodded. "I don't know how long I'll be gone. It could be three weeks. Hunter will help you find more suitable lodgings. You can't continue to stay in the hotel, not with the children. They need space to run and play."

"What time are you going to leave?"

"Early."

She pulled her hand away from his and untied the belt to her robe. The action broke his concentration. He watched as she slowly removed the garment and let it drop to the bed behind her.

He forced himself to gather his thoughts. "If you need anything . . . What are you doing?"

"Unbuttoning your shirt." She could hear the blush in her voice. She hoped he wouldn't notice. She didn't want to be timid or embarrassed tonight.

"I can do that."

"I know. I want to."

They were whispering now. Lucas's voice had taken on a gruff edge. She found the sound arousing. She tucked her head down so he wouldn't see her blush. Her fingertips trailed down his chest.

It felt like a butterfly's caress, and it was driving him to distraction. He grabbed hold of her hands to stop the gentle torment.

"Don't you want to know where I'm going?"

"Do you want to tell me?" She pulled her hands away from his grasp and reached down to undo the buttons of his pants.

He took a deep indrawn breath. "Taylor," he said. "We have to talk. We'll go in the other room and . . ."

He forgot what he was suggesting to her. Her fingers

slid into his waistband. He looked down and watched her slowly undo one button and then the next.

She couldn't believe her own boldness. She had to remind herself she was his wife now and that it was perfectly all right for her to touch him. And he was leaving tomorrow, she silently added. She wouldn't be able to touch him again for a long, long while.

She loved the feel of him. His stomach was hard, his skin hot to her touch. She undid another button. Her fingers splayed downward into his crisp, curly hair. Her fingers wrapped around his hard arousal.

"Stop," he demanded. "You're too tender. I'll hurt you."

It almost killed him to reason with her. His hands were in fists at his sides, and it took a supreme act of will and determination not to reach for her. He wasn't an ogre; he could control his lustful thoughts.

Taylor pulled away from him. "It doesn't matter if you hurt me," she whispered. "You're leaving tomorrow. We only have tonight, Lucas."

He wasn't abandoning her. He was coming back. Hadn't she been listening to him? "Just three weeks, maybe even two." He thought he got the reminder out, but his throat was so tight now, he couldn't be certain. His heart was thundering in his ears.

He forgot all about his plan to have a talk with her. It was her doing, of course. She took her nightgown off. Dear God, she was lovely. Each time he looked at her, he was stunned by her beauty. She was golden everywhere. Her breasts were full, her nipples rosy pearls. Her waist was narrow, and Lord but she had all the soft curves in all the right places. Her hips gently flared, and her legs were long, shapely, beautiful.

He pictured her wrapping herself around him. And then he tore his clothes off. He pulled her into his arms and held her and kissed her ravenously, and nothing else mattered but the feel of her against him. The world and all of his problems ceased to exist. There was only Taylor.

Their lovemaking was wild, intense, their hunger insatiable. He stroked her until she was ready for him, then moved between her thighs. He sank deep inside her. His mind reeled with each thrust. Her passion overwhelmed him, and her whimpers of pleasure drove him beyond his own control. His movements became rougher, more demanding. She tightened around him, squeezed him inside her, and whispered his name. His climax followed hers. His mouth covered hers for a long, searing kiss as he poured his seed into her.

The aftermath was just as fulfilling to him. He loved holding her in his arms and nuzzling the side of her neck while he listened to her heartbeat.

"Lucas, you're crushing me."

He immediately rolled to his side and pulled her up against him. She tucked her head under his chin. Tears were streaming down her face. She didn't want him to know she was crying.

"No man should have to give up his dreams."

He didn't know if she was asking him for his opinion or telling him a fact she believed. "What made you think about a man's dreams?"

"I was just wondering out loud. Even a man with responsibilities should be able to follow his dreams, shouldn't he?"

"What are you trying to tell me?"

"I'm tired tonight," she whispered. "I'm not making much sense."

"I guess we'll have to have our talk after I get back."

"You're going to Chicago, aren't you?"

"How did you know?"

"I heard Hunter tell you the man you were looking for was in Chicago."

"Yes."

"What was his name?"

"It isn't important."

"He's the man you want to hunt down, isn't he?"

"How would you know that?"

"On the ship, you told me you were going to go back to your mountains after you went hunting a man who'd done something to you. I asked you if he was evil."

Her memory impressed him. He let out a sigh. "And I told you he was evil."

"You want to kill him, don't you?"

He didn't know if he should tell her the truth or lie to her. She turned his attention with another statement. "You have responsibilities."

"Yes, I do," he agreed. He thought about the eight men Caulder had murdered. Lucas was the only voice left. The only gun. The others had been silenced forever. Only he heard their cry for justice. And revenge. He was going to kill John Caulder all right. He was going to feel good watching him die. The law wouldn't serve him or those eight men now.

Lucas closed his eyes. He had to deal with the past before he could turn to the future. He'd made a vow. He couldn't and wouldn't break it now. He knew all about responsibilities.

16

Love looks not with the eyes but with the mind.
— William Shakespeare,
Merry Wives of Windsor

Taylor seriously considered delaying their departure by another day. Getting all of their purchases packed and ready was going to take more time than she'd thought. The twins were into everything and made her task ten times more difficult. Georgie had made a pretend house in one of the extra trunks Taylor had purchased, and Allie was jumping up and down on anything that didn't move. Taylor's patience was sorely tested, and by noon, she believed it wasn't possible to get everything done. She fed the children, then put the twins down for a nap, and went back to organizing her things. Daniel was David today and he helped her.

Taylor tried not to think about Lucas. Tears sprang into her eyes twice during the morning for no apparent reason at all. She finally admitted the galling truth to herself. She missed him. Oh, how she wished she'd nagged the full story out of him about the man he was going to hunt down. She didn't think she would worry as much if she knew all the facts. She assumed Lucas was going after a wanted man, which translated to mean a dangerous man, and the longer she thought about it, the more concerned she became.

Her worries multiplied. She received a wire from Harry Sherman, the banker in Boston, informing her that her uncle Malcolm had petitioned the court to throw out his mother's last will and testament. He used the shameful reason that she was mentally incompetent and was under a terrible strain. Sherman added the news that until the matter was determined by the court, the accounts in England couldn't be touched. It was taking Malcolm's legal advisors longer to convince the American banks to cooperate.

Victoria had only just walked into the room when the wire arrived. She was alarmed by the news. Taylor wasn't at all surprised. She had expected her uncle to use every ploy possible to keep the money from slipping through his greedy fingers. It took her a few minutes to figure out how Sherman had tracked her down though, and then she remembered she'd given the banker in Cincinnati her temporary address when she'd signed the bank drafts and had a portion of her funds transferred.

The news of her whereabouts traveled with lightning speed. She and Victoria had only just agreed to wait until tomorrow to leave when a second wire was delivered. This one didn't just surprise Taylor. It scared the hell out of her. Malcolm had tracked her down. He wished to inform her that he had petitioned the court in London for custody of his grand-nieces and had just been awarded his request. He was sending armed escorts to collect the twins and bring them back to England, where he could watch over them.

"How did he find out about Georgie and Allie?" Victoria asked. "You were hopeful he wouldn't find out their father died, weren't you?"

"He's done his homework," Taylor whispered. She was in such a panic she couldn't seem to make her hands stop shaking. "Madam named the twins in her will. The money she left for Georgie and Allie is a considerable amount. As their guardian, Malcolm must think he'll have control over their inheritance. Oh, God, I don't know any of the legal ramifications. Will the authorities here help him take the babies? Do the American courts have some sort of agreement with England?"

"We'll have to find out," Victoria told her. "When we get to Redemption. I can be ready to leave in fifteen minutes."

They checked out of the hotel a half hour later. Taylor left a note for Hunter, purchased the tickets at the station, and they were all on their way to Montana Territory a short hour later.

Hunter spent the day combing the city, looking for suitable lodging. He returned to the hotel late that evening and was given the news of Taylor's departure. He had to read the note she'd left him twice before he believed it. The daft woman thanked him for his kindness, explained she'd paid for his room, and ended her letter with the wish that he would come calling for supper once she and Victoria and the children were settled in their new home in Redemption.

He thought she had lost her mind. He packed his bag, left a note with the hotel staff to give to Lucas when he returned, and then went running to catch the next train.

His mood was as black as the night. Taylor and her sickly friend were both crazy. What in God's name could they be thinking? They were out of their minds all right, and after he finished blistering the both of them with his opinion of their outrageous plan, he was going to take on the real culprit. Ross. By God, their friendship had limits. Chasing after two demented women went way over the boundary. Lucas owed him, and if that red-headed woman threw up on him one more time, he might have to shoot Lucas to even the score.

By the time Hunter boarded the midnight train, he was in a rage. He'd come to the conclusion he never should have befriended Lucas Ross in the first place. And if he had it all to do over again, he sure as certain wouldn't have stolen that useless, dull-bladed paring knife in the first place.

The journey to Redemption took Taylor and her crew eight full weeks. They went by train to Sioux City, Iowa. They stayed there for two days so the children could run and play, and so that Taylor could purchase a few last-minute supplies. The first on her list was a large wagon. There were plenty to choose from, and it didn't take her any time at all to complete the transaction. Finding four sound horses took her much longer. She spent a long while making up her mind. The cost was outrageous, but she knew that if she waited to make her purchases in Fort Benton, the price would be sky high.

Hunter caught up with them just as they were boarding the riverboat called the *Midnight Blue*. Taylor had chosen the larger more spacious riverboat because it carried both passengers and cargo. The cost for a cabin was an exorbitant one hundred and twenty-five dollars, which she was happy to inform Hunter when he tried to get her to turn back.

Lucas's friend had developed a rather severe twitch in his cheek by the time she finished explaining her plan to raise the children in Redemption. Then he tried to drag her, Victoria, and the three little ones back to the train station.

He didn't care how much money she'd spent. He suggested she throw all her money away. She wasn't going to need it once Lucas caught up with her. Dead women, he told her with a glare, didn't need cash.

Taylor wasn't impressed with his scare tactics. "You can either assist us or you can leave us," she announced. "We would dearly love to have your company," she graciously added. "Isn't that right, Victoria?"

Her friend snorted. Hunter's face started to turn red. Victoria marched up to him, folded her arms across her noticeably expanding middle, and said, "Either way, we're going to Redemption."

Taylor was praying he would decide to stay. They could certainly use his help, his strength, and his protection. She nudged Victoria in her side to get her to quit glaring at Hunter.

Victoria wasn't going to back down. "Yes, we would appreciate your company," she said. "But . . ."

"You're going either way, right?" Hunter snapped.

She nodded. He knew when he was beat. He threw up his hands in despair and then went to secure a cabin for himself.

Late that evening, after Taylor and the children had gone to sleep, Victoria went up on deck to get some fresh air. Hunter's room was directly across from hers. As soon as he heard her door open and close again, he followed the woman. He wanted to make certain she stayed out of trouble. She was a good-looking woman and would certainly attract attention. For the cost of just twenty-five dollars, anyone could secure passage on the riverboat, provided he was willing to sleep up on deck and bring his own supply of food. Men with unsavory backgrounds who traveled the river from town to town looking for easy money would find Victoria a sweet little morsel. She was too much of a lady to know how to ward off the drunken ones. She'd get into trouble all right. She was also Taylor's friend, which meant she didn't have a lick of sense either, and until Lucas caught up with them, Hunter felt it was his duty to look out for her.

Victoria was leaning against the railing looking up at the stars. There were two men sitting on the deck at the far end of the rail, smoking cigars and watching her. She didn't seem to notice her audience. One of the men started to stand. Hunter moved so that he stood between Victoria and her gawking admirers. The man sat back down again.

He couldn't blame them for looking. Victoria was a sight to behold tonight. She'd taken all those pins out of her hair and left the curls unbound. She looked beautiful. He had to remind himself he didn't like the woman. It didn't work. He still wanted to run his fingers through her thick, fiery curls.

"You shouldn't be up here alone, Victoria." He deliberately made his voice mean so he'd scare some sense into her.

"Have you ever seen so many stars, Mr. Hunter?"

"Yes," he answered. He stopped himself from smiling. "When did you decide not to be afraid of me?"

She didn't look at him when she gave him her answer. "When I realized you were a little afraid of me."

He leaned against the rail and looked up at the

heavens. "You've got it all wrong, lady. I've never been afraid of you."

She wasn't going to argue with him. The night was too lovely to be marred by bickering. She propped her elbows on the edge and looked out into the night.

"Captain says we'll make a hundred miles a day."

"We'll have to stop every morning to take on wood to use for fuel. Because of the size of the riverboat, I imagine we'll need around twenty-five to thirty cords a day."

"Will we be able to get off the boat and stretch our legs while the wood's being collected?"

"Yes," he answered. "When's your baby due?"

Her eyes widened over the question. Mr. Hunter had obviously noticed her thickening stomach. "September," she answered.

Neither one said another word for a good five minutes. It wasn't an awkward silence. Hunter shifted his weight, his arm touching hers. She didn't move away.

"Did your husband know you were pregnant before he died?"

"Yes."

"Do you have any idea of the hardships ahead? Giving birth in the wilderness will be difficult, Victoria. There won't be any medical help if it's needed. You'll be on your own, and if there are complications, there won't be a damned thing anyone can do about it."

"Are you deliberately trying to frighten me?" she asked.

"There's time to turn back," he countered. "I'm trying to make you realize you'll be better off in the city."

He sounded as though he really cared about her. Victoria started feeling guilty because she'd lied to him about having a husband. Hunter was a good, honest man. It wasn't right for her to deceive him. She'd seen the way he helped Mr. Ross search for the children.

She lied because she didn't want him to think ill of her. And that only made her guilt worse. Her own reaction to Hunter confused her. His opinion mattered more than she wanted to admit. She was drawn to him and thought perhaps it was because he was so strong. She always felt so unsure of herself. He was a commanding figure, intimidating really, with those dark eyes and that brooding look. His hair was long, almost shoulder length, and the color was as black as a panther's. He reminded her of the magnificent cat, for he moved with the same grace.

Victoria didn't realize she was staring at him until he pointed out her rudeness. She apologized. "Mr. Ross mentioned your grandmother was an Indian."

"Yes."

"I was wondering . . ."

"Yes?"

"Are all Indians as handsome as you are?"

She blushed as soon as the words were out of her mouth. She felt foolish and ignorant. She was an unmarried, pregnant woman. She should have known better than to act like a silly schoolgirl. "I shouldn't have said that to you. It was terribly forward of me. I meant no harm," she added in a rush. "And you must surely be used to hearing women tell you . . ."

"Was your husband handsome?"

Hunter didn't know why he was so curious about the man she'd been married to, and he knew he shouldn't be asking her questions about him. She was still in mourning, for God's sake, and here he was prodding at her to dredge up painful memories.

"He wasn't handsome," she answered. "But love is blind according to William."

"He said that?" he asked, jumping to the conclusion William was her late husband. "I'm not so certain that's true."

"Of course it's true. William wrote it down."

He shrugged. She asked him a question then. "Do you care what other people think about you?"

"No."

"I do," she admitted. "Some of the time," she hastily qualified. "And I only care what certain people think of me." *And so I lie,* she thought to herself. She let out a sigh. She suddenly wished she hadn't told Hunter she was married.

"'My stronger guilt defeats my strong intent,'" she whispered, repeating one of her favorite quotes from Shakespeare.

"What did you say?"

She repeated the quotation, then added, "They're William's words, not mine."

Hunter decided that the man she'd been married to must have been some sort of fancy high-brow scholar. She couldn't have lived with her husband very long. She wasn't old enough. But she'd certainly loved him. Why else would she have memorized everything he'd ever said to her. The longer he stood there staring at her, the more she quoted the Englishman.

"It won't matter that you're in mourning," he warned her. "Men will come calling. They'll fight each other to win your hand."

"I'm never getting married."

"Don't you mean you're never getting married again?"

"Yes, of course," she blurted out. "Again."

She sounded vehement. He wanted to argue with

her. Just because she had loved one man so passionately didn't mean she couldn't love again.

"Women are scarce where you're going," he pointed out. "Hell, people are scarce. You're going to get lonely. I'd wager you'll be married in a year. Mark my words."

She let out an inelegant snort. Then she turned the topic. "Are there many women in Redemption?"

"Not living in the town," he answered. "But there are two a day's ride away."

He didn't look like he was jesting with her. "Just two?" she asked.

"Ma Browley and her sister, Alice Browley. They're both pushing sixty."

"What about homesteaders?"

"What about them?"

She let out a sigh. Mr. Hunter was starting to get edgy. She wondered what had caused the change in his mood. He'd been perfectly pleasant for several minutes. Now he was becoming surly again.

"You'll probably die out there."

"Perhaps I will," she agreed. "What does it matter to you?"

"It doesn't."

She straightened away from the railing. "I'm a strong woman, Mr. Hunter. You might be disappointed."

She left him leaning against the railing and went back to her cabin.

The days and nights followed a set pattern. Every morning, the *Midnight Blue* stopped to take on the day's wood supply. The captain was usually able to purchase the cords they would need from enterprising families who had already cut and stacked the wood. Other days, the male passengers were asked to help with the cutting and the carrying.

The children were allowed to leave the riverboat and play along the shoreline. Hunter put a stop to the activity a few days later. He gave Taylor a one-word explanation: snakes. She immediately took the little ones back on board.

Hunter had his hands full watching out for the two women. They were too damned pretty for their own good. They attracted attention the way dogs attracted fleas. Thankfully Taylor was usually worn out by suppertime. She went to bed when the children did. Victoria was the problem. She was restless at night and liked to go up on deck. Hunter always followed her, and they always ended up in an argument. Inevitably she went back to her cabin in a huff. And that was fine with him. He had had his fill of all the clever little sayings her William had said to her. The man sounded like a pompous ass to him. Hunter never much cared for flowery language. If you had something to say, then say it.

It was a sunny Monday afternoon when Hunter notified the captain they would be leaving the riverboat the next morning. Then he went to tell Taylor to have her bags packed and ready.

"But we aren't even close to Fort Benton yet," she informed him.

It only took him a second or two to realize she wasn't jesting with him. Then he became furious with her. "You planned to go all the way to Fort Benton and then by wagon to Redemption?"

Taylor rushed over to her valise and pulled out her map. She waved the paper in front of Hunter's face. "According to my map, we must go to Fort Benton and then we backtrack."

He snapped the map out of her hand and looked at it. Whoever had drawn the thing had to have been drunk. There were forts all along the Missouri, but only one had been named and marked.

"Did you want to backtrack over a hundred miles?"

"No, of course not, but without proper trails, I thought . . . Do you mean we could take a shortcut?"

Hunter turned around and started for the door. He knew if he stayed a minute longer, he'd start shouting at her. The woman didn't even know where she was going.

"Be ready," he muttered on his way out the door.

The following morning, while Taylor kept watch over the children, the crew of the *Midnight Blue* unloaded their horses, wagon, trunks, crates, and valises. Hunter counted their supplies and decided they were going to need a second wagon. He found a suitable one in Jilly Junction. He separated the weight between the two wagons. He wasn't happy with Taylor's selection of horses, but after looking over the stock available for purchase in Jilly, he decided they would have to keep what they had. Oxen would have served them much better for the load they had to carry.

The wagon ride to Redemption took over a week. The landscape was magnificent. The colors of spring were everywhere. There were brilliant pink, red, purple, orange, and white flowers sprinkled all over the carpet of lush greenery. Taylor was overwhelmed by the beauty of the wilderness. Every afternoon she would collect a sampling of flowers she'd never seen before, and at dinner, Hunter would tell her what they were called. There were wood blossoms, Indian paintbrush, arnica, and white monkeyflowers and others he didn't know the names of and so he called them just plain wildflowers.

There wasn't anything plain about the area. It was a

kaleidoscope of color. Taylor felt as though she had been dropped into God's paradise. With each turn in the trail, there was something new and wonderful to see and appreciate. Sometimes she would become so overwhelmed by the sheer beauty of it all, her eyes would become teary and she would speak in a whisper.

The children were in awe of the animals they spotted. They laughed when they saw a mule deer because of his funny, giant ears. Georgie chased a whitetail doe and Daniel boasted he'd gotten close enough to almost touch one of her fawns.

The air affected Taylor as well. It was so pure and light, it made her dizzy. She felt such tremendous peace. Although she had never been to Redemption, she was already calling it home.

There were a few irritants, of course. Taylor wore white gloves to protect her hands the first day, but her fingers were still rubbed raw from gripping the reins. The following morning she put on a pair of old work gloves Hunter had. They were too big, brown in color, and really quite unattractive. She loved them.

Daniel had been a sweet, uncomplaining child until Taylor put Georgie in Hunter's wagon to ride with him for the morning. Allie wanted to sit next to Taylor and have a turn helping to hold the reins. The little boy couldn't be in two places at the same time and pitched a fit worthy of applause when his sisters were separated. His show of temper astonished Taylor. He was furious with her because she wouldn't change her mind. He kicked the wheel with his bare foot and then let out a howl of pain loud enough to scare a grizzly bear away. Taylor lifted him onto her lap and soothed his temper while Victoria rubbed the sting out of his foot. Daniel didn't want to be placated, however. He wanted things done his way. He ended up sitting in the back of Taylor's wagon and wouldn't talk to anyone for over an hour.

Taylor was secretly pleased with Daniel's behavior. He was obviously feeling safe and comfortable enough to let his guard down. The pretense of being a perfect little gentleman was finally wearing thin, and the real child was emerging. Daniel could be as obnoxious as any other seven-year-old, and she couldn't have been happier.

After the second day out, Hunter got stuck with Georgie. He didn't realize it was deliberate until the fourth morning. The little girl would squeeze herself up next to him on the seat, her baby doll in her lap, and talk from the minute the wagon started moving until they stopped for lunch. He was usually considering putting a gag in her mouth by then. Georgie rode with Taylor every afternoon and always took a long nap with her sister.

Victoria and Taylor both loved the evenings, for it meant they were another day closer to their destination. They prepared supper together over the fire Hunter started for them. They were terrible cooks and so they only fixed simple dishes. Taylor made pan biscuits every night. They weren't too bad if they were loaded with strawberry jam. Victoria fried and burned the fish Hunter caught and deboned for her. It was usually trout and incredibly delicious. They added apples from their store of supplies and whatever else they could think of that was easy to prepare.

Daniel and Georgie would eat anything Taylor put in front of them. Allie was the persnickety one. She wouldn't eat any food that touched any other food on her plate. If the biscuit were accidentally placed too close to the fish, the two-year-old wouldn't eat either offering. She was specific about her apples as well. Taylor had to peel it, core it, and then cut the apple into four sections, just like she'd done the first time she'd fixed the fruit for the child. And God help them all if Allie's fingers got sticky. The usually sweet-natured child would carry on something fierce until her hands were washed and dried.

Each one of them had his or her own peculiarity. Victoria always got a burst of energy as soon as the sun went down. Daniel still insisted on sleeping with his boots in his arms, and Georgie always talked until she fell asleep. The sound of her voice became her own lullaby.

Hunter became cantankerous every evening. He'd feel it was his duty to once again remind them that it still wasn't too late to turn back. When Taylor and Victoria wouldn't agree, he'd lose his patience.

Taylor was usually in a good deal of pain by the end of the day. The muscles in her shoulders and back would feel as though they were on fire. She didn't want to listen to Hunter's comments about how foolish she was, and on the night before they reached Redemption, her temper exploded. She told him she was pretty certain she had already aged at least twenty years, that she was sure she looked a fright, and that she ached from the top of her head to the tips of her toes. She couldn't do anything about her appearance or her pains. She could do something about his behavior, however, and if he didn't stop reminding her she was crazy, she just might have to prove him right.

She was too distraught to think of anything substantial enough to threaten him with. He wouldn't have believed her anyway. She turned around and walked back to her wagon. She hurt so much she wanted to cry, but she didn't give into the luxury because it would have required too much energy.

Hunter must have realized he'd been too hard on her, because the next morning, he didn't shake her awake at the crack of dawn. She and Victoria both slept until after nine o'clock. Georgie's laughter woke them up.

Victoria stayed behind to wash and dress, but Taylor put on her robe and went looking for the children. They were easy to find. She simply followed the sound of Georgie's voice.

Hunter had taken the trio to the creek. He sat on the bank, his rifle next to his side, watching over the children. Daniel had just put on his socks and pants and was struggling to put on his boots.

"Always turn your boots upside down and shake them real good before you put them on in the morning," Hunter advised.

"Why?" the child asked.

"Critters sometimes crawl inside during the night," Hunter explained.

Taylor ducked under a branch and walked forward. Her eyes widened when she saw the twins. They were both stark naked and soaking wet. Allie was sitting in the stream combing her baby doll's mop of hair while Georgie jumped up and down so water would splash up around her.

The water was as clear as air. Hunter had chosen a spot deep within a grotto where the water level was only a couple of inches. Further down the line of trees, the creek spilled into a much deeper pool.

Neither twin was shivering. Taylor assumed the water wasn't too cold for them. She suddenly wished she could join them. She longed to wash her hair and smell like her rose-scented soap instead of horses and old leather.

Allie was the first to spot her by the trees.

"Mama," she cried out. "I'm washing baby."

Taylor smiled. She took a step forward. "I can see you are," she called back.

"Good morning, Mother."

Taylor turned to her son. "Good morning, Daniel. Did you sleep well?"

"I'm going to be David today," he informed her. "I guess I slept well. I didn't wake up."

Taylor started walking toward the edge of the stream. Georgie was trying to carry handfuls of water to her. At least she thought it was Georgie. Taylor based her conclusion on the fact that the twin was chattering away about the game she was playing.

Taylor kicked off her shoes. She didn't stop when she reached the water's edge. She kept right on going, much to the children's delight. Hunter was as surprised. He let out a burst of laughter, which Georgie immediately imitated.

When she sat down in the middle of the stream, dressed in her nightgown and robe, even David cracked a smile.

Victoria came strolling around the bend in the trees to find out what all the commotion was about. She took one look at Taylor and burst into laughter.

While Taylor played with her daughters, Victoria went back to the wagons to fetch soap and towels. She washed Allie's hair and Taylor washed Georgie. David promised he'd already washed his own. He was thoroughly engrossed in the task of cleaning his boots.

After the twins had been scrubbed clean, Taylor put the pair on a blanket next to Hunter, and then went around the curve in the stream to the deeper water. She took off her gown and robe and then took her bath. Victoria stood on the bank with Taylor's gun in her hand, and it was only after her friend had washed her hair and finally started getting dressed that she admitted she didn't know how to shoot the weapon. Taylor promised to teach her as soon as they were settled in their new home.

Victoria took her turn next. David came to check on the women. Hunter had sent him to find out how much longer they were going to dally. Victoria sent back the message in a shout Hunter was sure to hear that she wasn't going to be rushed.

Taylor sat down on a blanket, put her gun in her lap, and started to dry her hair. Her gaze settled on the far bank, for she'd noticed a movement in the brush but couldn't see what was causing it. Victoria was oblivious to her surroundings. She was thoroughly enjoying herself. She'd lathered her hair up and was now rinsing the soap out. David grew bored and went back to play with his sisters.

Another movement caught Taylor's attention. She squinted against the sunlight but still couldn't see anything beyond. She made up her mind it was just the wind causing the leaves to sway. Then she saw the eyes. They were yellow. The outline of the body appeared next. It was a cat of some sort and without a doubt the biggest thing she'd ever seen.

She'd read in one of her novels that cats didn't go into water. They were afraid to get wet. This cat didn't know he was supposed to be afraid. Taylor slowly stood up and took aim. The animal was edging forward again. He looked ready to jump. She started to call a warning to Victoria. A hand clamped down over her mouth, effectively stopping her.

"Don't make a sound and don't move."

Hunter gave the command in a low whisper next to her ear. Taylor froze. She didn't even nod to let him know she'd heard. She guessed his worry. If Victoria stood up in the water, she would put herself between the cat and Hunter's rifle.

Neither Taylor nor Hunter was watching Victoria now. Their attention was riveted on the monstrous cat.

Victoria was having the time of her life. She made another lazy dive, rolled onto her back under the water so her hair wouldn't cover her face when she surfaced, and then stood up. She faced Taylor. She started to smile, but then she spotted Hunter and let out a gasp instead. Her hands covered her breasts under the water.

She suddenly realized they were watching the bank behind her. Hunter had his rifle ready. He was squinting through the sight. She was afraid to turn around. Her gaze frantically turned to Taylor again. Her friend silently mouthed the words "Get down." Victoria's knees went weak and she slowly sank down into the water.

The cat sprang into a high arch. Hunter fired twice in rapid succession, though he was certain he killed the mountain cat with his first shot. The animal landed with a splash just a few feet away from Victoria.

Victoria shot out of the water and stared at the animal as it sank to the bottom. Then she let out a piercing scream and collapsed backward into a dead faint. Hunter fished her out. Victoria was sputtering and crying. As soon as Hunter lifted her into his arms, she wrapped her arms around his neck and held on for dear life. Taylor tucked a blanket around her friend for modesty's sake.

The children came running to find out what had happened. Taylor took them back to the wagons. Victoria was sobbing now, and Taylor thought she could use a little privacy until she got control of her emotions. It had been a frightful experience. Taylor noticed her hands were shaking when she put her gun away in her apron. The twins were wide-eyed and silent while they listened to her explain what had happened. Georgie wanted to go and see the cat. Taylor wouldn't let her. She dressed the little girls, combed their hair, and had just finished tying their shoes when Allie let out a piercing scream. She had only just noticed her baby doll was missing.

Taylor's nerves were already frayed, but she held onto her patience. She put the twins side by side up on the seat, told them not to move, and then started to go back to the stream. Her son offered to go for her.

"You stay here, Daniel," she ordered. "I'll be right back. Allie, stop that screeching. I'm going to get your baby."

"I'm David today," her son reminded her. "Did you forget?"

This name business was getting out of hand. Taylor turned around. "Why don't I call you Daniel David until you make up your mind?" she suggested. "It would be easier for me to remember."

"Two names?" He smiled over the possibility.

"Yes," she agreed. "Two names."

"But what if I want to be David Daniel instead of Daniel David?"

Here we go again, Taylor thought. She left the boy to mull over his choices and muttered her way back to the creek. The doll was on one of the rocks near the water's edge. She didn't reach down to pick up the toy, however, but took a hasty step back instead. A snake with brown speckles all over it was coiled on the rock next to the baby doll. It was making a rattling sound and watching her. Taylor froze and started to call out to Hunter. She could hear Allie wailing in the background, and all that suddenly mattered to her was getting the doll so the child would stop screaming. Hunter wasn't always going to be around to take care of her and Victoria and the children. Lucas wouldn't be around either, she realized. She was going to have to stand on her own two feet, even when she didn't want to.

She took the gun out of her apron. She wished the snake would just slither away so she wouldn't have to kill it, and then another thought changed her mind. What if she had sent Daniel to fetch the doll?

Taylor took aim and killed the snake with one clean shot. The force of the bullet lifted the snake up and backward into the water.

Hunter was kissing Victoria and liking it entirely too much when the sound of gunfire pulled him back to reality. He put Victoria down, grabbed his rifle, and started toward the sound.

"Taylor," he roared.

"It was just a damned snake, Mr. Hunter," she called back.

Victoria had also started to go to her friend. Hunter stopped her by grabbing hold of her arm. He was going to tell her to stay put until he found out what had happened, but once Taylor shouted her explanation, he should have let go of Victoria. He didn't. She was adjusting the blanket to cover her breasts, her head bowed.

"She killed a snake," she whispered and then peeped up to look at Hunter.

"No, she killed a damned snake," he corrected.

Victoria nodded. "I would have gotten hysterical. Taylor got mad. Why did you kiss me?"

It didn't take him anytime at all to come up with a suitable lie. "To get you to stop crying."

"Oh," she sighed.

He couldn't make himself stop staring at her. God, she was lovely. Her eyes were the prettiest shade of green he'd ever seen, and her hair looked like bronzed fire to him. She had a splattering of freckles across the bridge of her nose. He resisted the urge to kiss them.

He was out of his mind to think about such things. For a moment, he'd forgotten who she was and what he was. A lady and a half-breed. It was an impossible combination. "You going to stand here all day?"

The anger in his voice stung her pride and pricked her temper. "Only until you let go of me."

He immediately pulled away from her and went back to camp. She followed him at what she considered was a respectable distance.

They were finally ready to leave a half hour later. Allie was still upset. She barely touched her breakfast. She didn't want a wet baby doll. She wanted a dry one. Taylor couldn't reason with the child. She finally took the doll and pinned it to the top of the canvas covering the wagon and explained to the teary-eyed twin that the sun would dry the doll in no time at all. When that promise didn't soothe Allie, Taylor declared the baby doll was having a nap.

Georgie wasn't helping matters. She was tormenting her sister with her own doll. It wasn't even noon yet and Taylor felt as though she'd already put in a full day.

They would reach Redemption by late afternoon, and that was the root of her worries. She was anxious about meeting the people who lived there and even more concerned about finding suitable lodgings.

Hunter added another worry by casually mentioning that Lucas could very well be in the town by now, waiting for them. She didn't believe it would be possible until Hunter convinced her. If his business in Chicago hadn't taken long, he could have taken the train from Cincinnati to Sioux City, then jumped on one of the many riverboats constantly traveling up and down the Missouri.

"That would still put him days behind us," she reasoned.

Hunter shook his head. "He won't be riding in a wagon," he pointed out. "Or spending time buying supplies like you did in Sioux City. He'll be riding a horse, Taylor, and taking all the direct routes a wagon couldn't get through. He could be there all right."

Taylor prayed Lucas hadn't gotten there ahead of her. She wanted to be settled in first. Then she'd deal with him. She knew he was going to be furious, and she couldn't help but become nervous over the prospect of facing his wrath.

Hunter was smiling while he hitched up the horses. Taylor concluded he wanted her to worry. She decided to get even with him. She waited until he'd taken up the reins of the second wagon and then carried Georgie over to him. He gave her a look that told her he knew why he was being saddled with the chatter-box. She shrugged back at him. Then she handed him Allie.

Georgie was squeezed up on his left side and Allie sat on his right. She was still wailing like a wounded animal.

Hunter looked down at the child. "You going to cry much longer?" he asked.

She nodded. Hunter laughed. The sound filled the woods around them. It proved contagious as well. Taylor found herself smiling, and when she looked at Victoria, she caught her smile as well.

Everyone waited on Daniel David now. He stood

between the two wagons, trying to make up his mind which one he wanted to ride in. He didn't particularly want to be separated from his sisters, he explained when Taylor asked him why he was taking so long, but he didn't think the two women should ride all by themselves.

Hunter made up his mind for him. He told the boy to get into his wagon and be quick about it. Daniel David didn't hesitate. Taylor concluded he liked having the decision made for him.

Hunter took the lead down the last hill into the valley. Daniel David sat in the back of the wagon watching Taylor for almost an hour. He'd wave every five minutes or so and then smile when she waved back to him. The child finally grew bored with his vigilance and climbed up on the seat next to Allie.

They reached the last gentle slope a little after two in the afternoon. They could see the town clearly now. It was nestled between snow-capped mountains and rolling hills. Mother Nature's glory was all around them. Taylor imagined she'd used her paintbrush to splatter the hillside with every color in the rainbow.

She'd run out of paint when she reached Redemption. Taylor's first impression of the town was one of disappointment. Victoria looked appalled by the sight. Lucas had been right when he told her the town wasn't more than twelve or fourteen buildings. She'd been prepared for that reality. She had to brace herself against the ugliness. Every single building was brown and dirty.

Hunter led them into the center of the town. There were wooden walkways on both sides of the dirt roadway. Everything had been constructed out of wood, and Taylor tried to imagine how pretty the town would be if the buildings were painted.

"Look, there's a general store," Taylor pointed out to her friend.

"There's a saloon right across the street," Victoria said. There was a bit of criticism in her voice.

"I wish it weren't so quiet."

The women kept their gazes straight ahead. They were attracting attention and trying not to notice the men gawking at them.

They were everywhere. They stood in doorways, hung out windows, and leaned over hitching posts. No two men looked alike, of course, but their expressions seemed identical. They all looked stupefied.

Word of the women's arrival spread as fast as a flash flood. Before the two wagons reached the hitching posts in front of the general store, the entire town had turned out to look them over. All nineteen of them.

Victoria didn't guess at the number. She counted just to be certain.

Taylor didn't know what was expected of her. Should she smile and call out a greeting? Or would that be considered too forward? She wanted to start out right. She just wasn't certain how.

The crowd was edging closer. Several started making hooping sounds. Hunter looped the reins over the posts and then turned to help Taylor to the ground.

"Why isn't anyone talking?" she whispered.

"They're having trouble believing what they're seeing," he answered.

Taylor let out a sigh, ordered herself not to be nervous, and then took off her bonnet.

Bedlam broke loose. Everyone pressed forward to meet the woman. Hunter waved them back. He lifted Taylor to the ground and then turned back to the crowd. "She's Ross's wife."

A man in a checkered shirt and baggy pants stepped

forward. He had an unruly gray-streaked beard, a giant-sized nose, and dark brown eyes. He squinted at Taylor and moved closer. "I haven't seen a pretty woman in so long I've forgotten what they look like."

"I ain't never seen any as pretty as these two," another man shouted. "We quit thinking of Ma and Alice Browley as women years ago."

"Back away, Cleevis," Hunter ordered. "Let the women breathe."

"I just want to get close enough to catch her scent," Cleevis admitted.

Taylor could feel herself blushing. She straightened her shoulders and edged her way around Hunter. She heard the man named Cleevis take a deep indrawn breath when she passed him, then cry out in what sounded very like ecstasy, "Roses. She smells like roses, men."

"If that don't beat all."

Taylor couldn't stop herself from smiling when she heard that odd comment. She made her way to the back of Hunter's wagon and pulled the flap back just enough for her to look inside.

Georgie was wide awake. She'd obviously just used the chamber pot and was now letting Daniel David fix her bloomers for her. Taylor took over the chore and then lifted the two-year-old into her arms.

The twin wanted to get down until she saw all the men staring at her. Then she wrapped her arms around Taylor's neck and buried her face in the crook of her neck.

Hunter was trying to assist Victoria to the ground. Every time he reached up for her, she'd shake her head at him.

"You can't sit there all day," he snapped. "I'm not going to let anyone hurt you."

"I didn't suppose you would," she whispered back. "Besides, I can take care of myself. I'm not afraid."

"Prove it."

She decided to do just that. She took off her bonnet, tossed it into the wagon behind her, and then accepted his assistance in getting to the ground.

Everyone was plying Taylor with questions. They spoke in low voices and when it dawned on her they were whispering so Georgie wouldn't become any more frightened, she lost her own nervousness.

"Where are you headed, Mrs. Ross?" a man with thick eyeglasses asked her.

"We have arrived at our destination, sir," she answered. "We're settling here."

"Is the red-headed one married?"

A young, freckle-faced man in the crowd called out the question. Taylor turned to look at Victoria. She thought she might want to answer the inquiry. Victoria wasn't paying any attention to her. She had latched onto Hunter's arm and wasn't going to let go. He was trying to peel her fingers away from him.

"She was married," Taylor explained. "Her husband died just a few months ago."

No one seemed to be particularly sorry to hear the news. Victoria received three marriage proposals before she'd circled the wagon to stand next to Taylor.

"I'm in mourning," she announced. "And I happen to be an expectant mother."

Neither statement made any difference to the men. They didn't even know her name and they were still pleading for her hand in marriage. One gentleman told her he'd be more than willing to let her keep the baby.

Victoria considered kicking the offensive man. Taylor laughed. Georgie was finally ready to explore her new surroundings. Taylor walked over to the steps and put her down on the wooden walkway. Georgie immediately ran inside the store.

Taylor straightened up and then took a hasty step back. Another man, wearing a thick, long-sleeved gray undershirt and blue overalls, had worked his way around the crowd and now stood towering over her. He was a giant of a man, at least six and a half feet tall, with huge shoulders and brawny arms. He had long brown hair and a thick beard. He was quite frightful looking, and he was waving a newspaper like a madman in front of her nose.

She swatted the paper away. "Whatever are you doing, sir?"

"You a reader?"

"Excuse me?"

He bellowed his question the second time. Taylor's ears started ringing.

"If you're asking me if I can read, the answer is yes."

Her admission pleased him. He let out a shout of satisfaction that very nearly knocked Taylor off the steps.

Victoria walked carefully around the giant and went into the general store. Several men chased after her.

Daniel David climbed out of the wagon and hurried to stand next to his mother. Taylor introduced him to her audience.

Hunter watched her. She told the men that Daniel David was her son. Someone tried to challenge the notion, but Taylor's stare stopped the protest cold.

"Daniel David is my son," she repeated. "I am his mother and Lucas Ross is his father."

She scanned her audience, daring them to disagree with her. No one said a word. Several nodded their acceptance. Taylor was satisfied. She happened to glance over at Hunter and saw him smile. Then she turned back to her son. She patted him and suggested he go inside the store and find out if there were any peppermint candies for sale.

"But Allie . . ."

"I'll get her," Taylor promised.

The little boy ran inside. Taylor walked back to the wagon. Allie was still sleeping soundly. She closed the flap and turned to Hunter. He nodded before she could ask him if he'd watch the wagon. She smiled at him and then turned to go inside.

The giant followed her. He had the newspaper tucked under his arm. Victoria was visiting with the owner. She introduced him to Taylor. The man's name was Frank Michaels, and he couldn't have been more pleased to meet her. He pumped her hand up and down for a good minute. His enthusiasm was heartwarming. Frank was approximately fifty years old. He wore spectacles with a crack in one of the lenses and had narrow shoulders and gnarled hands. His eyes held her attention. They were hazel in color and radiated warmth. So did his smile. He kept telling her over and over that he was as pleased as punch to meet her.

Georgie took off for the back of the store. A few seconds later, Allie appeared in the entrance. She was leaning against Hunter's leg, staring at the crowd.

"She's a quick one, she is," Frank Michaels announced. "She must have run like lightning to get around to the front so quickly."

Allie spotted her mother and ran to her. She had her baby doll in her hands. The owner squatted down close to the child. Allie immediately hid behind Taylor's skirts. Then Georgie came tearing around the corner. Mr. Michaels did a double take.

"Twins," he whispered.

"When you have a minute to spare, I'd surely appreciate your attention, Mrs. Ross."

The giant made the request from behind her. Taylor turned around and immediately dodged the newspaper he was waving in front of her face.

"Could you read this?"

"Yes, of course I could," she answered. She tried to hide her exasperation from the strange man. "I've been reading for years, sir."

"Now, Rolly, she only just got here. Let her catch her wind. You don't want to bother her with the paper." The owner made the protest on her behalf. He let out a little groan as he straightened up again and pressed the palms of his hands to his lower back.

"You have a handsome family, Mrs. Ross."

"Thank you, Mr. Michaels."

"I'd be pleased as punch if you'd call me Frank."

"Then you must call me Taylor," she replied.

"I'd be honored to," Frank told her.

Rolly wasn't going to be deterred or ignored. "She gave me her agreement, Frank. I heard her clear."

Taylor didn't know what he was talking about. Before she could ask what it was she had just agreed to, Rolly took hold of her hand, tucked it tight under his elbow, and pulled her back to the doorway. Rolly had to pass Hunter in order to get outside. The giant stopped, gave Hunter a worried look, then muttered, "Hunter." He added a nod to complete the greeting.

Hunter was just as ungracious. He frowned at Rolly, nodded his greeting, and then added his name in a grudging tone of voice. "Rolly."

They proceeded on. Rolly stopped when they reached the steps. He bellowed his order. "Get the crate, boys. We got us a reader."

A resounding cheer went up. Taylor was astonished

by the reaction. A crate appeared out of thin air and was placed on the boardwalk next to her. She stared down at it and then turned to look up at the giant again.

He handed her the paper and lifted her up to stand on the crate. Another man dragged out a rocking chair from the store. Rolly nodded to the man and then took his seat.

"Mama, what are you doing?" Georgie asked.

Taylor looked down at her daughter and shrugged. "I don't have the faintest idea," she whispered.

"Your mama's going to read us the news," Rolly explained. He gave Taylor a wave. "Get it started then."

Taylor looked at Hunter to see what he thought about the man's behavior. Hunter was standing just outside the entrance to the store, looking bored and unconcerned.

She unfolded the paper. It was the *Rosewood Herald*. She had never heard of the town. Then she noticed the date.

"Why, this paper's two weeks old."

"It's still going to be news to us," Rolly explained.

"We used to get lots of papers from the mining camps clustered up in the mountains," another man called out. "But we all prefer the *Rosewood Herald*, don't we, Rolly?"

"It seems we do," he agreed.

Taylor was dying to ask if her first impression was accurate. Didn't any of them know how to read? She didn't wish to offend their feelings, however. She had to be wrong, she thought. In this advanced day and age, surely some of them could read.

She decided to take a roundabout way of finding out. "Who read the paper before I was given the honor?"

Everyone looked to Rolly to answer. "Well, now, Frank usually did the reading. Then his glasses got cracked, and he hasn't had time to get them fixed."

"Then there was Earl," someone called out.

Rolly nodded. "We weren't partial to his reading. He had a hacking cough that got in the way of the news."

"Henry read once," Frank reminded Rolly from the doorway.

"He stuttered," Rolly interjected. "Drove me crazy," he added with a nod. "I almost shot him."

"You did shoot him," Frank reminded the giant.

Taylor's eyes widened. Rolly clarified his action. "That was for a different reason. Get it started," he ordered Taylor once again.

She looked over the crowd of men, their expressions earnest, expectant, and she did the only thing she could do. She read.

They wouldn't let her skip any section. She was expected to read every word in print. It took her close to forty-five minutes, as the paper was four sheets thick, and she counted her blessings Rolly hadn't handed her the *Denver Post*. It would have taken her hours to read the paper. She was interrupted with hoots of laughter over anything the least bit humorous and long discussions over the bad news.

Her audience was very appreciative. When she finished reading the last notice and folded the paper, they clapped and shouted their thank-yous. Someone she hadn't met yet told her she had a right nice pretty voice.

Taylor felt that she'd learned two things. The first was the fact that the men craved hearing news from the outside world. They obviously weren't content to live in their own little realm, they wanted to know what was going on all around them. They weren't passive Americans, and from the heated way they debated the issues, she realized they all took an active interest in their government. The second thing was about Rolly. The other townsmen gave the giant a wide path. He sat all by himself, and from the looks some of the others cast his way, she concluded they were afraid of the giant. He seemed harmless enough to her.

Taylor jumped down off the crate and handed the paper to the man. "Here you are, Mr. Rolly. Now if you'll excuse me, I have a hundred things to do before nightfall."

The giant stood up. "We'll see you Sunday then?"

"Sunday?"

"For the reading," he explained. "Harrison brings the paper on Fridays or Saturdays. We would all wait until Sunday to hear you read."

"I would be happy to read on Sunday," she agreed.

Rolly bowed to her. "I'd be willing to show you my appreciation, Mrs. Ross." He turned to glare at the crowd. "It's only right."

Heads bobbed up and down in rapid succession. Taylor surmised Rolly didn't want to be seen as thoughtful or courteous.

"Is there something in particular you might be needing?" he asked her.

"We need lodging, Mr. Rolly," Taylor explained. "Could you tell me if there are any vacant houses in the area? I know it's probably wishful thinking on my part, but we'll be more than willing to live in an abandoned soddie for a while. Do you know of anything?"

Rolly smiled at her and then turned to the audience watching from the street.

"She's wanting a house, men. Anyone disagree?"

The giant waited a full minute and then turned back to Taylor. "It's settled."

"What is settled?" she asked.

"Your house," he explained. "We'll start building you one tomorrow."

Her mouth dropped open. Rolly picked up the rocking chair and took it back inside. As he passed her, he suggested she pick her spot this afternoon.

He wasn't jesting with her. She told him he was being overly generous. He told her he didn't mind. No one else minded either, she realized. One gentleman told her the only way they could be certain she'd stay on is if they provided a home for her.

"We don't want Ross hiding you in the mountains," one earnest-looking young man admitted.

Frank Michaels had stayed outside to listen to Taylor read the paper. He had already scanned the news but he liked listening to the sound of her voice. "You could all sleep in Callaghan's house tonight," he suggested. "It's nice and sound."

"It's got wood floors," someone called out.

"Callaghan won't be back until summer," Frank told her.

"Won't he mind if we use his house?" Taylor asked.

"It ain't Callaghan's," Rolly explained. "He just took a liking to it. He ran the owners off years ago. They deeded the place to Lewis."

The freckle-faced young man named Billy stepped forward. "Whenever Callaghan comes to town, he stays in the house. No one knows how he gets inside. The house has four fancy glass windows, but none of them have been broken. He sure doesn't get in that way. There are locks on both doors, too. He's a crazy old mountain man," he added with a nod. "You don't want to be running into him."

"A real mountain man?" Taylor repeated the words in a whisper.

"I don't believe you should stay there unless your husband agrees. Where is Ross?" Frank asked.

"On an important errand," she answered. "He's really a mountain man?"

"Who?" Rolly asked.

"Callaghan," she explained.

"He's a real one, all right," Rolly confirmed with a nod.

"Would Mr. Lewis be willing to sell the house?" she asked then.

"He's wanting to sell it," Frank explained. "The couple who left made him their agent. Lewis holds the papers, and if he ever sells the place, he'll keep his cut and send the rest on to St. Louis. That's where the past owners were headed. You aren't thinking you want to buy the place, are you?"

"Lewis is the town's lawyer," Billy said.

Taylor was impressed. For a town this size to boast a legal advisor was quite a surprise. Then Frank pointed out the fact that Lewis had never had any formal schooling. He'd read a couple of books, followed a fancy attorney around for the year that he lived in Virginia City, and when he settled in Redemption, he put his own shingle out. Lawyers apparently didn't need diplomas.

"Does Mr. Lewis have specific office hours?"

The men found her question vastly amusing. When they stopped laughing, Frank explained Lewis didn't have an office. He owned the stable, and when he wasn't busy taking care of the horses, he took care of any legal matters.

"Why doesn't he read the paper for you?" Taylor asked then.

"He charged too much money," Rolly explained.

"Frank, I'm thinking she'll be safe enough. If Callaghan knows she's married to Ross, he'll leave her alone. He won't tangle with him."

Victoria came back into the general store with the twins trailing behind.

"Where's David Daniel?" Taylor asked.

"He's helping Hunter with the horses."

"I thought the boy's name was Daniel David," Frank commented. "I must have gotten it wrong."

Taylor shook her head. "You weren't wrong. He's both names until he decides which one he wants," she explained. "Mr. Rolly, would you please direct me to Mr. Lewis's stable?"

"I'd be honored, Mrs. Ross."

Taylor turned to give Victoria a quick summary of the conversation she'd missed.

"Does the house have wooden floors?" she asked.

Rolly told her it did. Victoria looked like she was going to swoon, so pleased was she with that bit of news.

One hour later, sight unseen, Taylor was the proud owner of a two-story house with wooden floors and four fancy glass windows. She and Victoria had also requested papers so that they could file for a hundred and sixty acres of land under the Homesteaders' Act. Lewis didn't believe either woman would qualify. Victoria was still a British subject and therefore might not be able to own land in America. He didn't know if Taylor could file either, since she was married and Lucas might have already filed.

It didn't take Taylor any time at all to come to the conclusion that Mr. Lewis was a complete nitwit when it came to understanding and interpreting the law. Even she realized that Lucas would have to sign the papers to transfer ownership, but Lewis was ready to record the deed on her signature alone. He used fancy words to muddle up the legal issue and hide his ignorance.

She insisted on taking the papers with her for her husband's signature. Lewis took the twenty dollars she gave him as a down payment. He congratulated her on her new home. She wasn't certain she owned anything, but she shook his hand anyway.

Hunter waited with Victoria and the children outside the stable. Taylor showed him the papers and then explained what she had done. He didn't try to argue with her or remind her that there was still time to turn around and go back to civilization. His reaction was actually quite bizarre. He laughed until tears came into his eyes.

Hunter, Victoria, and Daniel David walked down the center of the street. Taylor and the twins followed. Georgie needed her shoe retied, and by the time she got the child to stop dancing around her long enough for her to make a proper bow, the trio in front of her had made it all the way back to the general store.

Everyone wanted to see the house before nightfall. Hunter lifted Victoria up on the wagon seat and then put Daniel David next to her. He turned to wait for Taylor.

She caught hold of her daughters' hands and tried to quicken their pace. They walked toward the west. The sky was glorious with the sunset. A vibrant orange crown with red trimmings circled the sun and Taylor's breath caught in her throat while she stared up at the magnificent sight. She was entranced.

Georgie pulled her back to reality. "There's the man, Mama."

"What man, sweetheart?" she asked, barely pausing in her adoration to look down.

"Our man, Mama," Allie said.

Taylor came to a dead stop. Dear God, how could

she have missed him? Their man, as Allie had called him, was standing in the center of the road. The distance was too great for her to see his expression. She guessed he was frowning.

"We're in for it now," she whispered.

She wanted to turn around and run for safety. She immediately pushed the idea aside. She wasn't afraid of Lucas. Yes, he would be angry with her, but after a little while, he'd see the rightness in what she'd done. She sincerely hoped he wouldn't kill her first.

She straightened her shoulders and started walking again. The closer she got, the more alarmed she became. He was dressed in buckskin and wore both of his guns in his gunbelt low on his hips. His hands were at his sides. She suddenly had the bizarre feeling that she was walking toward a showdown. Or a shootout. Lucas had the advantage. Lord, she really needed to get hold of herself. It was the sunlight making him look magical and invincible to her. Golden streaks flowed all around him. By the trickery of the sunset, it appeared he had just walked out of the sun.

She was finally close enough to see his expression. Oh, God, he was furious all right. His eyes were as cold as ice.

She didn't know what she was going to say to him. She glanced over at Hunter and saw his smug now-you're-going-to-get-it expression and wished she was close enough to kick him. She continued to walk toward Lucas and finally came to a stop when she was just a few feet away.

They stared at each other for long seconds. Taylor noticed he was covered with a layer of dust. He had a beard, too. It made him look all the more intimidating. And wonderful. She was so happy to see him again she wanted to weep. He was everything she could ever want in a man, but what stunned her speechless was the realization that Lucas was beginning to look like a mountain man.

"Mama?" Georgie called out her name.

She snapped out of her trance. Then she took a deep breath, plastered a smile on her face, and looked down at her babies to give them her instruction.

"Say hello to your papa."

17

Our wills and fates do so contrary run.
—William Shakespeare,
Hamlet

"Are you out of your mind?"

Lucas asked her the question in a low whisper. He sounded hoarse. He was trying with all his might to control his temper, but the strain was taking its toll. His throat ached with the need to roar. He was shaking with relief because she was still alive and burning with fury because she'd taken such ungodly risks. But she was all right, he told himself for the tenth time. She hadn't gotten herself killed making the journey. He felt as though he'd died a thousand deaths worrying about her and the children on his race to get to them.

Taylor had never seen Lucas this angry. She found herself trembling in response to his fury. She wasn't afraid of him. She was just . . . nervous. She knew she was going to have to stand up to him. He needed to understand how things were going to be.

"I expected you to be upset," she began. "But seeing your anger is far worse than imagining it. I could appreciate it if you would try to calm down."

"Answer me, Mrs. Ross."

She had to force herself not to flinch. "Very well," she agreed. She tried to make her voice sound soothing. "No, I'm not out of my mind. Allie and Georgie and Daniel David have every right to call you father."

She straightened her shoulders and took a step forward. "And until they're old enough and strong enough to do without parents, they're stuck with the two of us."

She had completely misunderstood what he was asking her. He thought it was deliberate. He ignored her speech about fatherhood and turned her back to the question he most wanted answered.

"Why did you come here? What in God's name were you thinking?"

"We wanted to be close to you."

He wasn't buying it. "I was in Chicago," he reminded her. "You know where Chicago is, Taylor?"

"Yes, of course."

He nodded. "And so, in order to be close to me, you traveled over a thousand miles in the opposite direction. Have I got that right?"

"I don't believe it was even close to a thousand miles," she remarked.

He closed his eyes and counted to ten. Then he started over. "When did you decide to come here?"

She didn't believe telling him the truth would be a good idea now. He looked close to boiling over. He was spoiling for a fight, but she wasn't going to accommodate him. They were standing in the center of town, for heaven's sake, and their audience was growing by the second. She knew no one could hear their conversation. When Lucas got mad, his voice became softer, not louder. She counted that wrinkle in his personality a blessing.

"I don't wish to talk about this now," she told him. "When we have a moment alone, I'll be happy to answer all of your questions."

"I'm taking you back tomorrow," he announced.

She shook her head. She wasn't going anywhere.

He nodded. They would leave at first light.

Lucas didn't want to wait to get his questions answered, but he had calmed down enough to realize this was neither the time nor the place for their discussion.

"You know what, Papa? You know what?" Georgie was tugging on his pant leg and repeating the question for the fifth or sixth time. She was whispering, and Lucas realized she was trying to imitate him.

He picked her up and gave her his full attention. He stared into her wide blue eyes and suddenly realized she was going to grow up and drive some peace-loving man out of his mind . . . just like her mother.

"No, what?" he asked.

"Mama shot a damned snake."

His gaze flew to Taylor. "Is that so?" he asked.

She shrugged. "Children exaggerate."

"Up." Allie shouted her demand and put her arms out. Lucas lifted her into his arms and was surprised when she gave him a wet kiss on his cheek. She rubbed the palm of her hand over his beard, laughed with delight, and then told him her baby got wet and she had to cry about it for a long time. Lucas listened to every word. When she was finally finished with her story and had scrunched up her shoulders and smiled with self-pleasure, he asked her what else her mother had done.

The twins took turns telling on her. Taylor was astonished by their memories. She was also mortified.

Victoria would be, too, she realized, if she knew that Georgie had just told Lucas she was naked and crying and Hunter kissed her anyway.

Taylor started walking toward the wagon where Daniel David waited with Hunter and Victoria. She heard Georgie complain that her mama wouldn't let her see the dead cat and immediately quickened her pace.

Lucas followed her. He put the twins down when he reached Daniel David. The boy suddenly turned shy. He had his hands jammed in his pockets and was staring down at the ground. Lucas had a twin clinging to each leg, which made movement awkward. It didn't deter him, however. He lifted Daniel David up and gave him a hard hug.

The child squeezed him back. Lucas whispered something to him, and Daniel smiled while he nodded. Then Lucas settled the boy in one arm and turned to Hunter.

"I owe you."

His friend was in full agreement. "You got that right."

Frank Michaels called out to Lucas and started down the steps. The crowd had kept away during the reunion and now wanted to join in. Lucas was surrounded by friends who took turns congratulating him on his marriage.

The women weren't ignored. Both Taylor and Victoria were surrounded. Rolly asked for permission to touch their hair. Lucas heard the request and told the giant to keep his hands away from his wife and her friend.

Rolly immediately turned to Lucas. He had noticed he hadn't kissed his wife. Did that mean there was trouble brewing in the marriage? Lewis could see about the divorce if that was the case, and Rolly could start in courting Taylor within the month.

"There isn't going to be any divorce." Lucas's voice was emphatic. He stared at Taylor when he made the announcement.

He didn't speak to his wife again until late that evening. It took them two hours to get away from the town. Everyone offered them lodging. First Lucas refused, and then Hunter was asked. He also said no. Taylor was more diplomatic. She thanked them for their offer and then explained that the twins were used to sleeping in the wagon, and that routine was important with all the commotion going on around them. The twins were exhausted and needed a good night's sleep. The men finally agreed.

Routine really was important to all three children, Taylor supposed, but the real reason she didn't want to stay in town was because of her husband. He wasn't going to continue to ignore her and when the confrontation came, she didn't want an audience. Since he was being so difficult Taylor decided not to tell him about the house she'd purchased. They could all wait until tomorrow to move in.

Love and trust. The two words echoed in her mind and with it came the questions. *Did you have to have both or could one be enough?* She knew the answer but she stubbornly tried to ignore reason. How much did she have to tell Lucas about her past?

The answer was as clear as the air. She had to tell him everything. Taylor dreaded the task and turned her attention to her children. When she was busy, she could almost push the worries aside.

They made camp in a meadow just to the south of Redemption. There was a clear-water stream on one side, and the cloistered area was surrounded by trees.

After supper was finished and the children had been bedded down in one of the wagons, Victoria and Taylor decided to have another bath. Hunter led them to the deeper edge in the stream and then gave them privacy. He told them to call out if they needed him.

Victoria was a little nervous. The moon was bright enough to see where they were walking, but not sufficient to see beyond the far side of the water. She kept squinting her eyes and scanning the bank, looking for more wild animals ready to pounce, and Taylor was just as apprehensive, though for an altogether different reason. Lucas had her rattled, and dear God, what would she say to him to make him understand she really wasn't trying to trap him?

Lucas had disappeared right after supper. He came back to camp an hour later. Taylor and Victoria were sitting on a blanket in front of the fire Hunter had prepared. He sat across from them, and every now and then he would toss a couple of twigs on the blaze to keep it going.

Both women had put on clean day dresses so they would be modest, but Taylor hadn't bothered with undergarments. As soon as she climbed into the wagon to go to bed, she would change into her nightgown anyway.

The men were talking in low voices. Victoria turned to Taylor. "Lucas is still angry, isn't he?" she asked in a whisper.

"He'll get over it," Taylor whispered back. "As soon as he realizes I won't be making any demands on him, I'm certain he'll calm down."

"He doesn't want us here. I heard him tell Hunter he's going to take us back tomorrow."

"We aren't leaving."

"Can he make us?"

"No, of course not," Taylor replied. She changed

the subject just a little then. "Have you noticed he hasn't said a word to me in hours?"

"I did notice. Are you in love with Lucas?"

Taylor's gaze turned to her husband. He was leaning back against a tree trunk. His hand rested on his knee. He was listening to something Hunter was telling him. From his dour expression, he wasn't happy about what he was hearing.

"I do love him," she whispered. Her gaze lingered on her husband for a full minute before she forced herself to turn away. "I really must be out of my mind."

Victoria kept glancing over at Hunter. She couldn't seem to make herself stop. She remembered how wonderful it felt to be held in his arms. And when he kissed her . . .

She pushed the memory aside. Hunter was leaving tomorrow. " 'Men should be what they seem,' " she whispered.

"William?" Taylor asked.

"Yes," Victoria answered. "It's from *Othello*. Hunter should be hard and cruel and frightening."

"Was that your first impression of him?"

"Yes," she whispered. "Then he started being kind and sweet and considerate."

She sounded as though the man had tricked her. Taylor was sympathetic. She understood what her friend was feeling.

"Georgie told Lucas that Hunter kissed you."

Victoria started to blush. Then Taylor told her the rest of the story. "She also told him you were naked."

"Oh, God." Victoria's face turned bright pink.

Taylor smiled. "Did you want him to kiss you?"

Victoria started to shake her head, then nodded instead. "He's leaving."

"You're certain?"

"Yes. Why do I feel as though he's abandoning me? Isn't that the most ridiculous reaction? I barely know the man."

"You know him quite well," Taylor argued. "You've spent every waking minute with him from the minute we left Sioux City until this evening. You're falling in love with him."

"He's leaving," Victoria repeated again. "None of it matters. We're a sorry pair, aren't we? Neither one of us has learned from our pasts."

"Madam used to tell me I couldn't always have what I wanted. I can't seem to learn that lesson."

She let out a sigh and turned her gaze to her friend. "You should probably go to bed. You need your rest."

"I felt the baby move today. She's getting stronger."

"You're also strong," Taylor said. "It was a difficult journey and you never once complained."

"It didn't seem difficult. Hunter kept a slow pace, and if you remember, he insisted I walk by the wagon every afternoon."

"I remember he had to drag you out of the wagon on several occasions."

Victoria shrugged. "I realize now he had my best interests at heart."

"Did he tell you why he's leaving?"

"I don't want to talk about him any longer," Victoria announced. She gave Hunter a frown and then turned back to Taylor. "Do you think Lucas will want to talk to you tonight?"

"Probably. I'm dreading it," she admitted. "I honestly don't know what I'm going to say to him. I shouldn't have to soothe him, should I?"

"Just tell him the truth," Victoria advised. "If you love him, you're going to have to start trusting him."

"I do trust him." So easy to say and so difficult to do, she thought.

Victoria shook her head. "You've got an odd way of showing it. You trust him to protect your children, but I don't believe you trust him with your heart yet."

"Why should I?" Taylor realized she'd raised her voice and immediately lowered it to a whisper again when she added, "The man doesn't want to be married. How do you think he'd react if he knew I loved him?"

Taylor didn't wait for her friend to venture an answer. "Trapped," she whispered. She turned her gaze to Lucas and glared at him, while she wondered why he had to be such a difficult man.

"'Men are deceivers ever, one foot in sea, and one on shore, to one thing constant never.' William," she added with a nod.

"You've got that right," Taylor muttered.

Victoria let out a loud sigh. "I shouldn't be giving you advice," she said. "But I would suggest that if Lucas gets the upper hand in your discussion, and you can't come up with a logical argument, use William."

Taylor perked up. "And what quotes do you suggest I use?"

Victoria nibbled on her lower lip while she considered what would be most appropriate. A minute passed in silence, then she said, "I've got it. 'In a false quarrel there is no true valour.'"

Taylor repeated the quotation. Then she nodded. Victoria added another quote to use in the event Lucas's temper still hadn't cooled down. Taylor repeated the second quotation and nodded once again.

Victoria was yawning every other minute now. Taylor stood up and then helped her friend to her feet. Both women deliberately ignored the men. Victoria started to turn away, then stopped. "Don't you wonder why he rode so hard to get here? Hunter said he had to have set some kind of record. He seemed in an awful hurry for a man who doesn't want to be married."

She whispered good night and then circled the campfire to get to the wagon. She didn't look at Hunter. She knew she'd make a fool of herself if she tried to be civilized and say good-bye to him. She couldn't be sophisticated tonight. She was hurting too much. Why in God's name had she allowed herself to become so attached to him?

Victoria lifted the flap at the back of the wagon, stepped up on the crate, and then climbed inside. She was crying before she got the first button at the top of her dress undone.

Taylor was too restless to sleep. She didn't want to sit back down by the fire and be ignored by her husband any longer. She'd had enough of his rudeness. She decided to go for a walk. She needed a few minutes alone to get her emotions under control. The anticipation of the inevitable confrontation was making her a nervous wreck. She would have to explain everything to him. He deserved to know the truth, and oh, God, that meant telling him about Malcolm. She honestly didn't know if she had the strength or the courage. She turned away from her husband and hurriedly walked back to the stream.

The men watched her leave. Hunter was the first to speak. "Your face on fire yet? Your wife's glare was hot enough to burn you."

"Victoria was giving you the same attention," Lucas pointed out. "Are you going to walk away from her?"

"I can't see any other way," Hunter answered. "What happened in Chicago?"

Lucas took the hint. Hunter didn't want to talk about Victoria.

"Caulder was hiding out at his brother's place."

"You called that one."

"I didn't get him. A couple of bounty hunters got in my way. Caulder left in a hurry though. He didn't have time to pack."

"He left the gold behind."

Lucas nodded. "I wired Travis and told him where it was. Caulder thinks I've got his fortune."

"Are you going after him again?"

"I won't have to," Lucas explained. "He's going to come looking for me. They took Caulder's brother in. He was raving about Caulder blaming me for ruining his life. Said he'd get even. Can you believe it, Hunter? The bastard's talking revenge because I cost him his career and his gold? He's conveniently forgotten he ordered eight men killed and watched them die."

"He ordered nine men killed," Hunter reminded him. "You were also supposed to die, remember?"

"I remember."

"And you're still trying to figure out why you're still alive, aren't you?"

Lucas unfolded his legs and stood up. "Taylor's stewed long enough," he announced. He turned to go after his wife. "And I'm real curious to hear her reasons for coming here. They're bound to make me crazy."

Taylor had stood by the edge of the stream listening to the sounds of night. The crickets were out in force tonight. The sound they made in unison had a pulsating yet soothing beat. Every now and then an owl would add his voice, and Taylor was thinking how peaceful it was and how very beautiful the trees looked dappled in moonlight, when she heard a rustling of leaves being tread upon on the opposite side of the creek. The image of the huge mountain cat leaping at Victoria came into her mind, and she started shivering. Then she heard the howling of a lone wolf. The animal sounded close. Taylor whirled around and started back to the wagons.

Lucas blocked her path. He stood next to a tree not five feet away from her. One arm was draped over a low-hanging branch.

He hadn't made a sound. She didn't know how long he'd been standing there watching her. The noises of the night no longer frightened her. She felt safe again, and with that comforting feeling came courage.

She clasped her hands behind her back and stared up at her husband. He still hadn't shaved. The beard made him look all the more rugged, and she suddenly wanted to kiss him so she'd feel his whiskers rub against her skin.

"I did a lot of thinking on my way here," Lucas told her. His voice sounded mild, almost pleasant. "And I came to some interesting conclusions. Want to hear them?"

"If you want to tell me," she answered.

He crooked his finger at her. She took another step toward him.

"You and your grandmother had everything all figured out, didn't you? You weren't lying to me when you said I was your plan."

"We didn't have everything . . ."

He wouldn't let her finish. "I've been manipulated since the day I said I do. Isn't that right?"

She shook her head. "I didn't deliberately . . ."

Once again he interrupted her. "Yes, you did. Were you afraid I would say no if you asked me?"

"If I asked you what?"

"To be a father."

He answered his own question. It was beginning to become a habit. "Of course you were afraid. You didn't trust me at all, did you?"

With each question he asked, his voice became a little rougher and intense.

"Well?" he demanded.

"I'm waiting to hear my own answer," she told him. "I might as well go back to the wagon while you have our discussion. You have it all figured out, don't you?"

"Taylor, I'm trying to understand how I ended up chasing a wife and three children all the way to Redemption."

She bowed her head. "I know I have a lot to explain," she whispered. "I just need to figure out how." *And to find enough courage,* she silently added.

He shook his head. "No, that's not the way we're going to do this. I'm going to ask the questions and you're going to answer them. I've got quite a few stored up inside me. And no half answers, Taylor. I've run out of patience."

"Yes," she agreed. "I'll tell you everything." Tears welled up in her eyes. "And after you know the truth, I promise I won't try to stop you."

"Stop me from what?" he asked.

"Leaving."

He leaned back against the trunk. "Is that what you think I'll do?"

She let out a sigh and shook her head. "No," she whispered. "You won't leave. You're too honorable. But you'll want to," she predicted. "I won't blame you, Lucas."

She sounded heartbroken. He had to resist the urge to take her into his arms and comfort her. He knew that if he touched her, he wouldn't get any of his questions answered tonight, and he'd already vowed neither one of them was going to bed until all his nagging questions had been answered.

"Did you know you were going to raise the twins when you married me?"

"Yes."

"Did Madam know?"

"Yes."

"When were you going to tell me about Georgie and Allie?"

"Do you mean in the beginning?"

"Yes."

She took a breath. She knew he wasn't going to like her answer. She'd promised to give the truth, however, and she wasn't going to break her word. "You weren't ever supposed to know," she whispered. "We were going to part in Boston, remember? I was going to take the babies away."

"Where?"

"I was going to choose a city somewhere in the West. Oh, I had it all figured out, Lucas." She paused to shake her head over her own foolishness and naïveté. "I was going to hire a housekeeper and a cook and try to talk Mrs. Bartlesmith into staying on as their nanny. If she didn't want to, I was going to hire another qualified woman. I planned to disappear with the twins. Only Madam and I knew George had died. We didn't tell the rest of the family about the twins' father."

He mulled the information over in his mind and then asked, "So you did in fact marry me just to protect your inheritance?"

"No, I married you to protect the twins."

"Taylor, if I wasn't ever supposed to know about them, how was I going to protect them?"

His anger and his exasperation were both evident in his voice. She took an instinctive step back.

"You were my safety measure," she explained. "At the time, even I didn't fully understand. But Madam did. She insisted I marry you. She'd found out all about you. She had a file the size of a hatbox in her room. She'd gathered quite a bit of information about you and was certain that if I ever needed you to protect the babies, you would be there."

Lucas had tensed at the mention of the file. "Did you read the information she'd gathered?"

He wasn't able to keep the worry out of his voice, but reason pushed his initial panic aside. Her grandmother obviously hadn't had access to his war file. She never would have allowed her granddaughter to marry him if that was the case. There was also the possibility that Travis and his cohorts had softened the truth about him. By the end of the war, he had turned into a combination of a gunfighter and a bounty hunter, but the army hadn't looked at it quite that way. Hell, they'd given him medals for what they called valor. In Lucas's mind, killing was killing, and fancy medals couldn't change that fact. He'd put the medals away and never looked at them again. They were a part of his life he was determined to forget.

Taylor misinterpreted his reaction to her news about the file. She thought he was angry. She couldn't blame him. Madam had invaded his privacy, and that was terribly wrong, even though her intentions were honorable.

"No, I didn't read the file. I trusted my grandmother. She told me you were an honorable and courageous man. She even called you a prince among men. I believed her."

He relaxed against the tree trunk again. Taylor folded her hands together in front of her and turned her gaze to the ground.

"You told me about Redemption. Do you remember?"

"Yes," he replied. "You asked a lot of questions and I wondered why, but I sure as certain didn't think you were intending to come here."

"You said a man could walk for a mile and not see another person. I believed the twins would be safe here. Women have dreams, too," she added with a nod. "I always dreamed of one day living on the frontier, but I was going to be reasonable. I planned to wait until the twins were older. Then things changed."

"You needed my help in finding the children."

"Yes," she admitted. "And Madam died. She named the twins in her will. I wanted to believe Malcolm wouldn't look for them. Why would he care? They lived with their father and there wasn't any money to speak of that he would go after."

"Your grandmother left a considerable amount for each twin and that made Malcolm curious to find out where they were. Isn't that right?"

"He's their legal guardian now. I received two telegrams while I was in Cincinnati. You had already left for Chicago." She added that piece of information so he wouldn't think she'd hidden the wires from him.

"Tell me about them," he ordered when she didn't immediately continue.

"One was from the banker telling me Malcolm had protested the will. Until the matter is resolved, the money can't be touched. The other wire came from Malcolm. He knows that the twins' father is dead. He told me the court had granted him legal custody of the twins and that he was sending an armed escort to bring them home to him."

Lucas heard the fear in her voice and wanted to take her in his arms again. He forced himself to stay where he was. He was determined to find out everything while his wife was being so agreeable. "Keep explaining, Taylor. I'm listening."

She couldn't look at her husband now. She turned around and stared out into the night. Telling family secrets was difficult, but the shame in her family made the explanation almost unbearable. Marian had told her they were never to speak of the atrocity. It was too vile and sinful.

Taylor gripped her hands together and said a prayer for courage. Her voice echoed with sadness when she continued. "I have been running away from my uncle since I was a very little girl. Marian warned me about him. She told me what he would try to do to me. She protected me from the demon."

She turned around and looked at him. She was searching for signs of disgust. She didn't find any and decided he still didn't understand.

"I slept with the dresser in front of my bedroom door from that day on," she told him. "And I kept a knife under my pillow."

Lucas closed his eyes. The pain he heard in her voice washed over him. He pictured her as a little girl trying to defend herself against a full-grown man's sick cravings and started shaking with rage. He shouldn't have been surprised, for in the time they'd been together, she'd given him sufficient hints. Yes, he had guessed the truth, yet hearing the confirmation still stunned him.

"Did he ever try—"

She wouldn't let him finish his question. Her words were hurried now, for she was anxious to get the rest of the sins told before weeping.

"The little dresser wasn't an obstacle for Malcolm, of course. He came into my room late one night. I didn't wake up until he sat down on the side of the bed. God, I was so terrified. I found the knife under my pillow and when he reached down to cover my mouth with his hand, I cut him."

She took a long shuttering breath. "He didn't know I had a weapon, thank God, or he certainly would have been able to take it away from me. I almost blinded him," she added. "He let out a scream of pain. There was blood everywhere."

"And then what did you do?" he asked. Lucas kept his voice as soothing as possible. His rage was burning inside him, and it was all he could do not to shout with fury on her behalf.

"I ran and hid under Madam's bed. She was out for the evening and I remember I didn't go to sleep until I heard her come into the room. I still don't know what lie Malcolm told her about the injury."

"Why didn't you tell her what happened?"

"How could I?" she cried out. "I felt dirty and ashamed. Such things weren't discussed in our household. I remember I scratched my knee once and tried to show Madam. She was appalled I would raise my dress in her company. Showing a bit of ankle was shameful and there I was, flaunting my bare legs. Cook cleaned the abrasion."

Lucas shook his head. Taylor missed the action. She was staring down at her hands now, lost in her own thoughts. "I was trained to be a lady," she defended. "And ladies did not talk about such vile things. The truth would have killed Madam."

He didn't agree. "You do her an injustice, Taylor. She might not have wanted to hear the truth, but she would have done something about it."

As an adult, Taylor realized Lucas was right. Madam was her champion. She would have protected her and turned her wrath on her son. "Children don't think like grown-ups," she said. "At least I didn't."

"What about Marian?"

"She couldn't tell anyone but me. She didn't feel she could admit that Malcolm had come to her room. Oh, God, I don't know how long it went on. She eventually married George, and after the twins were born, she became desperate to leave England and—"

"Malcolm."

"Yes," Taylor agreed. "She didn't want her daughters near him. George wanted to go back home. He wanted to raise his daughters in America."

She took another step away from him. "Now you know everything," she said, her tone one of defiance.

"And this is when I'm supposed to leave or want to leave but won't because I'm so damned honorable?"

She nodded.

He shook his head. "I'm not going anywhere. Come over here, Taylor. I want to hold you."

She shook her head again, even as she started walking toward him. She burst into tears as soon as he touched her. Lucas held her close and let her cry. He didn't try to soothe her, for he knew she needed to weep. She'd been carrying a hell of a burden, and it was finally time to let it go. She wasn't alone any longer. He needed to tell her that as soon as she was able to listen to him.

All the while she was weeping, she was telling him she wasn't going to be a worry and now that she was safe in the wilderness, he really could leave if he wanted to.

He let her ramble. Long minutes passed before she gained control of her emotions. He didn't have a handkerchief with him, but he guessed it didn't matter. She used his shirt to dry her tears.

Taylor leaned against Lucas and considered the problems that were still facing her. Would Malcolm send men all the way to Redemption? She didn't have an answer and put the question to her husband.

"If he offers enough money, they'll come."

"I could go up into the mountains," she whispered.

"Listen to me," he ordered. He was careful to keep his voice calm and soothing. He could feel her panic taking hold again. She'd gone rigid in his arms. Her voice was shaking again as well. He wanted her to stay reasonable. "You're through running."

"He's their guardian," she cried out.

"In England," he reminded her. "Not here."

She pushed herself away from him and looked up into his eyes. "Meaning?"

"We're going to do exactly what he did," he told her. "We'll petition our court for legal custody. Their father was American," he added. "And it was apparent he wanted his daughters raised here. They were living in Boston when he died."

Taylor couldn't let go of her worry. "Will the authorities here honor a claim made in England?"

"Not if we've secured our own claim," he assured her.

"Don't use Lewis," she blurted out. "He doesn't understand the law."

"How did you figure that out so quickly?" he asked.

"I spoke to him about another legal matter this afternoon," she explained.

Before he could ask her to be more specific, she turned his attention. "I want to thank you for your help, Lucas. I know I've turned your life upside down . . ."

He didn't let her finish. "Don't thank me yet, Taylor. You're going to listen to what I have to say first. Then you can decide if you still want to thank me."

She agreed with a nod. She was still feeling incredibly relieved because Lucas was going to help her fight her legal battles against Malcolm. She could barely keep from smiling. Her husband sounded serious. His voice had taken on a hard edge, but she wasn't bothered by it.

"I'll be happy to listen to you," she said. *And then I'll thank you once again,* she silently added.

"I want you to understand how things are going to be from now on," he announced. "You could drive a man right out of his mind. You know that?"

She shook her head. He frowned. "You've driven me to distraction these past weeks. I'm still having trouble believing you actually dragged three children and a pregnant woman halfway across the country."

She felt the immediate need to defend herself. "I didn't drag Victoria. She wanted to come with me."

"Do you always think you know what's best for everyone else?"

He'd nailed her flaw right on the head. "I sometimes think I do," she admitted. "But I try—"

"Don't interrupt me," he snapped. "And listen carefully. You don't know what's best for me. Got that?"

She quickly nodded.

"Did you go and see Lewis about a divorce?"

She was astonished by the question. "No, of course not. Why would you think such a thing?"

"You said you went to see him about a legal matter. Damn it, Taylor, what else was I supposed to think?"

"I don't want a divorce," she whispered.

"You're not getting one," he snapped. "Answer another question for me. Did you decide to leave Cincinnati before or after you received the wire?"

"I was getting ready to leave before the wire came."

She didn't understand what was behind his motive in asking the question, but it was obviously terribly important to him.

Lucas's heart was thundering inside his chest. He was trying desperately not to ask her the one question that had plagued him night and day on his journey to get to her. The longer he looked at her, the harder it became to keep the words locked inside. He was aching with his need.

He was so damned tired of standing on the outside of life. He wanted a home, a family, and most of all, he wanted Taylor. He didn't want to live without her. She was everything he'd always believed he could never have and certainly didn't deserve. Yet she was here, standing just a few feet away, and all he had to do was reach out for her and he knew he could have it all.

The reasons had to be right, however. He didn't want a wife who was beholden to him. He didn't need her appreciation. He needed her love.

"Why did you run away from me?"

Her gaze flew to his. She saw the vulnerability in his expression and was astonished by it. "Is that what you thought? That I was running away from you? These mountains are your home. I wanted to be as close to you as possible. I knew you wouldn't bring me here. You told me it wasn't a fit place for a lady. But this is where your heart is, where you belong. Oh, Lucas, don't you understand. I was coming home."

She couldn't tell if she'd convinced him she was telling the truth or not. His expression became guarded. He wasn't giving anything away now.

"I took so much away from you," she admitted. Her voice shook over the guilt she was feeling. "You valued your independence and your freedom, and like a thief in the night, I stole both away from you. I ruined your life. I knew you wouldn't leave me alone to raise the children. You're too honorable. I didn't want to take all your dreams away."

"Do you honestly believe I would have allowed you to do anything I didn't want you to do?"

"You weren't given a choice," she cried out. "A man should be able to follow his dreams."

"So you came to my mountains?"

She nodded. "I thought we could live the way Daniel Boone and his wife lived. He left her for years at a time, and in all the stories I read, it was mentioned again and again that he would bring meat to her. I also read that she was very content."

"You really expected us to live like that?" His voice was incredulous.

She suddenly felt like a fool. "It sounded perfectly reasonable to me for a while," she admitted. "But I have had time to reevaluate. I, too, did a lot of thinking on the journey here. I hope I even grew up a little. I learned something interesting," she continued. "You can't always believe what you read in books. Just because it's written down doesn't mean it's true."

The smile caught Lucas by surprise. Taylor sounded as though she was telling him something that was going to stun him.

"Cats aren't supposed to like water. I read they were afraid to get wet. The cat who tried to pounce on Victoria apparently didn't know he was supposed to be afraid. And now I think that perhaps, if Mrs. Boone had truly loved her husband the way I love you, she wouldn't have been content when he left her. She must have been miserable. I know I was when you left for Chicago. I couldn't stop thinking about you."

"Look at me," he commanded. "Give me the words again." *And let me start living.*

"I was miserable," she cried out.

He thought those were the sweetest, most magical words he'd ever heard. His laughter echoed through the stillness. The sound was filled with joy. He suddenly was whole again and free.

She hadn't expected Lucas to be amused. Hearing him laugh after confessing her misery devastated her. He reached for her then, but she backed away from him. He was much quicker than she was, however. He grabbed hold of her hand and held tight. She struggled to pull free, but he wouldn't let go.

They stood at arm's length now. She finally quit trying to peel his hand away from hers and frowned up at him.

"Listen," he commanded. Then he slowly tugged her toward him. He took his sweet time, and he didn't stop until she was pressed up nice and tight against his chest.

"I don't hear anything," she whispered. "What is it?"

She nervously looked to her left to see if she could see anything lurking in the brush. She couldn't look to her right. Lucas's chin was in the way.

He let go of her hand and wrapped his arms around her waist. He wasn't going to explain. In his mind, he'd heard the sound loud and clear. That was all that mattered to him.

It was the gratifying sound of his wife being reeled in. She was miserable. He couldn't be happier. He had her completely now, and he was never going to let go. He would make her happy, and he could certainly give her everything she needed or wanted. She didn't ever have to know about his past. The future was all that mattered. His future with Taylor.

His hand moved to the back of her neck. He leaned down and brushed his mouth over hers. Her lips were so sweet and full and soft. She tasted like apples.

She reached up and caressed the side of his face. His whiskers tickled her lips and her fingertips. She hadn't realized how much she wanted him to touch her until he started nibbling on her mouth and teasing her with gentle kisses.

Her past didn't matter to him. He hadn't been offended or disgusted. Taylor was surprised by the relief she felt. She hadn't realized how important his reaction was to her.

Dear God, how she loved him. "Lucas, take me to bed."

The invitation intensified his hunger. They had been apart for long weeks, and all he'd thought about was holding her in his arms again. He became frantic to have it all once again, to feel her squeeze him tight inside her, to show her how much he loved her.

His mouth settled on top of hers. His tongue swept inside to duel with hers. He caressed her shoulders and her back and then lifted her up against his arousal.

The kiss turned ravenous, and when at last he tore his mouth away, they were both panting for breath. He knew he was fast losing control. He lifted her up into his arms with the intent of taking her back to camp. He would make love to her in the privacy of their wagon, and even if it killed him to wait, he would make certain she gained fulfillment before he did.

He felt smooth skin against his hand. He came to a dead stop. "Where are your underclothes?"

She was fervently kissing the side of his neck. "I'm not wearing any."

He almost dropped her. His stride became long and purposeful, and when they reached the second wagon, it dawned on him that Victoria was inside.

Taylor wasn't as rattled as he was. "She's sleeping with the children tonight," she whispered.

He helped her inside, then followed. Their bed was already made. A thick mat, wide enough for two, had been placed on the floor of the wagon. A sheet and blanket covered it.

When Lucas let the flap drop back down, the wagon was pitched into darkness.

He stripped out of his clothes before she'd taken all

the pins out of her hair. She was kneeling on their bed. Lucas stretched out next to her, then rolled onto his side and slowly began to caress a path up the inside of her thigh to the junction of her legs. His fingers brushed across her sweet flesh and then he began to stroke her.

Taylor's head dropped back. She closed her eyes and let out a low moan of surrender. The pleasure he was giving her was almost too much to bear. And when his fingers slowly penetrated her, her body instinctively reacted. Her hips slowly moved in the mating rhythm to gain more of the splendor.

He had to take her dress off. She couldn't seem to remember how. She was frantic over their separation and tried to pull him into her arms. They were both kneeling now, facing each other. His mouth covered hers in another long, drugging, tongue-thrusting kiss. His hands stroked her breasts and then dropped to settle on the tilt of her hips.

Taylor's hands were splayed against his chest. Her touch was feather-light, tantalizing. His breathing quickened when her caresses moved down his body and she grew bolder, and when at last her fingers closed over him, he let out a harsh groan of pleasure so intense, he felt consumed by it.

He very nearly lost his control then and there. His mouth never left hers as he pulled her hand away from him and then wrapped his arms around her and gently lowered her to the bed. He held her tight against him and rolled onto his back.

His hand cupped the back of her neck and his mouth captured hers again while he wedged one thigh between her legs. She rubbed against him, and his control completely scattered. His hand moved down low and into her warm, damp flesh. He tormented her with his fingers until she was writhing against him, and then he lifted her up and slowly penetrated her. She knelt on her knees now, straddling him, and with his gentle pressure pushing on her hips, she took him inside her. The warm knot of pleasure deep inside her seemed to explode into a thousand fragments. She couldn't go slow now. She squeezed him tight inside her and then began to move.

The pleasure they gave each other soon became unbearable. Neither could hold back. He was the first to climax. He arched up against her and gave her his seed, and the force of his release triggered her own. She whimpered his name and collapsed on top of him.

It took both of them a long while to float back to reality. He stayed inside her for as long as he could and held her close until her breathing had calmed.

"I didn't know we could . . ."

"Could what?" he asked.

"Like that," she explained.

He could hear the blush in her voice. He laughed in response. "You were a hellcat a few minutes ago," he reminded her.

She let out a sigh of contentment and closed her eyes. "I liked it," she whispered.

"I know," he replied. "I've got the marks from your nails to prove it."

He sounded very arrogant and pleased with himself. Taylor was too tired to take issue with him.

Lucas was starting to like her, she thought. In time, if she really tried not to be so bossy and act as though she knew what everyone else should be doing and if she was able to prove that she could do just fine in the wilderness, maybe then liking would turn into loving. She'd told him she was miserable, and now all she wanted in the world was for her husband to be miserable, too.

She was just drifting off to sleep when Lucas rolled

to the side and covered the two of them with the blanket. He pulled her back into his arms and closed his eyes.

"Taylor?"

"Yes?"

"We aren't going to raise our son and our daughters the way you were raised. They're never going to be afraid to tell us anything. They aren't going to be ashamed or embarrassed by their bodies, and by God, if anyone ever tries to touch them, they'll know how to scream."

18

*He that will have a cake out of wheat
must tarry the grinding.*
—William Shakespeare,
Troilus and Cressida

*L*oving Lucas was easy. Getting along with the impossible man was another matter altogether. Taylor hadn't realized how stubborn he could be until he refused to back down and listen to reason. The issue of where they were going to live was under discussion, though in truth she was the only one doing any discussing. Lucas had told her they were moving to a large city and refused to hear her argument against the plan. She was just as determined to stay where she was.

Time was on her side, however. Victoria was exhausted from their journey and needed to rest before she went anywhere. Her dear friend had just climbed out of the wagon when she heard Taylor tell Lucas she was ailing. She immediately jumped back inside and took to her bed.

Hunter was getting his things together with the

intent of taking off for the mountains. As soon as he heard Victoria was sick, he came up with one reason after another why he couldn't leave.

Rolly and three other men from town came marching into the clearing and inadvertently stopped the argument.

"We aren't finished with this discussion," Taylor whispered to her husband before turning to smile at the visitors.

"We aren't having a discussion," Lucas told her. "As soon as Victoria's feeling better, we're leaving."

Georgie and Allie were both demanding his attention. He squatted down to find out what they wanted.

Hunter was putting out the fire he'd started to cook their breakfast. Daniel was helping him.

"Ross, Hunter," Rolly called out, nodding after he shouted each name. He stopped in front of Taylor and bowed to her. "Morning, Mrs. Ross. Since you went and got yourself a house, me and the boys thought we'd go along and see to a few repairs. We'll make sure the place is clear of critters, so you won't have to worry about the youngsters stepping on something mean."

Lucas had stood up during Rolly's explanation. Allie hid behind his leg and stared up at the giant, but Georgie was bolder. She walked right up to Rolly and tugged on his pant leg until he looked down at her.

The child lost her balance staring up at Rolly and staggered backward. Then she put her arms up and waited.

Rolly looked at Taylor. "What's she wanting?" he asked nervously.

Georgie answered before Taylor could. "Up," she demanded.

Rolly looked thunderstruck. "I ain't never held me

a baby. Guess I could give it a try if you're agreeable, Mrs. Ross."

"Certainly, Mr. Rolly," Taylor replied.

"It's just Rolly," he instructed her. He bent over and gently lifted Georgie up. He held her up in the air at arm's length. "She don't weigh more than a feather."

"Taylor, what's Rolly talking about?" Lucas asked. He'd held onto his patience long enough. He wanted an immediate answer.

Rolly stepped forward. "She got herself a house. Can I put her down now? I don't want to damage her none."

Taylor reached up and took Georgie into her arms. The men smiled at the little girl, then followed their leader as Rolly turned and started back across the clearing.

"We'll be ready to help you move in by early afternoon, Mrs. Ross," Rolly called out.

Taylor put Georgie down and told her and her sister to go help Hunter. Then she turned to her husband. "I purchased a house yesterday. That's why I went to see Lewis," she said. Her words were hurried together when she added, "I haven't seen it yet, but I'm sure it's going to be fine. It has wood floors and glass windows."

There was only one house in Redemption with glass windows. Lucas let out a loud expletive.

"Callaghan's place," he whispered. "Lewis sold you that crazy old mountain man's house?"

He wasn't shouting, but he was close to it. Taylor hurried to soothe him. "It isn't his house. Even if we do leave soon, we still need somewhere to stay tonight."

"No."

"Lucas, be reasonable about this."

He took a step closer to her. "I am being reasonable. He's crazy, Taylor. You'll wake up and find him sitting at the table wanting breakfast. His smell will knock you over backward. I don't think he's had a bath in twenty years. He won't leave until he's good and ready," he added with a nod. "And then he'll take half of what you've unpacked with him."

Taylor hid her alarm. "Is he dangerous?" she asked.

Lucas wanted to lie, then decided on the truth. "No," he admitted. "He won't hurt you, but you'll want to kill him after being in his company for ten minutes. It's out of the question. We're staying in the meadow."

Victoria heard the argument and was peeking out the back of the wagon so she could watch the couple. She was ready to conclude that Lucas was going to win the argument. Then Taylor nudged the scales in her favor.

"My dear friend is sick," she announced. "She needs a proper bed. Are you willing to take all of us to your brothers' place and let us stay there until she's feeling better?"

He would have loved to do just that but knew it wasn't a good idea. "The ranch is a hard day's ride on a horse. With wagons and finding trails, it could take as long as four days."

"Lewis told me Callaghan doesn't usually come down from the mountain until the middle of summer."

"We'll be living in the city by then," Lucas told her.

"Then surely it will be all right if we stay in the house just one night."

Lucas finally gave in. He assured her it was only because of Victoria's health and only for one night.

He had the last word. "If she's better, we're leaving tomorrow."

The house was as wonderful as a palace in Taylor's estimation. There was a large glass window on either side of the entrance and one above on the second floor. The living area was quite spacious. To the right was a long wooden table with benches on each side that would surely seat eight or ten good-sized adults. Against the wall behind the table was a black iron kettle stove, and there was a little alcove with shelves and a long counter.

A small stone fireplace faced the front door. On the left side of the room was a bed and mattress Rolly assured her had already been aired out. And in the far corner of the room was a door that opened up into another bedroom. There was a bed against the wall, a crate next to it, and yet another glass window.

The steps leading up to the loft was on the other side of the fireplace. Taylor took the children up to look at their sleeping quarters. Her only worry was that one of the twins might try to climb over the railing, but Hunter assured her the girls had more sense than that. While he was defending them, Georgie got her head stuck between two of the banister spindles. Lucas had carried Victoria inside, for Hunter refused to get near her, and when Georgie started wailing, he put Victoria down on one of the benches and went up to free his daughter.

Taylor and Lucas both insisted Victoria take the back bedroom. She immediately became teary eyed over their thoughtfulness.

"Do you think you'll be feeling better tomorrow?" Lucas asked her.

Victoria looked to Taylor to find out the answer.

Hunter also looked at Taylor. When she gave a quick shake of her head, Victoria immediately put her hand to her forehead and said, "I certainly hope so, but it truly seems doubtful."

Hunter became furious. "Are you ill or aren't you?" he demanded.

Victoria was stunned by the anger in his voice. Her eyes widened and her hand dropped to the base of her neck as Hunter stomped across the room.

He didn't let her answer him. He stood there towering over her, glaring.

"I can't leave worrying about you," he snapped. "Answer me, woman. Are you really sick?"

Victoria latched onto his earlier comment and ignored his question. "You're worrying about me?" Her voice had gone all soft and breathless. Her eyes were as green as emeralds, and tears were already welling up.

"Don't make more of this than it is," he warned her. "What I feel and what I do are two different matters. You've got no business being here," he added. "No business at all."

"Why not?" she asked.

"Because you're a lady," he muttered. "And carrying," he added with a nod in case she'd forgotten.

She stood up. Her middle brushed against him. She couldn't back up; the table was in her way. He wouldn't back up; his pride was in his way.

"I have every right to go wherever I want to go," she told him.

"No, you don't," he told her, just to be stubborn.

"Why not?"

"Because you're pregnant."

It sounded perfectly logical to him. Victoria thought he was being ridiculous. Her face was turning pink with irritation and embarrassment. How dare he tell her what she could and couldn't do?

"'In a false quarrel there is no true valour,' Mr. Hunter," she quoted. "William wrote those very words."

"What the hell does that mean?" he demanded. His voice raised a note. "I'm going to be glad to be rid of you, Victoria. I'm sick to death of watching you mourn for your husband and telling me all the fancy words he said to you. The man's dead. You aren't. Get over it and move on."

Victoria's mouth dropped open. He believed William was her husband? She was speechless, though not because of his misinterpretation. It was the anger and the obvious jealousy she was seeing.

Chaos surrounded them. Lucas was going back and forth from the wagon, carrying what Taylor had promised him were only necessary items they would need for one night. The children were out back, watching Rolly and his men clear a yard. Taylor had gone up to the loft to make beds out of the mats and blankets Lucas had carried up for her.

Victoria was getting a crick in her neck looking up at Hunter. "I don't want you to leave," she whispered.

Hunter couldn't stop himself from touching her. He put his hands on her shoulders and gave her a gentle squeeze. He wanted to shake some sense into the woman. She was acting as though he had every right to stay.

A tear slipped down the side of her cheek. He caught it with his thumb. He wanted to make her understand how it had to be.

"My grandmother was a Crow."

"My grandmother was Irish."

He guessed he was going to have to be more blunt.

479

Victoria still didn't understand she was supposed to be prejudiced against him.

"I'm a half-breed," he reminded her in a low whisper.

"So am I," she immediately answered.

He got mad. "The hell you are."

She wasn't intimidated by his shout. She poked him in his chest. "I'm half Irish and half French, and you can't tell me any different. Facts are facts."

He gave up trying to argue with her because she refused to be logical. "I'm leaving."

She grabbed hold of his belt buckle. "I'm probably not in love with you."

"I hope to God you're not."

She stretched up on her tiptoes. He leaned down at the very same time. His mouth covered hers, and his arms went around her waist. He kissed her long and hard, and when he came to his senses and pulled back, she was breathless and staring up at him with a dreamy, bemused look on her face.

He wanted to kiss her again but didn't dare. His hands dropped to his sides. The woman was making him think impossible things could happen.

"Let go of me," he commanded.

"You can leave after the baby's born," she blurted out at the same time.

"No woman's going to tell me what to do."

She sat back down on the bench and bowed her head. "Go then. I don't need you or anyone else. I'd done just fine on my own."

He snorted. "What about your husband?"

He decided he wasn't going to wait around to hear her answer. She'd probably give him yet another one of the dandy's fancy remarks, and he knew he would completely lose his temper then.

He'd made it to the entrance when he heard her

whisper. "I've never been married. You're better off leaving a woman like me alone."

He stopped dead in his tracks. He didn't turn around. "Then who is William?"

"He was a famous playwright. William Shakespeare was his full name. He lived centuries ago."

Hunter stood there for a full minute without saying a word, then he walked outside. Victoria stood up and ran to the bedroom. She was weeping before she'd shut the door.

He made it halfway across the clearing before he stopped. He thought the matter over in his mind for a good five minutes.

Lucas was getting ready to chop wood. He'd taken his shirt off and turned to put it in the wagon when Hunter came storming out of the house. He could hear his friend muttering under his breath, and when Hunter stopped and didn't move for so long, he guessed exactly what was going on.

Georgie came running past him. He caught her in his arms and lifted her up.

"Don't bother Hunter now," he whispered to his daughter so his friend wouldn't overhear.

Then Daniel came hurrying past. Lucas grabbed hold of him and pulled him up against his side.

"Leave Hunter alone," he told his son.

"What's he doing?" Daniel asked.

Lucas smiled. "Struggling. Any minute now he's going to realize it's inevitable." He continued to keep his gaze on Hunter. "Why don't you two go and see what your mother's doing?"

As soon as he put Georgie down, Daniel took hold of her hand and led her back into the house.

Hunter finally made up his mind. He turned around and walked over to Lucas.

"I'll stay around for a little while," he announced.

"I'd appreciate your help."

Hunter nodded. He was glad his friend didn't ask him why he'd changed his mind. He hurriedly changed the subject. "Do you think Caulder might really show up here one of these days?"

"If he believes I've got his gold, he will," Lucas answered.

"They'll probably catch him before he gets as far as Sioux City."

"They might," Lucas agreed.

"Victoria shouldn't go anywhere until after the baby's born. The journey here was hard on her. She needs rest."

"Are you suggesting we stay?"

"Can't see any other way," Hunter replied.

Lucas was concerned about Victoria, of course, but he was also worried about his wife and his children. The wilderness was no place for them. He thought of at least ten reasons right away why it wasn't safe. One of them could step on a snake or drown in the creek or get mauled by a bear. The list was endless.

Yet Hunter was right. They had to stay until the baby was born.

Hunter went into town then to get some supplies he would need to reinforce the stairs.

Lucas told Taylor at supper that Hunter had agreed to stay on until Victoria had her baby. Taylor's friend burst into tears over the news. She stood up, excused herself, and went into her bedroom.

"What's wrong with her?" Daniel David asked.

"She's happy," Taylor explained.

Lucas shook his head. He thought Victoria's reaction was damned odd. Then he turned his attention back to his wife. She looked a sight tonight with her hair spilling down her back and her face rosy from cooking. He thought he could be content to look at her the rest of the night.

She wasn't paying any attention to him. Georgie had deliberately pushed a biscuit up against a piece of salted pork on Allie's plate, which caused an immediate uproar, and Taylor was trying to soothe one twin and lecture the other one at the same time.

Lucas slipped in the other bit of news when Allie paused to take a deep breath so she could scream again. "We're going to stay here until Victoria's had her baby. Then we're leaving."

She gave him a radiant smile. He immediately reminded her their living arrangement was temporary. "Don't think this means I've changed my mind. We aren't raising the children here."

"No, of course not," she replied.

He acted as though he hadn't heard her agreement. "It's too dangerous here for them and for you. You're too fragile for such primitive conditions. Come fall, we're moving to the city."

"But you hate the city."

"I'll get used to it."

With an effort, she was able to hold onto her temper. "Do you have a particular city in mind?"

"We're going back east."

She waited for him to elaborate. After a minute or two, she realized he wasn't going to say another word about his future plans for the family.

"I'm not fragile, Lucas."

He wouldn't listen to her. "Come fall, we're leaving. Don't even think about settling in."

She assured him she wouldn't.

The following morning, she put up yellow and white checkered curtains. She told Lucas it was just for privacy's sake, which was a ridiculous reason given the fact that they lived in the wilderness. Yes, she knew they were leaving. Of course she did. He'd told her so at least a hundred times. But that didn't mean they couldn't be comfortable in the meantime.

He noticed the tablecloth on the table that evening. And the dishes stacked in neat rows on the shelves. There was a new bedspread on their bed, and a glass vase stuffed with wildflowers on top of the mantel. The place was looking more and more like a home to him.

Rolly let them purchase the rocker from Frank with the condition that he be allowed to borrow it on Sunday afternoons for the reading of the newspaper. Taylor readily agreed. Frank didn't think Rolly had any business giving Taylor stipulations. Just because he'd made the thing didn't mean he could borrow it whenever he wanted. He had, after all, sold it to Frank if he would recall.

The giant didn't like being told what he could or couldn't do. He grabbed Frank by the collar and was about to give him a good shake when Taylor stepped between the two men.

"You made this beautiful rocker, Rolly?"

The awe in her voice gained the giant's full attention. She thought it was beautiful. He'd heard that compliment plain and clear. He forgot he was holding onto Frank. He gave her a nod, then muttered, "What of it?" so she wouldn't think he was pleased or proud of his work.

Taylor sat down in the rocker and trailed her fingertips along the polished wood. Rolly turned to watch her. He was still holding onto Frank and dragged him with him like Allie dragged her rag doll around.

"It's sound," he told her. His voice didn't sound surly now.

"It's magnificent," she declared. "I don't believe I've ever seen anything this well crafted in all of England," she exaggerated. "You're a true craftsman, Rolly."

The giant dropped Frank and hurried over to Taylor. "No nails," he announced. "I didn't cheat and use nails."

He made Taylor stand up so he could lift the rocker and turn it upside down. He wanted her to get a better look at the construction.

Frank quickly recovered from Rolly's burst of temper. Over the years he'd gotten used to being tossed or shaken or shoved by the giant. He wasn't afraid of him any longer. He knew Rolly would never kill him, for he thought of him as a friend. And friends in these parts were hard to come by. Frank knew the limits of Rolly's patience, however, and for that reason he didn't dare smile while he watched Taylor's compliments turn the fierce giant into a blushing boy.

Rolly told Taylor he had always been good with his hands, and he decided he might as well use them to turn a profit. He worked in his home and pointed to the last building down the road to show her where it was.

"I got enough wood stored up in the shed behind to make twenty rockers," he said. "And it takes me exactly two weeks, start to finish, to make one as sound as can be."

Taylor asked him if he would consider making a cradle for Victoria's baby. She was willing to pay a fair price, she assured him, and he would have all summer to work on it.

Rolly rubbed his whiskered jaw and then told her he'd have to think about it.

Late that evening, after everyone had gone to sleep, Lucas woke her up making love to her. She was so tired, she didn't think she had the strength or the inclination, but his warm caresses and hot kisses soon changed her mind. She became as demanding and desperate as he was, and when she found fulfillment, he silenced her scream of ecstasy with his mouth.

He collapsed on top of her and when she let out a groan, he rolled to his side and pulled her into his arms. She tried to keep the loving words locked inside. She didn't want to burden Lucas or make him think she was desperate for his pledge of love. She was desperate though, and no matter how hard she tried to be reasonable about it, she still couldn't talk herself out of her own longing.

She waited until he'd fallen asleep. "I love you, Lucas," she whispered then.

As exhausted as she was, sleep still eluded her. She told herself she should be thankful her husband didn't hate her. She had forced him to radically change his life. He hadn't been given a choice. The poor man detested marriage and was now saddled with a wife and three children.

Taylor spent a good long while feeling sorry for Lucas. Then she started feeling sorry for herself. It was a wonder her husband could even stand to look at her. She knew she wasn't very pretty like Victoria was, and she was certain she wasn't at all lovable. She had too many faults. She was bossy and opinionated and rigid. She used to think those were assets. She'd learned everything she knew about life from her grandmother. Madam taught her to be disciplined and controlled. One never complained or made demands. One took what one was given and made the best of it. No one liked a whiner, and if the need to cry couldn't be suppressed, then one should seek out privacy so no one else would see or hear. A lady was a lady from the moment she opened her eyes in the morning until she closed them again that night.

Taylor was sick and tired of being proper all the time. It was a terrible strain. The urge to scream when something bothered her was getting stronger and stronger, and the need to kick some sense into Lucas was becoming more and more appealing.

He was making her give up her dream, too. She knew that if she pointed out that fact to him, he'd only tell her what he'd been telling her almost from the moment he married her. She wasn't strong enough. Lord, he'd called her fragile. She thought that was probably the most insulting thing he could have said to her.

She would prove him wrong. Yes, that was it, she decided. Arguing that she was every bit as fit as he was wouldn't mean anything. Words were just words. She would have to show him. Taylor stopped feeling sorry for herself and turned her thoughts to the summer ahead. She had three months to prove to Lucas she wasn't fragile.

Once Lucas started thinking of her as his equal, she was certain he would begin to treat her like a real wife and share his hopes and his worries and his past with her. He'd been in the war. That was the only substantial fact she knew about him. What had he done before and after? What was his life like growing up? She'd certainly asked questions. She never got any answers. Lucas would close right up on her. She didn't even know if he'd caught the man he'd gone after in Chicago. What was his name? She couldn't remember.

Love and trust went hand in hand. Taylor fell asleep praying for both.

19

The prince of darkness is a gentleman.
— William Shakespeare,
King Lear

The following morning, Taylor put her plan into action. She was going to be the perfect wife, mother, and frontierswoman. She got out of bed an hour earlier than usual and had breakfast ready when the rest of the family stirred. If Lucas was surprised to see her working so diligently, he didn't show it.

After they'd eaten and the children had gone outside with Victoria, Lucas told Taylor he was leaving. "A man passing through told Frank there was a federal judge hearing cases in Rosewood the rest of this week and all of the next. If I press, I might be able to get the custody papers ready and the petition heard right away."

"Shouldn't I go with you?"

Lucas shook his head. "I don't think you need to," he said.

She didn't agree. Surely she would need to testify

and sign the papers. She didn't argue with Lucas, however, because he assured her that the judge was going on to Virginia City after Rosewood and if she was needed, he would take her there.

Taylor helped him pack and then followed him outside. Hunter had already saddled his horse for him. He handed the reins to Lucas and then walked away so that they could have a few minutes of privacy.

"Please be careful."

Lucas had been waiting for her to give him the order, and yet he was still surprised by how good it felt to hear her say the words. He didn't think he was ever going to get used to her worrying about him. Her love still overwhelmed him.

"I'll be careful," he promised. He leaned down and kissed her good-bye. When he pulled back, she sagged against him. "After we get custody of the twins, I'm going to find out what we have to do to make the boy legally ours."

She thought that was such a wonderful idea, tears came into her eyes. Lucas called the children over then and explained that he was leaving for a few days. He kissed the three of them, then told them all to mind their mother. Taylor noticed he stared at Georgie when he gave the order.

Allie cried when he left, then her sister joined in. Taylor didn't try to hush the little girls. They were doing exactly what she wanted to do. She said a prayer he wouldn't be gone long and then went back to work.

During his absence, Taylor put in a summer garden of cabbage, peas, turnips, and onions. Rolly stopped by to bring her a surprise, a second rocking chair identical to the first that he had started work on months ago and never got around to finishing. He thought Victoria might want to rock at the same time Taylor was using her rocker. She was thrilled with the gift, and after she'd given him sufficient praise and accepted the fact that he wasn't going to take any money for the chair no matter how long and hard she argued with him, she changed the topic to her garden and asked his advice.

Rolly ended up helping her with the chore. He made her dig up all the onions. They were buried so deep, they would never find their way up to the sun, he explained. It took her two full days of working from sunup to sundown to finish the garden.

Rolly put up wire fencing around the perimeter. He warned her the fence wouldn't keep out the rabbits, but he didn't have any suggestions to offer as to how she could keep them from eating the vegetables.

Victoria and Hunter usually went outside after supper while Taylor put the children to bed. The task shouldn't have taken her any time at all, but getting the twins to cooperate took at least an hour. Neither one of the little girls paid any attention to a word she said, and she didn't know what she could do to make them obey.

After they finally fell asleep, she turned her attention to Daniel. The bedtime stories were their special time together. The only problem was that she was running out of tales about Daniel Boone and Davy Crockett. She had already shortened her son's name to Daniel, and since he never corrected her, she thought he might be leaning toward that name. Yet when she asked him if he was going to choose Daniel or David, he shook his head and told her he hadn't made up his mind yet.

She tucked her son under the covers and fell asleep on the mat next to him. Hunter shook her awake. Victoria had sent him upstairs to make certain she was in the house. Taylor staggered to her feet. Hunter latched onto her arm on the way down the stairs so she wouldn't topple over.

"How long are you going to keep this up?" Hunter asked.

Taylor collapsed in the rocking chair and wearily began to unbraid her hair.

"Keep what up?" she asked.

"You're working yourself to death," Hunter explained.

"You are, Taylor," Victoria agreed.

"I'm just a little tired tonight," Taylor admitted. "After I get into a routine and do what I'm supposed to do each day of the week, I'll be more organized and less weary. Everything takes twice as long now but that's only because I'm learning as I go along. Making soap should have only taken one day but it took me three."

"Are you saying you are supposed to do certain chores on certain days?" Victoria asked. She glanced at Hunter to see if he knew what she was talking about. He wasn't paying Victoria any attention, however, for he was frowning down at Taylor.

"Yes, of course," Taylor answered. "The women in the wilderness have set days for each chore. Monday is wash day and Tuesday is ironing. Wednesday is baking day and . . ."

"For the love of God," Hunter muttered. "Where did you hear this nonsense?"

Taylor took exception to his tone of voice and his obvious ridicule. "I read it in Mrs. Livingston's journal. It seems very reasonable to me."

Victoria sat down on the bench and folded her hands together in her lap. "You're killing yourself," she told her friend. "You put in a garden, unpacked all the trunks, washed clothes, and made enough soap to last us three years."

"But I won't have to make it again for a long time," Taylor hastily pointed out.

Victoria turned to Hunter. "She mentioned she was going to make candles tomorrow. I can't imagine why we need them. We have plenty of lanterns."

Hunter kept his gaze on Taylor. "Exactly what is it you're trying to prove?"

She was too exhausted to lie or give him a clever half-truth. "That I'm not fragile."

He was taken aback by her answer. His eyes widened, and he almost smiled. She sure as certain looked fragile to him tonight. She looked half dead to him. Her complexion was as pale as flour and she had dark smudges under her eyes.

"Who said you were fragile?" he asked, already guessing the answer.

Victoria answered him. "I'll bet Lucas did."

Taylor nodded. "I want him to realize I'm capable of making it here."

"And then he won't make you leave," Victoria said with a nod.

"Yes."

"If that isn't—" Hunter began.

Taylor interrupted him. "I would appreciate it if neither one of you mentioned this conversation to my husband. I want him to see for himself that I'm strong and determined . . . and happy, damn it. Now if you'll both excuse me, I'm going to bed. I've had a long day."

"Why bother going to bed?" Hunter asked. "You'll be getting up in another hour."

She had secretly asked herself that question a dozen times in the last week. It did seem to her that as soon as her head hit the pillow and she closed her eyes, the sun was starting to climb back up in the sky.

"There is no need for sarcasm," she muttered.

She went into Victoria's room to wash and change into her nightgown. When she heard the front door close, she came back out.

Victoria had thoughtfully pulled the covers back on her bed for her. A faint blush covered her cheeks, and Taylor thought perhaps Hunter had kissed her again.

"How are things going with you and Hunter?" she asked. "Are you getting along?"

"Get into bed first. You look dead on your feet," her friend advised.

Taylor did as she was told. She smiled when Victoria tucked the covers around her. It felt nice to have someone look after her for a change. She patted a spot next to her on the bed and moved her legs out of the way so Victoria could sit down.

Her friend answered the question Taylor wanted to ask but knew she shouldn't.

"He kisses me good night every single night," her friend whispered. "Sometimes more than once. He doesn't seem to notice I'm getting big and awkward and ugly."

"You are radiant, not ugly, and that is what he sees."

"He still says he's leaving as soon as the baby arrives."

"He could change his mind."

Victoria nodded agreement, but the look on her face indicated she didn't believe it.

"Taylor, what can I do to help you?"

"Give me some advice," she answered. "Tell me what to do about Georgie and Allie. Be completely honest and tell me what you think of their behavior. They're old enough to listen and obey a few simple rules, aren't they?"

Victoria smiled. "You know I love and cherish Daniel and the girls, don't you?"

"Of course I do," Taylor replied.

"Daniel is such a delight. He's getting more opinionated and stubborn, I've noticed, but he listens to reason. He certainly isn't a problem. But the twins . . ."

"Yes?"

Victoria let out a sigh. "They're little hellions."

Taylor was in full agreement, yet as the twins' mother, she felt it necessary to defend the little girls. "They aren't always hellions. They listen to Lucas and Hunter. When one of them tells Georgie to get down off the table, she immediately obeys. They don't threaten her or plead with her and I know she isn't afraid of either one of them. She wouldn't be so sassy around them if she were afraid."

Taylor sounded bewildered. Victoria smiled in response. "It isn't the end of the world."

"They could drive a mother to drink," Taylor whispered.

Victoria laughed. "I'm certainly not an expert, but I do know this. You have to start saying no, and you have to mean it. You can't reason or negotiate with a two-year-old."

"I keep forgetting that," Taylor admitted. "I do try to reason with them."

"You try to placate them, too," Victoria told her. "They're old enough to understand certain rules. They're very intelligent." She sighed and added, "And adorable. It's difficult to say no when one of them is looking up with those big blue eyes and the tears start rolling down her cheeks."

Taylor knew what she was talking about. It was difficult not to give in.

"They are intelligent, and you're right, Victoria. I am going to have to be more assertive. They'll be completely out of hand if I don't."

After her friend went to bed, Taylor thought about the changes she was going to have to make to get the twins' attention. She fell asleep fretting, for the truth was difficult for any mother to admit, even an inept, thoroughly inexperienced one.

Her babies were brats.

Callaghan moved in the following night. Taylor rolled over in her bed, opened her eyes, and very nearly died of fright. The mountain man was sitting at her kitchen table, shoving day-old biscuits in his mouth two at a time.

A scream gathered in her throat, and her heart felt as though it had just stopped beating. Then his scent hit her, and she knew she wasn't going to die of fright at all. His smell would do her in. It was vile and rank and reminded her of skunks.

Taylor had never smelled anything like it. The stench made her eyes water and her stomach lurch. She didn't dare scream now. She'd have to take a deep breath first, and she simply didn't have the courage. She held the covers tight over her nose and her mouth and took tiny little pants of air while she stared at the deranged-looking man.

Callaghan. She remembered his name. She remembered Lucas's warning as well. He'd told her his stench would knock her over. He'd been right about that. He'd also told her he wasn't dangerous. She hoped to God he was also right about that.

He looked dangerous and wild. He was a good-sized man, but because he was hunched over the table, she couldn't guess his exact height. He wore dark brown buckskin pants and shirt and black boots with fur around the tops. His hair was long, stringy, and brown. She didn't know if that was his true hair color or if it was just as filthy as the rest of him and stained from years of going without a good scrubbing.

He turned and looked at her. She stared back. She wasn't at all afraid now. She knew that if she needed help, all she had to do was shout. Hunter was sleeping outside under the stars. He'd come running.

Callaghan wasn't a deranged maniac. His eyes were clear as day. She saw curiosity in his gaze and something else that started her temper boiling. There was a definite sparkle in those golden brown eyes.

"Aren't you going to scream?"

He asked her the question in a raspy voice filled with amusement. She shook her head no. He smiled, displaying brilliant white teeth, then turned back to the pan of half-eaten biscuits. He popped one into his mouth. "Needs salt."

Taylor finally got her wits back. She jumped out of bed, snatched the robe from where she'd left it draped over the back of one of the rockers, and hurriedly put it on.

Her gun was on the mantel. She edged her way close to the hearth to get the weapon just in case he turned hostile when she told him he was going to have to leave.

"Why did you think I would scream?"

"Most do," he answered with a shrug.

"And then what happens?"

"Their men throw me out. I don't stay out though. I come back inside. Yeap, I always do."

"When do you go back to the mountains?"

Taylor reached up to grab hold of her gun and only then noticed the bullets were all neatly lined up in a row behind the weapon. Callaghan was a whole lot more clever than she'd realized.

Her reaction surprised her: She started smiling.

"I leave when I'm ready."

"You're the real thing, aren't you, Callaghan?"

"Real what?" he asked.

"Mountain man."

She edged her way around the table with the intent of opening the door. If she didn't get some fresh air inside soon she feared she would faint.

"I'd appreciate it if you didn't call to your man until I finish my breakfast."

"I'm not going to call to anyone," she promised. "I want fresh air. That's all."

Taylor opened the door and both windows. It didn't help much. She leaned against the entrance and stared at the intruder. He had the manners of a hog.

"I'll be wanting coffee tomorrow morning," he announced. "And a proper breakfast."

He kept giving her quick glances to judge her reaction. Taylor kept right on smiling at him.

"It's all right if you want to scream now. I'm finished," he announced. He made the bench scrape against the floor when he stood up.

"I bet you have lots of stories to tell about life as a mountain man."

"Thousands," he agreed.

"Do you know who Daniel Boone and Davy Crockett were?"

"I'm not ignorant," he snapped. "Of course I've heard of them. They're dead, woman. I know that, too. They weren't from these mountains neither," he added with a nod. "We got our own tales to tell from our hills. Men like Tom Howard and Sparky Dawson and Montana . . ."

Victoria's scream interrupted Callaghan. Taylor jumped a foot in reaction. She had been so engrossed in the conversation, she hadn't noticed the bedroom door open. Her dear friend took one look at the back of the stranger and let out a screech that could wake Redemption.

Taylor moved out of the way in the nick of time. Hunter came running through the entrance with his gun drawn. "Callaghan," he roared.

"Morning, Hunter."

Callaghan called out the greeting. Taylor hurried across the room to help Victoria. Her dear friend was gagging now and looked like she was going to faint.

"He's harmless," Taylor whispered to Victoria. "If you go back in your room and close the door, the smell shouldn't bother you too much."

"That's what woke me up," Victoria whispered back. She gagged again. Taylor pulled the edge of her robe up to cover the lower part of her face. "Hold this close and take little breaths."

Victoria quickly did as she suggested. Her eyes were still wide with fright. Taylor left her friend sagging against the door frame and went to fetch her gun. She noticed her children peeking down from between the rails of the banister and smiled up at them.

She picked up her gun from the mantel and quickly loaded it. Hunter was threatening to kill Callaghan.

"You've got ten seconds to get out of here," he ordered. "And if I ever see you again, I'm going to kill you."

"He's not going anywhere."

Taylor had to repeat her decision a second time before she gained the men's attention. Hunter was certain he'd misunderstood her.

"What did you say?"

"He's not leaving." She smiled at Hunter. She wanted to laugh. He looked dumbfounded. "He told me he'll only just keep coming back."

Callaghan slapped the tabletop with his hand and started laughing. He stopped just as abruptly when she pointed her gun at him.

"You going to shoot me?"

"No," she answered. "But you aren't leaving until I say you can leave."

Callaghan turned to Hunter. His expression showed his concern. "She crazy?"

Hunter nodded. "She must be."

"She's overworked and exhausted and not thinking straight," Victoria cried out. Her voice was muffled by the fabric she held over her mouth. "Taylor, are you out of your mind?"

"Probably," Taylor answered. She laughed then and turned her gaze to the loft. "Daniel David?"

"Yes, Mother?"

"You know what we just captured?"

"What, Mother?"

"A real live mountain man."

The look of joy on Daniel's face made all the work she was going to have to do well worth the trouble.

"Hunter, get the tub."

Callaghan was their dream come true.

Lucas was away for three full weeks. He arrived home late Friday afternoon. Hunter met him in the yard. He knew something was wrong. There was lather on the horse's flanks. Lucas wouldn't have pushed his mount unless there was trouble.

"Where are Taylor and the others?"

"Inside," Hunter answered. "They're fine. What happened?"

"The judge agreed. I've got the signed papers."

He didn't need to explain further about the custody issue, for he had told Hunter all about Taylor's uncle so he would be forewarned if anyone came searching for the twins when he was away.

"Glad to hear it's settled," Hunter said, waiting for Lucas to tell him what else had happened.

"I trailed two men from Rosewood to South Creek. They're hired guns. They stopped in Cameron and were asking the quickest way to get to Redemption. I cut across and figure they're still a day's ride away."

"The rain we had last night should have slowed them down," Hunter interjected.

"The son of a bitch sent gunmen to take the twins."

"Are you going to tell Taylor or are we just going to take care of it and not bother her with the worry?"

Lucas didn't want to frighten his wife, but he knew he had to tell her. "She has to be on her guard. I'll tell her after supper."

"Guess we better stroll into town and talk to Frank," Hunter suggested.

"Guess we better," Lucas replied.

He was staring across the yard when he agreed with Hunter. He'd just spotted a stranger dressed in yellow-colored buckskin. The man turned the corner and started toward the front door. The fading sunlight dappled the stranger's face and the distance was too great for Lucas to get a good look. There was something vaguely familiar about him.

"Evening," the man called out.

Lucas took a step back. "Callaghan," he whispered in disbelief. He continued to watch the man until he disappeared inside the house. He acted as though he was used to coming and going during the daylight hours.

He said his name again. He bellowed it this time.

Hunter started laughing. "You didn't recognize him, did you?"

Lucas shook his head. "What in thunder happened to him?"

"Taylor happened to him," Hunter answered. "I'll take care of your horse. You go on inside."

Callaghan must have told the family Lucas was back because the front door suddenly opened and Taylor came running. She was followed by the children. Victoria stood in the entrance, looking happy and relieved to see him.

Taylor waited until Lucas had greeted the children before stepping forward to kiss her husband.

"Welcome home," she whispered. "Did you . . ."

He nodded. Then he pulled her into his arms and kissed the breath out of her. The three children were all talking to him at the same time. He reluctantly pulled away from Taylor, whispered, "Later," and then turned to the most demanding of the three.

"Yes, Georgie?"

"You know what, Papa?"

"No, what?"

"We got a man inside."

"So I heard." Lucas looked at Taylor when he made that comment.

"He tells us stories every night," Daniel interjected. "About real mountain men. There's one who lives real close, and Callaghan says I might meet him one day."

"Mama won't let him go home. He told me so," Allie blurted out.

Taylor turned to cross the yard and go back inside. Lucas grabbed hold of her hand and pulled her back.

"Why haven't you let him go home?"

"Daniel hasn't chosen a name yet," Taylor explained. "Callaghan sleeps outside, Lucas. He isn't any trouble at all. I understand why you don't like him. He explained he's been a thorn in your side for years."

"If he sleeps outside, why doesn't he sneak away during the night?" Lucas asked, his exasperation apparent in his tone of voice. He knew the answer. Callaghan was getting hot meals and plenty of attention.

"Mama told him she'd hunt him down and drag him back if he left before I chose my name."

"When's that going to happen, son?" Lucas asked. With an effort he was able to keep the irritation out of his voice. He didn't want Daniel to think he was annoyed with him.

"Soon," Taylor promised. Lucas's jaw was clenched tight. The telltale sign indicated his anger. "He's leaving soon."

"Supper's ready."

Callaghan shouted the news from the doorway. Lucas looked at Hunter. His friend quickly turned away but not before Lucas saw him smile.

"Shall we go inside?" Taylor asked.

He frowned over her eagerness. She was acting as though the president of the United States was having supper with them.

He let himself be pulled along. And when he finally went inside and shut the door behind him, he could have sworn he heard Hunter's laughter.

He was able to control his temper all evening. He listened to the outrageous tale Callaghan told his wife and his son and only interrupted a couple of times.

"That isn't how it happened," he snapped. "If you're going to tell it, then tell it right."

His sharp reminder didn't stop Callaghan from continuing to tell one outrageous story after another.

Taylor couldn't understand why Lucas was getting so upset.

Callaghan seemed to understand. When the mountain man started another story involving a black bear, Lucas knew where it was headed. He threw up his hands and stormed out of the house.

Taylor didn't understand what had come over him. She excused herself and went outside. Lucas was halfway to the creek before she caught up with him.

"He's a thief, Taylor."

He'd answered her question before she could ask it. "When he was younger, perhaps. He won't steal from us."

"I can tolerate almost everything else, but by God, what's mine stays mine."

"Like your knife," she agreed. "The one you left on the nightstand in Cincinnati so I'd know you wouldn't give up looking for the twins."

"Yes," he agreed. "Come here, Mrs. Ross."

She stepped into his arms and hugged him. His chin dropped to rest on the top of her head.

"Men are coming tomorrow," he began. "Your uncle sent them."

He tightened his hold on her and explained what he and Hunter were going to do. He promised he would force them to leave. He didn't add the fact that they were gunfighters.

Taylor didn't let the twins out of her sight from that moment on. The weather cooperated with her plan to keep them inside. It rained most of the morning and half the afternoon.

Lucas came home at sundown. He told her the men had left. They wouldn't be coming back.

Frank gave her more details the following Sunday when she went into town to read the paper for the men.

"They both knew who Lucas and Hunter were," Frank told her. "They weren't about to go up against them. They were talkative, too. Seems your uncle was going to pay a premium for the return of his nieces."

"Lucas and I have legal custody now," Taylor blurted out.

Frank hurried to soothe her. "We know you do. None of us will sit idle if anyone else comes looking. Don't worry, Taylor."

Rolly listened to the conversation and then took her aside. "I got a little present for you," he whispered. "I just finished it." She thought it was a cradle.

An hour later, Rolly carried the gift out to the house. She was extremely appreciative and only laughed because she was filled with such joy, she assured the giant. Then she led the way inside and chose a spot for her third rocking chair.

She insisted on paying. He insisted once again that it was a gift. The chairs were placed in a half circle in front of the hearth. Rolly wasn't in a hurry to leave. The twins were down for their naps, Victoria was outside arguing with Hunter about something or other, and Lucas had taken his son hunting.

Taylor invited Rolly to sit for a spell. He settled himself in one of the rockers. She offered him a cool drink, but he declined the offer.

"Is there something you wanted to ask me?" she prodded.

He nodded. "I'm getting ready," he told her.

It took him over twenty minutes to get his question stated. They both rocked back and forth in their chairs while she waited and he worried.

He finally blurted it out. Rolly wanted to learn how to read.

Taylor was astonished and pleased. He was embarrassed and worried sick someone would find out. If anyone snickered at him for being an old fool and trying to better himself, well then he'd have to kill him, wouldn't he?

She assured him that no one would laugh, and when he didn't believe her, she finally promised to keep his secret. She wouldn't tell anyone, not even her husband.

"It's time for Daniel to learn how to read," she said. "I could sit down between the two of you and—"

Rolly didn't want anyone, not even a seven-year-old, watching him struggle. He suggested she teach her son at night and tutor him during the noon hour when he closed his shop for supper. Taylor asked him to consider working together from one until two every afternoon because the twins napped then and it would be easier for her to slip away.

They began their lessons the very next day. Taylor told everyone she was going to stretch her legs and walk into town to say hello to Frank. She didn't want to lie, and so each day she walked in the front door of the general store and called out the greeting as she hurried down the main aisle and went out the back door. She passed through the store an hour later on her way back home. Frank must have thought she was out of her mind. She always gave him the same excuse, that she was out for a brisk walk because it was such a fine day, and he always gave her a look that told her he thought she was damned odd.

Teaching Rolly was a challenge and a joy and a delight, for he was eager to learn and really quite intelligent. It was also a respite for Taylor, as it was the only time during the day that she was able to sit down.

Rolly appreciated the effort she made to help him. Lucas didn't appreciate anything she did. He didn't seem to even notice the rigid schedule she was maintaining. Her husband became more and more distant and withdrawn. Taylor believed he was finally realizing the burden he'd taken on. She fretted and she worried, and every morning before she groaned her way out of bed, she said a prayer for patience.

Callaghan was getting ready to leave. He told the family he could hear the mountain calling to him, and while he'd enjoyed Taylor's hospitality, he'd done enough talking and visiting. He wanted his solitude and his privacy back. He told Daniel he felt free and at peace when he was standing on top of a peak looking down on God's paradise.

Taylor was going to miss Callaghan, but she knew it was time for him to leave. He was wearing on Lucas's nerves. Her husband hated to listen to the stories he told after supper. Most of them centered around a mountain man named Montana. Lucas would scowl at the mere mention of the man's name and leave the house. His reaction always caused Callaghan to slap his knee and let out a hoot of laughter.

Exhaustion was taking its toll on Taylor. She was so tense and worried and so sick with her pretense of being strong all the time, inside she felt as though she were going to explode. When things became too difficult, she would grab her bucket, tell whoever was listening that she was going to fetch water, and hurry to a secluded spot by the stream and cry until the tension let up. Sometimes she went for water three times in a single day.

Lucas was unknowingly pushing her toward her breaking point. It had become a ritual for him to warn her every evening that they were still going to leave in the fall. She interpreted his reminder to mean that she had yet to convince him she had the skill and the stamina to live in the wilderness. And so the next day she tried a little harder and worked a little longer, and the next day and the next and the next . . .

He had his ritual, and she had her obsession. She was determined to get him to start treating her like a wife. She wanted him to talk to her about his hopes, his dreams, his worries, and his past. She hungered for him to share with her a little remembrance from his past, and God only knew she tried to get him to talk. Yet no matter how innocuous her questions were, he still gave her only one-word answers. He seemed determined to hold a part of himself back, and she couldn't understand why.

Nothing seemed to be going smoothly. She'd been engaged in a battle of wills with the twins for over a week now. Victoria assured her she was making progress. Taylor wasn't convinced. When Allie or Georgie misbehaved, Taylor sat her down on one of the steps leading up to the loft and made her stay there until she promised to do what she was told. The first few times Georgie was put on the step, she didn't seem to mind at all. Then Taylor started ignoring her while she was being punished. She refused to talk to the child and wouldn't let anyone else speak to her either. It didn't take long for Georgie to realize it wasn't any fun to be left out. By Friday, she hated the punishment and was finally beginning to stay off the kitchen table and leave her sister's food alone.

Allie was far more difficult to discipline. She seemed to enjoy sitting on the step. She enjoyed crying, too. Her screams were ear piercing and Taylor was soon clenching her teeth together. She pretended to ignore the child. She acted as though the shrill noise didn't bother her at all. Allie was far more stubborn than she was. If Taylor went outside, the screaming stopped. Yet as soon as she came back inside, the child started up again. Allie apparently wanted an audience.

On Saturday morning, Taylor came up with an alternate plan. She put Allie up in the loft and told her she could cry all she wanted, but no one would hear her. It was a lie, of course, for the child's wails were loud enough to spook the horses, but Allie believed her. Crying finally lost its luster. Without someone to see and hear her, the power struggle didn't appear to be worth her effort.

The twins weren't always behaving like hellions, of course. They were usually sweet and loving. After their baths each night, they would cuddle up on her lap and take turns telling her everything they had done during the day. They seemed to have forgotten she'd been with them every waking minute. She gave them praise and affection as often as possible, and she was thrilled that both of them were adapting to the wilderness with such ease.

Daniel loved their new home. He followed Lucas around like a puppy and hung on his every word. The two of them spent quite a lot of time together. No matter how busy Lucas was, he always made certain he gave his son time and attention.

Taylor clung to the hope that her husband would eventually give her the time and attention she craved. It simply wasn't possible for her to keep up her rigid schedule forever, and on Saturday afternoon, Taylor's control snapped. Ironically it was her sweet, innocent son who inadvertently caused the dam to burst. He told her the name he'd chosen for his own.

Callaghan stood by Daniel's side with his hands clasped behind his back. He was rocking back and forth on the soles of his boots. He looked like he was gloating about something. She became intrigued. The mountain man liked to tease, and she wondered what game he was up to now. There was a definite sparkle in his eyes.

Daniel made his announcement. He explained he wanted to be named after the fierce and courageous mountain man everyone called Montana.

She understood his reason for making the choice for she had listened to Callaghan tell one magical story after another about the valiant and bold mountain man. She, too, had been enamored by the tales, but she still didn't feel the name was suitable. Did he really want to be named after a territory?

"Montana's the name everyone calls him, but not to his face. He hates the name, Mother. Callaghan told me so."

She nodded and waited for him to tell her the name. Daniel was stammering with excitement. She didn't rush him. This was an important moment for the child.

He took a deep breath and straightened his shoulders. And then he told her his new name. He was going to be Lucas Michael Ross.

She had to sit down. Her son didn't seem to notice how upset she was or how stunned. He had already jumped into one of his favorite stories about Lucas.

"He led forty settlers out of the canyon in the dead of winter and the Indians didn't bother them at all because, because . . ."

Callaghan was happy to supply the rest of the explanation while the boy paused for air. "They're afraid and they're respectful," he told her.

Her son nodded. "I can't be called Montana. Every mountain man has to earn his own nickname. Callaghan's called Bear. Isn't that right?"

"It surely is," Callaghan agreed.

"Rolly told me a story about Father, Mother. He said he could track his way—"

"Son, I don't believe your mama's up to hearing a tale now. She looks a might stunned to me. You didn't know, did you, Mrs. Ross?"

She shook her head. He burst into laughter. Taylor ignored the mountain man. She was remembering the crowd of men surrounding her husband in the lobby of the hotel in Boston. They were enthusiastically pounding him on his shoulder and begging him to shake their hands. She had believed their admiration had something to do with the war.

Dear God above, she was married to a mountain man. And everyone in America seemed to know who he was. Everyone but her.

"Callaghan said it would be confusing to call both of us Lucas," her son continued. "He suggested while I'm growing up I could use Father's middle name. I'm Michael now, Mother . . . if that is all right with you."

She didn't want to squelch his joy. She forced a smile. "Then Michael it is."

Callaghan left a few minutes later, and her son went outside to tell everyone else his new name. Lucas had already gone hunting. He would have to wait until later to find out what he was now supposed to call his son.

Taylor didn't move from the table for a very long time. Victoria and Hunter had taken the twins to the creek to play in the water. They were gone over an hour, and when they came back, Taylor was still sitting at the table.

Victoria had made a thick stew for supper. She announced it would be ready in another hour. She kept giving Taylor worried glances. Her friend looked flushed. She noticed she was trembling. Was fever the cause?

Taylor shook her head and stood up. "Not fever," she whispered to Victoria. "Fury." She tied her apron around her waist, tucked her gun in the pouch, and started for the door.

"Where are you going?" Victoria called out.

"To check the garden," Taylor answered. "Then I believe I'll go into town. I need to be alone for a little while," she added.

She thought her voice sounded calm, reasonable. Victoria didn't agree. "Is your throat paining you? You sound hoarse."

Taylor didn't answer her. She was pulling the door closed when her friend asked her how long she was going to be gone. She didn't want her to miss supper.

Taylor promised her she would be back before then.

Armed with her gun, she marched around the perimeter of her garden. She muttered over the damage the rabbits had already done to her budding vegetables and silently screamed inside over her miserable life.

Lucas knew something was wrong the minute he saw her. She stood on the opposite side of the garden, staring at him, and her expression was one he'd never seen before. She looked defeated.

She waited until he was about twenty feet away from her and then put up her hand in a signal for him to stop.

"I quit." She bellowed her announcement. His eyes widened in response. She nodded. "Did you hear me, Lucas. I quit."

He gave her a quick nod. "It's about time."

His reaction fueled her fury. "You expected me to fail, didn't you? You aren't at all surprised."

"No, I'm not surprised," he answered. "I've watched you work yourself to the bone these past weeks and seen what it's done to you." His concern about her made his voice harsh. "You've lost weight and you've got deep circles under your eyes. Thank God you came to your senses before you killed yourself."

She wanted to scream at him. She didn't suppress the urge. To hell with control. She'd come to the frontier to be free and by God she was going to be.

"Are you telling me my hard work convinced you I shouldn't stay here?"

"Taylor, you're shouting at me." He seemed astonished by the fact.

She didn't waste time agreeing with him. "Don't you dare tell me I'm fragile, Lucas, or I swear to God I'll scream you to death."

"You don't belong here," he argued. He was fast becoming as angry as she was. The longer he stared at his exhausted wife, the more furious he became. Didn't she realize she had become his whole world? If anything happened to her, he didn't know what he would do. She had responsibilities, damn it. The children depended on her. And so did he. Taylor needed to start taking care of herself, and he was going to make certain she did.

"I've stood by long enough," he told her. "I took you out of a ballroom and by all that's holy, I'm taking you back. You should be wearing diamonds and . . ."

She broke his concentration. She pulled the gun out of her apron, turned, and fired. A fat rabbit caught the bullet and was thrown backward against the fence.

Taylor put the gun away and then folded her arms together. She glared at her husband. "I quit," she shouted again. "Did you know your son has chosen his name? He wants to be called Lucas Michael Ross. We're supposed to call him Michael. What do you think about that, Montana?"

He took a step toward her. She backed away. "They're all exaggerations," he said. "I don't like to talk about it. I don't deserve the recognition. I'm a good tracker, that's all."

He was deliberately misunderstanding what she was trying to tell him. His expression became guarded. He obviously wanted her to drop the subject. She wasn't going to cooperate. "Everyone in America knows who you are. Everyone but your wife."

He didn't have anything to say about that. Taylor felt betrayed. She knew she needed some time alone to figure out what she was going to do.

"I'm not going to be a burden to you any longer," she announced. She picked up her skirts and started walking toward the path that led into town. "Now if you'll excuse me, I'm leaving."

"Go right ahead," he muttered. "But I'm warning you, Taylor. I'll only track you down and drag you back to me. What's mine stays mine."

She came to an abrupt stop. The panic she heard in his voice confused her. She turned around to look at him. She saw fear in his gaze. She didn't understand his reaction, yet she instinctively tried to calm him. "I'm going into town. I shall be back within the hour."

He couldn't hide his relief from her. Taylor thought about Lucas's behavior all the way into town. She ran part of the distance, and when she realized what she was doing, she slowed down. She was still so angry with the obstinate man she couldn't think straight. Her plan to prove to him that she had the gumption and the stamina to live in the wilderness had back-fired.

He was a full-fledged, bigger-than-life mountain man. If that wasn't galling, she didn't know what was. He knew she was fascinated with Daniel Boone and Davy Crockett. He heard some of the stories she told their son. Damn it, he knew how she felt about her heroes, and yet he never thought to tell her she was married to one.

Her temper flared again. Of course he didn't tell her. He would have to talk to her about his past and, God forbid, even share a few experiences with her.

Taylor threw her hands up in vexation. "I give up," she muttered. Then she burst into tears. Because she was in the habit of cutting through the general store, she took the pass through now. She cried her way down the main aisle, and because it was also customary for her to wave to Frank, she did that as well, and it wasn't until she'd gotten outside again that she realized how ridiculous she must have looked.

Taylor had promised to be back in an hour, but time got away from her. She went up the hill beyond Redemption, and when she reached the top, she looked down at the town below her, put her hands on her hips, and let out a loud, thoroughly liberating scream. It felt so wonderful, she screamed again. Only when her throat started aching did she finally stop.

She knew she was acting like a crazy woman. She didn't care. No one was around to hear or see her. It wouldn't have mattered if there were other people watching, she realized. She was a free woman. If she wanted to lose her control, then by God she was going to.

She let out a loud sigh of satisfaction and sat down. She spent a long while thinking about her husband. His reaction to her announcement that she was leaving kept nagging at her. He'd apparently thought she was telling him she was leaving their marriage, and while she thought that was a ridiculous conclusion for an intelligent man to jump to, what confused and fascinated her was the fact that she'd seen fear in his eyes. She hadn't been mistaken. There was fear and panic.

His reaction didn't make any sense to her. Did he truly believe she would walk away from him and the children? Or did he think she would leave the children with him and that was why he looked so panic stricken. She shook her head, denying the possibility. Lucas would know she'd never leave their children. How could he think she could leave him? She had told him she loved him. Did he think it was only a temporary affliction?

He hadn't been thinking clearly, she realized, and that wasn't at all like Lucas. He was always reasonable. He'd raised his voice to her as well. Yet Lucas never, ever shouted. He never allowed his emotions to get in the way of his control.

Until today.

There was only one conclusion possible, and suddenly what hadn't made any sense at all was perfectly clear.

He loved her.

She was overcome with joy. She wept for ten minutes before she felt like stopping. Then she started worrying. If he loved her, why hadn't he told her so?

Taylor mopped her face dry with the hem of her skirt and stood up. Love wasn't supposed to be confusing, was it? Perhaps Lucas hadn't realized he loved her yet. The possibility made sense to her, and since she couldn't come up with any other logical reason, she decided that was it.

Lord, she was going to have to be patient. She

honestly didn't think she had it in her. Lucas would eventually figure it all out, she knew, and she only hoped she wasn't dead and buried before the truth dawned on the obtuse man. Loving him could very well be the death of her. The thought made her smile.

It was time to go home. She brushed the leaves from the back of her skirt and started back down the hill. She suddenly found herself wondering what she had been doing a year ago and decided she was probably poring over Miss Livingston's journal. How naive she'd been back then. Miss Livingston didn't know poppycock about family life in the wilderness. Monday didn't have to be wash day and women didn't have to work until they dropped just to prove they were capable.

Life was too short for rigid schedules. Taylor knew she would eventually settle into a comfortable routine, but it wouldn't be demanding. She didn't need to prove anything to anyone. She wanted to live a long life with her husband at her side and watch her children grow up and follow their dreams.

She loved Lucas passionately, but she wasn't going to let him take her dreams away. She was stay'ng right where she was, and that was that.

The sun was setting. Taylor paused to admire God's handiwork, then picked up her pace and hurried back into town. The time had gotten away from her. She told Victoria she'd be back in an hour and more than two had already passed.

She took her shortcut through the general store, called out a greeting to Frank, and then hurried on out the front door.

She came face-to-face with her uncle Malcolm.

They almost collided with one another. She was so startled by the sight of him, she came to a dead stop.

He didn't seem to be at all surprised to see her. He grabbed hold of her arm just above her elbow, squeezed hard, and dragged her away from the entrance.

She was already trying to pull his hand away from her when he slammed her up against the wall. The back of her head struck wood. Pain shot through her, but she didn't cry out. She wasn't about to give him such satisfaction.

Malcolm was as ugly as she remembered, though he'd put on a considerable amount of weight around his middle since the last time she'd seen him. His hair was thinning on top, and there were thicker strands of gray along the sides. He was dressed in a black suit and white shirt. There were stains around the collar and down the front. He reeked of whiskey. Yes, Malcolm was every bit as repulsive as she remembered.

"Get your hands off me," she demanded, her disgust evident in her voice.

"Is that any way to greet your uncle?" he crooned. His face was just inches away from hers. She deliberately stared at the scar that crisscrossed his eyelid and brow. He finally noticed where she was looking and raised his right hand. He slapped her hard across the face just as Frank walked outside to see what was going on. He shouted and ran to help her.

Malcolm shoved him out of his way and pulled Taylor back into the store. He slammed the door shut, locked it, and then shoved her up against the counter.

"Did you think you could hide from me in this godforsaken place?"

She didn't answer him. "You were surprised to see me, weren't you?"

"Yes," she admitted. "I knew you would send more

517

men to try to take the girls, but I didn't believe you would come here."

"I'm taking them home with me," he announced. He patted the pocket of his jacket. "I've got papers proving I own them."

"No one owns them," she cried out. "Your papers don't mean anything here. We aren't in England."

He glared at her, then hurried to the back door. He pulled it closed and bolted it against intruders.

"We'll just wait here," he told her.

Taylor was looking out the front window. Frank was nowhere in sight. She assumed he had gone to get Lucas.

"I could kill you for the trouble you've caused me. It was your idea, wasn't it?"

She folded her arms in front of her and watched him pace back and forth down the aisle, frowning at her all the while.

"What was my idea?" she asked.

"To change the will."

She shook her head. "Your mother didn't tell me what she'd done. I found out when you did, after she died."

He snorted with disbelief. "I'm not leaving without the twins. I wouldn't have bothered if you hadn't cleverly talked the bitch into leaving a bloody fortune to Marian's brats. Thanks to your interference, I've got every creditor in London pounding at my door."

"Your loans were all paid off by Madam," she reminded him. "Have you already buried yourself in debt again?"

He didn't like her question. He took a threatening step toward her. She slipped her hand down into her apron. She wanted to be prepared for any eventuality.

"If I have to kill you, I will," he threatened.

"Do so and the money will go to my husband," she was happy to point out.

Malcolm smiled. "He should be dying right about now. I didn't hire cowards this time. I came prepared. I've got four gunslingers with me."

With an effort she was able to hide her alarm from him. "Only four?" she taunted.

He raised his hand to slap her again. A noise coming from the front turned his attention. He rushed over to the side of the window and peeked outside. He apparently didn't see anyone there, for he shrugged and turned back to her.

He strutted like a peacock as he came down the aisle again.

"Every bit of this is your fault," he snapped. "If there's killing done, you're responsible. I want every pound due me. I can't go after the money the old fool left to her charities, but I can take back what she set aside for you and the twins."

"How do you plan to accomplish that?" she asked. She didn't give him time to answer. "Let me guess. It won't be your fault or your responsibility, but I'm still going to have to die. Is that it?"

"I'm only doing what you forced me to do."

"Where did you get the money to hire gunfighters?"

"My daughter," he answered. "She sold her jewels. I'm giving her half of the inheritance. Jane sends her regards," he added with a chuckle.

"They hang men for murder around here," she told him.

Malcolm unbuttoned his jacket and reached into his pocket. Her hand was on her gun, but she didn't pull the weapon out of her apron. She didn't want to kill him unless she was forced to.

He had a gun tucked into the waistband of his

pants. It was squeezed between his belt and his roll of fat. He didn't reach for his weapon, however. He pulled out a handkerchief instead and began to wipe the sweat from his forehead.

"It's hot as hell in here," he muttered.

"Taylor!" Lucas bellowed her name. The glass in the windows shook from the force of his shout.

Malcolm went running to the window. He hid by the side and peeked out to see who was there. He didn't stand directly in front of the glass, for he didn't want to be a target.

"Who is it calling you?" he demanded in a low whisper.

There was laughter and relief in her voice when she answered him. "Lucas."

"No!" He howled the denial.

"Yes," she repeated. "Would you like me to answer him?"

"Shut your mouth, girl. Let me think," he ordered. He peeked outside once again, then flattened himself against the wall to stare at her. "They must not have gotten to him before he took off for town. Yes, that's it. They'll be on their way any time now. I'll keep him busy worrying about you until they get here. Answer him, damn you. Call out to him so he knows I haven't killed you yet."

"Do you expect me to help you?" She sounded incredulous. "God, you're despicable. You look like a cornered rat. You are cornered, you know. You might as well give up. Walk out of here while you still can."

"Answer him," Malcolm shouted again.

Taylor was going to refuse, but Lucas called her name again and she knew he must be worried about her. Men who loved their wives would worry. Lucas wasn't any different.

"Yes, Lucas?" she shouted.

"Are you all right?" His voice shook with terror.

"Yes," she shouted back. "I'm quite all right."

A full minute passed before Lucas called to her again. "I'm coming in."

Malcolm struggled to get his gun out of his waistband. He wasn't paying any attention to her.

"Tell him to stay where he is," he shouted.

"You don't need to come inside," Taylor called out. She pulled the gun out of her apron and took aim.

Lucas didn't know what to do. He was so scared inside and in such a rage he wanted to tear the door down and kill the bastard with his bare hands. All the way into town he blocked the possibility that she could already be dead, and when she called out to him and he knew she was still alive, his knees had gone weak and his heart had felt as though it had exploded inside him.

"Lucas, you're an easy target standing in the middle of the street," she shouted.

Malcolm was looking out the window again. He had his gun in his hand but down by his side. He hadn't taken aim yet. And that was the only reason he was still alive.

"I'm coming in," Lucas shouted to her again.

"You don't need to," she assured him.

She didn't sound frightened. Lucas didn't know what to make of the realization. And then she cleared it all up for him with a simple reminder.

"Why the hell not?" he wanted to know.

"I'm wearing my apron."

Malcolm didn't understand until he heard her cock the gun. He slowly turned toward her, raising his own weapon as he moved.

She shot the gun out of his hand. He let out a howl

of pain and fell back against the wall. The front door exploded into fragments. Lucas used his shoulder to break down the barrier. Then the back door crashed to the floor, and Rolly came storming inside.

Lucas glanced at Taylor to make certain she was all right, then turned to Malcolm. He lifted him up, slammed his fist into his jaw, and threw him backward. Malcolm went flying out the glass window and landed in a heap on the walkway.

He wanted to kill him. Taylor wouldn't let him. At first she thought justice would be served by sending him back to England. The life he would have to endure living as a pauper would be punishment enough. He was a broken-down, ruined man. But he still had the same appetites, the same sick cravings. No child would be safe as long as Malcolm roamed the streets of London.

And the children must always come first. Always.

She wanted him locked away for the rest of his life. Lucas finally agreed with her. He decided putting a bullet through Malcolm's black heart wouldn't be a good idea after all. He wouldn't suffer enough.

The entire town had gathered outside the store and were staring down at their captive while they debated what they wanted to do to him. Malcolm was sitting in the dirt, whimpering and cursing while he dabbed at his hand where Taylor's bullet had clipped his skin.

Rolly thought they should hang him then and there. Lucas wouldn't let him. He had his arm around Taylor's shoulders and was squeezing her tight against his side. She could feel him shaking, and from the look he was giving her, she thought he might be realizing he loved her. He looked ill.

Cleevis and Eddie stepped forward with the offer

to take Malcolm to the sheriff in Rosewood. Lucas agreed.

"What happened to the four men Malcolm hired?" Taylor asked.

Lucas had killed two when they tried to ambush him and let the third crawl away with a bullet in his gut. He wasn't going to give Taylor any of the details, however.

The gunfighters had set up their trap near the stream. While Hunter kept them busy with his gunfire, Lucas worked his way around to the side. He'd been consumed with panic, for Taylor always crossed over the path where the men were hiding on her way back from town. If she'd come home when she was supposed to, she could have gotten killed.

But she was late. She was always late, and Lucas thanked God for the blessed flaw. He vowed he would never criticize her again.

"Lucas, what happened to the four men Malcolm sent?" she asked again.

"I only counted three."

"I counted four."

Hunter made the comment from behind her back. She turned and smiled at him.

She had refused to look at her uncle. He'd called her name twice. She ignored him both times.

"I want to go home now," she whispered to her husband. "Frank? If you'll order glass for your window, my husband will be happy to pay for it."

Lucas let go of her and spoke to Hunter in a low voice. She couldn't hear what he was saying to his friend. She didn't wait for him. She suddenly needed to get away from Malcolm and breathe fresh air. She said her farewells and started walking home. Lucas caught up with her at the bend in the dirt road.

She told him what Malcolm had said to her. "He

has never taken responsibility for anything in his entire life. He was very clever making others feel as though they were somehow at fault for what he did."

"Marian?" he asked.

"Yes. She believed she had done something wrong. Will Malcolm be locked away?"

"The charge will be attempted murder," Lucas told her. "Yes, he'll be locked away. Taylor?"

"Yes?"

"Never mind." His voice was trembling. He was still having difficulty getting his emotions under control. He had never felt stark terror until he realized Taylor was inside with the bastard. He never wanted to feel like that again. He was still sick to his stomach and his nerves were strung tight enough to pop.

"Lucas, quit glaring at me."

"I'm never going through that again. Do you hear me, Taylor. I'm never going to be scared like that again."

"Why do you think you were scared?" She held her breath while she waited for his answer.

"That's an ignorant question."

Lord, he could be impossible. They walked along for several more minutes before she spoke again.

"When I left for my walk, I had made a decision. I decided I didn't want to be married to a man who didn't love me."

"You aren't." He sounded furious with her.

"I know." She sounded thrilled.

"Have you stopped loving me?"

It wasn't what he asked but how his voice shook when he asked that stunned her. His anguish was almost unbearable to witness. He looked as though she was about to destroy him with her answer. He believed he had it all figured out as well, for he was beginning to nod.

"I will never stop loving you," she whispered. She grabbed hold of his hand and held tight. "How can you ask me such a question? Do you think that if you say or do something wrong, I'll stop? Honest to God, Lucas, you're going to drive me out of my mind. My love isn't conditional or temporary. It's forever."

"Then stop asking questions about my past," he ordered. "Leave it alone, Taylor. I'm damned sick of worrying you'll . . ."

He didn't go on. He pulled away from her and quickened his pace.

"Realize what?" she asked.

He shook his head. She wouldn't give up. "Answer me," she demanded in a near shout.

He turned around and looked at her. "I'm a bastard, remember?"

"I am aware of the circumstances surrounding your birth," she replied. "Madam told me, you told me, and I believe William Merritt told me. It didn't matter then and it doesn't matter now."

"Why the hell doesn't it matter to you? When are you going to realize I'm not . . ." He stopped suddenly, shook his head again, and then muttered, "I know I don't deserve you. I won't give you up though, no matter how unworthy I am. If you knew all the things I've done, you wouldn't be able to look at me. I started living the day I met you. Let my past alone. And this is the last time I'm ever going to talk about this. Do you understand?"

He didn't wait to hear her agreement. He turned around again and started walking.

The truth was finally out. Lucas was afraid. Dear Lord, why had it taken her so long to understand? He was ashamed of his past and believed that if she knew about his childhood and his war years, she would stop loving him. At the root of his fear was the stigma of being born out of wedlock. She hadn't realized until this very minute how much it had affected him or what his life as a young boy must have been like.

He never called William Merritt by name. He called him a son of a bitch. She had also heard him call William a bastard. He wasn't illegitimate. Neither was her uncle Malcolm, but Lucas called him a bastard, too. She finally understood why. In Lucas's mind, being called a bastard was the most horrible, contemptible, and dishonorable curse one man could put on another.

Seeing such vulnerability made her love him all the more. Her heart was suddenly pounding a furious beat, and all she wanted to do was throw herself into his arms and cry with joy because he loved her.

She was going to have to get his attention first, and then convince him he was more than worthy. He was the man of her dreams.

She called out to him. He ignored her. She shouted his name the second time. He acted as though he hadn't heard her.

She let out a sigh and reached for her gun. She aimed and shot a pebble off the ground a yard or two in front of him.

He whirled around to face her. "What in thunder do you think you're doing?"

"Getting your attention."

He shook his head. He didn't want to stay and talk until he'd gotten his emotions under control. She had seen enough of his weakness and his vulnerability.

"Put that gun away. I've got things to do. I'm leaving, damn it."

She smiled at him. "Go ahead," she shouted back. "But I'm warning you. I'll only track you down and bring you back home where you belong. I love you, Lucas. You are everything I could ever want."

He turned away from her. She shot a piece of bark off a tree twenty feet away from him.

Then she tucked her gun back into her apron, picked up her skirts, and went running to him. She was sobbing by the time she threw herself into his arms.

He shook with emotion. He couldn't stop telling her how much he loved her. He kissed every inch of her sunburned face and whispered all the words he'd held inside for so long. He wanted to prove to her first that he was worthy. He would give her the kind of life he was certain she wanted and deserved, and once they were living in their fancy house and she was draped in velvet and diamonds, he would tell her he loved her.

She thought that was the most beautiful, loving, and foolish fantasy she'd ever heard. She was already living in a paradise and she never wanted to leave.

Their kisses and their pledges made them hungry for more. She tried to pull him toward the yard that led to their house, but he shook his head and took her to a secluded spot nestled between the pines. They made love then with an intensity and passion that overwhelmed them.

They lazily washed in the stream and made love again. They kissed and stroked each other while they put on their clothes, and the ordinary task took them a long, long while.

Taylor didn't want to go home just yet, but she knew Victoria would be worried. Lucas told her Hunter knew they were going to be late.

Her husband stretched out on his back on a carpet of grass and let out a loud sigh of contentment.

"How did he know we would be late?"

"I told him."

"But you were in such a hurry to get home," she reminded him.

He grinned. "Only when you started pressing me," he told her.

Taylor sat down next to him and stared up at the stars. "I am surrounded by luxury," she whispered. "The stars are my diamonds, and I'm sitting on a carpet of emeralds."

"You're really determined to stay?"

"Oh, yes."

"It will be hard on you. There will be times you'll want to give up."

"I'm sure there will be."

"What will you do?"

"Scream."

He laughed. "Like today."

"Yes."

"You aren't fragile."

She was so pleased with his realization, she leaned over and kissed him.

"When did you figure that out?"

"The rabbit."

She didn't understand. She had to wait until he stopped laughing to hear his explanation.

"It was your concern about your garden, I suppose," he said. And the way she had pulled out her gun to protect what belonged to her.

"What's mine stays mine."

She was throwing his words back at him. He nodded. "That's right."

He cupped the back of her neck and drew her down for another long kiss. When she finally pulled away, he let out another satisfied sigh.

She stretched out next to him. They stared up at the night. She thought about their future. He thought about his past.

Neither spoke for several minutes. Taylor thought the night was filled with magic. She inhaled the sweet mountain air and closed her eyes. She had never known such contentment or peace.

"I used to fall asleep every night staring up at the stars. I would pretend I was the only one who could see them. They belonged to me and only me. I didn't have anything to call my own back then, not even a legitimate name."

He continued to talk for almost an hour about his growing-up years. She didn't interrupt or ask any questions. She simply listened. She smiled when he told her about some of the pranks he and Hunter had pulled, and became teary eyed when he told her about some of the more painful experiences he'd endured.

Lucas didn't tell her about the war until they were on their way back home. It was difficult for him to talk about and nearly unbearable for her to hear. And when he told her what a man named John Caulder had done to him and eight other men, she wept with compassion and sorrow.

"I was the fortunate one," he told her. "I survived. I couldn't understand why. The others had families waiting for them. I didn't have anyone. Hunter told me there was a reason and eventually I would figure it all out. You helped me do that, sweetheart. I think you and the children are the reason why I was supposed to stick around."

She smiled over the wonder in his voice. He turned the topic back to Caulder and called him a bastard. She gently corrected him by pointing out that being born out of wedlock wasn't the baby's fault. He hadn't made the choice or done some terrible deed. Caulder deserved to be called every vile name Lucas would think of, but bastard wasn't allowed.

"Will they tell you when they've captured him?"

"Yes."

"He needs to stand trial. The world needs to know what he did to your friends."

Lucas knew she was right. He would be their voice when he testified against Caulder.

Lucas told her another war story and when he was finished, he turned the subject to his brothers. He talked about the ranch they were building and how beautiful the land was there. She wanted to know when he was going to get around to introducing his family to his brothers.

He promised her he would take her and the children over the pass as soon as possible. He thought it might be a good idea to bring Kelsey home with them. The boy could use a little mothering and Daniel, or rather Michael, would have the opportunity of getting to know his young uncle. Taylor thought that was a splendid idea.

He wanted to know why she was spending so much time with Rolly. She refused to give him an answer. Lucas assured her he wasn't jealous, but he kept prodding her until she finally told him enough to satisfy him. She said they were working on a special project and he would have to wait to find out what it was.

Lucas decided she must have finally talked Rolly into making a cradle for Victoria's baby and was helping him with the task.

Three weeks later, he realized his guess had been wrong. Rolly stopped by with another gift he was certain they would appreciate. It was yet another rocking chair.

Lucas told Rolly they didn't need it. The giant was just as certain they did. Lucas eventually gave in. He took the rocker and put it with the others.

"Don't you know how to make anything else?" he asked.

"I'm partial to rocking chairs," Rolly replied.

That evening, after the children had gone to sleep, the four adults sat in the chairs and rocked back and forth. Taylor was the first to start laughing. Then Victoria joined in, and it wasn't long before Hunter and Lucas began laughing too.

They made so much noise, they woke the children. Taylor dabbed at the corners of her eyes while she explained to the little ones that she was laughing with happiness because they had so many fine chairs.

"Guess I'll start work on a cradle," Hunter told Victoria.

"Guess I'll have to build another room," Lucas drawled out. "If Rolly doesn't run out of wood soon, we'll need the space."

That statement started everyone laughing again. The twins were cuddled up on their father's lap. They didn't understand why everyone was so amused, but they laughed all the same.

Taylor's son sat with her. He thought his parents were crazy.

"We're just enjoying ourselves, Daniel," she explained.

"It's Michael now, not Daniel, Mother. Please get it right."

His sassy tone of voice astounded her. She burst into laughter again. She wrapped her arms around her son and hugged him. "I'll try to get it right, Michael."

She kissed him good night and sent him up to bed. Lucas carried his daughters.

Victoria stood up, took hold of Hunter's hand, and led him outside. From the way the two of them were gazing at each other, Taylor knew there would be a wedding soon.

She leaned back in her chair, closed her eyes, and let the sounds of the night float around her. She could hear the twins giving their father fits. Allie was upset because her papa hadn't tucked her baby under the covers just right. Then Georgie started in. She gave her papa several reasons why she couldn't go to sleep. Lucas finally got the two of them settled down by starting a bedtime story he let his son select from his favorites.

Lucas was far more patient with the children than she was. He wasn't perfect, however. She was going to have to ask him to stop using blasphemies, for just the other day Georgie had settled herself at the table, propped her face up in her hands with her elbows on the tabletop, and asked, "What the hell's for supper, Mama?"

Lucas was definitely going to have to start guarding his language.

Taylor's thoughts flittered from one lazy thought to another. She knew she was about to drift off to sleep, and so she said her prayers. She thanked God for her blessings, and when she was finished, she whispered good night to Madam.

She had to have known. Oh, yes, she'd known Lucas was the man of her dreams. She would have found out all about him from the information she'd gathered in her file.

Tell the babies kind stories about me. Taylor hadn't forgotten Madam's request. She would tell the children hundreds of stories about their great-grandmother, but the one she would most enjoy relating would be about the gift the grand lady had given her. She would tell them how she met and married Prince Charming.

Visit

JULIE GARWOOD

online!

For a preview excerpt of Julie Garwood's
upcoming hardcover, *Heartbreaker*, go to:

www.SimonSays.com/juliegarwood

Read excerpts from her other books,
find a listing of future titles, and
learn more about the author!

**POCKET BOOKS
PROUDLY PRESENTS**

Mercy

JULIE GARWOOD

**Now available in paperback
from Pocket Books**

**The following is a preview of
Mercy. . . .**

Theo Buchanan couldn't seem to shake the virus. He knew he was running a fever because every bone in his body ached and he had chills. He refused to acknowledge that he was ill, though; he was just a little off-kilter, that was all. He could tough it out. Besides, he was sure he was over the worst of it. The god-awful stitch in his side had subsided into a dull throbbing, and he was positive that it meant he was on the mend. If it was the same bug that had infected most of the staff back in his Boston office, then it was one of those twenty-four-hour things, and he should be feeling as good as new by tomorrow morning. Except, the throbbing in his side had been going on for a couple of days now.

He decided to blame his brother, Dylan, for that ache. He'd really nailed Theo during a family football game on their parents' lawn at Nathan's Bay. Yeah, the pulled muscle was Dylan's fault, but Theo figured that if he continued to ignore it, the pain would eventually go away.

Damn, he was feeling like an old man these days, and he wasn't even thirty-three yet.

He didn't think he was contagious, and he had too much to do to go to bed and sweat the fever out of his body. He'd flown from Boston to New Orleans to speak at a law symposium on organized crime and to receive recognition he didn't believe he deserved for simply doing his job.

Tonight was the first of three black-tie affairs. He'd promised to attend a fund-raiser, and he couldn't back out. Dinner was going to be prepared by five of the top chefs in the city, but the gourmet food was going to be wasted on him. The thought of swallowing anything, even water, made his stomach lurch. He hadn't eaten anything since yesterday afternoon.

He sure as certain wasn't up to pointless chitchat tonight. He tucked the room key into his pocket and was reaching for the doorknob, when the phone rang.

It was his brother Nick calling to check in.

"What's going on?"

"I'm walking out the door," Theo answered. "Where are you calling from? Boston or Holy Oaks?"

"Boston," Nick answered. "I helped Laurant close the lake house and then we drove back home together."

"Is she staying with you until the wedding?"

"Are you kidding? Tommy would send me straight to hell."

Theo laughed. "I guess having a priest for a future brother-in-law does put a crimp in your sex life."

"Five more weeks and I'm gonna be a married man. Hard to believe, isn't it?"

"It's hard to believe any woman would have you."

"Laurant's nearsighted. I told her I was good-looking and she believed me. She's staying with Mom and Dad until we all head back to Iowa for the wedding. What are you doing tonight?"

"I've got a fund-raiser I have to go to," he answered. "So what do you want?"

"I just thought I'd call and say hello."

"No, you didn't. You want something. What is it? Come on, Nick. I'm gonna be late."

"Theo, you've got to learn to slow down. You can't keep running for the rest of your life. I know what you're doing. You think that if you bury yourself in work, you won't think about Rebecca. It's been four years since she died, but you—"

Theo cut him off. "I like my life, and I'm not in the mood to talk about Rebecca."

"You're a workaholic."

"Did you call to lecture me?"

"No, Laurant's been bugging me to call you."

"Is she there? Let me talk to her," he said. He sat down on the side of the bed and realized he was feeling better. Nick's fiancée had that effect on all the Buchanan brothers. She made everyone feel good.

"She isn't here. She went out with Jordan, and you know our sister. God only knows what time they'll get home. Anyway, I promised Laurant that I'd track you down and ask . . ."

"What?"

"She wanted me to ask you but I figure I didn't need to," he said. "It's understood."

Theo held his patience. "What's understood?"

"You're gonna be my best man in the wedding."

"What about Noah?"

"He's in the wedding, of course, but I'm expecting you to be best man. I figured you already knew that, but Laurant thought I should ask you anyway."

"Yeah?"

"Yeah, what?"

Theo smiled. "Yeah, okay."

His brother was a man of few words. "Okay, good. Have you given your speech yet?"

"No, that's not until tomorrow night."

"When do you get your trophy?"

"It's a plaque, and I get it right before I give my speech."

"So if you blow it and put all those armed officers to sleep, they can't take the trophy back, can they?"

"I'm hanging up."

"Hey, Theo? For once, stop thinking about work. See the sights. Get laid. You know, have a good time. Hey, I know . . . why don't you give Noah a call. He's in Biloxi for a couple of months for a training conference. He could drive over to New Orleans, and the two of you could have some fun."

If anyone knew how to have fun, it was Noah

Clayborne. The FBI agent had become a close friend of the family after working on several assignments with Nick and then later assisting Theo with his investigations as a federal attorney for the Justice Department. He was a good man, but he had a wicked sense of fun, and Theo wasn't sure he could survive a night out with Noah just now.

"Okay, maybe," he answered.

Theo hung up the phone, stood, and quickly doubled over from the pain that radiated through his right side. It had started in his belly, but it had moved down, and, damn, but it stung. The muscle he'd pulled felt like it was on fire.

A stupid football injury wasn't going to keep him down. Muttering to himself, he grabbed his cell phone from the charger, put it into his breast pocket with his reading glasses, slipped his gun into his belt holster, and left the room. By the time he reached the lobby, the pain had receded and he was feeling almost human again. That, of course, only reinforced his own personal golden rule. Ignore the pain and it would go away. Besides, a Buchanan could tough anything out.

It was a night to remember.

Michelle had never attended such an extravagant affair before, and as she stood on the steps overlooking the hotel ballroom, she felt like Alice about to fall through the looking glass into Wonderland.

There were flowers everywhere, beautiful spring flowers in sculptured urns on the marble floors and in crystal vases on all the white linen tablecloths. In the very center of the ballroom, beneath a magnificent crystal chandelier, was a cluster of giant hothouse-nurtured magnolia trees in full bloom. Their heavenly fragrance filled the air.

Waiters moved smoothly through the crowd carrying silver trays with fluted champagne glasses while others rushed from table to table lighting long, white tapered candles.

Mary Ann Winters, a friend since childhood days, stood by Michelle's side taking it all in.

"I'm out of my element here," Michelle whispered. "I feel like an awkward teenager."

"You don't look like one," Mary Ann said. "I might as well be invisible. I swear every man is staring at you."

"No, they're staring at my obscenely tight dress. How could anything look so plain and ordinary on a hanger and so—"

"So devastatingly sexy on you? It clings in all the right places. Face it, you've got a killer figure."

"I should never have spent so much money on a dress."

"For heaven's sake, Michelle, it's an Armani . . . *and* you got it for a song, I might add."

Michelle self-consciously brushed her hand down the side of the soft fabric. She thought about how much she'd paid for the dress and decided she would have to wear it at least twenty times to make it cost-effective. She wondered if other women did that—rationalized a frivolous expense to appease the guilt. There were so many more important things she could have used the money for, and when, in heaven's name, was she ever going to have another opportunity to wear this beautiful dress again? Not in Bowen, she thought. Not in a million years.

"What was I thinking? I never should have let you talk me into buying this dress."

Mary Ann impatiently brushed a strand of white blond hair back over her shoulder. "Don't you dare start in complaining about the cost again. You never spend any money on yourself. I'll bet it's the first really gorgeous dress you've ever owned, isn't it? You're absolutely beautiful tonight. Promise me you'll stop worrying and enjoy yourself."

Michelle nodded. "You're right. I'll stop worrying."

"Good. Now let's go mingle. There's hors d'oeuvres and champagne out in the courtyard, and we've got to eat at least a thousand dollars' worth each. That's what the tickets cost. I'll meet you there."

Her friend had just gone down the stairs, when Dr. Cooper spotted Michelle and motioned for her to join him. He was the chief of surgery at Brethren Hospital, where she had been moonlighting the past month. Cooper was usually reserved, but the champagne had rid him of his inhibitions, and he was quite affectionate. And effervescent. He kept telling her how happy he was that she was using the tickets he'd given her and how pretty she looked all dressed up. Michelle thought that if Dr. Cooper got any happier, he was going to pass out in the soup.

A few minutes later, Cooper's wife joined them with another older couple in tow. Michelle used the opportunity to sneak away. She walked around into the adjacent hallway with the bank of elevators.

And that's when she noticed him. He was leaning against a pillar, hunched over, tilted protectively to one side. The man was tall, broad-shouldered, well built, like an athlete, she thought. But there was a sickly gray pallor to his complexion, and as she walked toward him, she saw him grimace and grab his stomach.

He was definitely in trouble. She touched his arm to get his attention just as the elevator doors opened. He staggered upright and looked down at her. His gray eyes were glazed with pain.

"Do you need help?"

He answered her by throwing up all over her.

She couldn't get out of the way because he'd grabbed hold of her arm. His knees buckled then and she knew he was going to go down. She wrapped her arms around his waist and tried to ease him to the floor, but he lurched forward at the same time, taking her with him.

Theo's head was spinning. He landed on top of the woman. He heard her groan and desperately tried to find the strength to get up. He thought he might be dying and he didn't think that would be such a bad thing if death would make the pain go away. It was unbearable now. His stomach rolled again, and another wave of intense agony cut through him. He wondered if this was what it felt like to be stabbed over and over again. He passed out then, and when he next opened his eyes, he was flat on his back and she was leaning over him.

He tried to bring her face into focus. She had pretty blue eyes, more violet than blue, he thought, and freckles on the bridge of her nose. Then, as suddenly as it had stopped, the fire started burning in his side again, so much worse than before.

A spasm wrenched his stomach, and he jerked. "Son of a bitch."

The woman was talking to him, but he couldn't understand what she was saying. And what the hell was she doing to him? Was she robbing him? Her hands were everywhere, tugging at his jacket, his tie, his shirt. She was trying to straighten out his legs. She was hurting him, damn it, and every time he tried to push her hands away, they came back to poke and prod some more.

He felt her open his jacket, knew she could see the gun holstered above his hip. He was crazed with pain now, couldn't seem to think straight. He only knew he couldn't let her take his weapon.

She was a damned talkative mugger. He'd give her that. She looked like one of those J. Crew models. Sweet, he thought. No, she wasn't sweet. She kept hurting him.

"Look, lady, you can take my wallet, but you're not getting my gun. Got that?" He could barely get the words out through his gritted teeth.

Her hand pressed into his side. He reacted instinctively, knocking her back. He thought he might have connected with something soft because he heard her yell before he went under again.

Theo didn't know how long he was out, but when he

opened his eyes, the bright lights made him squint. Where the hell was he? He couldn't summon up enough energy to move. He thought he might be on a table. It was hard, cold.

"Where am I?" His mouth was so dry, he slurred the question.

"You're in Brethren Hospital, Mr. Buchanan." The man's voice came from behind him, but Theo couldn't see him.

"Did they catch her?"

"Who?"

"J. Crew."

"He's loopy." A female voice he didn't recognize made the comment.

Theo suddenly realized he wasn't in any pain. He felt good, in fact. Real good. Like he could fly. Odd, though, he didn't have the strength to move his arms. A mask was placed over his mouth and nose. He turned his head to get away from it.

"Are you getting sleepy, Mr. Buchanan?"

He turned his head again and saw her. Blue Eyes. She looked like an angel, all golden. Wait a minute. What the hell was she doing here? Wait . . .

"Mike, are you going to be able to see what you're doing? That eye looks bad."

"It's fine."

"How'd it happen?" the voice behind Theo's head asked.

"He clipped me."

"The patient decked you?"

"That's right." She was staring into Theo's eyes when she answered. She had a green mask on, but he knew she was smiling.

He was in such a happy daze now and so sleepy, he was having trouble keeping his eyes open. Conversation swirled around him, but none if it made any sense.

A woman's voice. "Where did you find *him*, Dr. Renard?"

"At a party."

Another woman leaned over him. "Hubba, hubba."

"Was it love at first sight?"

"You decide. He threw up all over me and ruined my new dress."

Someone laughed. "Sounds like love to me. I'll bet he's married. All the good-looking men are married. This one's sure built. Did you check out the goods, Annie?"

"I hope our patient is sleeping."

"Not yet," a male voice said. "But he isn't going to remember anything."

"Where's the assist?"

"Scrubbing."

There seemed to be a party going on. Theo thought there were at least twenty or thirty people in the room with him. Why was it so damned cold? And who was making all the clatter? He was thirsty. His mouth felt like it was full of cotton. Maybe he ought to go get a drink. Yeah, that's what he would do.

"Where's Dr. Cooper?"

"Probably passed out in the dessert by now." Blue Eyes answered the question. Theo loved the sound of her voice. It was so damned sexy.

"So you saw Cooper at the party?"

"Uh-huh," Blue Eyes answered. "He wasn't on call tonight. He works hard. It was nice to see him having a good time. Mary Ann's probably having a great time too."

"You." Theo struggled to get the word out. Still, he'd gotten her attention because when he opened his eyes, she was leaning over him, blocking out the glaring light above him.

"It's time for you to go to sleep, Mr. Buchanan."

"He's fighting it."

"What . . ." Theo began.

"Yes?"

"What do you want from me?"

The man hiding behind him answered. "Mike wants your appendix, Mr. Buchanan."

It sounded good to him. He was always happy to accommodate a beautiful woman. "Okay," he whispered. "It's in my wallet."

"We're ready."

"It's about time," the man said.

Theo heard the chair squeak behind him, then the stranger's voice telling him to take deep breaths. Theo finally figured out who the man behind him was. Damn if it wasn't Willie Nelson, and he was singing to him, something about Blue Eyes cryin' in the rain.

It was one hell of a party.

Theo slept through recovery. When he awoke the following morning, he was in a hospital bed. The side rails were up, and he was hooked to an IV. He closed his eyes and tried to clear his mind. What the hell had happened to him? He couldn't remember.

It was past ten o'clock when he opened his eyes again. She was there, standing beside the bed, pulling the sheets up around his waist. Blue Eyes. He hadn't imagined her after all.

She looked different today. She was still dressed in surgical scrubs, but her hair wasn't hidden underneath a cap. It was down around her shoulders, and the color was a deep, rich auburn.

She was much prettier than he remembered.

She noticed he was awake. "Good morning. How are you feeling? Still a little drowsy?"

He struggled to sit up. She reached for the controls and pushed a button. The bed slowly rose. Theo felt a tugging in his side and a mild stinging sensation.

"Tell me when."

"That's good," he said. "Thanks."

She picked up his chart and started writing while he blatantly stared at her. He felt vulnerable and awkward sitting in bed in a hospital gown. He couldn't think of anything clever to say to her. For the first time in his life he wanted to be charming, but he didn't have the faintest idea how to go about it. He was a die-hard workaholic, and there simply wasn't room for social graces in his life.

"Do you remember what happened last night?" she asked, glancing up from her notes.

"I had surgery."

"Yes. Your appendix was removed. Another fifteen minutes and you definitely would have ruptured."

"I remember bits and pieces. What happened to your eye?"

She smiled as she started writing in his chart again. "I didn't duck fast enough."

"Who are you?"

"Dr. Renard."

"Mike?"

"Excuse me?"

"Someone called you Mike."

Michelle closed the folder, put the lid back on her ink pen, and tucked it into her pocket. She gave him her full attention. The surgical nurses were right. Theo Buchanan was gorgeous . . . and sexy as hell. But none of that should matter. She was his physician, nothing more, nothing less, yet she couldn't help reacting to him as any woman naturally would react to such a fit specimen. His hair was sticking up and he needed a shave, but he was still sexy. There wasn't anything wrong with her noticing that . . . unless, of course, he noticed her noticing.

"You just asked me a question, didn't you?" She drew a blank.

He could tell he'd rattled her, but he didn't know why. "I heard someone call you Mike."

She nodded. "Yes. The staff calls me Mike. It's short for Michelle."

"Michelle's a pretty name."

"Thank you."

It was all coming back to Theo now. He was at a party, and there was this beautiful woman in a slinky black evening gown. She was breathtaking. He remembered that. She had killer blue eyes and Willie Nelson was with her. He was singing. No, that couldn't be right. Obviously, his head hadn't quite cleared yet.

"You were talking to me . . . after the surgery," he said.

"In recovery. Yes," she agreed. "But you were doing most of the talking." She was smiling again. "And by the way, the answer's no. I won't marry you."

He smiled, sure she was joking. "I don't remember being in pre-op. I remember the pain though. It hurt like a son of a . . . "

"I'm sure it did."

"You did the surgery, didn't you? I didn't imagine that?"

"Yes, I did the surgery."

She was backing out of the room. He didn't want her to leave just yet. He wanted to find out more about her. "You don't look old enough to be a surgeon." Stupid, he thought, but it was the best he could come up with at the moment.

"I hear that a lot."

"You look like you should be in college." That statement, he decided, was worse than stupid.

She couldn't resist. "High school, actually. They let me operate for extra credit."

"Very funny."

"Dr. Renard? May I interrupt?" A male aide was standing in the hallway, shifting a large cardboard box under his arm.

"Yes, Bobby?"

"Dr. Cooper filled this box with medical supplies from his office for your clinic," the young man said. "What do you want me to do with it? Dr. Cooper left it at the nurses' station, but they wanted it moved. It was in the way."

"Would you mind taking it down to my locker?"

"It's too big, Dr. Renard. It won't fit. It isn't heavy, though. I could carry it out to your car."

"My father has the car," she said. She glanced around, then looked at Theo. "Would you mind if Bobby left my box here? My father will carry it down to the car for me just as soon as he arrives."

"I don't mind," Theo said.

"I won't be seeing you again. I'm going home today, but don't worry. You're in good hands. Dr. Cooper's Chief of Surgery here at Brethren, and he'll take good care of you."

"Where's home?"

"In the swamp."

"Are you kidding?"

"No," she said. She smiled again, and he noticed the little dimple in her left cheek. "Home is a little town that's pretty much surrounded by swamp, and I can't wait to get back there."

"Homesick?"

"Yes, I am," she admitted. "I'm a small-town girl at heart. It isn't a very glamorous life, and that's what I like about it."

"You like living in the swamp." It was a statement, not a question, but she responded anyway.

"You sound shocked."

"No, just surprised."

"You're from a big, sprawling city, so you'd probably hate it."

"Why do you say that?"

She shrugged. "You seem too . . . sophisticated."

He didn't know if that was a compliment or a criticism. "Sometimes you can't go home. I think I read that in a book once. Besides, you look like a New Orleans kind of woman to me."

"I love New Orleans. It's a wonderful place to come for dinner."

"But it won't ever be home."

"No."

"So, are you the town doctor?"

"One of several," she said. "I'm opening a clinic there. It's not very fancy, but there's a real need. So many of the people don't have the resources to get regular medical care."

"Sounds like they're very lucky to have you."

She shook her head. "Oh, no, I'm the lucky one." Then she laughed. "That sounded saintly, didn't it? I am the lucky one, though. The people are wonderful, at least I think they are, and they give me far more than I can give them." When she spoke, her whole face lit up. "You know what I'm going to like best?"

"What's that?"

"No games. For the most part, they're honest, ordinary people trying to scrape a living together. They don't waste a lot of time on foolishness."

"So, everyone loves everyone else?" He scoffed at the notion.

"No, of course not," she replied. "But I'll know my enemies. They won't sneak up behind me and blindside me. It isn't their style." She smiled again. "They'll get right in my face, and I'm going to like that. Like I said, no games. After the residency I just finished, that's going to be a refreshing change."

"You won't miss the big beautiful office and all the trappings?"

"Not really. There are rewards other than money. Oh sure, it would be great to have the supplies and equipment we need, but we'll make do. I've spent a lot of years getting ready for this . . . besides, I made a promise."

He kept asking her questions to keep her talking. He was interested in hearing about her town but not nearly as much as he was fascinated with her expressions. There were such passion and joy in her voice, and her eyes sparkled as she talked about her family and friends and the good she hoped she could do.

She reminded him of how he had felt about life when he had first started practicing the law, before he'd become so cynical. He too had wanted to change the world, to make it a better place. Rebecca had changed all that. Looking back, he realized he had failed miserably.

"I've worn you out, going on and on about my hometown. I'll let you rest now," she said.

"When can I get out of here?"

"That's Dr. Cooper's call, but if it were up to me, I'd keep you another night. You had quite a nasty infection. You need to take it easy for a couple of weeks, and don't forget to take your antibiotics. Good luck, Theo."

And then she was gone, and he'd lost the only chance he had to find out more about her. He didn't even know where her home was. He fell asleep trying to figure out a way to see her again.